CW00601141

Praise for *T*

'One of the reasons this boo[...]
you know you're in the hand[...]
understands the tension of dealing with someone who's
intent on taking their own life; a man who has experienced
these problems first hand and writes about them with great
authority; introducing us to a world that makes the book
fascinating and unputdownable'   Jeffrey Archer

'Superb. An incredible blend of gripping characters, fabulous
plot and chillingly authentic political corruption'
                                                    Graham Bartlett

'A compelling and timely tale of political corruption'
                                                    Daily Express

'Not only does *The Fallen* drip with authenticity and insider
secrets (unsurprising, given Sutherland's background), it's
also full of charm, compassion and emotion. The plot is
intricate, frighteningly plausible and superbly paced; I raced
through it in two sittings. Recommended'   M. W. Craven

'A hugely enjoyable thriller'   *Daily Mirror*

'Breathtakingly tense . . . A firecracker of a book'
                                                    Neil Lancaster

'A compelling page-turner you'll struggle to put down'
                                                    Women & Home

'Finely constructed as *The Fallen* is, it is his palpable anger
at the police being starved of resources and the toll the work
takes that stays with you'   *The Times*

'Superbly authentic'   *Peterborough Evening Telegraph*

John Sutherland is a father of three who lives with his wife and children in south London. For more than twenty-five years he served as an officer in the Metropolitan Police, rising to the rank of Chief Superintendent before his retirement on medical grounds in 2018. John is a sought-after public speaker and commentator on a broad range of issues, who regularly appears on TV and radio and writes for major newspapers. His first book, *Blue*, written and published while he was still serving in the Met, was a *Sunday Times* bestseller.

Follow John on Twitter @policecommander

Also by John Sutherland

Blue
Crossing the Line
The Siege

THE FALLEN

JOHN SUTHERLAND

ORION

First published in Great Britain in 2023 by Orion Fiction,
This paperback edition published in 2024 by Orion Fiction,
an imprint of The Orion Publishing Group Ltd
Carmelite House, 50 Victoria Embankment
London EC4Y 0DZ

An Hachette UK Company

1 3 5 7 9 10 8 6 4 2

Copyright © John Sutherland 2023

The moral right of John Sutherland to be identified as
the author of this work has been asserted in accordance
with the Copyright, Designs and Patents Act of 1988.

All rights reserved. No part of this publication may be
reproduced, stored in a retrieval system, or transmitted
in any form or by any means, electronic, mechanical,
photocopying, recording, or otherwise, without the
prior permission of both the copyright owner and the
above publisher of this book.

All the characters in this book are fictitious, and any resemblance
to actual persons, living or dead, is purely coincidental.

A CIP catalogue record for this book is
available from the British Library.

ISBN (Paperback) 978 1 3987 0886 0
ISBN (eBook) 978 1 3987 0887 7

Typeset at The Spartan Press Ltd,
Lymington, Hants

Printed in Great Britain by Clays Ltd,
Elcograf S.p.A.

MIX
Paper | Supporting
responsible forestry
FSC® C104740

www.orionbooks.co.uk

In memory of Kodjo, Ben, Milad and Dogan

'All money corrupts, and big money corrupts bigly.'

Oliver Bullough (*Moneyland*)

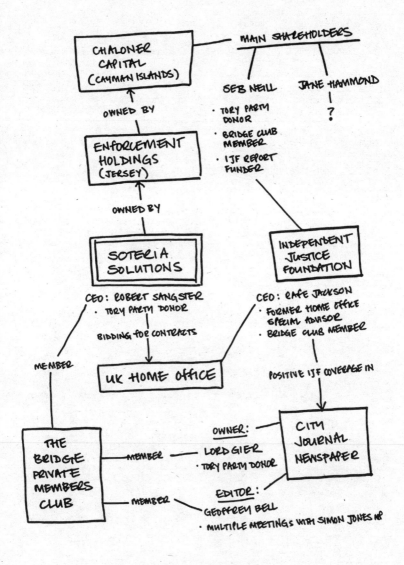

A page from Rowan Blake's notebook

Prologue

It was the last hour before dawn, on a Monday morning in late-October. Becca Palmer had been wandering the backstreets of Westminster and Pimlico since a little after midnight: seemingly oblivious to the cold, losing all track of time, drinking too much alcohol and steadily falling apart. Her head was bowed, her body was stooped and her movements laboured: as though despair itself had somehow taken on human form. And all of it apparently brought on by a conversation that had taken place the night before – when, out of nowhere, her boss had delivered the shattering news that he no longer wanted her.

Shuffling and swaying her way along the road that runs behind the famous old Tate Britain art gallery, she paused to steady herself against a lamp post, before reaching a trembling hand into her coat pocket and pulling out a near-empty half-sized bottle of Smirnoff. She twisted the cap off and let it fall onto the pavement, where it bounced with a faint *tink* before rolling into the gutter. As she lifted the bottle to her lips and tilted her head to drain its remaining contents, shafts of sodium light from above fell onto her face.

In almost any other setting, at almost any other time, her simple, natural beauty would have been plain to see – but each one of her features had been dimmed and diminished

1

by her circumstances. Her hazel eyes were hooded and salted red with tears. Her face was puffy and grey. Her light brown, shoulder-length hair was in a state of tangled disarray and the small amount of make-up that she had so carefully applied the day before was smeared across her cheeks. She was in her early twenties but looked at least ten years older. The sleeves of her coat were scuffed with dirt and her navy-blue jeans were torn at the knee – evidence not of fashion, but of falling. The cuts and grazes on her legs and on the palms of her hands offered proof of the fact.

She dropped the empty vodka bottle onto a nearby flowerbed and resumed her stumbling journey east, in the general direction of the Houses of Parliament. On either side of the road, pollarded plane trees towered above her, their naked branches extended in a series of awkward, angular shrugs, as though troubled deeply by the state of her, but powerless to intervene.

Ten blurry minutes later, Becca found herself standing opposite the main entrance to the Home Office in Marsham Street. Her place of work. She was just about to cross the road when she stopped herself. The lone, bored-looking security guard standing just inside the glass doors represented the prospect of more human contact than she seemed capable of dealing with.

Slowly, she turned and walked back the way she had just come, following the building line round into Horseferry Road. There were plenty of CCTV cameras, but no guard at the staff entrance, which afforded twenty-four hour access to those in possession of the correct ID card and accompanying four-digit security code. Becca stared at the three revolving doors, each enclosed in a vertical cylinder of reinforced glass. She patted herself down and, hands still shaking, searched through the pockets of her trousers and coat. Locating her pass – one of two attached to a dark green lanyard – she pressed it against the keypad for the door closest to her. As the pad illuminated to reveal a set of numbers and symbols, her face screwed up in drunken concentration. Her first attempt at inputting her code was met with a stern buzz and a red light. Her second too.

'Oh, for fuck's sake!' she slurred to herself.

She finally managed to get it right at the third attempt and the glass cylinder rotated open. She stepped onto the pressure pad and edged forward as the door began to turn.

Once inside the strip-lit emptiness of the ground-floor lobby, she took a deep breath before summoning the lift. The doors opened with a ping a few moments later. Selecting the button for the fourth floor, she glanced at the girl reflected in the lift's mirror and appeared not to recognise her. The reflected girl, in turn, seemed to stare straight through her. Becca turned and faced in the opposite direction.

Arriving on the fourth floor, she turned left and walked along the corridor, as if on autopilot, emerging a few moments later in a well-ordered, open-plan office that was all business, no character. The overhead lights came on automatically, affording the room an anaemic glow. Becca stood and leaned against the edge of a desk as she stared at the closed door on her right-hand side. It bore a brass nameplate that read: 'Policing Minister'. Her boss. At least, that's what he had been until the previous evening's conversation. A flicker of incomprehension passed across her face as her red eyes filled once more with tears.

She wandered slowly across the room and came to a stop behind a desk piled high with a disorderly clutter of files. She pulled the chair out from beneath it and slumped down, before absent-mindedly picking up a wooden photo frame that was sitting in front of her. It contained a picture of her, smiling, with her arms wrapped tightly around a slightly older woman who bore a certain resemblance to her. Becca lifted the picture to her lips, closed her eyes and kissed the glass.

As though she was remembering. And saying goodbye.

She was jerked back into the present by the sound of a vacuum cleaner being switched on somewhere along the corridor, on the other side of the lifts. Her body tensed and she started pulling open the drawers beneath the desk, her movements suddenly urgent, as though she was determined to be gone from the office before anyone found her there.

From the bottom drawer, she retrieved an empty burgundy tote bag. She placed the wooden photo frame carefully inside it. From the middle drawer, she pulled out a couple of well-thumbed paperbacks: *The Testament* by John Grisham, and *The Voyage of the Dawn Treader* by C. S. Lewis. Both went into the bag, along with a pencil case and a hairbrush. In the top drawer, she found a box of pills. *Fluoxetine*. The details on the packet suggested they were long past their use-by date. She left them where they were and was about to stand up when a thought seemed to occur to her. She eased her weight back into the chair, reached into the top drawer for a pen and across the desk for a blank piece of A4 printer paper. Then she started to write.

She had filled almost half the page by the time she put the pen down. She folded the note and put it into a plain envelope. Leaving the outside blank, she stood up and walked uncertainly over to the door with the brass nameplate on it. She tried the handle, but the door was locked. So she crouched down gingerly and pushed the envelope through the narrow gap beneath it.

The sound of the vacuum cleaner was closer now. Becca went back to her desk, picked up the tote bag and, without looking back, stumbled tearfully towards the stairs and down to the ground floor. A broken-hearted, broken-headed girl.

As she stepped back out onto the pavement, the overcast early-morning sky was streaked with red.

The old shepherd's warning.

Chapter 1

'Are you ready to save a life?'

The dreams, whenever they returned, always began with the same simple question, asked by a distant female voice at the other end of a telephone line. There was something both familiar and reassuring about the sound of her; something about the way she spoke and the very particular set of words she used; something that prompted the faintest twitch of a smile, even as he slept. But, as surely as the seasons change, her voice would fade and his face would fall and those same dreams would curl and twist into desperate nightmares that only ever ended in horror: with the staccato sound of gunfire and the sight of a critically wounded man crumpling to the ground in front of him; or, in a different part of the city, at a different point in time, with a sudden *whump* of flame and a different, screaming man catching fire just a handful of metres away from where he was standing.

And that was when Superintendent Alex Lewis would always wake up, covered in sweat and gasping for air.

Though the nightmares had lessened both in frequency and intensity over the course of the past few months, the potential for their return was always there, and always would be. Alex Lewis was a man haunted by ghosts. Of both the living and the dead.

So it was, that in the early hours of Monday morning — with the house still shrouded in darkness and silence — he woke with a violent start, his eyes wide and his chest heaving. As he sat bolt upright in bed, staring at the flickering, fading images playing out like scenes from a film on the bedroom wall, his partner, Pip, stirred alongside him.

'Alex?' she said sleepily, reaching a hand across to him.

He didn't respond straight away. He was frightened and disorientated; still trying to distinguish between what was real and what was not.

Pip sat up slowly and slid her arm behind his back, seemingly unfazed by the state he was in. The T-shirt he was wearing was damp to the touch, as were the pillows and sheets on his side of the bed. 'More nightmares?' she asked gently as she eased herself closer to him. It had been a few weeks since anything like this had last happened, but the situation was a familiar enough one to both of them.

Alex continued to stare in silence at the wall opposite the foot of the bed. Whatever it was that he thought he had seen there had now disappeared from view, but his mind was still occupied by a confusion of echoes and shadows. Of gunfire and flames. He was like a prize fighter in the split seconds after taking a fierce right to the chin: his thoughts temporarily scrambled and his balance momentarily gone. He groaned.

'Let's get you out of this, shall we?' Pip suggested, lifting his T-shirt up and easing it over his head. As she dropped it on the floor next to the bed, Alex allowed his full weight to lean against her.

'Bloody hell,' he murmured.

'I've got you,' she whispered as she wrapped both her arms around him and held him tight.

And, in the moments of silence that followed, Alex could

feel the tension in his body starting to ease, as his pulse and breathing began to recover some semblance of normality.

'What did you see?' Pip asked him quietly.

'The same as I always do,' he said.

Alex Lewis had been a police officer for more than twenty years and a hostage negotiator – a voluntary role he performed in addition to his day job as Superintendent (Operations) for the north London Borough of Camden – for almost ten of those. In that time, he had seen endless things that he knew he could never unsee: faces and places that he would never forget. So much so that his geography of London was defined as much by the locations of major incidents and serious crimes as it was by any more conventional set of landmarks, or a map of the Underground. The things that he saw in his dreams and nightmares were not some product of the darkest recesses of his imagination; they were founded almost entirely in reality.

The gunshots and the falling man were from Romford in East London, at the scene of a domestic siege that had taken place two years earlier. Alex had been one of the Met's on-call nego-tiators on the day it happened and, over the course of many hours, he and his colleagues had been able to save the lives of four innocent people: a mother and her three young children, aged nine, seven and three. But it was the memory of the life they hadn't been able to save that continued to weigh heavily on him: that of a man high on a cocktail of booze and cocaine; an abusive father to the three rescued children; a relentlessly violent partner to their mother; a bare-chested maniac, armed with two kitchen knives, who had charged in demented fury at the thin blue line of armed police officers. There was absolutely nothing that Alex, or anyone else, could have done to save him. But still, the memory of the man remained. And, whenever Alex heard a firework going off, or an engine backfiring, or some other such noise, he was immediately back in Romford, staring at the dead.

The flames and the burning man were from Herne Hill in South London, at a church hall where, just over twelve months before, a terrorist had taken nine hostages and threatened to kill them all. Alex had been the first negotiator deployed to the scene and had remained at the heart of the protracted – and ultimately successful – police attempt to free all nine of them: men, women and children. But it was the image of the man in flames that lingered: a right-wing extremist, a Nazi fanatic, who had declared repeatedly that he was willing to die for his cause. The fact that he had survived his act of self-immolation – and had later been sentenced to life in prison, with a recommendation that he serve a minimum of fifteen years – had done little to ease the burden of recollection.

Faces and places. Alex Lewis remembered them all.

Pip kissed him tenderly on the cheek. 'Do you want to talk about any of it?' she asked him.

Like Alex, Detective Inspector Philippa Williams – to give Pip her full name and proper title – was a long-serving police officer and hostage negotiator. They had been close friends and colleagues for a number of years before their relationship had developed into anything more than that. Pip had been alongside him at the Herne Hill siege. She had seen and heard it all. And she knew every last detail of what had happened at Romford. She had read the reports and listened to Alex telling her the story a dozen times or more. She understood as well as anyone what he had been going through. What he was *still* going through.

'I think I'm all right,' he said to her. And he meant it. The fact that she was there in the bed next to him made the ordeal a great deal more bearable than it would otherwise have been.

And the knowledge that they had been through – and recovered from – similar experiences on a number of previous occasions drew at least some of the sting from it all.

'Come over here,' she said quietly, moving back across to her side of the bed, where the sheets were warm and dry.

He lay down next to her, his head resting on her shoulder.

'I'm guessing that it has something to do with the fact you're back on call this week,' she said as she gently ruffled his hair.

'What do you mean?' he asked. His eyes were growing heavy and his mind was starting to slow. It was obvious that Pip was thinking much more clearly than he was.

'The last time you had a bad night like this coincided with the last time you were on the negotiator call-out list,' she explained. 'It's not difficult to imagine that there might be a connection between those two things.'

Her suggestion certainly made sense, though the realisation it prompted in Alex was a sobering, somewhat depressing one. 'I thought I was past all that,' he said wearily. 'I thought I was better.'

'You *are* better,' Pip responded quickly. 'Certainly a whole lot better than you were when all of this first started happening.' She turned onto her side so that she was facing him and kissed him on the lips. 'This is just one of those bumps in the road that we always knew would happen from time to time,' she said. 'You're going to be just fine.'

'You really think so?' he asked.

'I know so,' she replied, holding his gaze and kissing him again.

'How can you be so sure?'

'Because I know you.'

Alex sighed. 'Sometimes I think you have more confidence in me than I do in myself,' he said.

Chapter 2

Alex couldn't remember exactly how their middle-of-the-night conversation had ended, or what time he had fallen back to sleep, but when he woke just after six, he was feeling unexpectedly peaceful. More often than not in the past, his nightmares had left him with a kind of psychological hangover that had persisted well into the following day, but, to his immense relief, he sensed that it might somehow be different this time. His heart felt steady and his mind was still. There was no haunting, no sense of being overwhelmed by the past.

Turning his head on the pillow, he looked over at Pip, who was still fast asleep. Perhaps she was right, he thought. Perhaps he really was getting better. And, as he watched the gentle rise and fall of her breathing and the hint of light from the street outside resting on her face and bare shoulders, he felt a sense of deep gratitude. She, more than anyone or anything else, had got him through the past few months.

At the time of the Herne Hill siege, Alex had been stuck in the last days of a failing marriage. It meant that, in the immediate aftermath of the siege – at a time when he was struggling both psychologically and emotionally – there had been no one at home for him to turn to. In the days and weeks that followed, Pip had become that person. During the formal debriefing process after Herne Hill, Alex had done his best to maintain the illusion that all was well. But Pip had seen straight through him. She had recognised what was really going on and had made it clear to him that she was going to do whatever she could to help get him through it. Initially, there had been no more to it than that, but as the weeks went by, the intensity of their shared experiences had brought them steadily closer. Six months after Herne Hill, they had moved in together.

Pip was the one who had convinced him of the need to seek professional help – and who had reassured him repeatedly that there was no shame in his doing so. They were both products of a policing generation that considered asking for help to be a sign of both personal and professional weakness, but times were changing and Pip was having none of it. Encouraged by her, Alex had attended a series of medical appointments – initially with his local GP and, later, with a specialist who had diagnosed him with complex post-traumatic stress disorder – CPTSD. Up to that point in his career, Alex had never once stopped to consider the long-term effects of all that he had seen and done as a police officer. To him, it had always just been 'the Job'. It was what he did and, in countless different ways, it defined who he was.

At Pip's suggestion, he had also been seeing a therapist for several months and, somewhat to his surprise, it had been doing him a great deal of good. The antidepressant medication was helping too. He was starting to learn that, when faced on an almost daily basis with the very depths of human pain and suffering, the most natural, normal, healthy thing in the world was to *feel*. Like so many of his colleagues, Alex had spent a large part of his professional life attempting to do precisely the opposite.

In the end, it was also Pip who had persuaded him to carry

on working as a hostage negotiator. In the weeks immediately following the siege, with his mental health fractured and the memories still vivid and incredibly raw, Alex had seriously considered stepping back from the role. But Pip had convinced him not to. She knew how much he loved it, and she knew how good he was at it.

Hers was the familiar voice in his dreams, asking him if he was ready to save a life.

Alex slipped quietly out of bed and put on his running gear. A steady five kilometres, three or four mornings a week, was another recent development in his life. He had discovered that it was as good for his head as it was for his body: it helped him settle his mind and ready himself for whatever the day ahead might hold.

When he got home, sweaty and exhilarated, some forty minutes later, he found Pip sitting at the kitchen table, her hands wrapped around a large mug of steaming coffee. She worked in one of the Met's specialist sexual offences units and Alex knew that she savoured the moments of relative stillness and calm that fell before the start of the working day.

'Morning!' she smiled.

'Morning!' he replied, with a smile of his own. He steadied himself against the kitchen door frame with one hand, as he reached down with the other and slipped off his trainers.

'How are you doing?' she asked him.

'Good,' he replied.

'No more nightmares?'

Alex shook his head.

Pip looked pleased. 'And how are you feeling about being back on call?' she asked.

'I'm looking forward to it,' he said, his face brightening

13

further. 'I've got the negotiator van for the week. I'm picking it up from the Yard on my way up to Camden.'

Pip had been right, of course. As she was about most things. Alex really did love being a hostage negotiator. He loved the opportunity it gave him to get out of the office, away from the humdrum routine of paperwork and meetings, back to the realities of frontline policing. He loved the unpredictability of it, and the fact that it allowed him to remain involved in the real lives of real people.

More than anything, though, he understood that there was no greater duty – no greater privilege – for any police officer than to save the life of another human being.

Alex pulled the front door shut behind him. He and Pip had signed a two-year lease on a small terraced house in the back-streets of Stockwell, South London – chosen for its geographic proximity to Alex's two teenage sons, who were still living with his ex-wife in the Clapham home he'd once shared with them. He saw his boys most weekends and on at least one evening during the week. Having acknowledged his failings as a husband, he had been determined to do better as a dad. And his efforts were being rewarded: his relationship with his sons seemed to him to be about as good as it could have been, given the circumstances. That the same could not always be said of his relationship with his ex was a fact that Alex preferred not to dwell on.

He walked the short distance to Stockwell tube station, pausing at the entrance to pick up a copy of the free *Metro* newspaper, before taking the escalator down to the platforms. It was still before 8 a.m. and there was plenty of space on the northbound Victoria Line train.

As the doors to his carriage slid shut, he found a seat

and turned his attention to the *Metro*'s front-page headline: 'Gridlock! Thousands of protestors plan to bring the Capital to a standstill'.

The accompanying article provided details of a large anti-government demonstration that was scheduled to take place in central London later that day. The piece concluded by suggesting that it was likely to be another busy afternoon for the Metropolitan Police.

Alex puffed out his cheeks and exhaled slowly. Busy afternoons were just about all that he and his Met colleagues had known in recent times. Busy mornings, evenings and nights too. Most of the time, it felt as though they were fighting a losing battle. And a huge part of the blame for that fact – certainly as far as Alex was concerned – lay squarely at the feet of the people who were supposed to be running the country.

Alex had never much cared for politics and politicians – whether those in office or those in opposition – but he cared a great deal about policing. And the people who were currently in charge had spent the best part of ten years making his job progressively harder to do. They had cut huge numbers of police officers and staff. They had slashed hundreds of millions of pounds from operational budgets. They had closed and sold hundreds of police stations. Crime squads and proactive teams had been disbanded. Local neighbourhood policing had all but disappeared. And all of it at the whim of a procession of Westminster types who seemed to have very little grasp of the real world and none whatsoever of 'the Job' and its people.

Alex could feel his blood rising. *Bloody politicians*, he thought to himself. *The ignorance and the arrogance and the endless harm done*.

He put the newspaper down on the empty seat next to him, closed his eyes and tried to forget about them.

The train rattled and swayed its way through the next couple of stops. When it pulled in at Victoria, rather than change to the District Line, Alex decided to get off and walk the remainder of the distance to New Scotland Yard. He planned to pick up the negotiator van from the basement car park at the Met's headquarters and drive it up to Kentish Town police station where he was based.

Not far from Victoria Station, just across the road from the Home Office building, Becca Palmer was sitting alone on a wooden bench in St John's Gardens. She was drinking from a bottle of cheap gin as the last of the light faded from her eyes.

Chapter 3

It was just after two o'clock on Monday afternoon when Alex's mobile rang. He was sitting on his own in his office on the first floor at Kentish Town, studying the latest set of borough crime figures. They made for particularly troubling reading. Violent crime was up significantly – knife crime and domestic violence in particular. Street crime was rising too – caused in significant part by a rapidly growing number of robberies and mobile phone snatches committed by youths on stolen mopeds. In recent weeks, he had found himself under almost constant pressure from his boss – the local Area Commander – to get the situation under control, and these latest numbers were only going to make things worse.

The problem was that – as a direct consequence of the decisions taken by the '*bloody politicians*' – Alex was hopelessly short of both the officers and the financial resources he needed to make any sort of sustainable difference to the situation. The majority of his counterparts in the other London boroughs were in a very similar position. '*More for less*' had been the Government's mantra, but, like so many other Westminster slogans, it had turned out to be meaningless nonsense. Actually, it was worse than meaningless. It was dangerous. Members of the public were at greater risk of becoming victims of violent crime and police officers were at greater risk of confrontation with violent criminals. Alex and his colleagues understood that, most of the time, all you get for less is less.

All of which meant that the distraction provided by his ringing phone was a welcome one.

He reached across his desk and grabbed the handset. The screen was displaying the name of DCI Richard Wells, the Met's Negotiator Co-ordinator for that week – the individual with responsibility for any decision to deploy negotiators to the scene of an incident.

Alex's pulse quickened.

'Afternoon, Rich,' he said as the line connected. There was an expectant tone in his voice. The two men were long-standing colleagues and friends. Rich was the full-time head of the Met's Hostage and Crisis Negotiation Unit. A year earlier, he had been with Pip and Alex at the scene of the Herne Hill siege.

'Are you available for a call?' Rich asked.

'Absolutely,' Alex replied eagerly.

'In which case, I need you on Westminster Bridge,' he said. 'We've got a young woman apparently threatening to jump. No more details at this stage, other than the fact that local officers are already on scene, trying to engage with her.'

'No problem,' Alex responded. 'I've got the van with me here, so I can deploy straight away.'

'Thanks, Alex,' said Rich. 'You were my first call. I'll see who else is available, then I'll start heading in your direction.'

'No problem,' Alex reassured him. 'I'm on my way.'

Westminster Bridge spans the River Thames in the very heart of London. On the north side of the river stands the magnifi-cent Elizabeth Tower – more commonly known by the name of Big Ben, the great bell that chimes inside it – alongside the equally spectacular Houses of Parliament, where grown adults bicker like small children and the Speaker pleads repeatedly for 'Order!'. On the southern side of the bridge, the handsome, classical structure of the old City Hall sits on one side of the road, with the rather more prosaic form of St Thomas' Hospital on the other.

On the bridge itself – on any ordinary day – red buses and black taxis shuttle back and forth while feral pigeons mingle with visitors from almost every nation on earth. Everywhere you look, people with their phones out and selfie sticks extended are posting pictures on social media for the benefit of the folks back home. All the while, a ragtag assortment of street musicians provide a varied soundtrack – though mostly bagpipes – that mingles with the noise of the traffic and the occasional horn sounded by the captain of a passing boat. Taking up whatever space might remain elsewhere along the pavement, watchful, weaselly hustlers run crooked three-card tricks while rogues of other kinds open small suitcases and offer for sale bottles of rip-off perfume that *'haven't been stolen, miss, I promise you; they just haven't been paid for yet'*.

Sometimes, though, the traffic stops flowing and the pavements empty of people. In the aftermath of a terrorist attack, for instance.

Or when someone has climbed over the green parapet and is standing on the wrong side, ready to jump.

The bridge had been closed at both ends. Police cars were parked at angles across the roadway – one with its blue lights still flashing – while PCs stretched lengths of blue and white tape between lamp posts and batted away the questions being asked by the inquisitive and the inconvenienced. The centre of the bridge was almost completely deserted, save for a lone PC in uniform trying – and failing – to elicit a response from the young woman staring down at the water below.

Back at Kentish Town police station, Alex had changed quickly into a set of warm, comfortable clothes. He had checked the weather forecast – possible rain showers later in the afternoon – and double-checked the contents of his rucksack: extra layers, waterproof coat and trousers, a selection of biros and marker pens, several pads of yellow Post-it Notes, a digital Dictaphone with a set of spare batteries, and an unopened packet of Silk Cut cigarettes. He was only an occasional smoker – usually at moments of particular stress or after one too many drinks – but cigarettes had proven uses as negotiating tools. On more than one occasion in the past, the simple offer of a smoke had been all that was required for Alex to persuade a person to climb down from a roof or to put down the weapon in their hands.

Bag packed, he poked his head into the next office along the corridor. 'Can you cover the performance meeting for me this afternoon, Ronnie?' he asked.

Chief Inspector Veronica Egan – or 'Ronnie', as she preferred to be known – was Alex's very capable deputy.

'Sure,' she replied, looking up from her computer screen. 'I take it you need to be somewhere else?'

'Someone on Westminster Bridge. Apparently thinking about jumping,' Alex responded. 'I could be gone for a while.'

'No problem,' Ronnie said, 'I'm here all afternoon.'

'Thanks,' said Alex. 'I really appreciate it.'

And, with that, he turned and hurried along the corridor, down the stairs and out into the station yard.

Over the years, the majority of Alex's negotiator deployments had begun with calls not dissimilar to this one – individuals who weren't guilty of committing any crime but, rather, had reached the end of themselves and were in desperate need of a helping hand. Armed sieges and full-blown hostage situations were the things that tended to grab the headlines and the wider public imagination, but they remained a comparative rarity. Mostly, Alex would spend the hours following a call-out listening and talking to troubled strangers whose stories were unlikely ever to make the local paper, much less the rolling news on national TV. But every single one of them mattered to him. Whoever they were, wherever they were from, and whatever had led them to the situation they had found themselves in, his job was to save their lives.

Whenever a friend or colleague asked him why he continued to volunteer for the significant additional burdens and responsibilities associated with being a negotiator, Alex would respond by quoting a phrase often used by the RNLI – the Royal National Lifeboat Institute: 'Every life is precious,' he would say.

Those were the exact words in his mind as he ran over to the van. From the outside, it looked like an unremarkable black VW Transporter. But it was fitted with covert blues and twos – lights and sirens – and the rear of it had been converted into a mobile negotiation cell, complete with a fixed table and seats, a series of small whiteboards mounted on the side walls and a range of power sockets and mobile phone charging points. At the very back was a metal cage containing three sets of ballistic vests and helmets, together with a variety of ropes and harnesses. Just in case they were needed.

Alex climbed into the driver's seat and started the engine. He reached down to his left to switch on the blue lights and two-tone sirens and, after waiting impatiently for the station's automatic back gate to open, he accelerated out into the afternoon traffic.

*

In the meantime, the PC on Westminster Bridge had been struggling to make any kind of headway. A female colleague had been sent to join him in the hope that she might be able to elicit a different response, but to no avail. The woman hadn't jumped, thank goodness, but neither was she responding to anything they were saying to her.

There was a burgundy tote bag lying on the ground, at the spot where she had apparently climbed over the parapet. Some of the contents had spilled out onto the pavement and, among them, next to a smartphone with a smashed screen, the female PC noticed what appeared to be some kind of work pass attached to a green lanyard. She reached down to pick it up and found that it was actually two passes: one for the Home Office and one for the Houses of Parliament. Both carried a photograph that was an obvious match for the woman on the parapet. Both bore the name 'Becca Palmer'.

As Alex raced south in the van, lights blazing and sirens wailing, the traffic parted for him like the Red Sea for Moses. Heading through Camden Town and King's Cross, turning towards Holborn, his thoughts were racing too. He wanted to know what was happening on the bridge. He hadn't had any update from Rich since the initial phone call and the police radio in the van seemed to be on the blink. He would have to get that sorted out later on. In the absence of facts, he found himself imagining what a successful outcome to the negotiation might look like: one involving the girl accepting the offer of his outstretched hand and climbing back to safety.

He continued to speed along New Oxford Street, slowing a fraction whenever he approached a set of red lights, then accelerating across the junction as soon as he was sure that everyone else had given way to him. Bicycles were the things to be particularly wary of: bicycles being ridden by idiots wearing headphones, oblivious to their surroundings and indifferent to the requirements of the Highway Code. Alex had been involved in his fair share of near-misses over the years.

As he swung left onto Tottenham Court Road, his senses quickened even further. Not too far to go now. Snatching a look at his watch, he reckoned that he should be there in the next five or six minutes. But, at more or less exactly that moment, the traffic around him began to thicken and slow. Even with the blues and twos still going, the progress of the van was soon reduced to a crawl, and then to a complete standstill.

Alex thumped the steering wheel in frustration. What the hell was going on? Up ahead of him, he caught sight of a number of people weaving in and out of the traffic, waving placards and banging on the bonnets and roofs of stationary vehicles. A group of them were even attempting to hang a large banner between a pair of lamp posts on either side of the road.

Shit, he thought to himself. He'd completely forgotten about the march that had been planned for that afternoon. The people up ahead must have broken away from the main demonstration route and decided to make their point in a different part of town.

Furious at his own mistake, and even more so with those who had made good on their promise to bring central London to a standstill, Alex craned his neck in every direction, looking for options. Cars and taxis were trying to pull up onto the pavements in front of him, but the buses had nowhere to go. *Shit!*

With no way forward, he realised he was going to have to go backwards. To find a way through, he would have to turn around and head back the way he had just come. It would add at least another fifteen minutes to his journey. And what would that mean for the girl on the bridge? Despite knowing that there were local officers with her, Alex felt an enormous sense of personal responsibility for whatever might happen to her. And he couldn't help her if he wasn't there.

Hands clammy and with beads of perspiration running down the small of his back, he lowered the window of the van and began waving frantically at vehicles on both sides of the road to get out of his way. In a series of rapid and jerky backwards and forwards movements, the drivers around him did the best they could and, eventually, Alex was able to make the turn. Trying to slow his breathing, he began to steer a course through the backstreets, in search of the quickest alternative route to his destination. And, as he did so, each new knot in the traffic tightened the knot in his stomach.

Chapter 4

It was approaching 3 p.m. when Alex finally pulled up outside St Thomas' Hospital on the southern approach to Westminster Bridge – more than three quarters of an hour after he had originally received the call from Rich. He should have been there much sooner, but he couldn't afford to dwell on the thought. He now needed to focus fully on the task in hand.

He grabbed his rucksack from the front passenger seat and swung it onto his shoulder as he jumped out of the van and locked the doors. Then he hurried towards the thin strip of cordon tape spanning the road in front of him and produced his warrant card for the benefit of the nearest PC.

'I'm Alex Lewis, your negotiator,' he said. 'Can you tell me where the Duty Officer is?'

'She's somewhere over there on the other side of the bridge,' replied the PC, gesturing in the general direction of the Houses of Parliament. 'Do you want me to get her over here?'

'Tell her I'll meet her halfway,' Alex replied, already ducking under the tape.

Up ahead and to his left, he could see the two uniformed police officers – one male, one female – standing on the pavement a few feet away from a young woman who was on the wrong side of the parapet, holding on with one hand, facing out towards the river. The two PCs were as still as statues, perhaps afraid of the consequences of movement; of somehow upsetting the balance in the air. Neither of them appeared to be saying anything.

Alex's gaze settled on the figure of the girl as three pressing questions established themselves right at the front of his mind:

Why her?

Why here?

Why now?

The answers to those questions were the keys to unlocking her story and, in turn perhaps, to finding a way to help her back from the edge.

As he moved towards the middle of the bridge, Alex felt a surge of nerves and fresh adrenaline and reminded himself that both were necessary if he was going to be able to do his job well: the adrenaline to sustain him; the nerves to guard him against any kind of complacency.

A second female officer was hurrying towards him on the other side of the road. The Duty Officer, Alex guessed. As she got closer, he could see the inspector's pips on the shoulders of her uniform.

'Alex Lewis,' he said as he reached out to shake her hand. 'I'm one of the on-call negotiators.'

'Jenny Haith,' she responded. 'Thanks for getting here.'

'No problem,' said Alex, his voice calm and reassuring. 'What can you tell me?'

'Not a great deal to be honest,' Inspector Haith replied. 'We've found a security pass with her name on it – we think she probably works at the Home Office. I've asked for some calls to be made, but I haven't heard anything back yet. We've been with her for about ninety minutes and, so far, she hasn't said a single word. I've got two of my best PCs with her and neither of them have been able to get any kind of response out of her.'

'Well she's still with us,' Alex responded, 'and that's a good sign.'

'Meaning?' queried the Inspector.

'Meaning that if she'd made up her mind to jump, I suspect she'd have done it by now,' explained Alex. 'The fact that she hasn't suggests that there might be some doubt in her mind. And that gives us something to work with. It certainly gives me some hope.'

The Inspector raised her eyebrows, seemingly unsure whether or not she shared his positive outlook on the situation. 'What do you need from me?' she asked.

'Just the names of the two officers over there with her,' said Alex, gesturing across to the other side of the road.

'Steve and Emma,' she replied. 'Both with plenty of years in "the Job". Both with their heads screwed on.'

'Are you happy for me to go across and join them?' Alex asked, wanting to get started.

'Yes, of course,' said the Inspector, taking a step to one side.

If the fall doesn't kill you, then the cold and the currents almost certainly will.

In any given year, as many as fifty people lose their lives in the murky, fast-flowing waters of the River Thames. Alex knew the numbers and the risks, but he was also an optimist – and his was an optimism born of experience. He had never lost a person on a London bridge, and he had been called out to several of them over the years. If he got there in time, experience had taught him that the chances of success were high.

That was the principal thought in his mind as he walked the last few metres towards the stranger on the parapet.

'You must be Steve and Emma,' he said quietly to the two PCs, who nodded at him in acknowledgement. 'And who have you got here with you?' he asked, looking past them at the young woman.

The female PC handed Alex the lanyard with the two photo passes attached to it. Alex studied the photos and the name: Becca Palmer.

'Has Becca told you why she's here?' Alex asked them.

'She hasn't told us anything,' the male officer replied. 'She hasn't said a word in all the time I've been with her.' The concern in his voice was mixed with a hint of frustration.

'That's OK,' Alex reassured him.

Over the years, Alex had found that uniformed PCs often turned out to be natural negotiators. They might not have done the official training course, but they spent a large part of their working lives dealing with people in every kind of crisis: victims with heartbreaking stories and life-threatening injuries; suspects armed with weapons and rage; traumatised witnesses struggling to remember a single thing they have seen; drinkers with demons; street sleepers with habits to feed and nowhere to go; people in agony, trying to make it through the worst days of their lives.

But, in this particular case, Alex could see that the two officers were struggling. They hadn't done anything wrong as far as he could tell, but neither had they managed to find a way to break whatever spell the girl was under.

Alex put his rucksack on the ground next to the discarded tote bag. 'Let me talk to her for a bit,' he suggested to them.

The two PCs moved a short distance along the pavement in the direction of Big Ben – out of immediate earshot, but close enough to be of swift assistance should the need arise.

Alex double-checked that his phone was switched to silent. He still hadn't heard from Rich. He didn't know which other negotiators had been called out, or how long it would be before they eventually got there, but he wasn't prepared to wait for them. Having already taken too long to get to the bridge himself, he couldn't afford to − and it certainly wouldn't be the first time he'd started a negotiation on his own.

Standing about three metres away from the girl, he leaned his elbows on the top of the balustrade and closed his mind to every possible distraction. For as long as it was going to take, saving her life needed to be the only thing that mattered to him.

Slowly, he turned his head and looked in her direction, taking care not to unsettle her with any sudden movements. Her hair was moving constantly in the breeze, one moment obscuring her profile, the next flicking out behind her in tangled disarray. From where he was standing, Alex only had sight of one side of her face. Her right eye was screwed tight shut and he could see the fading streaks of make-up on her freckled skin. She looked a complete mess.

Why her? Why here? Why now?

When the wind switched briefly in his direction, he could smell the booze on her breath.

'You must be Becca,' he said gently.

The girl didn't respond.

'Would it be all right if I talked to you for a while?' he asked her.

She ignored him.

'My name is Alex,' he continued. 'I'm with the police and I'm here to help you.' Almost every negotiation he had ever taken part in had begun with those same words, or something

29

very like them. *This is who I am*, he was telling her. *And this is why I'm here.*

But the girl offered no indication that she had even heard him.

The air temperature was falling. Alex reached into his coat pocket and pulled out a pair of fleece gloves. As he put them on, he looked across at the girl's right hand, gripping the inside edge of the balustrade, and reminded himself that she'd already been there for the best part of two hours. There was surely no way she was going to be able to hold on for very much longer.

Chapter 5

A mile or so away, on the fourth floor of the Home Office, a phone was ringing. It was answered by a man in his late twenties wearing round, gold-rimmed glasses and an earnest expression. His plaid shirt – no tie, sleeves rolled halfway up his forearms – and rumpled chinos afforded him a look that was more postgrad than civil servant.

'Yes, this is the office of the Policing Minister,' he said politely. 'How can I help you?'

His female colleague, sitting at the desk opposite him, seemed oblivious to the interruption as she continued to sift through a large pile of files and documents on her desk. She was older than the man, in her mid-forties perhaps, and dressed much more smartly than him: in a pale blue silk shirt and navy-blue trouser suit that was either brand new or fresh from the dry-cleaners. Her name was Camilla Lane and she was the no-nonsense, highly capable senior advisor to the Minister.

'Yes, she works here,' said the young man in response to what must have been a question at the other end of the line. 'But I'm afraid she isn't in at the moment. Can I take a message?' As he said this, he glanced across the open-plan office and his eyes settled on Becca Palmer's empty desk. 'Oh,' he said after a short pause.

And there was something about the way he said 'oh' that caused Camilla Lane to look up from her work. Immediately, she saw the look of concern on the man's face.

'What is it?' she asked in a loud whisper.

The man put his hand over the mouthpiece of the phone. 'It's Becca,' he said.

His boss rolled her eyes in exasperation. 'Oh, for God's sake! What is it this time?' she asked him.

'I'm talking to the police,' he said, gesturing at the phone handset. 'Apparently, she's on Westminster Bridge. It looks as though she might be about to jump into the Thames.'

The girl on the bridge remained silent. Alex studied the parliamentary pass he was holding. It told him where she worked and suggested what he should call her, but it offered no more than that. And Alex understood that people are so much more than the names they are given and the jobs that they take. His responsibility was to find out who she really was and why she was in such a terrible state.

'It looks to me as though you're having a really tough day,' he said softly. It might have been a statement of the blindingly obvious, but Alex was attempting to establish a connection with her. He was identifying with her distress, whatever the source of it might have been. 'Why don't you climb back over onto the pavement and we can talk about it,' he suggested.

But she continued to pay no attention to him.

Despite his concerns about the amount of time she'd already spent out in the cold, Alex allowed the silence to rest for a while. So much of policing happened at speed – in the headlong rush from one emergency call to the next – but Alex knew that hostage and crisis negotiation was often different. Years of being deployed had taught him that negotiation frequently requires a conscious slowing down – a deliberate curbing of a copper's natural instinct to get things done in a hurry. Of course, he would always try to get a vulnerable person to safety as soon as he possibly could, but he understood that, sometimes, the only way to achieve that was to take the long way round.

His eyes followed the course of a lone cormorant as it arrowed downriver, flying just inches above the surface of the water. How did they manage to do that, he wondered, without ever catching a wingtip and cartwheeling into the swell? The only other movement in his immediate line of sight was on the deck of the *Nina Mackay II*, one of the boats from the Met's Marine Policing Unit, whose crew were silently watching and waiting. In case the girl jumped or fell.

'I don't know what's happened today, Becca,' Alex said after an extended period of quiet, 'but I want you to know how sorry I am about whatever it might be.' He looked sideways at her hunched form. She didn't appear to be shivering, but Alex was sure that the cold was having an effect on her. How could it not have been? 'I'd like to help you if I can.'

Still nothing.

Alex wondered for a moment whether she might be deaf – whether she might not be responding because she couldn't actually hear. But he could see no sign of a hearing aid. At least, not in her right ear. He glanced in the direction of Parliament and made eye contact with the two PCs, raising his eyebrows in acknowledgement of the fact that he too was finding it difficult to get through to her.

Beyond the two officers, on the far side of the cordon tape, he could see the inevitable crowd that had gathered. Voyeurs armed with smartphones were documenting events as they were unfolding – hoping to be the ones to take the picture or record the clip that would later go viral. Because that was how success so often seemed to be measured nowadays: not in the saving of a life, but in the amassing of *clicks* and *likes* and a few fleeting moments of online fame.

Alex would have much preferred it if the crowd wasn't there, but at least none of them was yelling at the girl to get on with it and jump. Unbelievably, that had happened to him before: during a negotiation with a teenager on the top floor of a multistorey car park. An audience had gathered in the street below and Alex had heard one or two voices shouting up at the boy to get it over and done with. Fortunately, the teenager had listened to him and not to them, but how could anyone be so utterly devoid of basic human compassion?

Alex pushed the memory from his mind as he turned back to face Becca. He knew full well that a significant proportion of all human communication is non-verbal. He understood that, if he was paying proper attention, his eyes would be able to tell him at least as much as his ears.

Beneath her tangled hair, her eyes were still closed. Her skin was a washed-out grey colour and there were deep lines set into her forehead. If he could read those lines, what would they say? Though the depth of her distress made her seem a good deal older, Alex guessed she was probably in her early- to mid-twenties. Far too young, he thought, to be overwhelmed by burdens apparently so great. But what were those burdens? What had gone so wrong for her? What had brought her to this place?

She was wearing a black Puffa coat and, beneath that, a white cotton shirt and a light grey V-necked jumper, both of which were rumpled and creased, as though she had slept in them the night before. If, indeed, she had slept at all. Her jeans were covered with streaks of dirt and he noticed the rip at the knee. He suspected that she must have tripped and fallen over at some point. Did she have any physical injuries? Alex couldn't see what she was wearing on her feet, but he hoped sincerely that it was something practical. Anything that might offer her some form of grip.

In the face of her continuing silence, Alex tried to pause the flow of his thoughts in order to take stock of the situation. She was very obviously in a bad way, though he was no closer to understanding why. She was standing on an extremely narrow ledge and had been for a considerable length of time. She had drunk an unknown, though clearly significant, amount of alcohol – Alex could still smell it every time the breeze shifted. And it was cold and getting colder. He told himself that Becca could hardly have been in a more precarious situation.

It was at almost exactly that moment that Alex felt the first spot of rain on his cheek.

Simon Jones MP was sitting at his desk in the Home Office, looking the part. He was wearing a crisp white double-cuffed shirt and a racing-green tie with white polka dots on it. The tailored, single-breasted jacket of his dark-grey suit was hanging on the back of his chair. He looked good for a man of forty-seven, the flecks of grey in his neatly trimmed black hair lending a hint of gravitas to his otherwise remarkably youthful appearance.

He was reading the executive summary of a report on disproportionality in the police use of stop and search – and making a mental note to add it to his growing list of policing problems that needed fixing – when he was interrupted by a knock on his office door. He checked the time on his Breitling watch – a recent birthday gift from his wife – and pushed the report to one side.

'Come in,' he said loudly, the evidence of his Yorkshire heritage clear, even in those two syllables.

Simon Jones was Sheffield born and raised, and immensely proud of the fact. He had been the Member of Parliament for Fulwood – a constituency on the edge of the old industrial city – for the past six years, having retained the once-safe Labour seat with a significant majority at the previous general election. It was clear that the locals there absolutely loved him. He was that rare thing among his contemporaries: an MP who looked genuinely at home in a pub, pint of beer in hand, talking to ordinary people. With his local roots, state-school education, degree from an unheralded university and track record as a self-made businessman, he was a politician with no background in politics – the antithesis of the old-Etonian cabal who had so alienated voters in recent years. His reputation was such that some of his political allies had taken to describing him as 'the future of the Party': a man capable of reversing the Government's parlous position in the polls. Certainly, his reputation was burgeoning among the Westminster commentariat – many of whom were tipping him for higher office, with several suggesting that he might well be destined for the highest office of them all. Even among the Conservatives' most entrenched opponents, there was a certain amount of grudging respect for Simon Jones.

The door opened and Camilla Lane's face appeared. 'I'm so sorry to disturb you,' she said. 'Have you got a moment?'

'Of course,' he replied with a warm smile.

She closed the door behind her and approached his desk.

'It's about Becca,' she said.

'Oh?' he enquired, indicating for her to take a seat.

'Have you spoken to her since Friday?' she asked.

'I spoke to her yesterday actually,' he replied, appearing

unconcerned by the question. 'She rang me up at some point during the evening.'

'And?' Camilla prompted him.

'I talked to her about the things that you and I discussed last week,' he said.

'And how did she take it?'

'As you might expect,' he replied. 'Why do you ask?'

At this, the usually unflappable Camilla Lane hesitated.

'Go on, what is it?' the Minister said, leaning forward in his chair, an expression of passing concern on his face.

'It's just that . . .' Camilla tried to gather her thoughts before continuing. 'It's just that she appears to be on Westminster Bridge.' She hesitated again.

'And?' the Minister asked, looking more troubled.

'And the police are concerned that she might jump into the river.'

'Seriously?' Jones replied, sounding worried now.

'Seriously,' Camilla confirmed.

Rain is most often a police officer's friend. '*PC Rain*', Alex and his colleagues called it, on account of its unerring ability to clear the streets of criminals and troublemakers of almost every kind. But when you are a police officer dealing with a distressed young woman standing on the wrong side of the parapet of a bridge, rain is just about the last thing you want or need.

Alex looked nervously up at the sky as he felt a few more drops fall. The clouds were by no means thunderous, but they bore shadows. He tried to recall the detail of the forecast he'd read back at the station. Light showers, he thought it had said. His task was becoming more urgent by the moment.

'Becca,' he said, a little more loudly than before.

She didn't move. More drops of rain, a little heavier this time.

Alex looked back up at the sky, then down at the river beneath him. He looked at the pair of PCs who were staring up at him from the deck of the *Nina Mackay II*. They were two of a much larger number of people who were looking on from various vantage points – including from the terrace outside the House of Commons – and waiting to see what happened next. The knowledge that he was being watched did nothing to alleviate the pressure of the situation.

Alex felt a twitch of anxiety. How the hell was he going to get her back to safety before the rain set in? Becca seemed unaware of the change in the weather. The whitening around the knuckles on her right hand showed how tightly she was gripping the inside of the balustrade, but how much longer was she going to be able to hold on for? Another twitch of anxiety, more insistent this time. In all his years of negotiating, Alex had never known anyone to remain silent for this long. Right at the moment when he needed it most, his natural ability to get people talking seemed to have deserted him.

There was still no sign of Rich or any of the other negotiators, and no indication of when they might eventually arrive. It occurred briefly to Alex that they might have been held up by the protests in the centre of town. He thought about calling Rich to ask where on earth he was, but immediately dismissed the idea. There really wasn't any point. It wouldn't change anything and it would use up precious time – time that he knew he didn't have.

He looked again at the sky. Again at the water below. The rain was continuing to drizzle and every drop that was landing where Becca was perched was placing her in ever greater jeopardy. The anxiety was starting to hum almost constantly at the edges of his thoughts – nudging his imagination ahead of reality. For a fleeting moment, he thought he could see Becca slip. He thought he could see her fall.

He balled his gloved hands into tight fists, clenched his jaw and told himself to snap out of it. He wasn't going to be of any use to Becca Palmer if he couldn't keep his head together. He took a couple of slow, deep breaths and willed his mind to settle. *Every life is precious*, he insisted to himself as he looked back across at her.

His choices were extremely limited. He could keep trying the same approach – attempting to engage with her from the pavement – but that had yielded nothing so far. If the rest of the team had been there, he would have stepped aside and allowed one of the other negotiators to take over. A simple change of voice had been known to bring a change of fortunes. But that wasn't an option immediately available to him and, in any case, it hadn't worked earlier on – when his uniformed colleagues had handed over to him. Of the remaining alternatives, there was no way that he was going to attempt to make any sort of grab for her. On his original negotiator training course, Alex and his colleagues had been shown CCTV footage of two officers on a bridge trying – and failing – to do exactly that. The grainy images of the falling man had been etched into his imagination ever since.

In that moment, it seemed to Alex that there was really only one thing left to do. He was going to have to climb up onto the balustrade.

Chapter 6

Simon Jones and Camilla Lane remained deep in conversation. His office door was still closed, despite the fact that his next appointment was waiting outside.

'Can you remember exactly what you said to Becca on the phone last night?' Camilla asked him.

The Minister stared up at the ceiling as he tried to recall the precise details. 'As far as I can recall,' he began, 'I told her exactly what we agreed I should say.'

'Which was?'

'That we were concerned about both her attendance and her performance. I pointed out the fact that she has missed something like thirty days of work in the last four months.'

'And?'

'That we had spoken to her about our concerns on a number of occasions before.'

'Keep going.'

'That we knew how bright she was and how much potential she possessed, but that we felt she needed to prioritise her health.'

'Her health? Were you any more specific than that?'

'Well, yes.' He hesitated for a second or two. 'I think I did make specific mention of her mental health.'

'And what was her response?'

'She was in denial.'

'About her mental health or about her performance at work?'

'About her mental health. She didn't really say anything about work.'

'So, how did you leave it with her?'

'I told her that I was genuinely sorry, but that I thought it was best – not least for her – if we went our separate ways.'

'And?'

'And then I ended the call.'

'That was it?'

'More or less, yes.'

'And she didn't give any indication that she was going to do anything stupid?'

'She was upset, of course. But, no, there was no suggestion that anything like this might happen.'

If only you'd waited until this morning to tell her, was what Camilla wanted to say to him, *until we were in the office and I could pick up the pieces*, but she thought better of it. The next few weeks were going to be critical for Simon Jones's political future and she needed to keep his head in the game.

'I feel very sorry for her,' the Minister said.

'I'm sure we all do,' Camilla replied without obvious emotion. 'But she'll be in safe hands with the police.'

Of course, the safer thing for Alex would have been for him to keep both feet planted firmly on the pavement. But he knew that, when it came to saving people's lives, risks were sometimes unavoidable. And, in any case, there was no one to stop him.

He placed his gloved hands on the top of the balustrade. The metal surface was damp and greasy from the rain. 'Would it be all right if I climbed up and joined you, Becca?' he asked.

He stood very still while he gave her a chance to reply. If she said 'no', he would need to reconsider.

But she didn't say anything. She showed no sign of having even heard him.

'Becca, if it's all right with you, I'm going to climb up now,' he said. 'But don't worry, I'm not going to come too close. I just want to make sure that we're able to hear one another.' He intended to keep at least a couple of metres' distance between them: partly to show that he had no intention of making a sudden grab for her and partly to offset the possibility that she might take hold of him and send them both plunging into the water below.

His eyes didn't leave her as he lifted himself slowly onto the top of the balustrade. As he did so, he could feel his anxiety easing a little. It felt good to be doing something positive – something practical – to try to influence the situation. It helped him to feel just that little bit more in control of what was happening.

He didn't climb all the way over. That would have been a risk too far. Instead, he straddled the balustrade as though he was sitting on a horse: one leg on the pavement side, the other dangling in space.

There was another knock on Simon Jones's door.

'Come in,' he said, breaking off from his conversation with Camilla.

The door opened and the young man in the plaid shirt appeared. 'I'm so sorry,' he began, 'but your next appointment has been here for the last few minutes and I know you don't like to keep people waiting.'

Camilla made no attempt to disguise her annoyance at the interruption. She fixed the young man with an irritated stare, but the Minister spoke before she had the opportunity to express her displeasure any further.

'Yes, yes, of course,' he said. 'Thank you. Please can you apologise to him for me. We'll just be a couple of moments.'

The young man nodded and backed out of the room, closing the door behind him.

'I suppose there isn't a great deal we can do at this stage,' the Minister said to his senior aide. 'Unless you can think of anything?'

Camilla had worked with him long enough to know when he was keen to move on. There was a whole lot more they needed to talk about, but it would have to wait. 'Not for now,' she replied, 'but I'll let you know how the situation develops.'

'Of course, yes, thank you,' he said as she got up to leave.

Camilla crossed the room and held the door open as the highly influential editor of the *City Journal* – the country's leading right-of-centre broadsheet newspaper – walked in.

'Geoffrey!' said the Minister, rising from his seat with a broad smile on his face. 'I'm so sorry for the wait. It's very good to see you!'

Camilla Lane left them to it.

Returning to her desk in the main office, she retrieved the blank envelope from beneath a stack of files. She had found it on the floor of the Minister's office first thing that morning, before he had arrived for work. As she opened it and slowly re-read the handwritten note, she reaffirmed her earlier decision to keep the contents to herself. She saw no point in troubling the Minister. Or anyone else for that matter.

Sitting on the balustrade with his back to Big Ben, Alex absorbed the subtle change in perspective. He had turned ninety degrees to his left. The river was now down on his

43

right-hand side – rather than in front of him – and he was looking directly at Becca. Beyond her, he had a clear view of St Thomas', the hospital where his two sons had been born and, more recently, where his father had spent his final days. A place where life began and life ended. But also where lives were saved.

The rain was easing and Alex was still trying to work out what to do next when Becca Palmer suddenly opened her eyes. He was still processing the fact when she turned her head and looked straight at him.

'What did you say your name was?' she asked.

Chapter 7

'My name's Alex,' he said to her, stumbling a little over his words. The unexpected change in her demeanour and the sudden sound of her voice had caught him completely by surprise – knocking him momentarily off balance, both psycho-logically and emotionally. He gripped the balustrade tightly with his knees. He needed to switch on quickly because she was talking again.

'What are you doing here?' she asked him.

'I'm here to help you, Becca,' he said as his training and years of experience started to come back to him.

'Why am I here?' she asked him uncertainly. Her voice was almost childlike. She looked utterly bewildered.

'I was hoping you might be able to tell me that,' Alex responded quietly.

'I've got a headache,' she said.

'I'm so sorry about that,' Alex replied. 'Would you like me to get you a drink of water?' He didn't have any immediately to hand – or even in his rucksack – but he could send one of the PCs to fetch some if necessary. It would provide evidence of the fact that he was there to help, not harm her. And, having given her some water, he might be better placed to ask her for something in return.

But she didn't answer the question. Instead, she looked around her, as though she was taking in her surroundings for the first time. Her gaze settled on the lumpy flow of the water beneath them.

'Please be careful, Becca!' Alex said – a little more loudly than he had intended – as her feet shifted on the ledge. He'd been relieved to see that she was wearing a pair of trainers, but was still enormously concerned about the potential for her to slip and fall. He could hear the scuff of rubber sole against damp and grimy metal. 'Keep looking at me,' he said firmly.

She turned her head back to face him. 'What did you say your name was again?' she asked.

'Alex,' he replied, reassured by the renewal of eye contact.

'Hmm,' she murmured, before retreating back into temporary silence.

Alex had often observed that negotiations with people in deep distress rarely followed what might be described as the 'normal rules' of conversation: where answer followed question and both parties had a reasonable sense of where things might be headed. His exchanges with Becca Palmer already looked set to pursue their own unique and erratic path.

'It seems to me like you're having a really tough day, Becca,' he said, in a deliberate repetition of his earlier statement. On the negotiator training course, what he was doing would have been called 'emotional labelling'. To Alex, it was simple human empathy.

'He told me we were finished,' she said.

'Who told you that?' Alex replied, doing his best to keep pace with the chaotic unfolding of her thoughts and words.

'Simon.'

'Who's Simon?'

'He's the man I'm in love with,' she said.

46

*

'You know she's told some of them that she's in love with you?'
said Camilla Lane. She was back in Simon Jones's office, the
editor of the *City Journal* having just departed.

'What? Who?' the Minister replied distractedly as he
searched for something in the top drawer of his desk.

'Becca,' Camilla said. 'She's told at least three members of the
team that she's in love with you.' She paused for a beat. 'And
that you're in love with her.'

Simon Jones stopped what he was doing and stared at her.
'You've got to be kidding me,' he said.

'His name is Simon Jones,' said Becca.

'Simon Jones?' repeated Alex, trying not to sound surprised
as he made the immediate mental connections: the parliamentary pass, the job at the Home Office. Of course, there might
be more than one person with that name working in Marsham
Street, but, somehow, Alex already knew the answer to his next
question. 'Would that be Simon Jones, the Policing Minister?'
he asked. Alex had never met him, but he certainly knew who
he was: a self-described compassionate Conservative; a happily
married father to three young children; a people's politician; the
man who had declared his intention to reform British policing.
Alex had never much liked him. But then, he had never much
liked any politician.

'Yes,' Becca replied, 'Simon Jones, the Policing Minister.' She
didn't seem to have noticed the expression on Alex's face or
the change in his tone. 'He's my boss at work,' she said. 'Or
rather, he *was* my boss. Until last night, when he told me it
was all over.'

'Last night?'

'Yes, last night at his flat. We were eating dinner and, just like that, he told me we were finished.' She slurred her words a little as she said this.

'I'm so very sorry, Becca,' Alex said.

And, whether it was because of the obvious kindness in his voice or for a different reason entirely, the words began to tumble out of her – as though she could no longer hold them in. Like the surge of water from an underground drain after a mains pipe has burst. Alex had spent a great deal of his time on the bridge fearing that she might never speak. Now he couldn't stop her.

Becca Palmer told him that all she'd ever really wanted was a career in politics – an ambition motivated, she said, by nothing more than the simple desire to make the world a better place. She had started out in life with not very much: sharing a bedroom with her older sister in a small two-up, two-down terrace tucked away in a working-class corner of suburbia. Her parents had spent most of her childhood fighting with one another – staying together, but falling apart. At least, that's how Becca remembered it. During their teenage years, she and her sister had responded to the chaos by burying themselves in their schoolwork and her efforts had been rewarded with a place a Cambridge University and a first class degree in Modern History. Her parents had barely noticed her achievement – they were still too busy finding fault with one another to pay much attention to anyone else – but she had made her big sister proud and that was all that had really mattered to her.

When words tumble, they don't always make perfect sense, but, in spite of her occasional incoherence and the lingering effects of the alcohol she'd consumed, Alex was able to follow most of what she was saying.

At the age of twenty-two, she had moved to London to work as a research assistant for The Independent Justice Foundation

– a Westminster-based think tank set up, according to their blurb, to develop solutions to a range of challenges faced in policing and the wider criminal justice system – and, two years later, she had been recruited to work at the Home Office in a junior advisory role.

The new job was everything she had hoped it would be – all that she had been working towards. She loved being in the thick of things, close to the heart of Government. The subsequent development of her relationship with Simon Jones was the only thing that hadn't formed part of any conscious plan she'd made for herself. It had just been one of those unexpected things that happened to people sometimes. Yes, he was handsome and charismatic and capable – that much was obvious – but there had been so much more to it than that. He came from the sort of humble beginnings that were familiar to her, and he had risen high above them to make something extraordinary of his life. Like her, he saw politics as a force for good and he was determined to use whatever power he had to improve the lives of ordinary people. They had been together for almost a year and, so far, they'd managed to keep it a secret from everyone else. As far as Becca was concerned, they had been making plans for their shared future. At least, they had been until yesterday.

'I didn't mean to fall in love,' she said plaintively. 'And now I've lost everything,' she added as her eyes brimmed with tears.

'Everything?' Alex responded.

'My job. My relationship. My reputation. Everything.' The words seemed to catch in her throat. Her face folded up in regret as the tears began to flow.

Encouraged though he had been by her willingness to talk, Alex felt suddenly nervous about the direction the conversation might now be headed in. Without meaning to, he edged a fraction closer to her. 'I'm so sorry, Becca,' he said. 'I really am.'

'I can't do this any more,' she said, and her knees seemed to buckle a little.

'Can't do what?' asked Alex, dreading the likely answer.

'Life,' she replied, with exhausted finality. 'There's nothing left for me now.'

'That's not true,' Alex said as his earlier anxieties resurfaced with renewed intensity. His chest felt tight and his breathing was shallow. Now, more than ever, he needed to hold it together. 'I know it feels like that at the moment,' he reflected, making no attempt to diminish her pain, 'but I promise you that it won't always be that way.'

She responded with a look of complete incomprehension, as though he was speaking to her in a language she didn't understand.

'I can't do this any more,' she mumbled through her tears, as her feet shuffled once more on the hopelessly narrow ledge.

Chapter 8

Alex edged along the balustrade another centimetre or two, suddenly terrified that he was losing her. Terrified that she was about to fall. The freezing cold river continued to run at pace beneath them. The tide was out and it was a long way down.

'Look at me, Becca,' he pleaded.

She responded with a heave of her shoulders and a sigh that seemed to come from the very depths of her being.

'What about your sister?' Alex asked suddenly. The question came to him in a single, split second of clarity. She had mentioned her sister earlier in the conversation. A sister who was proud of her. Surely, that had to be a good thing. In that moment, it was all he had.

'My sister?'

Her voice was barely louder than a whisper. But, thank God, she was still talking to him. She hadn't jumped. Not yet.

'Yes, you talked about your sister a little while ago,' said Alex. 'She sounded amazing.'

'She is.'

'What's her name?' Alex had somehow managed to re-establish a connection with Becca and he was desperate not to lose it.

'Helen,' Becca replied. 'Her name is Helen. She's older than me.'

'Are you still in touch with her?' asked Alex, wanting to establish the nature of their relationship. Were they close? If they were, might he be able to make use of the fact to try to influence whatever Becca chose to do next?

'Of course,' Becca replied as though the question was an unnecessary one. 'We talk all the time. She knows everything about me.'

'And what would Helen say if she was here with us now?' Alex asked, feeling a little more certain of what he was trying to achieve.

Becca stared at him. And then she studied the empty space to his left, as though she was imagining her sister standing there on the pavement. Alex watched her as she tried to process her thoughts.

'She'd tell me not to give up,' Becca said eventually.

'She'd tell you not to give up,' Alex repeated. And it felt as though the weight of the entire world was lifting from his shoulders.

'But I'm not as strong as Helen,' she said.

'I think you're stronger than you'll ever know,' Alex replied. 'I think that today hurts like hell and that tomorrow will too. But I think you're going to get through this. And I think Helen would say the same.'

'Really?' she asked, sounding unconvinced.

'Really,' Alex answered. 'Sometimes, when it feels as though the sky is falling on our heads, it can be difficult – impossible even – to believe that things will ever get better. But I promise you that they will.'

'How do you know?' Becca asked him. 'How can you possibly be so sure?'

'Because I've been there,' he replied.

*

On the south side of the bridge, a marked traffic car with its blue lights flashing pulled up next to Alex's van. DCI Rich Wells climbed out of the back seat and thanked the driver before introducing himself to the PC on the cordon. He was about fifty metres from the centre of the bridge when Alex saw him approaching. With the smallest of hand gestures, he indicated to Rich that he wanted him to stay back. Becca was still talking to him.

'Can I talk to Helen?' she asked.

'Of course you can,' Alex said. 'As soon as you're safely back on the pavement, we can call her.'

'Do you promise me?'

'You have my word.'

'But my phone's broken,' she said.

'No problem,' he said reassuringly. 'Do you know your sister's number?'

'Yes.'

'In which case,' Alex replied, 'you would be welcome to borrow my phone.'

Becca took a second or two to consider the situation. 'In which case, I think I'd like to climb back over now,' she said.

The wave of relief that swept over Alex was tempered immediately by the realisation that the next few moments would be as critical as any in the past few hours. Becca was still standing on a very narrow ledge. She was still on the wrong side of the balustrade. The rain had left everything damp and unpredictable. Alex found himself thinking about the stories of climbers who reached the summits of mountains, only to lose their lives on the descent.

'You're being incredibly brave, Becca,' he said. 'If it's all right with you, I want you to stay exactly where you are and I'm going to move a little bit closer. Would that be OK?'

She nodded and kept looking at him.

Moving in slow motion, Alex eased himself carefully towards her. 'Now,' he said, 'I want you to keep your right hand exactly where it is – holding on tight to the bridge. OK?'

She nodded again, her eyes not leaving him.

'And, when you're ready,' he continued, 'I want you to reach across with your other hand and take hold of mine.' He held out the open palm of his right hand as he said this. 'Take all the time you need,' he added, 'we're not in any rush.'

Becca's left hand was quivering as she reached slowly across the front of her body, towards him. As she did so, her shoulders rotated naturally and her feet started to follow. Alex took a firm, reassuring grip on her hand and guided her carefully round, until her back was to the water and she was facing the pavement.

'Well done, Becca,' he whispered as the relief threatened almost to overwhelm him. 'You're doing so well.' He let her settle in her new position before he continued. 'Now, if it's all right with you, I'm going to ask a friend of mine to come and help us with this last bit. Would that be OK?' Again, she nodded. 'His name is Richard and he's a good person.'

Alex looked over at Rich and nodded at him. Without the need for any sort of explanation, Rich walked straight over to join them.

'Rich, I'd like you to meet Becca,' Alex said. 'Becca, this is my friend Richard.'

'I'm very pleased to meet you, Becca,' Rich said.

'Becca would appreciate a bit of help climbing back over,' Alex explained.

'No problem,' replied Rich. He placed a gentle hand on Becca's right wrist. 'It's OK,' he said to her, 'I've got you. You can let go of the bridge now.'

Without releasing his grip on her other hand, Alex slipped his right leg back over the balustrade and put both feet on the pavement. 'All right, Becca,' he said, 'your turn now.'

The two men leaned forward and lifted her gingerly up and over the balustrade. They helped her down onto the pavement and Alex put a firm arm around her shoulders. She started shivering uncontrollably.

Alex turned to the two PCs who were still close by. 'Can one of you grab us a blanket from somewhere?' he asked them.

Alex and Rich eased Becca into a sitting position on the ground and Alex sat down next to her. He pulled his mobile phone out of his pocket and offered it to her.

'Would you like to call your sister now?' he asked.

Simon Jones had just walked back into his office from a meeting elsewhere in the building when Camilla Lane appeared with the news that Becca Palmer was safe.

'Thank God for that,' the Minister said as he sank into his chair. 'Have they said what's going to happen to her?'

'I imagine they'll either take her to hospital or to the nearest police station,' Camilla replied.

'Why on earth would they take her to a police station?'

'Because police stations are designated places of safety under the Mental Health Act.'

'But she obviously needs medical help. Surely hospital is the best place for her?'

'I agree,' said Camilla. 'I think she may well end up being sectioned.'

'Really?' said the Minister.

'I would think so,' she replied, 'particularly when you think about some of the other things she's said and done over the course of the last few months. We've known that she's not been well for a while now.'

Simon Jones looked at the large framed photograph of his wife and three children that had pride of place on his desk. 'Did she really tell people that she was having an affair with me?' he asked.

'She did,' Camilla replied. 'But – and I hope I don't sound too unkind saying this – everyone in the office knows that she sometimes has a habit of saying things that turn out not to be true.'

Alex was standing next to Rich as they watched Becca being helped into the back of an ambulance, a red blanket wrapped around her shoulders and a female PC at her side. Chances were, that would be the last Alex ever saw of her. He'd done his job as a negotiator and she was someone else's responsibility now.

'You're an idiot,' said Rich as the ambulance pulled away.

'What do you mean?' Alex replied, though he knew exactly what was coming.

'Climbing onto the balustrade,' Rich remarked. 'Putting yourself in unnecessary danger. Potentially making things much more difficult for the rest of us.' His tone was much gentler than the words he was using, but he was making a serious point. He was emphasising the fact that Alex had done something that wouldn't be found in any negotiation manual – at least, not without a full team around him and a whole series of safety measures in place.

'She's alive, isn't she?' Alex responded. 'And, in any case,' he insisted, 'I know you'd have done exactly the same thing.'

'So that's the full extent of the debrief is it?' asked Rich with a half-smile of resignation.

'More or less,' Alex replied. 'What the hell happened to the rest of the team?'

'I think they're still stuck in the middle of a crowd of angry demonstrators,' Rich answered, 'somewhere on the other side of Trafalgar Square.'

Three quarters of an hour later, Westminster Bridge was open again. The cordon tape had been removed and the last of the uniformed police officers had left the scene. Rich had gone too. The traffic was moving slowly and the pavements were once again full of tourists and card sharks and bagpipe players. It was as if the events of the past few hours hadn't happened.

But the black negotiators' van was still parked outside St Thomas' Hospital. Alex was sitting alone in the back of it. His hands were shaking as he lit a cigarette.

Chapter 9

'I thought I was going to lose her, Pip,' Alex said. It was just before 10 p.m. and the two of them were sitting at their kitchen table, talking through everything that had happened that afternoon. Alex had barely touched the bowl of stir fry in front of him.

'But you didn't,' Pip replied. 'You saved her life.'

'I could see her falling,' he said, taking a sip from a half-empty bottle of beer. He was still on call and knew that he ought to have been sticking to soft drinks, but he had needed something stronger. He would just have to rely on the phone not ringing for the rest of the night. 'I was sitting right there, opposite her, and I was imagining it happening.'

'But it didn't happen, did it?' she responded, placing a reassuring hand on his forearm as she spoke. Given her own extensive negotiating experience, Pip had a clear understanding of the unique set of pressures and demands that went with the role.

Leaning back in his chair, Alex rocked his head slowly from one side to the other in an effort to release some of the tension in his neck. 'I do sometimes wonder why I keep doing this to myself,' he said.

'Keep doing what?'

'Why I keep putting myself through it as a negotiator,' he clarified, though he was only being half-serious. It had certainly been a testing day, but it had turned out all right in the end. Becca Palmer was safe.

'You already know the answer to that,' she said as if reading his mind. 'You keep putting yourself through it because, number one, you love it and, number two, you're bloody good at it. And, in any case, you're hopeless at sitting on the sidelines. You and I both know that it's always better to be involved – especially when there are lives at stake.'

Listening to her, Alex was reminded of the story he'd once heard about a young boy who lived next to the ocean. Early one morning, in the aftermath of a great storm, the boy had found thousands of starfish washed up on the sand. He knew they would die in the heat of the day if he didn't do something, so he began picking them up, one at a time, and throwing them back into the water. Further along the beach, an old man was watching him. After a while, he approached the boy. 'Really, what is the point?' the old man asked. 'There are far too many of them – what possible difference are you going to make?' The boy paused for a moment to consider the question before bending down, picking up another starfish and throwing it into the sea. 'All the difference in the world to that one,' he replied.

Alex knew Pip was right. If it took a day or two for his mind to settle, then so be it. He would still be ready for the next call. Because there would always be more starfish washed up on the sand.

Alex woke the following morning having slept all the way through the night. Given all that had happened on the bridge, he had half-expected the dreams to return. But the ghosts had stayed away.

Pip had left for work by the time he got back from his morning run, so he ate breakfast alone while he checked the morning headlines on his laptop: wars and rumours of wars in the Middle East; refugees massing at European borders; the latest sobering facts about global warming; a serving junior cabinet minister – a nondescript man whose name Alex didn't recognise – caught offering political access in return for financial donations; a second successive day of anti-government protests planned for central London.

He checked the time and reckoned that he should be able to make the journey up to Kentish Town before the crowds started to gather.

'So how did the performance meeting go yesterday?' Alex asked. He was sitting in his office, with his feet propped up on a low table, talking to Chief Inspector Ronnie Egan.

'As you would expect,' his deputy responded with a note of exasperation. 'The Area Commander was his normal completely unreasonable self: the crime figures are too high; the teams on the ground aren't doing enough; the press are asking awkward questions; the Commissioner is under pressure from the Home Office.'

'The same as always then,' said Alex. 'Did the Commander actually offer us anything by way of practical support?'

'Of course he bloody didn't,' Ronnie replied. 'He actually used the phrase "*more for less*".'

'I swear that man is more politician than police officer,' Alex responded irritably. 'He's actually part of the problem.'

'He's not bright enough to be a politician,' observed Ronnie.

'Nor are some of the politicians I've met,' Alex replied.

*

An hour later, Alex wandered out of the police station to buy his lunch. Turning right onto Kentish Town Road, he walked into the local Tesco Metro in search of something healthier than the usual sandwich-and-crisps meal deal. As he walked past the display of newspapers and magazines, he was startled by the sight of Simon Jones MP staring at him from the front cover of *The Economist* magazine. The undeniably statesman-like head-and-shoulders photograph accompanied a byline that read: 'Could this man be our next Prime Minister?'

Alex couldn't remember the last time he had read an article in *The Economist*, but he was intrigued enough to buy a copy along with his chicken salad and can of Diet Coke. He realised that he wanted to know more about the man Becca Palmer claimed to have fallen in love with.

Back at the station, as he sat down at his desk and started to read, it immediately became clear to him that the author of the article held his subject in particularly high regard. Simon Jones certainly stood out from the political crowd. One of five children, he had been raised by a father who had worked hard in the local steel industry and a mother who had worked even harder in the family home. If it wasn't exactly a working-class upbringing, Jones certainly hadn't come from any kind of money. Emerging from university with a second class degree in Business Management, he had set up his own technology company in the heart of Sheffield and, ten years later, he was employing close to two hundred people and turning over several million pounds a year. He was happily married to Frances – whom he'd met not long after graduating – and they had three children. They were a genuine Sheffield success story, sharing local newspaper column inches with the likes of Jessica Ennis-Hill and the Arctic Monkeys.

His journey into politics had begun when he was in his

mid-thirties. He'd made a small fortune selling his business and decided that he wanted to give something back to the local community. He and Frances had set up a foundation to support disadvantaged local children with their education, and his charitable endeavours – combined with his commercial achievements and telegenic good looks – had caught the eye of someone senior in the local Conservative Party machine. They had approached him to stand as their candidate in the next general election and he'd won the Fulwood seat at his first attempt.

Wearing his political philosophy very much on his sleeve, he had written a short book – more of a booklet, really – that set out his vision for the country. He called it –rather too grandiosely, Alex thought – *Making Britain Great Again: The Road Back to Prosperity*, and he used the text to rail against what he described as the 'twin evils' of government overspending and overregulation. He wanted to roll back the state and set the market free to secure the nation's success. And the general public seemed set on buying whatever he was selling.

Simon Jones was a no-nonsense, plain-speaking, highly relatable, genuinely popular politician. In short, he was a complete breath of fresh air – considered by a growing number of people in the Conservative Party and beyond to be the Prime Minister-in-waiting.

As Alex was absorbing the detail, he was conscious of the clear disconnect between his own perception of the Minister – not least in light of what he had heard from Becca – and most of what was written on the page. And he was also struck by the fact that he was reading it in *The Economist*: a serious publication with a serious audience. This was not some puff piece in a glossy magazine, complete with air-brushed pictures and PR-infected prose. This was proper journalism.

Had Becca Palmer been telling him the truth about her relationship with Simon Jones?

Had she been telling him the truth about anything?

The following Saturday, Alex and Pip were enjoying a late pub lunch and reading the weekend papers. Alex was partway through an article in the sports pages about the decline of Manchester United in the post-Ferguson years when Pip interrupted him.

'Have you seen this?' she said. There was a clear note of indignation in her voice.

'Seen what?' Alex replied.

'This,' she repeated, holding up a copy of that day's *City Journal*. 'A full-page article written by none other than the Policing Minister.'

'He seems to be everywhere at the moment,' said Alex, only half looking up from his own article. 'I was reading something about him in *The Economist* earlier this week.'

'*The Economist*? You?' asked Pip in mock surprise.

'I read it all the time,' said Alex with wide eyes and a knowing grin.

'Well, have you seen *this*?' she pressed, waving her newspaper at him as she did so. She was clearly annoyed by what she'd been reading.

'I haven't, no,' he replied, his grin a counterpoint to her grumpiness. She could be entertaining company when she got worked up about something. 'What does it say?'

'It says – and I'm paraphrasing here – that policing in this country is in a shit state and that he's the man to sort it out.'

'Is that actually what it says?' asked Alex, his smile turning to a frown. Listening to *bloody politicians* handing down pompous and ill-informed judgements about the job he loved

– the job he had devoted almost his entire adult life to – was something that never failed to darken his mood.

'Not in exactly those words,' Pip admitted, 'but that's the general gist of it. Policing is, apparently, the last unreformed public service. We're going to have to modernise, become more accountable, more efficient. He's drawing on his own business experience and suggesting that the police service has a whole lot to learn from the private sector.'

'Has he said that we're going to have to do more for less?' Alex asked, now sounding every bit as resentful as he looked.

'That's exactly what he's said,' Pip replied.

Two weeks later, it was Pip's turn to take her place on the hostage negotiation rota. Since setting up home together, she and Alex had made a specific point of keeping their negotiation duties separate from one another. It helped them to maintain a healthy distance between their work and home lives.

But all of that was about to change.

Chapter 10

Alex had just got home from work when his mobile rang. He checked the call display.

'Hey, Pip,' he said cheerfully. 'What time are you back?'

'Are you doing anything at the moment?' she asked, side-stepping his question.

'It's Tuesday, remember?' he said. 'I'm just about to head out to meet the boys.' Other than when he was on call or away on leave with Pip, Tuesday evenings tended to be the ones set aside for Alex to spend time with his two sons. During the football season, when the Champions League was on, they would find a pub with a big screen and enjoy a match together. It was practically the only commitment in his diary that Alex would never think about cancelling. And Pip had never dreamed of asking him to.

'Shit! Sorry! I'd completely forgotten what day it was,' Pip apologised. There was an edge in her voice that Alex picked up on straight away.

'Are you all right?' he asked, unable to mask his concern.

'Yes, yes, I'm absolutely fine,' she reassured him.

'What is it then?'

'It's Becca Palmer,' Pip replied. 'Remember her? The girl you dealt with a couple of weeks back?'

'Of course I do,' Alex replied. 'Why? What's happened?'
An image of Becca's face immediately filled his mind. In it, she
was crying.

'She's back on the bridge.'

'She's what?' Alex replied, his mind somehow slow to catch
up with what Pip was telling him.

'She's back on Westminster Bridge,' Pip replied. 'And she's
refusing to speak to anyone except you.'

'She's what?' said an unsettled Simon Jones to Camilla Lane.

'Apparently she's back on Westminster Bridge,' Camilla replied. 'In exactly the same place as last time.'

'But I thought she was in hospital?'

'She was. I visited her there last week.'

'You did?' the Minister seemed surprised. 'That was kind
of you.'

Camilla shrugged. 'It's my job,' she replied.

'So why isn't she still in hospital now?'

'She must have discharged herself.'

'Can she even do that?' asked the Minister.

'She can if she's a voluntary patient,' Camilla replied.

The Minister rubbed his face and ran his fingers through
his hair. It had already been a very long day and he was due
to leave for an evening function in less than an hour. 'So what
do we do?' he asked.

'Have you tried telling her that you know all about what happened last time?' Alex ventured.

His head was spinning. His immediate professional instinct
was to grab his coat and head straight back out of the door, just
as he'd always done in the past. Because he understood that,
when you're a police officer, the calls never stop coming. And

so he'd always kept going. On any other evening of the week, he wouldn't have hesitated. But this was a Tuesday evening and his time with his boys was sacrosanct – the realisation of a promise he'd made to them not long after his separation from their mother. And it was a promise he'd managed to keep ever since.

But that didn't change the fact that someone out there was in terrible trouble, and that they were asking for his help. Should he go to her? Or should he honour his commitment to his sons? Of course he should. He wasn't even on call. But what if she jumped and he wasn't there? Back and forth the arguments went in his mind. It felt like an impossible dilemma.

'Have you explained that you're just as able to help her as I am?' he asked Pip.

'Of course I have,' Pip replied, trying to remain patient. 'I've been trying to reason with her for the past hour and a bit. But she's flat-out refusing to talk to anyone except you.'

'Why?'

'If I knew the answer to that question, it might give me something to work with,' Pip said. 'But I don't.'

Alex really didn't want to ring his boys and cancel their plans. His repeated past failures to put family before work was a large part of the reason why his marriage had fallen apart in the first place. But Becca Palmer was asking specifically and directly for his help. Was he ready to save her life?

'I know it's terrible timing,' Pip continued, 'but I just can't seem to get through to her.'

'I struggled to get through to her last time,' Alex replied, continuing to wrestle with what was being asked of him. 'But we got there in the end.'

'I know,' Pip responded. 'But I've got a strange feeling about this one. I really hate to ask, but I think I need you here.'

Alex fell silent. He rattled through a mental inventory of all his failings as a father, set alongside his more recent attempts to make amends. He hadn't missed a planned evening with his boys in more than a year. Surely a single postponement wouldn't undo all that investment of time and love. But it was also true that the reliable consistency of their get-togethers had been fundamental to the mending of his relationship with them. Having got it so wrong for so long, why on earth would he do anything that might jeopardise what he and his sons now had?

'The boys will understand,' said Pip, apparently sensing what he was thinking. 'You can rearrange something for tomorrow.'

Maybe the boys would *understand*, Alex thought to himself. He could make it up to them. Perhaps he could try to get actual tickets to see a Champions League football game later in the season, rather than just watching it with them on TV. He could talk to his counterpart at Islington – the Superintendent who looked after Arsenal matches at the Emirates Stadium. She might be able to help him out. Yes, that's what he'd do. He'd call his sons. He'd make it right. Then he'd go to Becca Palmer.

'All right,' he said to Pip at last. 'I'll be with you as soon as I can.'

He sincerely hoped that he was doing the right thing.

'I don't think we need to do anything,' Camilla Lane said to Simon Jones. 'Not least, because she doesn't actually work here any more.'

'That's a bit harsh,' said the Minister, reproachfully. 'Surely we have some sort of duty of care for her?'

'Of course. That's the reason I went to see her in hospital,' Camilla said bluntly. 'But, right at this moment in time, I don't think there's a great deal we *can* do. It's in the hands of the police now – and whoever is responsible for her medical treatment.'

'It just doesn't seem right to me,' he said.

'Maybe not,' she replied, 'but it can't be helped. And, in any case, you've got a dinner to attend and a speech to make this evening. Those are the things I need you to be concentrating on.'

Much to Alex's relief, the phone call with his oldest son had gone unexpectedly well. *No problem*, he had said. He and his younger brother were both free the following evening and they were more than happy to rearrange. Perhaps the three of them could go and see the latest *Mission Impossible* film together. That had sounded great to Alex. At the same time, though, he had told himself that it was absolutely a one-off – that he was not going to make a habit of changing their plans at the last minute. There was no way he was going back to the days when he disappointed them so routinely that even his ex-wife had given up commenting on the fact.

He locked the house and was hurrying in the direction of Stockwell tube station when he happened to see a marked police car heading in his direction. He stepped off the pavement and flagged it down. The driver pulled up alongside him and lowered the front passenger window. He looked as though he was just about to deliver a lecture on the inadvisability of walking out in front of a moving vehicle – and a police one at that – when Alex produced his warrant card.

'Superintendent Alex Lewis,' he said, slightly breathlessly.

The look of annoyance on the PC's face vanished the moment Alex mentioned his rank. He sat up a little straighter in his seat.

'Can I help you, sir?' he enquired.

'Are you in the middle of anything important?' Alex asked him.

'Nothing that can't wait,' the PC replied.

'In which case,' said Alex, 'I need you to get me to Westminster Bridge as quickly as possible.'

'What's at Westminster Bridge?' the PC asked.

'I'm a negotiator,' Alex explained. 'I've been called there to help with someone who might be about to jump.'

'In that case,' the officer responded, 'we'd better get going.'

As Alex opened the car door and got in, the PC called up on his radio to explain what was happening and to get himself assigned to the call.

'Sorry for the interruption,' Alex said.

'No problem,' replied the PC as he switched the blues and twos on, spun the car around and put his foot down.

Chapter 11

The last light of the autumn day had faded to a deep orange glow as the liveried Vauxhall Astra Estate hurtled east along South Lambeth Road.

Alex got his phone out to text Pip. '*With you in 5,*' he typed. Seconds later, he received a single '*x*' in reply. This would be the first time they had been deployed together since Herne Hill; the first time since they had been together as a couple. Would it make any difference? Alex didn't know. In any case, for the time being, he was more preoccupied with thinking about Becca Palmer.

In his imagination, he was replaying moments from his previous negotiation with her: his arrival on the scene; his first sight of her; for some reason, the green colour of the paint on the balustrade; the close-up mess of her physical appearance; the strong smell of booze on her breath; the stubborn, unsettling silence; the first drops of rain; the growing sense of unease; the eventual, unexpected sound of her voice.

How was it going to play out this time? What kind of state was she going to be in? The fact that she had asked to talk to him seemed to be a good sign. But what was she going to say?

The driver continued to pick his way expertly through the traffic, through Little Portugal and the Vauxhall one-way system, onto Albert Embankment and towards Lambeth Palace. The back end of the car kicked out a little at the next round-about and, despite the pressure and intensity of the situation, Alex couldn't help smiling to himself. The *Boy's Own* thrill of a blue-light run was still there, even after more than two decades in 'the Job'.

As they approached the A&E entrance at the back of St Thomas' – with the inevitable queue of ambulances backed up on the forecourt – the traffic started to slow for the first time, no doubt as a consequence of the latest closure of Westminster Bridge.

'You can let me out anywhere along here,' Alex said to the PC, reckoning that it would be quicker to cover the last few hundred metres on foot.

'You're sure?'

'Absolutely,' Alex replied as the driver pulled over at the side of the road. 'Thanks again for the ride.'

He was out of the car and running before the PC had a chance to reply. He turned the corner onto the bridge just as Big Ben was striking seven. Up ahead of him, in exactly the same place as before, Becca Palmer was once again on the wrong side of the balustrade. Pip was standing on the pavement close by, along with a male negotiator whose face Alex recognised, but whose name he couldn't immediately recall.

As soon as she saw Alex, Pip headed straight over to him.

'Thanks for coming,' she smiled wearily. 'Were the boys OK?'

'Actually, they were fine,' Alex replied. 'I'll see them to-morrow instead.'

'That's good,' she said.

'So how are you doing?' he asked.

'We're not making any progress at all,' Pip replied. 'But I've told her that you're on your way and I'm hoping that, once she knows you're here, she'll climb back over and talk to us. Or to you at least.'

'What sort of state is she in?' Alex asked.

'Well, she's definitely been drinking,' Pip replied.

'And?'

'She's in a bad way.'

Not far away – a little over a mile as the river flows – Simon Jones was enjoying the moment. He had just been introduced to his black-tie audience in the main banqueting hall at one of the City's most prestigious livery companies and they had responded with the sort of ovation that most of his fellow parliamentarians could only dream of. Camilla Lane was nodding approvingly from her vantage point at the back of the room.

The Minister leaned in towards the microphone that had been placed on the top table in front of him. 'You are all far too kind,' he said, while motioning for everyone to take their seats. He had to repeat the gesture several times before people eventually complied.

He took a handful of index cards out of his inside pocket and squared them off as though they were a poker deck. He paused and studied the notes he'd written on the first of them while he waited for the hum in the packed room to fade.

'My lords, ladies and gentlemen,' he said grandly. 'Thank you for such a kind and generous welcome. It is a great pleasure to be able to spend some time with you here this evening.'

He paused and scanned the room, ensuring that he made direct eye contact with several notable guests. He and Camilla had studied the seating plan in advance and he knew exactly where to look and who to look for.

He glanced back down at his notes. 'For the benefit of those in the room I've yet to have the privilege of meeting, there are four things that I want you to know about me.' He paused for a beat or two. 'The first is that I'm a proud Yorkshireman. Second, that I'm a proud family man. Third, that I'm a proud businessman.' Another beat. 'And, fourth, that I'm a proud Conservative.' He'd been practising the delivery of these few sentences for the previous couple of days and the preparation paid off handsomely. By the time he had finished saying the word 'Conservative', half the people in the room were back on their feet. Everyone was applauding.

He responded to them with a broad smile, while gesturing once more for them all to take their seats.

'Given those facts about me,' he continued, 'I'd like to take a few minutes of your time to explain why I think that the public sector in this country would benefit from far greater levels of private involvement in the work that they do.'

Back on Westminster Bridge, Alex was moving slowly and deliberately as he approached Becca Palmer. As had been the case two weeks earlier, he wanted to avoid doing anything that might take her by surprise. He walked in a slow arc behind her back, and only started to move closer to her when he was confident that she could see him. There was a flicker of recognition in her eyes as he reached the balustrade.

If anything, she looked worse than the last time he'd seen her. She had visibly lost weight and her face was pale and drawn, with large black circles beneath her eyes. Her hair was limp and greasy and the only reason her make-up wasn't a mess was the fact that she didn't appear to be wearing any. She was wearing the same black Puffa coat as before, zipped up to her chin. Below her, the tide was high and the surface of the river was rippling with light: red from the warning beacons on the arches of the bridge, yellow from the street lamps on either side of the road, an undulating pillar of gold where the angled reflection of Big Ben fell.

'Hello, Becca,' Alex said quietly as she half-turned her head towards him. 'I don't know if you remember me,' he continued, 'but my name's Alex. We met a couple of weeks ago.'

'I remember you,' Becca said. Her voice was brittle and whispery. There was no mistaking the smell of alcohol on her breath and even on her coat. Alex watched as a single teardrop rolled down her cheek.

'I'm so sorry that you're having another bad day,' he said quietly and gently.

Becca stared at him, but didn't respond.

'My friend Pip rang me and said that you wanted to speak to me,' Alex continued.

Becca nodded slowly. She was looking straight at him but seemed to be having trouble getting her eyes to focus.

'Why don't I help you back over here, onto the pavement, and we can find somewhere a bit more comfortable to have a conversation,' Alex suggested, seizing on the earliest possible opportunity to try to get her back to safety.

'Maybe,' she murmured. But she didn't move.

The *Nina Mackay II* was back with them on the water below and, this time, she had been joined by a bright orange lifeboat from the nearby RNLI station.

Every life is precious, thought Alex once more.

He glanced over to where Pip was standing. With a subtle circular movement of her hand, she encouraged him to keep going.

'What did you want to talk about?' Alex asked.

Becca didn't respond straight away. She seemed to be finding it difficult to gather up her words into any kind of coherent order.

'Take as long as you need to, Becca,' Alex told her. 'We've got time.'

Simon Jones sat back down with the applause still echoing off the walls of the banqueting hall. He adjusted his bow tie and acknowledged the succession of replenished wine glasses being raised in a toast by his dining companions. Off to one side of the top table, a well-heeled queue was forming: a spontaneous gathering of the rich and the powerful, all hoping to grab a few moments with the Minister or, at the very least, to have their photograph taken with him.

His star was very much in the ascendant.

Becca sighed deeply. The same kind of sigh that Alex had heard the last time he'd encountered her.

He tried to read the expression on her face. He could see the exhaustion and confusion, but he knew that there was a whole lot more going on below the surface. 'What's on your mind?' he asked her.

She opened her mouth to respond, hesitated and closed it again, as though she was struggling with the weight of the words she was trying to use.

'It's all right, Becca,' Alex reassured her. 'Take as much time as you need.'

When she eventually spoke, it was with an uncertain, wavering voice. 'Are you going to leave me?' she asked him.

'Leave you?' Alex replied, caught unawares by her question and failing to hide his surprise. 'Of course I'm not going to leave you. I'm right here and I'm not going anywhere.'

'You're here now,' Becca said, her words starting to slur a

little into one another. 'But you won't be later on. You'll leave me, just like you did last time.' And, as she spoke, Alex realised for the first time that he could hear something beyond the desperate sadness in her voice. Something that sounded to him like fear.

'I only left last time when I was certain you were safe,' he said to her, rather more defensively than he had intended.

She turned her head away from him and stared back down at the water below. 'But I wasn't safe,' she said, her voice trailing away.

Chapter 12

'Look at me, Becca,' Alex pleaded, unnerved both by the loss of eye contact and by the implications of what she had just said.

Several long seconds passed before she eventually turned her head back towards him, her face a picture of ever-deepening despair. And he realised with increasing certainty that it wasn't only despair he was looking at. Alex thought that he'd heard it in her voice a few moments earlier and now he could see it, in the tensing of her jawline, and in the distressed flicker in her darkened eyes – she was afraid.

'I'm so sorry you didn't feel safe, Becca,' he said gently. 'Are you able to tell me why that was?'

She looked at him blankly, as though she had lost her place on the page of their conversation.

'Just now, you said to me that you didn't feel safe when I left you last time,' Alex prompted her. 'I was telling you that I was sorry and I was wondering whether you might be able to tell me why?'

'Camilla came to see me in hospital.'

Alex couldn't immediately tell whether this was an answer to his question, or simply the next thought to have entered her troubled mind. 'Who's Camilla?' he asked patiently.

'She brought me some flowers.'

'That was kind of her,' Alex said, trying his best to remain in step with what Becca was saying to him.

'She brought a document for me to sign as well.'

'A document?' Alex asked, confused by the apparently random nature of the things she was telling him. Camilla. Hospital. Flowers. Document. It didn't seem to make a great deal of sense. 'What sort of document?'

'She told me that I wasn't allowed to talk about it,' Becca replied nervously.

Alex could hear the hesitation in her voice, but he was none the wiser. He realised that, if he was going to be able to make any sort of sense of what she was saying, he needed to retrace the last few steps of their exchange.

'Forgive me, Becca,' he said. 'I've managed to get myself a little bit muddled. Can you tell me who Camilla is?'

'Camilla from work.'

'One of your colleagues?'

'My boss, I suppose.'

'I thought Simon Jones was your boss.'

'He is. Or he *was*,' Becca said with regret. 'Camilla is his senior advisor.'

'Do you know what her surname is?'

'Lane,' Becca responded quietly. 'Her name is Camilla Lane.'

'And Camilla came to see you in hospital?' In most other circumstances, Alex would have avoided asking so many closed questions – those demanding only a 'yes' or 'no' answer – but he was conscious of the need to establish some basic facts.

Becca nodded.

'And she brought a document for you to sign?'

Becca seemed to shrink away from him. 'She said that I wasn't allowed to talk about it,' she reiterated, her anxiety becoming ever more apparent. She looked back down at the river and, as she did so, the soles of her trainers scratched on the narrow surface of the ledge.

Alex winced at the sound. 'Please be careful, Becca,' he insisted, raising his hands in a plea to her to stand still. The two boats were maintaining their stations on the river below, their crews standing by.

Becca stopped moving and renewed her grip on the balustrade. Alex breathed a little more easily, but his mind was whirring as he tried to work out what he should say next. He reminded himself that he was there – standing in the biting cold on Westminster Bridge – because she had made a specific request for him to be there. He told himself that she had refused to talk to anyone else, but that she had asked to talk to him. And, reluctant though she was now sounding, Alex sensed that she really did want to talk.

'I can tell that you're frightened, Becca,' he said cautiously, 'and I very much want to help you. Would it help if you told me just a little bit about the document?'

Becca looked distressed and uncertain. Once again, it took a seeming eternity for her to respond.

'If I do tell you about it,' she said falteringly, 'you have to promise me that you're not going to tell anyone else.'

'How did the speech sound from the back of the room?' Simon Jones asked Camilla. A procession of silent staff dressed in black waistcoats were clearing away the main course and the Minister had taken the opportunity to step away from his table – and the queue of well-wishers – for a few moments.

'Outstanding,' his senior advisor replied. 'I actually don't think it could have gone any better.'

'That's good,' he replied. 'Thank you for all your help in putting it together.'

'That's what I'm here for,' she acknowledged.

'Well, I want you to know that I don't take it for granted.'

'Thank you,' she said. 'And before you head back to your table, there's someone I want you to meet.'

'Who?'

'His name's Seb Neill and he's a significant party donor. He's funded a couple of the recent reports from The Independent Justice Foundation.'

'Seb Neill?' replied the Minister. 'The name sounds vaguely familiar, but I don't think I've met him before.'

Alex steadied his mind, knowing that he needed to choose his next words incredibly carefully. Becca was asking him to make a promise that he might not later be able to keep and, in all his years as a negotiator, that was something he had never done. It had never been for high-minded, moral reasons, but rather, for hard-nosed, pragmatic ones. Because broken promises led inevitably to broken trust and, in a negotiation, trust might well end up being the only thing you have to rely on.

'It's difficult for me to make a promise when I don't know exactly what it is that you might want to talk about,' he ventured carefully. 'But I guarantee you that, whatever it is, I will treat it with absolute discretion.'

Becca lifted her head and looked up at the darkening sky. She seemed to be weighing his reply, and her response to it. Silently, Alex willed her to overcome her fears.

'Here's a promise that I definitely *can* make,' he said, in an attempt to further reassure her. 'I promise you that you can trust me.'

'Can I?' she asked nervously. 'Camilla said that I must never talk to anyone about it,' she murmured. 'She said that there would be consequences if I did.'

'What sort of consequences?'

'She didn't say.'

'Did she threaten you in some way?' Alex asked with concern.

'No,' replied Becca uncertainly. 'At least, I don't think so . . . I can't really remember.'

'But you *felt* threatened,' Alex suggested.

Becca nodded. She looked lost and trapped and scared and alone. All of those things, all at once, Alex thought. Her shoulders sagged and she began to cry.

'I'm so sorry, Becca,' Alex said. 'It all sounds really, really horrible. I'm incredibly sorry that you've had to go through it all.'

'The thing is,' she said through her tears, 'in spite of whatever it was she said to me, I can't help feeling that I really do need to tell you about Simon.' There was a pleading look in her eyes.

'About your relationship with him?' Alex asked.

'About much more than that,' Becca replied.

Several miles away in East London, oblivious to the unfolding events on Westminster Bridge, a petite woman in her mid-thirties was sitting in the living room of her cramped first-floor flat, a laptop and hardback A5 notebook open on the small table in front of her. She had striking blue-grey eyes and collar-length brown hair that she kept tucked behind her ears. She was gripping a biro between her teeth like an old-fashioned cheroot and she had a look of intense concentration on her face. There was work to be done. Important, urgent work.

Much of the available floorspace in the room was taken up with large piles of paperwork – complete with a mass of coloured sticky tabs and strokes of orange, green and yellow

highlighter pen marking out text and data of apparent importance. Her only company in the room was a plump goldfish
turning unhurried circles in a small tank on a nearby bookshelf.

The woman's name was Rowan Blake and she was an investigative journalist – formerly of the *Guardian*, now working
freelance – who spent the majority of her time chasing down
stories that others had missed. While many of her colleagues
in the media seemed to devote most of their time and attention
to those – whether politicians, celebrities or anyone else – who
shouted the loudest (that is, when they weren't doing the
shouting themselves), Rowan Blake had a different approach.
She listened for the whispers. And then she went in search
of the truth. Relentlessly so. If she had a reputation in some
quarters for being difficult, it was only among the people who
didn't like the questions she tended to ask them.

She might have been small in stature, but she was fearless
and she was fierce. She was also incredibly capable, with an
almost photographic memory and a forensic attention to detail
that had secured her many an exclusive.

Her laptop screen was displaying the homepage of a company
called 'Soteria Solutions'. At the top of an otherwise blank page
in her notebook, she had written a single question:

What is the truth about Simon Jones?

Chapter 13

'What do you need to tell me about Simon?' Alex asked.

Becca said nothing at first and Alex allowed the silence to linger, recognising that he needed to remain incredibly patient. He could tell that she wanted to talk to him, but he also understood that it needed to be on her terms and in her own good time. Studying her haunted body language, he felt a sense of deep compassion for her. More than anything else at that moment in time, he just wanted her to be all right. At least, as all right as a person standing on the parapet of a bridge ever can be.

'Alex?' she said eventually.

'Yes?' he replied expectantly.

'I do trust you.'

'I'm really glad that you do,' he replied with a kind smile. He wondered whether it might have been the reason she'd asked for him to come back to the bridge.

'But I don't trust anyone else.'

'I understand.'

She took another deep breath. 'If I climb back over,' she whispered, 'will you stay here with me?'

The mention of climbing back over seemed to have come from nowhere. But the immediate surge of elation that Alex experienced on hearing it was tempered by a strong note of inner caution. He was perfectly prepared to remain with Becca for as long as it took to get her to safety, but, at the same time, he was acutely conscious of needing to avoid doing anything that might encourage her to start forming some sort of unhealthy dependency on him. He was immediately starting to imagine a succession of future phone calls from overstretched colleagues telling him that they were trying to help a young woman in crisis, but that she was refusing to speak to anyone apart from him. It had happened tonight and, given Becca's very obviously vulnerable mental state, it could so easily happen again. And he wouldn't be able to respond on every occasion. Nor would it be appropriate for him to do so. He was a police officer, not a doctor; a negotiator, not a mental health professional. His responsibility was to help her back from the edge, and then to place her in the care of people who were trained and qualified to give her the specialist medical help and care that she so obviously needed. Once again, he had to take immense care with his choice of words.

'I can't promise to stay indefinitely,' he said gently, 'but I do promise that Pip and I will stay with you for the rest of this evening.' That seemed to him to be a sensible compromise, and introducing Pip to the conversation was one way of trying to dilute Becca's potential fixation on him. There had been no opportunity to discuss any of this with Pip, but he was confident that she'd agree with what he was suggesting.

'Who's Pip?' asked Becca uncertainly.

'Pip is a very good friend of mine,' Alex replied, feeling enormously relieved that Becca hadn't reacted badly to his suggestion. 'She's just over there,' he said, turning and pointing to where Pip was standing, just a few metres away from them. Pip responded by smiling at the two of them. 'Pip is really good at listening to people who are having a tough time,' Alex added.

'I don't know her,' Becca said.

'I know you don't,' Alex replied. 'But I do.'

Once again, Becca took her time before responding.

'Do you trust her?' she asked at last.

'I would trust Pip with my life,' Alex said.

'You're sure?'

'I'm certain of it.'

'All right then,' said Becca reluctantly. 'If you absolutely promise me that you're going to stay here with me, I'll climb back over and talk to you.'

'That's really good news, Becca,' Alex said, his spirits lifting. 'And you have my word: Pip and I will stay with you for the rest of this evening if that's what you want and need us to do.'

Becca looked at Alex and then at Pip. She looked down at the water and then back at them both. 'All right then,' she repeated.

Pip stepped forward and she and Alex helped Becca back over. Becca's legs buckled the moment her feet touched the pavement, but Pip was swift to throw an arm around her and stop her from falling. 'It's OK, Becca,' Pip said, 'I've got you.'

Becca promptly hunched forward and threw up all over the pavement. The sharp-edged smell of alcohol-infused vomit filled the air.

'It's all right,' Pip said, without missing a beat. She produced a packet of tissues from her coat pocket and handed them to Becca before easing her a handful of paces towards the north side of the bridge.

Alex followed them, opening his rucksack as he walked. He pulled out a large fleece and wrapped it around Becca's shoulders. 'Why don't we find somewhere a little bit more discreet to talk?' he suggested.

Becca didn't reply. Her head was down, her clumped hair obscuring her face. She was shivering.

'Where's the van?' Alex asked Pip.

'Just outside Portcullis House,' replied Pip, gesturing in the direction of the large parliamentary office building situated next to Westminster Underground station. She reached into her pocket and handed him the keys.

Alex looked at Becca, who appeared to him to be disappearing into new depths of fear and despair. 'Becca,' he said, 'I'm just going to leave you with Pip for a couple of minutes, but *I promise* that I'm coming straight back.'

When Becca didn't respond, Alex looked at Pip with an unspoken question. Should he just go and fetch the van? Pip nodded that he should.

Alex hurried across the bridge, stopping halfway to tell the third member of the negotiating team that he was free to head home. When he reached the cordon on the north side, he paused a second time to briefly explain his intentions to the inspector in charge of the scene. What he was suggesting was irregular – the negotiators had done their job and the next step would normally have been to place Becca in the care of their uniformed colleagues, but when Alex pointed out that he was trying to limit the likelihood that Becca would return to the bridge for a third time, the inspector was only too happy to agree to the plan.

Half an hour later, Becca was sitting with Alex and Pip in the back of the negotiator van. It was cramped with all three of them in there, but it served a clear purpose, providing them with both warmth and privacy. Alex had collected the two women from the bridge and driven them south of the river in search of a quiet backstreet where they could park up and talk. He had found a place close to the Imperial War Museum, just around the corner from a late-night cafe, and Becca was nursing the large polystyrene cup of sugary tea that he had just handed to her. Some of the colour was returning to her cheeks, but she remained quiet and withdrawn.

'How are you doing?' Alex asked her, recognising that, while she was no longer at immediate risk of harm, he and Pip were still going to need to draw on all their skill and experience as negotiators if they were going to be able to provide her with any more help.

'A little bit better, I suppose,' she said quietly. 'Thank you for the tea,' she added.

'No problem,' Alex replied brightly. 'I bought you something to eat as well.' He pulled a bar of chocolate out of his coat pocket and offered it to her.

'No, thank you,' she said. 'I'm not feeling very hungry.'

He put it down on the small table in front of her. 'I'll leave it there in case you change your mind.'

'Thank you,' she said again, blowing on her tea and taking a cautious, shaky sip. She seemed to be more or less sober, but the lingering evidence of the alcohol remained on her breath and in her movements.

As on the bridge, Alex allowed the silence to remain for a while. Becca's earlier intimation that she might have something of significance to tell them about Simon Jones had piqued his natural copper's curiosity, but he was prepared to wait. He reckoned that she would tell them when she was ready.

'I don't suppose you've got a cigarette, have you?' Becca asked after a while.

'Actually, I have,' Alex said, reaching through to the van's front passenger seat and grabbing his rucksack. He retrieved the packet and offered it to her.

'Mind if I join you?' Pip asked.

'Of course I don't,' Becca replied shyly.

Alex knew that it was Pip's way of breaking the ice, of putting Becca at her ease. He offered them both a light, before deciding to light one for himself. In the moments of quiet that followed, the gentle streams and swirls of exhaled smoke had a strangely calming effect on the atmosphere in the van.

'Thank you,' Becca said softly.

'For what?' Alex asked her.

'For staying with me,' she replied.

'I promised you that we would,' Alex said. 'And I always keep my promises.'

Becca took another draw on her cigarette. 'I'm scared,' she said.

'I know you are,' Alex responded gently. 'I can tell.'

'I think you're being incredibly brave,' Pip said, choosing that moment to join the conversation.

'Brave?' Becca asked. The expression on her face betrayed her obvious doubts.

Pip nodded her affirmation.

'I don't feel brave,' Becca said.

'Sometimes,' Pip observed, 'the bravest thing of all is to keep going.'

Becca took her time absorbing this thought as she sipped her tea and smoked the last of her cigarette. She held the filter between her thumb and forefinger and looked enquiringly at Alex. He opened the side door of the van and she flicked it out onto the pavement. He and Pip did the same with the remains of their own cigarettes.

'I still love him, you know,' Becca said after a further pause.

'Simon Jones?' Alex queried.

'Yes.'

'Of course you still love him,' Pip said. 'You don't suddenly stop loving someone just because they've ended a relationship with you.'

Becca hesitated. 'I'm *really* not supposed to talk to you about it,' she said uneasily.

Alex studied the changing expression on her face: the narrowing of her eyes, the pursing of her lips, the flush of her cheeks. In spite of her very obvious anxieties, it seemed to him that she really did want to talk to them. He could sense it. 'Earlier, when we were still on the bridge,' he said, 'you suggested to me that your relationship with Simon wasn't the only thing you'd been warned not to talk about.'

Becca nodded slowly.

'What else is there?' Alex asked.

'You won't believe me if I tell you,' she replied.

Chapter 14

'Why wouldn't we believe you?' Pip asked Becca.

'Because nobody else does,' Becca replied, quietly.

'Nobody?' Pip queried. 'Who do you mean?'

'The people in the office,' Becca explained. 'They don't take anything I tell them seriously. They never have done.'

'Why not?' Pip asked.

'Oh, I don't know,' said Becca, her voice beginning to sound weary. 'Probably because, to them, I'm just a girl. I'm only twenty-four. I haven't been working there for all that long. I'm the youngest and least experienced member of the team. All of which means that I'm a bit of a nobody to them.' She paused for a second before continuing. 'Or, maybe, they just don't like the fact that Simon was in love with me.' She took another sip of tea. 'They didn't believe me when I told them about that either.'

'I believe you,' said Alex, looking her straight in the eye. And he meant it. He might not have been able to square her story with the public image of the Policing Minister – not least as portrayed in the article he'd read in *The Economist* – but all his instincts were telling him to trust her. He had spent his entire professional life being lied to by people of violence and ill will. And Becca Palmer was nothing like any of them.

'I believe you too,' said Pip, taking hold of Becca's hand.

Becca's eyes widened. 'Really?' she said, looking from one of them to the other, her voice a blend of incredulity and faint, far-off hope.

'Really,' Pip replied.

'Really,' Alex agreed.

Becca was on the verge of tears again. She took a deep breath. 'The thing is,' she said uncertainly, 'I think Simon might be involved in something criminal.'

'Something criminal?' Alex replied, trying hard not to look or sound startled. Of all the things that Becca Palmer had so far said to him, this was the most extraordinary – the most sensational – by far. He recognised that his commitment to believing her was going to be challenged at the very first time of asking.

'Hmmm,' Becca responded uncertainly, suddenly sounding frightened again.

'It's all right, Becca,' Pip said, sensing her unease. 'You're completely safe here with us.'

'What sort of crime do you think he might be involved in?' Alex asked. He was conscious of the need to maintain Becca's trust. Which meant a suspension of any reservations that he might be feeling.

'I don't really know,' Becca confessed. 'I think it might be some kind of fraud.'

'Are you able to tell us any more than that?' Pip asked. If she was sharing any of Alex's inner doubts, she certainly wasn't letting them show.

'Not really,' Becca replied, her words becoming more tired and laboured. 'But I think it might have something to do with Home Office contracts.'

'What sort of contracts?' Pip asked.

'I honestly don't know,' Becca said.

'That's all right,' said Pip, who could see how exhausted Becca was. 'You really don't have to keep answering our questions if you don't want to.'

Becca lifted her head and looked at Pip. 'No, it's fine,' she replied. 'You can keep going.' More than anything else, she seemed grateful that Pip was paying proper attention to what she was saying.

'Only if you're absolutely sure,' Pip said.

Becca nodded. Alex could see very clearly that Pip had gained Becca's trust. There was no need for him to do anything other than settle back in his seat and listen.

'OK then,' said Pip. 'Do you remember what it was that first raised your suspicions?'

'Things I heard him say on the phone,' Becca replied. 'When we were in his flat and he was in a different room and didn't think I was listening.'

'What sort of things did you hear him say?'

'Things about money. Bank accounts. Wire transfers. That sort of thing.'

'Anything more specific than that?'

Becca thought for a moment. 'There was one name I heard him mention a few times,' she said. '*Soteria Solutions*.'

'I've never heard of *Soteria Solutions*,' Pip said. 'Do you know how to spell the first part of their name?' She pulled her phone out of her pocket, ready to make a typed note of it.

'Actually, I do – but only because I've seen it on a couple of documents at the flat.' She spelt out the name.

'And what is *Soteria Solutions*?'

'I don't know,' Becca admitted.

'Is there anything else you can tell us?' Pip asked.

'I don't think so,' Becca replied. She yawned and looked at Pip apologetically. 'I'm so sorry,' she said. 'I know that I'm not giving you very much to go on, but I promise you that I'm telling the truth.'

'I know you are,' Pip replied. She looked at Becca's tired face. 'Do you think you might have enough energy left for a couple of final questions?' she asked.

Becca nodded and yawned again.

'Did you ever talk to Simon about your concerns?' Pip asked her.

'Kind of.'

'Meaning?'

'Meaning that I mentioned it to him once. But he closed the conversation down straight away – told me that it wasn't anything I needed to worry about.'

'And that was it?'

'That was it.'

'And when Camilla came to see you in hospital, did she talk about it?' Alex interjected

'No.'

'She didn't mention anything at all about it?' Alex queried.

'Not directly, no,' Becca reiterated. 'But she told me that I mustn't say anything about Simon to anyone. She told me that I was in danger of ruining a good man.'

Alex raised an eyebrow. Simon Jones – a good man? A married man with young children, yes. A successful businessman, evidently. A charismatic politician, undeniably. But a good man? Not if he was involved in any kind of criminality. Not if he was trying to cover up an affair with a vulnerable young woman half his age.

'And she made you sign a document?' Alex asked.

Becca nodded. Her eyes looked heavy and her head was starting to nod. Somehow, she looked both younger and older than her years: the soft, freckled skin on her face lined with sadness and anxiety and exhaustion.

'I think that's maybe enough talking for now,' Pip said.

'I want to see my sister,' Becca said quietly.

'Her name's Helen, isn't it?' Alex asked, remembering it from his first encounter with Becca.

'Uh-huh.'

'I think I still have her mobile number in my phone from when you borrowed it to call her last time,' Alex said. 'Would you like me to give her a ring?'

'Yes, please,' Becca murmured.

Alex slid open the side door of the van and walked a few paces along the pavement to make the call. Helen Palmer – she had kept her maiden name when she married – picked up at the other end almost immediately, her voice bright and kind. Alex introduced himself and briefly explained the situation, having been swift to reassure her that Becca was safe. Helen didn't seem to want to ask him any questions. Instead, she gave Alex her address and insisted that they should bring Becca over straight away.

Alex thanked her and returned to the van, where Becca was sitting with her head resting on Pip's shoulder. 'I've spoken to Helen,' he said, 'and she's looking forward to seeing you. She said that she'll have the spare room made up by the time we get there.'

Half an hour later, the three of them were in Wandsworth, sitting with Helen at her large kitchen table. Becca had spent the remainder of the van journey struggling to stay awake and, aside from a quiet greeting to her sister, she had said almost nothing since their arrival. Helen had offered all of them a helping of reheated lasagne, but, while Alex and Pip had gratefully accepted, Becca had said that she wasn't hungry. Helen had put a helping in front of her, just in case, but it was starting to go cold. Every now and then, Becca prodded at it with a fork, but she didn't seem inclined to eat any of it.

Helen's husband was overseas on business and their infant son was already asleep upstairs. Alex guessed that she was four or five years older than her sister. She didn't seem at all unsettled by the state that Becca was in – as though it was familiar to her.

'This happens from time to time,' she explained to Alex and Pip as she leaned across and wrapped a comforting arm around her younger sibling. 'The poor thing hasn't been feeling too good for the last little while.'

Becca didn't react and Helen continued to fill the silence. She explained that Becca had struggled on and off with her mental health for a number of years. She had first been diagnosed with anxiety and depression in her mid-teens and had been taking medication ever since. But, sometimes, she stopped taking it and that always turned out badly. She was bright and she was brilliant, but she had missed several weeks of work during the past twelve months and Helen knew that Becca's bosses had been raising concerns about her attendance. Apparently, Becca hadn't disclosed her full medical history when applying for the job and her employers had latterly accused her of being less than honest about her circumstances. Helen knew all of this, because her sister told her everything. She always had done. The situation had spiralled downwards in the past month – both in terms of her health and her work – resulting in her apparent dismissal two weeks earlier.

Helen paused what she was saying and turned back to her sister, who had pushed her plate to one side and was now slumped forward, with her forehead resting on the tabletop.

'You look completely shattered,' she said tenderly. 'I've got some of your sleeping tablets upstairs,' she continued. 'Why don't we get you into bed?'

Becca offered no resistance as her sister eased her to her feet and began to lead her out of the room.

'Do you mind waiting for a few minutes?' Helen asked Alex and Pip. 'I won't be long.'

'Of course,' Pip said.

Meanwhile, in East London, Rowan Blake was sitting cross-legged on her living-room floor, working her way slowly and methodically through the large pile of documents closest to her. The paperwork she was studying represented a tiny fraction of the vast quantity of material that had entered the public domain following the recent 'Jersey Papers' scandal – the latest in a series of huge data leaks from law and accountancy firms based in offshore tax havens such as Bermuda, the British Virgin Islands and Jersey itself. A consortium of investigative journalists from around the world had been working on the content for several weeks and the headline findings – involving a succession of the world's wealthiest and most dishonest individuals caught in the act of trying to conceal billions of pounds, dollars, euros and yen from the world's tax authorities, via a vastly complex web of secretive corporate structures and bank accounts – had already been reported on the BBC's *Panorama* programme and printed in the *Guardian*.

But Rowan Blake was trying to look deeper even than the BBC and the newspaper that had previously employed her. She believed passionately in holding powerful people to account and the focus of her attention in this case was on members of the current government and anyone connected with them. Her instincts told her that there was likely to be plenty to uncover, but the size of the leak made it painstakingly slow work. It was less a question of finding needles in haystacks than finding specific, individual needles in a needle storage warehouse. Her laptop remained open on the floor next to her and she had filled a page in her notebook with a succession of bullet points:

- *Who owns Soteria Solutions?*
- *What other companies do they own?*
- *Any connections with UK political donors?*
- *Who funds the Independent Justice Foundation?*
- *Content of recent IJF reports: what do they say/recommend?*
- *What connections between Soteria/IJF and Government Ministers?*
- *Any connections with the Home Office in particular?*
- *What impact on policing/law enforcement policy?*
- *What are the newspapers saying – particularly the* City Journal *and* GB Today?
- *Who benefits?*
- *FOLLOW THE MONEY*

The last bullet point was written in block capitals and underlined several times. Beneath it, she had written a question that echoed the one at the top of the page: *Where is Simon Jones in all of this?*

She couldn't find him.

Back in Wandsworth, Helen had reappeared in the kitchen. 'Thanks so much for waiting,' she said. 'Becca's fast asleep.'

'Is she going to be all right?' Alex asked.

'We've been here before,' Helen replied, 'and we've always managed to get through it. We'll get through it this time too.'

'Will you take her back to the hospital?'

'I'll wait and see how she is in the morning,' Helen said. 'She doesn't like it there. During the last couple of weeks, I visited her most days and she made no secret of the fact she wanted to come home with me. I would happily have said yes, but the doctors had just put her onto some new medication and they wanted to keep a close eye on her.'

'Do you happen to know if anyone else visited her while she was there?' Alex asked, without explaining the reason for his question.

'Not that I'm aware of, no,' Helen replied.

'We don't want to outstay our welcome,' Alex said, 'but would you mind if we asked you about a couple of other things?'

'Of course not,' Helen said, 'particularly after all you've done for her.'

'I don't think we've done a great deal,' Pip replied. 'We were just doing our jobs.'

'Well, you did them incredibly well, and I want you to know how very grateful I am,' Helen said. 'What can I do for you?'

'We just want to try to make sense of one or two of the things Becca has said to us,' Alex responded.

'I'll certainly help you if I can.'

'Has she mentioned anything to you about being in a relationship with Simon Jones?' Alex asked.

'The Minister?' Helen looked and sounded surprised.

'Yes.'

'Is that what she told you?'

'Yes,' Alex replied. 'When I spoke to her on Westminster Bridge the first time. She told me that he had ended their relationship the night before. I imagined that was the reason – or certainly one of the reasons – for the state she was in.'

Now Helen looked confused. 'No, she's not said anything to me about that.'

'Nothing at all?' Alex checked.

Helen opened her mouth to speak a couple of times before closing it again. She was clearly weighing up what she ought to tell them. 'How can I put this?' she said carefully. 'The fact is that, on occasions, Becca says things that aren't actually true. I don't know why she does it – or even if she knows that she's doing it – but this wouldn't be the first time it's happened. I love that girl with every fibre of my being and there's nothing that I wouldn't do for her, but there's no doubt that she makes things difficult for herself sometimes.'

'Right . . . I see,' replied Alex as he tried to absorb the implications of what he was hearing. 'Becca told me that she and Mr Jones had been keeping their affair a secret from everyone,' he said.

Once again, Helen took her time replying.

'The thing is,' she said eventually, 'as far as I'm aware, Becca's never actually had a boyfriend.'

Chapter 15

It was beginning to rain quite heavily as Alex and Pip said their goodbyes to Helen and hurried back to the van. With Alex at the wheel, they travelled in companionable silence, while they both took the opportunity to reflect on the events and conversations of the previous few hours.

'So what do you think?' Pip asked eventually.

'About which bit in particular?' Alex replied, glancing across at her before turning his attention back to the road.

'About any of it?'

'To be honest, I'm not sure I know where to begin,' he conceded.

'I suppose we could start with the question of whether or not we actually believe her?' Pip suggested.

'Becca you mean?'

Pip nodded.

Alex considered the question for a moment. 'I like her,' he said. 'And I feel desperately sorry for her.'

'I do too,' Pip replied. 'But that doesn't actually answer the question. Do you believe what she's been telling us?'

Alex slowed the van on the approach to a pedestrian cross-ing. 'That's where it all starts to get a bit more difficult,' he admitted. 'I know what my instincts are telling me. But I also know that the evidence seems to be suggesting something different.'

'So, talk me through it,' said Pip. 'Tell me what you're thinking.'

'My first instinct was to accept without question what Becca told us about her relationship with Simon Jones.'

'*Was?*'

'I really meant it, in the back of the van, when I told her that I believed her.'

'I know you did,' Pip responded. 'I did too.'

'But now we've got Helen telling us that Becca's never even had a boyfriend.'

'As far as she knows.'

'As far as she knows,' Alex agreed. 'But the first time I spoke to Becca on the bridge – two weeks ago – she told me that she talks to Helen about everything. And Helen has just suggested more or less the same thing.'

'Maybe Becca made an exception in this case,' Pip replied.

'But Helen didn't appear to know about Camilla's visit to the hospital either,' Alex said.

'That's assuming Camilla did actually visit her.'

'So you think Becca's making that bit up?'

'That's not what I said,' Pip replied. 'I think Becca genuinely believes that she's telling us the truth. But I also know that she's not very well. Who knows what might be going on in her mind?'

'So you think she might be imagining some of what she's saying?'

'I don't know,' Pip answered. 'But it has to be a possibility, doesn't it? I mean, what do you make of her extraordinary suggestion that Jones is involved in some sort of criminal activity?'

'It sounds like too much to believe, doesn't it,' Alex replied. 'But how do you explain the fact that she seemed so anxious when she was talking about it? Frightened even?'

'Because she believes that what she's saying is real.'

'But what if it is real?'

Pip stared out at the puddling pavements on Clapham High Street. Most of the shops were closed, but the bars and restaurants seemed to be doing a brisk trade. She could see diners and drinkers in a succession of brightly lit doorways shaking off umbrellas and ducking inside. 'Is that what your instincts are telling you?' she asked him.

'I'm honestly not sure,' Alex replied. 'All I do know is that Becca Palmer doesn't seem to me to be the kind of person who would deliberately try to mislead us. And I definitely don't trust Simon Jones.'

'Yes, but that's because he's a politician,' Pip said, 'and you've never trusted politicians. You've never even met the man.'

'I don't need to meet him,' Alex insisted. 'I only have to look at what he and his kind are doing to the police service in this country to know what kind of person he is.'

Pip conceded the point. Alex definitely wasn't the only one with concerns about the government's attitude and approach to policing. Most of their colleagues in the Met had serious reservations of one kind or another. 'All right, so you don't trust him,' Pip said. 'For what it's worth, I don't trust him either. But it's a bit of a leap from that to suggesting that he's a criminal.'

'Maybe,' said Alex as he turned left into the road where they lived. He pulled into an empty parking space opposite their house. 'What was the name of that company?' he asked as he switched the engine off.

'Which company?'

'The one Becca mentioned. The one she said she'd heard Jones talking about.'

'Oh that,' Pip replied as she rummaged in her pocket for her phone. She tapped on the screen a couple of times. 'Soteria Solutions,' she said.

'I think we should look it up,' Alex said.

'Remind me what we've got in the diary for tomorrow?' Simon Jones said to Camilla Lane. It was late and they were sitting in the back of his ministerial car, en route to his flat on Albert Embankment. The City dinner had been an unqualified success. The conversation with Seb Neill had been an enormously productive one. Several other important connections had been made. And the applause was still ringing in his ears.

'You're seeing the Home Sec first thing,' Camilla replied.

'Of course I am,' he said. 'Any issues from his team?'

'None at all,' she responded. 'I think they recognise that you're on the way up, even as he's on the way down. He won't be standing in the way of anything you have planned. In fact, don't be surprised if he tries to claim that some of it was his own idea all along.'

Simon Jones laughed. 'I mind less about who gets the credit for it than I do about getting it done,' he said.

'I know.'

'First up is the implementation of last year's Independent Justice Foundation recommendations about private-sector involvement in public-service delivery. I was talking to Seb about them earlier. Can you remind me which roles we've put out for private tender for the first time?' he asked.

'Hold on a moment,' she said, reaching for her phone and scrolling rapidly through a succession of screens. She found what she was looking for and read from a list: 'Crime scene management. Custody supervision. Community patrol. CCTV investigations. Those, and a handful of others.'

'Excellent,' he replied. 'Do you happen to know whether we've had any bids from Soteria Solutions?'

'S-O-T-E-R-I-A.' Pip was spelling the name of the company and Alex was typing it into his laptop. They were sitting at their kitchen table. Alex had opened a bottle of beer. Pip, still on call, was drinking tea.

'Soteria Solutions,' said Alex as the results of his search opened up in front of him.

'Go for the top one,' Pip suggested.

Alex clicked on the link. It took them straight to the company's homepage.

'Let me see,' he said, scanning the text. 'It says here that they are a global company offering commercial solutions for the UK criminal justice system.'

'What does that mean exactly?'

Alex continued to read the text. 'It means that they're involved in things like forensics and prisoner transport.'

'Like Securicor and G4S, you mean?'

'I suppose so.'

Sitting side by side, the two of them continued to read. Soteria were proud of their track record and their website was filled with glowing endorsements from apparently satisfied clients.

'So Soteria are the people charging double the amount we used to pay for the same services when they were delivered in-house?' Pip asked.

'I think that's how the system works, yes,' said Alex. 'Another in a long line of corporate con acts taking the taxpayer for a ride.'

'What else is there about them online?'

'Just the usual, I suspect,' began Alex, returning to the list of search results. 'Wikipedia entries. Articles from the financial press. That sort of thing.'

'What about that one?' said Pip, pointing to the bottom of the screen and an article titled, '*What are the Home Office not telling us?*'

When Alex clicked on the link, it brought up a blog written by someone called Rowan Blake.

'Who's he?' Alex asked.

Rowan Blake put her spoon down in her empty bowl and pushed it to one side. It was late, but there was so much more to do and she was a woman on a mission. On a fresh page of her notebook, she had written a new set of names and notes, connected by lines and arrows in the form of a kind of flow chart:

- *CEO of Soteria Solutions: Robert Sangster*
- *Sangster: Conservative Party donor*
- *CEO of Independent Justice Foundation (IJF): Rafe Jackson*
- *Jackson: former Home Office special advisor*
- *IJF advocating greater privatisation in criminal justice system*
- *Extensive positive coverage of IJF reports in* City Journal
- City Journal *edited by Geoffrey Bell – who has had at least three 1-2-1 meetings with Simon Jones in the last six weeks*
- *Simon Jones has also written a recent column in the paper*
- City Journal *owned by Lord Peter Gier*
- *Lord Gier: also owns* GB Today *tabloid newspaper*
- *Lord Gier: major Conservative Party donor who lives in Jersey. Has paid virtually no tax in the UK in the last 10 years*

Rowan Blake was making connections.

*

'Isn't Rowan a girl's name?' Pip asked.

'Could be,' said Alex. 'Either way, I've got no idea who Rowan Blake is.'

'That's what the internet is for,' Pip replied. She gave Alex a good-natured shove and pulled his laptop across the table towards her. She adjusted the screen and started typing.

Alex stood up and walked over to the fridge in search of another beer.

'He or she is a journalist,' Pip said.

'Oh?' said Alex as he eased the top off a bottle of Peroni.

'Used to work for the *Guardian*.'

'And?'

'Now freelance . . . They carry out their own investigations.'

'Is he or she credible?' asked Alex warily.

'Seems to be,' Pip replied. 'I'm looking for a photo, but I haven't found one yet.'

'So what does the article itself say?'

'Give me a minute to read it,' said Pip.

Alex wandered over to the window and looked outside. Even after midnight, the local London streets were full of life and movement. Night workers. Nightclubbers. Late homers. Cab drivers. Inhabitants of a restless city. He wondered about Becca. Was she still sleeping?

'It's about the privatisation of policing and the wider criminal justice system,' Pip said after a while.

'I don't like the sound of that,' Alex replied, watching a man in his late twenties weaving his tipsy way along the pavement below.

'It actually talks about lots of the things that Simon Jones was saying in that article I read in the *City Journal* – albeit in far less positive terms.'

'Does it mention Jones by name?' The drunk outside had paused to steady himself against a parked car.

'No it doesn't,' Pip replied. 'But it does mention Soteria Solutions.'

'Hence it coming up in the web search.'

'Indeed,' Pip replied. 'It says that Soteria already have a number of contracts with the Home Office and that they're in the process of bidding for several more.'

Alex turned around and looked at her. 'Didn't Becca say something to us earlier on about Home Office contracts?'

'Yes, she did,' confirmed Pip.

'Hmmm . . . What else does the article say?'

'Well, the rest of it is worded very carefully – but the clear suggestion is that a small handful of private individuals are pocketing vast sums of public money.'

'The rich just keep getting richer,' Alex remarked.

'So what do you think we should do about what Becca's told us?' Pip asked, standing up and wandering over to the kitchen sink to rinse out her mug. The laptop remained open on the table behind her.

'Well, we can't just leave it,' Alex replied. The content of Rowan Blake's piece had put him in a determined frame of mind.

'Why not?' Pip responded. 'We've done our job as negotiators.'

Alex knew that Pip wasn't necessarily trying to disagree with him. Rather, her question was designed to check and challenge his thinking before he started to get too far ahead of himself. 'Because you can't just ignore an allegation of crime that's been made against a government minister,' he said.

'But is that really what it is?' Pip replied, continuing to play the role of devil's advocate. 'It seems to me to be rather more of a suggestion than an allegation.'

'Either way, we still can't ignore it.'

'I'm not suggesting that we should,' Pip responded. 'But haven't you got enough on your plate with the day job? I know I have.'

'We both have,' Alex said. 'But that's not really the point, is it?'

'No, it's not,' Pip agreed. She wandered back over to the table and woke the screen up on the laptop. She scrolled back down to the bottom of the article. 'There's a contact number here for Rowan Blake,' she said. 'Maybe we should get in touch.'

Chapter 16

The following morning, sitting at the kitchen table in his running gear, Alex decided to do as Pip had suggested. He picked up his phone and composed a WhatsApp message to Rowan Blake. He introduced himself and explained who he was. Without saying anything about Becca Palmer or Soteria Solutions, he mentioned the fact that he'd read the online blog and asked whether Rowan might be willing to speak to him. As he pressed send, he didn't hold out much hope of getting any kind of reply, but he knew that he needed to try.

Believing Becca was one thing. Finding actual evidence of crimes that might have been committed in the corridors of power was something else entirely.

An hour later, Alex walked into Ronnie Egan's office at Kentish Town police station.

'Can I run something past you?' he said.

'Do I have a choice?' his deputy responded with a smile.

Alex ignored the gentle jibe and sat down opposite her. Although he and Pip had reached some sort of consensus the night before, he knew that it would be no bad thing to get another perspective from a trusted source – particularly someone who wasn't going to be influenced by any sort of emotional connection to Becca Palmer. Beginning with the first call to Westminster Bridge two weeks earlier, he talked about the two negotiations; about Becca's description of her affair with Simon Jones; about the allegation – *the suggestion* – that the Minister might be involved in some form of criminal activity; about the possibility that Becca might have been asked to sign some kind of non-disclosure agreement. All the while, he was trying to gauge Ronnie's unspoken reaction to what he was saying.

'What would you do if you were me?' he asked.

'Do you believe her?'

'Yes, I do,' Alex responded. 'At least, I think I do.'

'But do you have any actual proof to back up what she's saying?' Ronnie pressed.

'Not really, no,' Alex answered with a shrug.

'Do you have any lines of enquiry that you might reasonably be able to follow up on?'

'I've sent a WhatsApp message to a freelance journalist,' Alex replied, knowing full well that it didn't represent much of an answer.

'And what did that message say?'

'It was a query about a blog of theirs that I'd read.'

'And that's it?' asked Ronnie with a dismissive roll of her eyes.

'Pretty much, yes,' Alex acknowledged.

'So there isn't really a whole lot you *can* do,' Ronnie said.

'I suppose I could try speaking to someone at the Yard,' Alex suggested.

'What? And tell them that you're in possession of information supplied by a young woman who is known to be mentally unwell – someone also known to have what might best be described as an occasionally tenuous relationship with the truth – alleging that the current Policing Minister is a criminal?

Never mind the fact that she seems to be struggling to specify exactly what those crimes might be or, indeed, to provide you with any evidence in support of her claims.'

'Well, when you put it like that . . .' Alex began.

But Ronnie was warming to her theme. 'As if we aren't in enough difficulty with the Home Office already,' she said. 'What with the current tidal wave of crime and all.'

Before either of them could say anything more, Alex's phone buzzed. He pulled it out of his trouser pocket to discover that he'd just received a WhatsApp reply from Rowan Blake.

'*I don't trust police officers,*' was all it said.

Having apologised to Ronnie for the interruption, Alex had returned to his office. He was sitting at his desk as he composed his reply to Rowan Blake.

'*I don't trust some of them either,*' he wrote, in an effort to establish some sort of an initial connection. It was the Area Commander he was thinking of as he sent the message, but there were others too – colleagues who were so preoccupied with their own advancement that they rarely, if ever, gave much thought to anything that might resemble the greater good.

Seconds later, the icon on his phone screen told him that a reply was being typed.

'*What do you want?*' it said.

And so began Alex's first conversation with Rowan Blake.

'*To talk.*'

'*About what?*'

'*About your recent blog – the one that mentions Soteria Solutions.*'

'*What about it?*'

'*It might be easier to talk about in person.*'

'*How do I know you're a real police officer?*'

Alex used his phone to take a picture of his warrant card – including his name, rank and warrant number – and sent it by way of a reply.

'*How do I know you're not wasting my time?*' came the response.

'*You don't. The only way to know is to have a conversation.*'

This time, the reply was slower in coming and Alex hoped he hadn't pushed it too far.

He sent a follow-up. '*For what it's worth*,' he typed, '*I think you might be interested in what I have to say.*' He considered mentioning Simon Jones by name, but thought better of it. Journalists had an even lower trust rating among the general public than police officers did, and he still had no idea who Rowan Blake actually was.

'*Tomorrow evening. 6 p.m. Coffee shop opposite the Young Vic.*'

Like something from a spy novel. Alex actually grinned as he read the message.

'*Would it be OK to bring my partner?*' he typed.

'*If you must*,' came the reply.

Alex sent Rowan Blake a clearer and more recent photograph of himself than the one displayed in his warrant card. '*So you know who to expect*,' he wrote.

With no further response forthcoming on WhatsApp, he leaned back in his chair and thought through his earlier conversation with Ronnie. It had been a useful reality check. He had his instinctive belief in Becca and his instinctive dislike of Jones, but he recognised that he didn't have a whole lot in the way of substance to support either of those positions – certainly nothing that he might reasonably mention to anyone at the Yard. Not if he wanted to be taken seriously.

But still, he had an allegation, even if it really wasn't much more than a suggestion. He also had a litany of unanswered questions. More than any of those things though, he felt a sense of deep responsibility for a vulnerable and frightened young woman who had placed her trust in him. There was no way he was going to walk away from her.

The following evening, just before 6 p.m., Alex and Pip walked into The Daily Grind, an independent coffee shop situated opposite the Young Vic theatre, just around the corner from Waterloo station. There were a handful of other customers in there, but none who looked up and made eye contact with them.

'Let's sit over there,' Pip suggested, pointing to a table in the corner that would afford them a view of the front door. They had spent much of their time the previous evening and over a shared breakfast that morning looking through a number of other articles written by Rowan Blake. The subject matter had ranged from society and politics, to economics and religion, to generational injustice and institutional failure. A recurring theme in much of the writing had been Blake's obvious contempt for the current government, who she described at one point as a 'crooked cabal of charlatans and chancers'. Alex had found himself in willing agreement with much of what he'd read.

He and Pip had also talked at length about the approach they should take to their conversation with the journalist – with 'cautious' and 'wary' being two of the words that had featured more prominently in the conversation. Over the years, they had both encountered the media at its worst – stories that had been misrepresented; sensitive information that had been printed without permission; criticisms of colleagues that had been misinformed and wholly unfair – and they understood that they would need to be careful about what they said. But, at the same time, they were also conscious of the need to build a level of rapport if they were to stand any chance of finding out what Rowan Blake might know. To get something, they had to be prepared to give something. After all, it wasn't as though they had an abundance of other investigative options to pursue.

Alex ordered two cups of tea from the waiter who appeared alongside them, pen poised over a small notepad. Just then, the door to the cafe opened and a young man in his early twenties walked in. He headed straight for the counter, paying no attention to anyone else.

'Not him then,' said Pip.

A couple of minutes later, the front door to the cafe rattled again. This time, a woman in her mid-thirties walked in. She couldn't have been much taller than about 5'2". She was wearing a long, dark woollen coat and an oversized scarf that was wrapped several times around her neck. Her collar-length brown hair was tucked behind her ears. She spotted Alex and Pip and walked straight over to them.

'You must be Alex,' she said without ceremony and without offering a hand for him to shake. Alex was in the process of standing up when she gestured impatiently to him to sit back down. 'And this must be your partner,' she added, looking closely at Pip.

'Yes, this is—' Alex started to introduce Pip, but the woman interrupted him.

'In life or in work?' she asked.

'What?' Alex replied, taken aback by a conversational style that was blunt, verging on rude.

'Your partner in life or in work?' she repeated impatiently.

'Oh . . . right,' said Alex, still flustered. 'Both actually.'

Before Rowan Blake could say anything else, the waiter appeared with a large mug of tea in each hand.

'Thank you,' said Pip, indicating for him to put the cups down on the table. 'And what can we get you to drink?' she asked Rowan.

'I'll have the same,' she said, ignoring the waiter and addressing her reply to Pip. And with that, she pulled out a chair and sat down opposite them. 'I don't trust police officers,' she added in a provocative repetition of her earlier WhatsApp message to Alex. She fixed them both with an unsympathetic stare.

Meanwhile, Simon Jones was on his way to the Anvil Theatre in Basingstoke, venue for that evening's broadcast of the BBC's flagship programme *Question Time*. As usual, Camilla Lane was sitting alongside him in the back of the ministerial car.

'So what's likely to come up tonight? he asked her.

'Much as you'd expect,' she replied, 'but there are likely to be a couple of questions that will be perfect for you.'

'Oh?'

'One on stop and search and the need for police reform and one on the apparent failures in the privatisation of the probation service that will give you an opportunity to talk about how it should have been done – and will be done in the future.'

'Excellent,' the Minister replied. 'That should coincide very nicely with my article in tomorrow's edition of the *City Journal*.'

'And a full-page news article in *GB Today*,' Camilla added.

Simon Jones smiled. Everything was going according to plan.

Well, I don't trust bloody journalists, was what Alex would have liked to say to the woman with apparently limited social skills who was now sitting in front of him. But that wouldn't have got him anywhere and, in any case, it wasn't his normal style.

'Then it's up to the two of us to earn your trust,' was what he actually said.

'So what do you want to talk to me about?' Rowan Blake asked, seemingly ignoring the olive branch he was trying to offer her.

'Are we off the record?'

'Are you asking me or telling me?' she responded impatiently.

'Well, we're both off duty,' Alex said, glancing at Pip before looking back at Rowan, 'and I'd appreciate it if we could remain off the record. For the time being at least.'

'As you wish,' she replied, before folding her arms in a 'come on then, impress me' sort of way.

'It's about Simon Jones, the MP.'

And the simple mention of his name seemed to have a remarkable effect on Rowan Blake. Her eyes widened a little and her demeanour softened a degree or two. She leaned in closer to them and began to unwrap her scarf.

'Well, go on then,' she said briskly. 'I'm listening.'

Chapter 17

'Before we get to Simon Jones,' Alex said, 'it would be really helpful to understand a little bit more about Soteria Solutions.' He didn't want to show his full hand straight away. Instead, he wanted to hear from Rowan Blake. She was an unknown quantity to them, who, so far, had given away nothing of herself. More than anything, he wanted to know whether they could trust her. He had no doubt that she would be asking herself the same question about them. 'We know broadly what they do,' he continued, 'but we don't know very much about them as an organisation.'

'Why the interest in Soteria?'

'It's just something that was said to us by someone who used to work for Simon Jones at the Home Office.'

'*Used* to work for him?' she replied, unprepared to let the detail pass.

'Until very recently, yes.'

'Who?' asked Rowan, with sudden, whispered intensity. Alex realised that he had her full attention.

'We'll get to that,' he said. 'But, first, what can you tell us about Soteria?'

Rowan huffed and looked over her shoulder before beginning. There were no other customers within earshot. 'The company is run by a man called Robert Sangster,' she said. 'He made his money in hedge fund management, before taking over as Soteria CEO about five years ago. Prior to taking up the post, he regularly donated large sums of money to the Conservative Party and he remains remarkably well-connected in Whitehall.'

'Which must help when it comes to securing Government contracts,' Alex prompted.

'It absolutely shouldn't do,' Rowan replied, 'but of course it does. Sangster was a rich man before he took over at Soteria. He's considerably richer now.'

'So how many Home Office contracts do they have?' Alex asked.

'A dozen or more, I think,' Rowan replied, her eyes fixed on a blank spot on the wall and her head bobbing from side to side as she rechecked her mental calculations. 'And they're currently in the process of bidding for several more.'

'How much money are we talking about?' Alex enquired.

'Millions,' she replied. 'Tens, if not hundreds of millions.'

The lone tea light in the middle of the table flickered as the waiter put a third mug of tea down next to it.

'Thank you,' said Rowan, acknowledging his existence for the first time.

'Do you want something to eat?' asked Alex, sensing the slight thaw in her manner.

'I'm fine,' she replied, but she seemed to appreciate the offer. For the first time since she'd walked into the cafe, she was regarding them with something other than pure suspicion.

'So, let me try to get this straight in my head,' Alex said. 'We have a very wealthy man who has, in the past, given significant amounts of money *to* the party in government, and is now in charge of a company that is earning vast sums of money *from* the Government – with the potential to earn a whole lot more?'

'That sounds about right,' said Rowan with a rueful nod.

'So why is no one asking any questions? Raising any concerns?' asked Alex, still trying to make sense of his own analysis.

'Some of us are trying to,' Rowan replied.

Pip had waited until now to join the conversation. 'So is there any kind of connection between Soteria Solutions and Simon Jones?' she asked.

In Wandsworth, Helen Palmer was sitting in her kitchen when she thought she heard her front door click shut.

'Becca?' she called out. 'Is that you?'

Hearing no reply, she walked out into the corridor. The house was silent. Her son was asleep and, the last time she'd checked, Becca had been resting in the spare room. She opened the front door, but there was no one standing outside – either on the path, or on the pavement beyond. She wondered whether she might have been imagining things.

She walked up the stairs to the spare bedroom at the back of the house. The door was ajar and the light was on inside. She could hear the sound of the TV. Feeling immensely relieved, she poked her head around the door to ask whether there was anything that her sister needed.

But Becca wasn't there.

'It's a perfectly reasonable question,' said Rowan Blake. 'But, so far, I haven't been able to find a direct connection between Soteria Solutions and Simon Jones – aside from the rather obvious fact that he's the Policing Minister and Soteria deliver work for the Home Office.'

'But you think there might be something beyond that?' Pip asked.

'Well, if there is, I'll find it,' Rowan replied. 'But I've looked in all the obvious places. In some of the less obvious ones too. And Simon Jones comes up clean. He's never worked for Soteria and he doesn't own shares in the company. Nor does anyone he's immediately connected to – relatives, close friends, that sort of thing. He's never received any direct political donations from Robert Sangster. As far as I can tell, the two men have never even met one another. And I've checked through every single one of his official meetings for the last twelve months. Nothing with anyone representing Soteria. So far, I've drawn a complete blank.'

'But you still have your suspicions?'

'Call it old-fashioned journalistic instinct; call it world-weary cynicism after years of being repeatedly disappointed by people in positions of power; but, yes, I have my suspicions. I just haven't found the proof I need to back them up yet,' she replied. She looked first at Alex and then at Pip. 'But it sounds as though you have some suspicions too,' she said to them. 'And I think it's about time you told me why.'

'Fair enough,' Alex replied.

He began with the first call to Westminster Bridge, his voice not much louder than a whisper. Rowan planted her elbows on the table and rested her chin on her interlinked hands. She was listening intently. Alex decided not to mention Becca by name as he described the scene on the bridge and the early stages of the negotiation that followed.

'And did you believe her?' asked Rowan when Alex paused a few minutes later to drink the last of his tea. 'About the affair, I mean?'

'I did, yes,' Alex replied.

'It sounds like she was in a really bad place,' Rowan said sympathetically.

'She was,' Alex acknowledged. 'I'm just pleased that we managed to get to her in time.'

*

Helen raced back down the stairs. She checked the living room and the ground floor loo. Then she ran out to the front of the house, calling Becca's name. There was no way Helen could move far from the house with her baby alone and asleep inside, but she checked the street in the immediate vicinity as thoroughly as the circumstances allowed. And there was no sign of her sister.

Experiencing a growing sense of dread, Helen ran back into the house and through to the kitchen to look for the contact card that the police negotiator had left with her earlier in the week.

Once Alex had finished describing the first call-out, attention had shifted to Pip, who took up the story of their second encounter with the girl on the bridge. She and Alex passed the narrative back and forth between them and were just reaching the part where Becca had made the allegation of criminality when Alex's phone rang.

'I'm so sorry,' he said, planning to ignore it. But as he pulled his phone out of his pocket to switch it to silent, he saw who was calling. 'It's Helen – Becca's sister,' he told Pip, clumsily and unintentionally revealing both of their names. He turned to Rowan. 'I really am sorry, but I'm going to have to take this.' He stood up. 'Pip will explain,' he added as he headed for the door of the cafe. He connected the call as he stepped out onto the pavement.

'Helen?' he said.

'She's not here,' said the distressed voice at the other end of the phone. 'Becca's disappeared.'

Chapter 18

Alex walked straight back into the cafe. 'We need to go,' he said to Pip, the urgency obvious in his voice. 'She's gone missing.'

'I thought it must be something like that,' Pip noted grimly.

Alex looked anxiously at Rowan, then back at Pip.

'It's all right,' Rowan said, her tone much softer than when she had first spoken to them. 'Pip explained the likely connection between the call and our conversation. You need to go. We can pick this up another time.'

'Thank you . . . yes . . . yes we can,' said Alex, anxious to leave, but not wanting to break the rapport they had begun to build up with the journalist.

'Go, go,' urged Rowan, making shooing gestures with her hands. 'I hope you find her.'

Alex dropped a ten-pound note on the table as he and Pip grabbed their coats from the backs of their chairs. 'I hope that's enough to cover the bill,' he said. 'We'll be in touch,' he added as they hustled towards the door.

As Rowan Blake watched them leave, she waved the waiter over. 'I'll have another cup of tea, please,' she said.

*

'What did Helen say?' asked Pip as they hurried along the pavement. The fact that she was still on call meant that they had travelled to the cafe in the van. It was parked a couple of streets away.

'Not a great deal,' Alex replied as he tried to catch his breath. 'She was in her kitchen when she thought she heard her front door click shut. She went upstairs to check the spare bedroom and that's when she discovered Becca was gone.'

'Bloody hell,' Pip muttered. 'Could she think of any reason why Becca might have disappeared?'

'Sort of,' Alex replied. 'Apparently, Becca came downstairs earlier this evening and told Helen that there was a dark grey car parked across the road from the house and that there were two men sitting in it.'

'The significance of that being?'

'Becca claimed they were watching her. Apparently, she looked genuinely frightened, but, when Helen checked the front of the house, there was no sign of any car, or of the two men.'

'No trace at all?'

'None,' Alex confirmed.

'So Becca imagined it?'

'Or they'd driven away before Helen went to look.'

'Has Helen tried calling her?' Pip asked.

'Becca's phone is broken.'

'Poor woman.'

'Who? Becca or Helen?'

'Both of them,' Pip replied.

'Absolutely,' murmured Alex, his feeling of compassion for the two women mingling with a sense of nagging disquiet.

'So what did you tell Helen to do?' Pip asked as they reached the van. She pressed the remote on the key and opened the driver's door.

'I told her to dial 999 and report Becca missing,' Alex answered as he climbed into the passenger seat, 'and said that we would head straight for Westminster Bridge.'

'How long has it been since she disappeared?' asked Pip as she started the engine and pulled out of the parking space.

Alex checked his watch. 'About twenty minutes,' he said, 'so she's unlikely to have made it all the way to the bridge.'

'If that's actually where she's heading,' cautioned Pip.

'Where else could she be going?'

'She could be going anywhere.'

Alex slumped back in his seat. 'You're right, of course,' he said, 'but we've got to start somewhere.' An all-too-familiar sense of anxiety was starting to gnaw at him again.

'Get your phone out,' said Pip, recognising his unease and giving him something constructive to occupy his thoughts with. 'Find us the most obvious route from Helen's house to Westminster Bridge. She might have taken a bus or taxi, or the Underground, but I have a feeling she'll be on foot. We'll start from the bridge and work our way back from there.'

'It's as good a plan as any,' said Alex, without sounding – or feeling – particularly hopeful.

Backstage at the Anvil Theatre in Basingstoke, Simon Jones was making small talk with the BBC make-up artist who was powdering his nose and forehead in preparation for his appearance under the lights.

He was feeling quietly confident. Not overconfident, because that wasn't his way, but certainly confident enough. He knew that this was his time.

*

125

Pip wasn't using the lights and sirens. She was actually driving at less than twenty miles an hour as she and Alex constantly scanned their surroundings. He was covering the nearside of the road; she had taken the offside. They had started outside St Thomas' Hospital and were trying to second-guess – in reverse – the route that Becca might be taking. If she was heading for the bridge. If she was above ground. If she was on foot. If she was still on the move. If she was somewhere that was visible from the road. With the addition of each new variable, Alex recognised that their chances of finding her were vanishingly slim. Add in her likely state of mind and her consequent unpredictability and Pip was right: Becca could be anywhere. Alex was feeling progressively more uneasy with just about every minute that passed.

The pavements were busy – with office workers heading home; with young lovers heading out; with street sleepers heading nowhere – but there was no sign of Becca Palmer.

They were on South Lambeth Road and Alex was on the verge of giving up hope completely when Pip suddenly jammed on the brakes. Despite their comparatively low speed, the sudden change in momentum threw Alex forward. His seat belt dug into his collarbone.

'Back there,' said Pip loudly as she threw the van into reverse, the engine whining in protest at the pace she was suddenly demanding from it.

'Where?' asked Alex, trying to shake off the sense of malaise that had been crowding in on him.

'Down there,' directed Pip as she hit the brakes again. She was pointing towards a pedestrian walkway that appeared to lead into the heart of a residential estate.

'But there's no one there,' Alex responded as his anxieties attacked him with renewed intensity.

'I'm sure I saw her,' insisted Pip, 'wearing the same black coat she had on earlier this week.' She was already getting out of the van. 'Come on!' she demanded.

Alex was doing his best to pull himself together. He unclipped his seat belt and got out.

Pip was already on the other side of the road. 'Hurry up!' she shouted at him.

'For fuck's sake,' Alex muttered in self-admonition as he coaxed his legs into a jog, then a run.

He caught up with Pip just as she was entering the estate. The walkway was empty, but Pip wasn't giving up. She knew what she'd seen. More to the point, she knew *who* she'd seen.

They reached a junction in the walkway. There was still no sign of Becca, or of anyone else for that matter.

'Left or right?' Pip asked urgently.

'Right,' replied Alex instinctively. Right was in the general direction of central London. They might be chasing phantoms and shadows, Alex reasoned, but Westminster Bridge remained the only fixed point on the map that offered them any kind of assistance with their search. Right was as good a direction as any to be heading in.

While Alex and Pip were looking for Becca, Rowan Blake was looking for clues. She was sitting on a tube train with her laptop open, looking through a series of documents that she had scanned and saved the day before.

The week before, she had drawn up a list of Soteria Solutions' directors and board members and had been running a series of background checks on all of them to see if she could establish any kind of link with Simon Jones. But it had proved to be a frustrating process that, so far, had yielded nothing of real interest. Having reached a series of dead ends, she had decided to shift her focus away from the people associated with the company and onto the company itself. And this was where she had caught a break. Or at least the glimmer of one.

One of the documents she had found among the millions released in the Jersey Papers leak revealed that Soteria Solutions had been purchased a year earlier by a Jersey-based venture capital firm called Enforcement Holdings. By following the online paper trail, she had been able to establish that Enforcement Holdings was, in turn, owned by Chaloner Capital, a company registered and incorporated in the Cayman Islands. Neither of those names had appeared in the public domain prior to the leak.

As with almost everything contained in the Jersey Papers, the ownership, structure and banking arrangements of the two organisations were shrouded in secrecy, but, whereas Enforcement Holdings appeared to be little more than a shell company, she was now looking at a set of documents associated with Chaloner Capital that provided her with the names of the firm's two principal shareholders: Sebastian Neill and Jane Hammond.

Neither of those names meant anything to her, but they would certainly give her something to work with.

She glanced up and realised that the next stop on the Underground was hers.

Alex and Pip had split up in order to be able to cover more ground. The sprawling housing estate was a jumbled mixture of tightly packed red-brick terraces and grey-slab high-rise blocks, all connected by an internal warren of roads, paths and raised walkways. It had been built in the 1960s and it was showing its age. The walls were damp and tagged with graffiti; the lighting was poor; and the stairwells were strewn with litter. Underfoot, the pavements were cracked and the roads potholed. It wasn't that the people who lived there didn't care – quite the opposite, in fact – it was that none of it had ever been built to last and the council no longer had the money or the resources to keep pace with the decay.

Pip had run back out to South Lambeth Road and was covering the perimeter of the estate. Alex was somewhere in the middle of it all, trying to make sense of the maze. They kept in frequent touch by mobile and neither of them was having any joy. Alex's mood was a match for his surroundings: dark and despairing. The whole undertaking seemed hopeless to him.

But he kept going, because that is what he had always done. Because that is what his ever-present sense of duty demanded of him. Because he didn't know any other way. And, at the moment when he least expected it, he saw her. Or, at least, he thought it was her.

He spotted a lone figure in a familiar black Puffa coat on the far side of a children's playground, tucked away in the middle of the estate. She was about a hundred metres away from him and he couldn't be absolutely certain it was Becca. But she was the right height and the right build and his gut was telling him that it was her.

'Becca!' he shouted at the top of his voice, quickening his pace as he did so.

The moment he called out, the woman started running.

'Shit!' said Alex as he broke into a sprint. 'Becca!' he shouted again. 'It's me, Alex.'

But the figure in the black coat didn't stop. If anything, she started running even faster.

Alex pulled his phone out of his pocket to call Pip and, as he peered down at the screen to find her number, he tripped on a kerbstone. The palm of his left hand hit the ground first, followed by his face. He lay on the ground for a moment, stunned and disorientated. There was a sharp pain running the length of his left arm and he could taste his own blood – the result of an ugly cut that had appeared on his forehead, just above the bridge of his nose.

He sat up and tried to gather himself. Becca! Where was she?

He raised himself gingerly onto his haunches just in time to see the woman disappearing around a corner at least eighty metres away.

Alex forced himself onto his feet. His phone had survived the fall and, this time, he dialled Pip's number before he started running again. The pain in his left arm was starting to intensify.

'She's heading east in the middle of the estate,' shouted Alex as soon as Pip answered.

'Where are you now?' Pip asked. She could hear that he was running. She could hear him sucking the air into his lungs.

'No idea,' Alex replied, between breaths. 'And I've lost sight of her.'

'Keep going,' Pip urged him.

Meanwhile, live on national television, Simon Jones was in full flow.

'We are stuck with a policing model in this country that was designed in the nineteenth century and is no longer fit for purpose,' he declared, to murmurs of approval from some sections of the *Question Time* audience. 'The last Labour government poured hundreds of millions of pounds of public money into law enforcement and we have seen very little in the way of corresponding improvements in performance.'

Warming to his theme and allowed to continue uninterrupted by the programme's host, he explained that people wanted change. That *he* wanted change. That it was long past time to bring the expertise of the private sector much more significantly to bear.

'And it's not just me saying this,' he insisted. 'Look at the reports published in the last year or so by the Independent Justice Alliance.' Here, he placed particular emphasis on the word 'independent'. 'The experts are telling us about the need for change,' he declared, starting to sound positively evangelical about his message. 'The evidence is telling us the same. And, as a former businessman, expertise and evidence are what matter to me. The police service in this country is losing the trust and confidence of the public it is supposed to serve – and we are all suffering as a consequence. It is for that reason that I intend to set in motion the most significant police reform programme we will have seen in this country in any of our lifetimes.'

He settled back in his chair to more than a smattering of applause from the live audience. It didn't really matter what anyone else on the panel might say in response to his remarks. He knew he had the backing of the Home Secretary and the Prime Minister. He knew he had the backing of the right-wing press. And he knew that the Government had more than enough votes to push through the changes he was looking for.

It had been another excellent night's work.

Alex reached the place where he had last seen Becca. She was nowhere in sight, but there was only one direction she could have gone in. He kept running, spitting blood onto the ground as he did so, his physical discomfort and his anxieties drowned out by a single-minded determination to catch up with her.

He reached a T-junction on the pathway through the estate. He looked to the left. Nothing. He looked to the right and there she was, leaning against a wall just at the point where the pathway rejoined the pavement on South Lambeth Road. She looked completely exhausted.

This time, Alex didn't shout. Instead, he walked cautiously towards her, talking quietly to Pip on the phone as he did so.

'I'm not far from the van,' Pip said. 'I'll get to it and head your way.'

'Thanks, Pip,' Alex whispered before ringing off.

As he got closer, he could see that it was definitely Becca. She appeared to be wearing a pair of blue and white striped cotton pyjamas under her coat and Alex noticed for the first time that her feet were bare. He felt a swell of renewed sympathy for her. She could hardly have looked in a worse state. She was leaning forward with her hands on her knees, staring at the ground, apparently lost somewhere inside her own head. She didn't seem to notice that he was there.

He was still about thirty metres away from her when she straightened up suddenly, pushed herself away from the wall and stumbled out of the estate, onto the pavement. She didn't even stop to look before stepping out into the road.

Alex's whole body seized as he heard the terrifying screech of brakes and tyres. He buried his face in his hands and waited for the inevitable, sickening impact.

Chapter 19

Pip was behind the wheel of the van, racing towards the location Alex had given when she saw it all happen up ahead of her. She saw Becca in the middle distance, stepping blindly out into the road. Horrified, Pip watched the front of a silver Ford Focus dip violently as the driver slammed on the brakes. She stifled a scream as, in seeming slow motion, the silver car began to skid and slew sideways across the road.

Back in her East London flat, Rowan Blake had just switched the television off. After her return from the meeting at the cafe, she had planned to continue with her research, only to be distracted by the appearance of Simon Jones on *Question Time*. The content of the programme had served only to renew and intensify her dislike of the man. Though she had yet to find any hard evidence of wrongdoing on his part, she had never subscribed to the view – held by many of her journalistic contemporaries – that Jones was somehow different from the rest. His politics and apparent worldview – not least his unwavering belief in the power of the free market to decide a nation's future – left her stone cold. She wondered from time to time whether she might be lacking in a certain amount of objectivity, but her judgement had rarely failed her in the past, and if there was one group of people she distrusted even more than police officers, it was politicians.

She yawned and stretched and checked the time on her watch. Before heading through to her bedroom, she picked up her phone and typed a WhatsApp message to Alex Lewis.

'*Have you managed to find her?*' she asked.

Somehow, the car had missed Becca.

Inconceivably, unfathomably, the driver of the Ford Focus had managed to avoid hitting her.

Pip was staring at Becca, standing unharmed in the middle of the road, and she was struggling to comprehend what she had just witnessed. She was replaying the events of the previous few seconds on a rapid loop in her mind, and none of it was making any sense to her. How on earth was Becca still on her feet?

The silver car was now stationary on the wrong side of the road, at right angles to the kerb. It had come to a stop outside a Portuguese restaurant. The driver had succeeded not only in missing Becca, but in missing everyone and everything else as well. Passers-by were standing on the pavement staring at the scene, too stunned even to get their phones out and start filming.

Pip had the presence of mind to switch the van's blue lights on as she pulled over on the nearside of the road and, as she did so, she spotted Alex emerging from the pedestrian entrance to the estate, looking thoroughly shaken. She could see the blood on his face and noticed his left arm hanging limply by his side, but, before she could do anything to help him, she knew that she needed to get to Becca – to get her off the road and safely into the back of the van.

As she jumped out and ran towards her, she was reassured to see that one of the staff from the restaurant, a portly, middle-aged man wearing a red and white striped apron, had gone to check on the shellshocked driver of the car.

When Pip reached her, Becca was rigid and rooted to the spot. As had been the case on the bridge earlier in the week, Pip could smell the alcohol on her breath and skin.

Pip put an arm around her. 'It's OK, Becca, you're safe now,' she said as she nudged her gently but firmly out of harm's way. She slid the side door of the van open. 'Sit down in there for me,' she encouraged Becca, helping her into the back and easing her into one of the seats. Pip took her coat off and placed it over Becca's knees.

Alex was hugely relieved to see that Becca was with Pip. Having had his hands over his face, he hadn't seen quite how close the car had come to hitting her, but, even so, he was struggling to believe that she had survived. As he walked towards Pip, he could still hear the squeal of the tyres and he was picturing Becca's body being thrown through the air like a rag doll.

'What on earth happened to you?' Pip asked as he approached, her face a picture of concern.

'You should see the other bloke,' Alex replied, as much in an attempt to lift his own spirits as hers.

'Very funny,' she said without laughing. 'What actually happened to you?' She placed a gentle hand on his cheek as she studied his face.

'I fell over,' he said.

'How the hell did you manage to do that?'

'It was dark,' he replied defensively. 'I was trying to ring you and I didn't see the kerb.'

In a less serious set of circumstances, it might almost have been funny: a grown man – and a police officer at that – falling flat on his face in the middle of a housing estate. But neither of them was feeling much like laughing.

'Are you hurt?' Pip asked, immediately regretting the clumsy phrasing of her question.

'What do you think?' he replied testily.

'Sorry,' she said. 'Stupid thing to ask. I mean, *how badly* are you hurt?'

'I'm all right,' he shrugged, though his face and arm suggested otherwise. 'But what about Becca?' he asked, looking over Pip's shoulder and into the back of the van. 'Is she OK?'

In truth, Alex was struggling much more with his emotions than he was with the injuries he'd sustained. It was as though he needed to be sure that Becca was OK in order to feel all right himself. There was something almost symbiotic about it.

His capacity for deep empathy had always been both a blessing and a burden to him. A blessing, because he found it easier than most to connect with people in crisis. It was a large part of what made him so effective as a negotiator. But a burden too, because he found it harder than most to disconnect once the crisis was over. And, given that this was now his third encounter with Becca Palmer, the likelihood was that the process of disconnection would become harder still. In all his years as a negotiator, she was the first person he had ever dealt with more than once. And the danger was that his own sense of wellbeing was becoming tangled up with the fate of someone he barely knew.

'Physically, she seems fine,' said Pip, unaware of what was going on in Alex's head. 'The rest, I'm not so sure about,' she added quietly as a marked police car arrived on scene.

*

As Pip crossed the road to speak to the two local officers who were getting out of their response car, Alex climbed into the back of the van and joined Becca.

'Hey there, Becca,' he said softly as he sat down opposite her. She was curled into a sideways foetal position on her seat, with her knees drawn up tightly to her chin. She slowly turned her head and looked at him.

'What happened to your face?' she asked as his injuries came into focus. Alex could tell that she'd been drinking, but it was also obvious that the experience of the last few minutes had sobered her up significantly.

'I fell over,' he replied, without elaboration.

'You're bleeding,' she said, looking concerned.

Instinctively, Alex put a hand to his forehead. He could feel the clotting stickiness of the blood beneath his fingertips. 'Oh, it's nothing serious,' he said lightly. 'Just a couple of bumps and bruises.'

'But it looks really painful.'

'I promise you I'm fine,' he reassured her. The expression on her face suggested that she wasn't convinced. 'But what about you, Becca? he asked. 'How are you doing?'

Becca responded with a barely audible groan that conveyed more to Alex than whole sentences of words could have done. It was the sound of weariness and shame. Of uncertainty and anxiety and frustration.

'Why did you run away from me?' he asked her. His tone wasn't accusatory or angry. He simply wanted to understand what had happened, and why.

'I didn't know it was you,' she replied hesitantly, almost apologetically. 'I heard someone shouting and I got scared.'

Her explanation made sense. 'I'm so sorry, Becca,' Alex said. 'I didn't mean to scare you.'

Slowly, she started to uncurl herself in her seat, some of the more obvious signs of her angst fading as she did so. 'I didn't mean to step out in front of the car,' she said sincerely. 'I was confused. I didn't know where I was ... or what I was doing.'

Alex was continuing to pay as much attention to Becca's demeanour as he was to what she was saying. There was now an earnest expression on her face and it seemed to him that she was wanting somehow to make amends for the trouble she'd caused.

'I understand,' he said. 'The most important thing is that you're safe now.' But there was something else that he knew he needed to say to her. It wasn't the sort of thing he would ever have considered saying to someone he was dealing with for the first time. But the situation with Becca was different and Alex knew that he needed to draw a line. 'We can't keep doing this,' he said gently.

Becca looked at him with a mixture of contrition and concern. 'You mean me doing something stupid and you having to come to my rescue?' she said.

Alex nodded.

'I know,' she responded quietly. 'I'm incredibly sorry.'

'Why did you leave your sister's house this evening?' Alex asked her.

Instantly, the shadows returned to her face and her voice. 'I was scared,' she replied, her eyes widening as she spoke. Her bottom lip began to tremble and Alex could see her hands starting to twitch in her lap. He realised that she was remembering – visualising – whatever it was she thought had happened earlier on.

'What was it that scared you?' he asked her.

'They were watching me,' she replied anxiously.

'Who was watching you?' he asked, choosing not to make

138

any immediate mention of what Helen had told him on the phone. He wanted to hear what Becca had to say about it first.

'Two men,' she replied, drawing her knees back up to her chin. 'They were in a car outside the house and they were watching me.'

'What did they look like?' Alex asked, making a conscious choice to set aside any doubts he might have been feeling about what she was telling him.

Becca ignored the question. 'I saw them earlier today as well,' she said.

'Did you?' asked Alex. 'Where?'

'I went to the local shop to buy some milk,' Becca replied. 'Helen said that the fresh air would do me some good.'

'And?'

'And they followed me.' She looked down at the floor of the van and shifted uneasily in her seat.

'Can you describe what happened?'

'They were standing on the other side the road when I walked out of the shop. One of them crossed over, but both of them followed me all the way home.'

'That must have been very frightening for you, Becca,' Alex said sympathetically. 'Did you tell Helen about it?'

'Not until I saw the same two men sitting in the car later on,' Becca replied. She reached out suddenly and caught hold of Alex's uninjured right arm. 'Who do you think they are?' she asked in a voice that was starting to sound panicky. 'Do you think Camilla sent them?'

'I don't know,' Alex replied calmly. He studied her eyes and the expression on her face. He could feel the tremor in her hand as she gripped his forearm. There was no doubt in his mind that she believed what she was telling him. For the time being, the question of whether or not he actually believed her was less important than the need to reassure her. 'All I do know,' he said, 'is that you're safe now.'

'I don't think I am,' she replied.

'Look at me, Becca,' Alex said to her. She lifted her head a fraction and met his gaze. 'I promise you that you're not going to come to any harm,' he insisted.

He only hoped that he was right.

Chapter 20

Their conversation was disturbed by the noisy arrival of an ambulance.

Pip appeared at the side door of the van a few moments later, accompanied by two paramedics – one male, one female. 'Sorry to be the one to interrupt,' Pip said to them, 'but we ought to get the two of you checked out.'

'Sounds sensible to me,' Alex replied, grateful for an opportunity to take some time and space to think. Becca's situation was becoming more complex and he wasn't at all certain what he ought to do next. 'Why don't you stay here with Becca,' he suggested to Pip, 'and I'll head across the road?'

'Well, I'm as certain as I can be that it's not broken,' said the young man in the green uniform, following a careful examination of Alex's left wrist and forearm. They were sitting together in the back of the ambulance. 'But it's definitely sprained,' he continued. 'Do you want me to give you some painkillers to take?'

'I'm all right for now,' Alex replied, glad that he wasn't going to have to spend the next few hours sitting and waiting in an overcrowded A&E department. 'I've got some at home if I need to take them later on,' he said.

'In which case,' said the young man, 'let's take a look at your face.' He gently cleaned the cut on Alex's forehead and carefully wiped away the streaks of blood from his nose, cheeks and chin. 'Not too bad,' he remarked with a smile. 'I think you'll live.' He closed the wound with a couple of Steri-Strips and covered it with a piece of white surgical tape, before rummaging in his kitbag and producing a tubigrip bandage that he eased carefully over Alex's hand and wrist.

Having been patched up, Alex stepped gingerly out of the ambulance and looked back across the road to where the van was still parked. He was feeling stiff and sore. He was also feeling troubled. On the one hand, the conversation with Becca had eased some of his most pressing concerns about her. She was safe – for the time being at least – and she was sober. More than that, she had, for the first time since he'd met her, seemed able to acknowledge both the seriousness of her situation and the need for her to do something about it. *We can't keep doing this*, he had said, and he'd been reassured by her acceptance of the fact. On the other hand, he was bothered by the apparent inadequacy of the mental healthcare she was being provided with. It was obvious that she remained incredibly vulnerable.

He was also bothered by the potential implications of what she'd told him about the two men. What if they weren't just a product of her imagination? What if she really was being watched and followed? And the questions didn't end there. What if there was some sort of a connection between the two men and Camilla Lane's possible visit to the hospital? What if someone – or more than one person – really was trying to keep Becca quiet? What should he and Pip do?

Deep in thought, Alex wandered back over to the van, where Pip and Becca were sitting and talking to the female paramedic.

Pip greeted him with a broad smile. 'You look a whole lot better,' she said.

Alex responded with an attempt at a smile of his own. He wasn't sure that he was feeling any better, but he chose not to mention the fact – not least because Becca was looking much better herself. He had no immediate way of knowing whether she'd repeated to Pip any of the things she'd earlier said to him, but she seemed much more settled than when he'd left her to get his injuries treated. There was none of the twitchy anxiety that had been there before. He supposed that swift and sometimes significant alterations in her moods and behaviour were another symptom of the state of her mind. Once again, he felt his heart going out to her.

'How about the two of you?' he asked. 'How are you getting on?'

Pip replied for them both. 'I think we're doing all right,' she said. 'We've been talking about what's best for Becca, and we think we've come up with a plan.'

'Let's hear it then,' Alex said.

'Well, I think it would be fair to say that Becca definitely isn't keen on the idea of going back to hospital,' Pip began. Becca nodded vigorously. Hospital was clearly the very last place she wanted to go to. 'Though it turns out that it probably wasn't an option in any case,' Pip continued. 'We've just found out that the Bethlem Royal doesn't actually have any crisis beds available tonight. They're completely full.'

'It's the same in most places,' the female paramedic inter-jected. 'Too many people needing help and not enough help to go round.'

'So we've agreed that Becca can go back to her sister's house,' Pip added, 'provided she agrees to a number of specific condi-tions.'

'Those being?' Alex asked.

Becca leaned right forward, seemingly eager to answer the question for herself. The positive expression on her face was a long way removed from the fear and concern that had been so apparent less than half an hour earlier. 'I'm going to go back on my medication – starting tonight,' she said keenly. 'Then I'm going to contact my GP first thing in the morning to sort out some proper counselling. And I'm going to stay at my sister's house until I'm feeling much, much better. I'm not going to leave again.'

It was as clear and coherent as Becca had sounded on any of the three occasions that Alex had spent time with her. He watched her as she relaxed back into her seat and wondered whether there was something in particular that had prompted the change in both her outlook and her demeanour. Perhaps it was simply the result of spending a bit of time in Pip's company. Alex certainly knew from repeated personal experience how much kindness and calm Pip was able to bring to a challenging situation. Or maybe Becca had taken a bit of time to think through her terrifyingly close encounter with the silver car and was now embracing the realisation that she'd been given an opportunity to make a fresh go of things.

Whatever the reason might have been, Alex felt both pleased and relieved by her response to the situation. 'Well, it sounds like a good plan to me,' he said.

They rang Helen to say that they were on their way and when they pulled up outside her house, she was waiting for them on her front doorstep. As she wrapped her younger sister up in a tearful embrace, she expressed her repeated and sincere gratitude to Alex and Pip.

'It's honestly not a problem,' Pip told her. 'It was our pleasure in fact.'

As before, they followed Helen through to the kitchen and, as before, she offered to make them tea.

'Would you mind if I went up to bed?' Becca asked them.

'Of course not,' Helen replied.

'Are you sure you're all right?' Alex asked her.

Becca nodded. 'I'm sure,' she replied. Once again, there was no obvious trace of her earlier unease. It was almost as if she'd forgotten about the car and the two men. She walked over to her sister and hugged her again. 'Sorry for all the trouble,' she said.

'I'm just glad you're home,' Helen replied.

Alex watched as Becca walked out of the room and listened as she padded up the stairs.

'What about you?' Helen asked as the kettle finished boiling. She had seen the bandage on Alex's wrist and was looking at the cut on his forehead. 'Are you all right?'

'I'm fine,' he answered.

'He fell over,' Pip explained, without going into detail.

'Can I get you anything apart from a cup of tea?' she asked him. 'Paracetamol perhaps?'

'Just tea would be great,' Alex replied, before changing the subject. 'Would it be all right to ask you a couple of quick questions about earlier today?'

'Of course it would,' Helen replied as she filled the first of three mugs with boiling water.

'Curiouser and curiouser,' Pip mused as she started the engine and put the van into gear. Having finished their tea and said their goodbyes, they were both feeling more than ready to head home.

'That would certainly be one way of describing it,' Alex remarked.

Helen had done her best to answer all the questions he'd put to her. Yes, she had sent Becca out to the local shop earlier that afternoon. Yes, she had told her that she thought it would be good for her to get some fresh air. No, Becca hadn't mentioned anything about being followed home. Not at the time anyway. Yes, Becca had run downstairs later in the day to say that there was a car parked outside and that there were two men in it who were watching her. And, yes, she had seemed to be genuinely frightened. But there had definitely been no sign of the car, or of the men, when Helen had gone outside to look. Like Alex, she hadn't doubted Becca's belief in what she was saying, but, like Alex, she wasn't certain how much, if any of it, was real, and how much was in her sister's mind. 'Here's the thing,' she had said to them, 'I know I mentioned to you before that Becca sometimes says things that aren't actually true. Well, on occasions, I've also known her to *see* things that aren't actually there.'

'Sometimes she sees things that aren't actually there,' Pip said, quoting Helen as she turned left at the next junction.

'It sounds like something from an M. Night Shyamalan film, doesn't it?' Alex commented. He angled his head to one side and stared at his bloodied and bruised reflection in the van's nearside wing mirror. 'The thing is,' he continued, 'Becca was definitely genuinely scared when she was talking to me about it in the back of the van.'

'I don't doubt it, the poor thing,' Pip replied sympathetically. 'What do you think we should do?'

'Well, I could call my counterpart at Wandsworth and ask if one of the local community officers could keep half an eye on the house,' Alex suggested. 'Just in case.'

'OK.'

'I also think I should call into the Home Office on my way to work tomorrow morning,' Alex added.

'To do what?' Pip looked surprised.

'To see if this Camilla person is there and to find out what she might be able to tell us about Becca.'

'What might you say to her?'

'I'd say that, between you and me, we've now been called out to deal with Becca on three separate occasions,' Alex replied, 'and that I'm looking for any possible information that might help us to ensure that it doesn't happen a fourth time.'

'Seems reasonable enough,' Pip agreed.

'And who knows what else I might find out along the way,' Alex said.

It was just after nine o'clock the following morning when Alex walked through the main entrance of the Home Office in Marsham Street. His first meeting at Kentish Town wasn't until eleven, so he had plenty of time. He produced his warrant card for inspection and was waved through security. As he approached one of the chest-high reception desks, he showed his warrant card again and asked the member of staff on the other side of the plexiglass divide whether it might be possible to speak to Camilla Lane in the Policing Minister's office. He explained that he didn't have an appointment.

Camilla was in the open-plan office on the fourth floor when her desk phone started to ring. Simon Jones had decided to travel straight back to his Sheffield constituency after his *Question Time* appearance the previous evening and it had left her with an unexpected – and much-needed – opportunity to catch up on some paperwork.

'The office of the Policing Minister,' she said briskly.

The young man wearing the round glasses sitting at the desk opposite could only hear her end of the conversation.

'You're speaking to her,' Camilla said. 'What can I do for you?'

'Who?' she asked after a pause. Evidently, the person at the other end of the line had given her a name she didn't recognise.

'What does he want?' she said.

The young man in the glasses couldn't help noticing the dip of her eyebrows and the expression of mild concern on her face.

'Oh,' she said a moment later. 'Well, in that case, you'd better send him up.'

Alex followed the directions given to him by the receptionist. When the lift doors opened on the fourth-floor landing, he was greeted by an elegantly dressed middle-aged woman with a businesslike manner and a penetrating gaze.

'Camilla Lane,' she announced, offering her hand for him to shake. 'And you must be?'

'Alex Lewis,' Alex replied, handing her a business card with his contact details on it. 'I'm a superintendent in the Met. Thank you so much for seeing me at such short notice.'

'At *no* notice,' she corrected him.

'At no notice,' Alex affirmed. He was barely out of the lift and he was already on the back foot. 'I promise not to take too much of your time,' he said, in an attempt at conciliation. His instincts were telling him that he needed to tread extremely carefully for the next few minutes if he was going to be able to find out anything of use from the Minister's senior advisor. The need to establish a level of rapport with her was just as important as it would have been in any of his negotiation work.

'This way,' she directed him as she turned and started walking down the corridor.

He followed her into a large office occupied by at least a dozen staff. One or two of them looked in his direction – including a young man wearing round glasses – but most of them ignored him. Alex couldn't help noticing the empty desk on the far side of the room.

'We'll use the Minister's office since he's not here today,' Camilla announced. 'It will give us some privacy.' She opened the door and ushered him in. 'I'll be with you in a moment,' she said. 'I'm just going to grab my notebook.'

Alex stood in the middle of the room and took in the detail: the high-backed swivel chair behind a large desk that was empty, save for a large silver framed photo of a smiling Simon Jones, sitting on a bench with his wife and children in the garden of an extensive and impressive house; the triptych of urban landscapes – Sheffield, Alex guessed – hanging on the wall, alongside a portrait of the Queen; the inevitable line-up of grey metal filing cabinets, next to a set of shelves containing a series of books chosen, it seemed, more for display than reference. Taken together, the contents of the room – those that Alex could see, at any rate – offered little by way of substantial insight into the character and personality of the man who normally occupied it.

'Why don't we take a seat,' said Camilla as she reappeared in the room and closed the door behind her. Her voice and manner were a little less abrasive than they had been out in the corridor and in the open office. Alex wondered whether his initial encounter with her had contained an element of performance, put on for the benefit of her colleagues. Perhaps she had a reputation to maintain.

'Thank you,' Alex said.

'How can I help you?' she asked, adjusting the sleeves of her jacket and checking her watch.

'It's about Becca Palmer,' Alex replied, noting that he was on the clock and choosing to get straight to the point.

'So the receptionist told me,' Camilla replied. She didn't seem ruffled by the mention of Becca's name.

'We were called to deal with her again last night.'

'Oh really? I hadn't heard about that. Is she all right?' Camilla asked, sounding more concerned than she actually looked. Alex decided to give her the benefit of the doubt.

'She's safe,' he replied. 'Perhaps, I could bring you up to date with her situation?'

'By all means.'

Beginning with the previous night, Alex provided an abridged and redacted account of the events of the past two-and-a-bit weeks. At this early point in the conversation, he made no reference to the alleged affair with Simon Jones. Camilla Lane listened closely, interjecting periodically with observations and comments of her own. All the while, she jotted notes in the book lying open on her lap.

'I want to make sure that she now gets all the help she needs,' Alex said as he reached the end of his initial summary. 'Not least to make sure that my colleagues and I don't keep getting called out.'

Camilla nodded. 'And how can I assist you with that, Superintendent?' she asked.

'I was hoping you might be able to help me with a couple of minor queries.'

'I'm running a little short of time,' Camilla replied, checking her watch again. 'But go ahead.'

'I'm really grateful,' Alex said. 'I only need another minute or two.'

Camilla nodded at him to continue.

'Becca mentioned that you went to visit her in hospital after the first encounter that I had with her on the bridge,' Alex said.

'I did, yes.'

'She also mentioned some paperwork that you asked her to sign?'

'And the relevance of that is?' Camilla replied in slightly more clipped tones. She was frowning.

'It's just that Becca seemed rather upset by it,' Alex explained, 'and I was trying to understand why.'

'I'm not sure why that would be,' Camilla responded. 'It was just a standard form.'

'Would I be able to see it?' Alex asked.

For the first time in the conversation, Camilla Lane hesitated. 'I'm not sure that would be appropriate,' she said after a pause. 'It's a confidential personnel document.'

'I'm sure Becca wouldn't mind,' Alex replied, trying to push home any small advantage he might have gained in the exchange.

Her response, when it came, was not the one he was expecting. 'Well, I suppose it wouldn't do any harm,' she said. 'Particularly if it helps to put the poor girl's mind at rest.' Whatever her initial reservations might have been, she appeared to have made a choice to be amenable.

'As long as it wouldn't be too much trouble,' Alex said.

'Not *too* much,' Camilla replied, her expression easing. 'If you don't mind waiting for a moment or two, I'll find it and have a copy made for you.'

'Of course. Thank you very much.' Alex watched her as she walked out of the office. He retrieved his phone from his trouser pocket. '*Curiouser and curiouser*', he texted to Pip.

151

Chapter 21

'I've just spent the last half an hour with Camilla Lane,' Alex said. He was speaking to Pip on his mobile, having just walked out of the Home Office.

'What did you make of her?' Pip asked.

'She's an interesting character,' Alex replied. 'I'm not sure what to make of her, to be honest – and I'm definitely not inclined to trust her – but, to be fair to her, she answered all of my questions.'

'So what did she tell you?'

'That Becca has always had enormous potential, but that she appears to have been unwell for quite some time,' Alex relayed. 'In the relatively limited period that she's been working with them at the Home Office, she's already been off sick on something like a dozen occasions. Usually only for a day or two at a time, but they'd reached the point where, reluctantly, according to Ms Lane, they were about to start the formal part of their unsatisfactory attendance procedures with her.'

'I thought Becca said that she'd been fired?'

'Not according to Camilla Lane.'

'So what gave Becca the impression that the decision had already been made?' Pip asked.

'Apparently the Minister might have said something to her in a phone call – the day before I first spoke to her on Westminster Bridge.'

'A phone call?'

'That's what Ms Lane said.'

'But didn't Becca tell you that she'd been with the Minister at his flat the night before she ended up on the bridge?' Pip queried.

'Yes, she did.'

'So, someone's not being straight with you.'

'It certainly looks that way,' Alex agreed.

'I take it you kept that knowledge to yourself?'

'Of course I did,' Alex replied. 'Like I said, I'm not sure that I trust Ms Lane.'

'Did you ask her about the hospital visit?' Pip enquired.

'I did.'

'And about the paperwork?'

'Yes.'

'So what did she say?' Pip pressed.

'She went and got me a copy of the document.'

'She did?' Alex could hear the surprise in Pip's voice.

'Absolutely,' he replied. 'I'm looking at it right now.' He glanced down at the single sheet of A4 paper that he was holding in his bandaged left hand.

'What does it say?'

'Well, it certainly isn't a non-disclosure agreement.'

'So what is it then?' Pip asked, sounding disappointed.

Alex had felt much the same when Camilla had first handed the document to him. He realised that he'd been hoping to be given some sort of smoking gun – something to back up the unsubstantiated possibility that Becca was being silenced by unseen forces with something to hide. But the piece of paper he'd been given was nothing of the sort. 'It's just a standard Home Office attendance management form,' he said.

'Nothing more than that?' Pip asked.

'Nothing more.'

'And is it genuine?'

'Seems to be,' Alex replied. 'It's got her name at the bottom of the page, and a signature to go with it.'

'So that's the end of that then.'

'Maybe,' Alex replied. 'I'd like to show it to Becca if we get the chance. Just to check.'

'What about the affair?' Pip asked. Like Alex, she was still looking for anything that might resemble evidence in support of Becca Palmer's claims. 'Did you mention that to her?'

'Uh-huh.'

'And how did she react?'

'It didn't seem to surprise her – the suggestion, I mean. She told me that Becca had said the same to some of her colleagues in the office.'

'And?'

'Ms Lane said that it wasn't true. And, to be honest, she sounded pretty convincing on the subject. She pointed out that she currently spends more time with Simon Jones than anyone else does – more even than his own family at this particular point in his career – and she told me very clearly that she would know if he was having any kind of affair.'

'And you believed her?'

'Hmm...'

'What does "Hmm" mean?'

'It means that I need to think about it,' Alex replied. 'It's possible that the affair was going on without Camilla Lane's knowledge.'

'Or that Camilla Lane is covering for him?' Pip suggested.

'There is that possibility too.'

'And Becca?' Pip asked.

'What about her?'

'Do you still believe *her*?'

'I want to.'

'Even if the available evidence is pointing in the other direction?'

'Even if the available evidence is pointing in the other direction,' Alex replied.

'And you're sure it's not just a case of your prejudices affecting your judgement?'

'Which particular prejudice might we be talking about?'

'The one that means you're rarely – if ever – inclined to trust politicians,' Pip replied. 'Particularly when the politicians in question are members of the party that's done so much damage to policing during the past decade.'

Alex knew that Pip had a point. Of course it was entirely possible that his preconceptions were clouding his thinking. He was just as susceptible to them as the next man. He knew perfectly well that there were trustworthy politicians on both sides of the House, even if they didn't appear to be the ones who were actually in charge of the country at that particular moment in time. He understood that they weren't all bent – that many of them were dedicated public servants who, just like him, had set out on their careers wanting to make a difference in the world. It might even be that Simon Jones was one of them.

'Maybe,' he replied.

'Did this Lane woman have anything else to say?' Pip asked.

'There was one other thing she mentioned just as I was leaving. It was almost a word-for-word repetition of something Helen has mentioned to us on more than one occasion.'

'What did she say?'

'She suggested that Becca has a bit of a reputation among her Home Office colleagues for saying things sometimes that turn out not to be true.'

155

*

An hour later, Alex was back in his office at Kentish Town police station. He was with Ronnie Egan, going through the latest bleak set of overnight crime figures, when they were interrupted by the insistent buzz of the mobile phone lying on his desk. Alex reached for it, took one look at the call display and rolled his eyes as he showed the screen to Ronnie. It was the Area Commander.

'Morning, sir,' Alex said as politely as he could muster.

'What were you doing at the Home Office this morning?' the Commander demanded, dispensing with any form of greeting and getting straight to the point.

Alex was taken aback. He had grown accustomed to his boss's charmless manner, but the subject of the call was un-expected. He hadn't told anyone apart from Pip that he was going to see Camilla Lane – it hadn't occurred to him that he should – and, immediately, he was trying to work out if he'd done something wrong. He didn't think that he had. Ronnie looked at him enquiringly.

'Er . . . I was following up on a hostage negotiation job,' Alex ventured.

'At the office of the Policing Minister?' The voice at the other end of the phone was irritable and impatient.

'Yes.'

'What the fuck did you do that for?'

Alex held his mobile away from his ear and looked at it in bemusement. He switched it to speaker so that Ronnie could hear both ends of the conversation. It was never a bad idea to have a witness on your side when things looked as though they might be going wrong. 'Because the very vulnerable person I've been dealing with worked there until about three weeks ago,' he said into the phone's microphone, 'and I was trying to find a bit more out about her.'

'And you didn't think to mention it to me?'

'Should I have done?' Alex might have been startled by the timing and content of the call, but he didn't feel in the least bit intimidated by a man he had no respect for. As a result, he was quickly finding his feet in the conversation.

'Of course you fucking should have done,' the Commander replied, oblivious to the diminishing returns that his approach to the conversation was delivering. 'I've had the Commissioner in my ear about it for the last ten minutes.'

'The Commissioner?' Alex replied, genuinely bemused. 'What's it got to do with him?'

'Are you being deliberately naive?' the Commander rumbled back. 'Crime is up. Detection rates are down. The Met is under all sorts of pressure from Number 10. Questions are being asked in the press. The very last thing the Commissioner needs is for you to be stirring up trouble.'

'Trouble?' responded Alex, unable to hide his surprise. 'What trouble? I was just doing my job.'

There was an exaggerated sigh at the other end of the line. 'Oh, for fuck's sake, Alex,' the Commander said testily. 'Your *job* is to do something about the crime wave that's currently sweeping through North London. And that means staying away from the fucking Home Office.' With that, he hung up.

Alex stared at Ronnie Egan in disbelief.

'The man's an idiot,' Ronnie said.

'I think we knew that already,' Alex replied. 'But what the hell was that all about? Stirring up trouble for the Commissioner? I wasn't doing anything of the sort. And, in any case, why on earth would the Commissioner be concerned about a negotiation job on Westminster Bridge?'

Chapter 22

'He said what?' asked Pip, looking incredulous. She was sitting opposite Alex in a small cafe just around the corner from Kentish Town tube station. She was due at a case conference at Holborn police station later that afternoon and had called him on the off chance that he might be free to meet for a quick bite to eat beforehand. He was partway through telling her about that morning's call from the Area Commander when she interrupted him with her question.

'He told me to stay away from "*the fucking Home Office*" – and advised me to concentrate on the day job.'

'Seriously?'

Alex nodded.

'The man's an idiot.'

'Funnily enough,' Alex said, 'those were the exact words Ronnie used.'

'Well, we can't both be wrong,' Pip replied.

'But why would my going to the Home Office for a perfectly legitimate reason have the potential to cause trouble for the Commissioner?' Alex asked.

'It really shouldn't do,' Pip acknowledged. 'But think about it for a moment. How long has the Commissioner been in post?'

Alex paused to do the maths. 'Coming up for four years,' he said.

'And what does he want?'

'Apart from a knighthood, you mean?'

'Apart from that.'

'An extension to his contract – he wants another four years.'

'And who makes the final decision about that contract?'

'The Home Secretary.'

'So there's your most likely answer,' said Pip with a shrug. 'Don't make waves at the Home Office while the Commissioner is waiting on a contract extension.'

'And a knighthood,' Alex reminded her.

'That too,' Pip agreed.

'But I really wasn't making any waves,' protested Alex. 'I was just asking some very basic questions concerning a young woman's welfare.'

'You know that and I know that,' Pip replied, 'but you also told them that the same young woman is alleging she's had an affair with one of the highest profile politicians in the country. Someone at the Home Office was concerned enough about your visit to pick up the phone to the Yard.'

'That someone being Camilla Lane?'

'Who else could it be?' Pip said.

'I told you I didn't trust her,' Alex remarked.

'I'm so sorry to bother you when you're at home,' Camilla Lane said to Simon Jones, 'particularly since you're seeing so little of your family at the moment.' She was sitting in his office with the door closed, speaking to him via WhatsApp audio. Like many of their Westminster contemporaries, they used encrypted apps for most of their important messages and calls.

'No problem,' he replied. 'My wife has gone to collect the

kids from school and I was just catching up on some reading. What can I do for you?'

'I just wanted to let you know about a visitor we had in the office earlier today.'

'Oh?' It sounded as though his mind was elsewhere. Camilla could hear the rustling of paper at the other end of the line.

'The visitor was one of the police officers who helped Becca when she was on Westminster Bridge.'

'Really?' said the Minister, immediately sounding more engaged. 'What did he want?'

Camilla responded by telling him about Alex – about the reason for his visit and about their conversation. The Minister sounded relieved to hear that Becca was safe and being cared for.

'There was one other thing,' Camilla said, somewhat reluctantly.

'Yes?'

'He asked me if you had been having an affair with Becca.'

'You're kidding?' Simon Jones sounded shocked.

'She must have said something when he was talking to her on the bridge. I suppose we shouldn't be unduly surprised, given that she's said similar things to people here in the office.'

'And what did you tell him?'

'I told him the truth, of course,' Camilla replied. 'I told him that I currently see more of you than your wife does – and that I would certainly know if you were having an affair.'

'Thank you, Camilla,' the Minister replied. 'I appreciate it. I know that politicians have all sorts of things said of them that aren't true, but it can be particularly hurtful when it's something so personal.'

'I don't doubt it.'

'Actually, I was bothered enough when you first mentioned it to talk to Frances about it,' he said. 'Partly to ask her advice and partly to avoid any unwelcome marital complications should Becca decide to spin her stories to anyone other than the police.'

'And what did she say?'

'She was remarkably relaxed about it. There have never been any secrets between us and she understands that this kind of thing goes with the territory sometimes.'

'I'm glad you've spoken to her,' said Camilla, 'and she's right. I don't think you need give it another thought.'

'I just can't imagine being unfaithful to my wife,' he remarked. 'What was it that the actor Paul Newman once said? Something about the senselessness of going out for a burger when there's steak available at home?'

'I'm not comfortable with any analogy that portrays a woman as a piece of meat,' Camilla replied bluntly.

'Fair point,' the Minister conceded. 'But you understand what I mean?'

'I do.'

'Was there anything else?' he asked, already sounding as though he'd moved on.

'I called the Commissioner's office,' Camilla said. 'Just to let them know what had happened.'

'Did you need to do that?' he asked.

'I don't want him coming back,' she explained. 'There's no reason why he would need to, of course, but I need to make sure that the team in the office are free from any kind of distraction. The work you're doing is far too important to allow their minds to wander or their tongues to wag.'

'That makes sense,' said the Minister. 'Thank you,' he added, for the second time in as many minutes.

*

Alex was cooking supper that evening when his phone pinged with a text notification. It was from Rowan Blake.

'*Did you find her?*'

As he looked at the screen, Alex realised that it was the second message she'd sent asking the same question. He'd been so preoccupied with the search for Becca that he'd completely missed the first one.

'*Yes we did,*' he typed. '*I'm so sorry not to have replied before. I didn't actually see your last message.*' He put his phone down briefly to crack open the oven door and check on the food.

'*Thank God for that,*' came the response. '*Is she OK?*'

'*Sort of. She nearly got hit by a car. But she's safe now.*'

'*I'm glad,*' said the reply. It was followed quickly by another message. '*Could we meet again?*'

Alex put his phone down and called through to Pip, who was reading a book in the next door room. 'It's Rowan Blake,' he said.

'And?'

'She's asking to meet us again.'

'What have you said?'

'I haven't said anything yet,' Alex replied. 'I wanted to check with you first.'

'Is there any reason not to?' Pip asked, appearing at the kitchen door.

'None that I can think of.'

'Unless the Area Commander finds out,' said Pip, with a mischievous smile.

'Not funny,' said Alex. 'If anything, the conversation with Camilla Lane and the subsequent phone call from him has left me feeling more concerned about Becca.'

'Do you genuinely think that there might be some sort of grand conspiracy in play here?' asked Pip doubtfully.

'I've honestly no idea,' Alex replied. 'But I can't help feeling that we've got unfinished business with Rowan Blake.'

'I'd certainly be interested to know whether she's managed to find anything else out about Soteria Solutions,' Pip noted.

'That's decided then,' Alex said as he picked up his phone from the work surface next to the oven. '*Sure*,' he typed to Rowan. '*When did you have in mind?*' Pip came and stood next to him while they waited for her to reply.

'*I have to go away for the next few days. Can you do next Tuesday evening? Same time and place?*'

Alex looked at Pip.

'What about the boys?' she said. 'Won't you be with them on Tuesday?'

'We're doing Wednesday next week,' Alex replied. 'They've both got something on at school on Tuesday.'

'All right then,' Pip said.

'*We'll be there*,' Alex typed.

'*Thank you*,' came the response. '*I've got plenty to tell you – and a very important question to ask.*'

Chapter 23

The weekend passed fairly uneventfully. Pip had been called out on a negotiation job late on Saturday afternoon, only to be cancelled before she'd even made it to the scene. Local officers had managed to resolve the situation – some sort of protest by an Italian man perched on the roof of a three-storey house – without the need for additional help. She'd made it back home in time to spend a quiet evening with Alex, who'd been with his boys for the day.

Sunday was quieter still: a morning run for Alex, followed by a shared shower with Pip; an afternoon stroll through Borough Market and along the South Bank together; a bottle of decent wine over dinner; an early-ish night in preparation for the week ahead. Reassuringly for Alex, there had been no phone calls from Helen about Becca. He hoped that meant that all was well with them – at least, as well as it could have been, given the precarious nature of Becca's health and the events of recent days. As he lay in bed on Sunday night, it was Becca he was thinking of as he began to drift off – his limbs twitching every now and then as he relived the chase through the estate and the near miss with the silver car.

Monday couldn't pass quickly enough. Alex spent the morning with Ronnie Egan, going through the weekend's crime figures, followed by an afternoon at Scotland Yard – together with his counterparts from five other London Boroughs – doing his best to explain those same figures to an increasingly agitated Area Commander.

As ever, the story told by the operational officers was one of the inevitable long-term consequences of decisions taken by a clueless bunch of politicians and their special advisors. These were the people who had cut policing to the bone. And these were the same people who, with a startling lack of self-awareness, were now expressing their surprise and concern that – exactly as predicted by anyone with even a passing understanding of reality – crime had started to rise rather significantly. It was as though they had deliberately broken the legs of policing and were now blaming it for being unable to run. These were the things that Alex and his colleagues had tried to explain to the Area Commander, but the senior officer hadn't been interested in any of it. He'd ended the meeting irritably by demanding 'solutions, not excuses,' from an audience of women and men who thought him a fool.

By the time Tuesday evening came around – at the end of another day of pressurised meetings and difficult conversations about crime rates – Alex was more than ready for anything that might provide some sort of diversion from it all. He was actually looking forward to seeing Rowan Blake.

He met up with Pip outside Waterloo station and they walked the short distance round the corner to the cafe where they'd met Rowan the week before. As before, they got there first. And, as before, they took the table in the corner with its view of the door.

Rowan arrived a few minutes later, stumbling through the door of the cafe, looking flustered but expectant. She was wearing the same oversized woollen scarf. As she approached their table, her manner was markedly different from the first time they'd met. She smiled as she shook their hands and she thanked them for taking the time to be there. And, as she settled into her seat, there was none of the latent suspicion she'd carried with her before. It seemed to Alex that any reservations she might have had about speaking to a pair of police officers had been replaced by something that almost approached kinship. Whatever was going on, she seemed to think that they were in it together.

'Lots to tell you,' she said in hushed tones as she unwound her scarf and draped it over the back of her chair. 'But let me order us something to drink first,' she added as she waved at the lone waiter who was chatting to his female colleague behind the counter. 'What can I get you?'

Pip asked for tea, Alex for a can of Diet Coke. Rowan placed the order, with the addition of a milky coffee for herself.

'So, what have you got for us?' Alex asked as the waiter walked away.

Rowan allowed for a moment of dramatic silence before delivering her first piece of news. There was an unmistakable look of mischief on her face when she spoke. 'I followed him yesterday evening,' she said with a grin.

'Followed who?' Alex asked.

'Simon Jones,' she replied with an even broader smile.

'You did what?' Alex replied, leaning back in his chair and shooting a slightly nervous sideways look at Pip. Immediately, he was thinking about the phone call from the Area Commander and the unequivocal instruction to stay away from the Home Office. He wouldn't have been unduly concerned if it had only been the Commander saying it, but, apparently, the direction had come all the way down from the Commissioner's office. And the fact that Rowan was now telling him that she'd followed the

Policing Minister made him feel like a co-conspirator in something illicit. But, from the expression on her face, Pip didn't seem to share his concerns. In fact, she didn't seem bothered at all.

'I followed Simon Jones!' responded Rowan, evidently enjoying Alex's reaction. 'From his office after work.'

'And?' Pip prompted her.

For the next few minutes, Rowan described what had taken place, taking her time with the details, savouring each small turn in the tale. She explained that she hadn't really had any sort of clear plan – she'd checked Jones's online schedule of official appointments, and didn't know for certain whether he was even at the Home Office that afternoon – but that she was determined to find out anything she could about a man she suspected of things she so far hadn't been able to prove. She didn't immediately elaborate on exactly what it was she suspected him of doing, but she was finding her flow and any questions would have to wait. She readily acknowledged that her approach had been speculative at best.

'But,' she explained to them, 'you have to cast a line to catch a fish.' If nothing else, she wanted to find out where he went on a Monday night.

The drinks arrived and Alex started to relax. If Pip wasn't concerned by what they were hearing, there didn't seem to be any need for him to be either. After all, it wasn't as though they had played any part in the events that were now being related to them. He opened his can of Diet Coke and took a first sip as Rowan continued.

She'd been sitting in a Marsham Street coffee shop – almost directly opposite the main entrance to the Home Office – for the best part of two hours when Simon Jones had finally emerged from the building. He was on his own and she'd been relieved to see that there was no driver waiting for him. Following him on foot would be a whole lot easier than flagging down a taxi and trying to keep up with a ministerial car. He had turned left out of the Home Office and started walking briskly towards Westminster, his phone clasped to his ear. She'd hoped that he wasn't simply heading for Parliament. That wouldn't have helped her to prove anything.

She had left the coffee shop, hurried across the road and started following a safe distance behind him. The ebb and flow of people on the pavement made it a good deal easier to remain anonymous, but she'd taken the precaution of wearing a dark-coloured hat and coat that she could later take off if she needed to alter her appearance.

In spite of his initial reservations, Alex couldn't help smiling at the details. For the second time in his dealings with Rowan Blake, he felt as though he was a bit-part player in some sort of improbable spy story. As a police officer, he would never have got away with what she was describing – not without risk of significant censure. But he recognised that journalists weren't subject to the same set of constraints as him. If Alex had wanted to put someone – never mind a government minister – under any kind of surveillance, he'd have needed a whole lot more than a hunch to go on. He would have needed to complete a mountain of exhaustive paperwork setting out the justification for his intentions, after which he would have had to obtain the written authorisation of a senior colleague. Rowan had been faced with no such limitations.

Alex listened intently as she continued to describe what had happened. At the end of Great Smith Street, rather than turn right towards Parliament, Jones had carried straight on into Storey's Gate and, from there, into St James's Park. This was the point at which Rowan had started to feel a little more confident that she might not be wasting her time. Once in the park, the number of people on foot had started to thin out, so she had allowed the Minister to get a little further ahead of her.

He'd walked around the lake and out of the other side of the park. He'd been on his phone almost constantly since leaving the office, though Rowan had been much too far behind him to hear anything he might have said. He had crossed the Mall and climbed the steps that led up to Carlton House Terrace. From there, it was a short walk to The Bridge Club – a Union Jack-draped private members' establishment just off Piccadilly.

'And guess who he just happened to bump into in the street right outside?' Rowan asked them. Her question was articulated in a tone that suggested the encounter was unlikely to have been an accident.

'I've no idea,' said Alex, still smiling at the conspiratorial style of her storytelling.

'Geoffrey Bell and Lord Peter Gier.'

'Isn't Bell the editor of the *City Journal*?' asked Pip.

'The very same,' Rowan replied. 'And Lord Gier owns it. He also owns *GB Today*. There was a fourth man with them who I didn't recognise, but I managed to get a slightly blurry picture of him on my phone.'

'What were they all doing there?' Alex asked her.

'It might have been nothing out of the ordinary,' Rowan acknowledged. 'But I'm not so sure. Something about it just didn't feel right to me. They certainly seemed in a hurry to get inside the building – as though they didn't want to be seen in public together. I'd have a better idea about what might have been going on if I knew who the fourth person was.'

*

'I happened to see Geoffrey Bell at the club last night,' Simon Jones remarked. He and Camilla Lane were working late in his office. The rest of the team had left for the day.

'How was he?' Camilla asked, looking up from the file that was open on her lap.

'On good form, as ever,' the Minister responded. 'He wants me to write another piece for the paper. He told me that the last article I wrote went down very well with their readers.'

'Excellent news,' Camilla replied. 'Perhaps we can link it in with your speech at the party conference in two weeks' time?' Only four days earlier, the Prime Minister had been in touch, asking him to give one of the keynote addresses at the annual gathering of the Tory faithful.

'My thoughts exactly,' Simon Jones said. 'In the meantime, have you got any update on the progress of the latest contract bids from Soteria Solutions?'

'Politicians and newspaper people talk all the time,' Alex said.

'Of course they do,' Rowan replied. 'But the timing of this particular encounter is interesting.'

'Why?' asked Pip.

'Because I checked online and there's no mention of it in Jones's official diary. Because we're entering party conference season. Because Simon Jones is pursuing a very clear agenda when it comes to policing and law enforcement – and my sources tell me that he's planning to use his conference speech to make some significant policy announcements. Because Soteria Solutions are getting closer to securing millions of pounds' worth of new Home Office business. Because the *City Journal* and *GB Today* appear to be offering their uncritical support to everything that Jones says and does.' Rowan paused and looked at Alex and Pip. 'And because I don't trust a single one of them,' she said.

'What do you think it all means?' Pip asked her.

'That something dodgy is going on,' Rowan replied. 'And that they're all in on it.'

Alex raised his eyebrows. 'But can you actually prove the things that you're suggesting?' he challenged.

'I'm working on it,' she replied, with a look of determination on her face that matched the tone of her voice. 'But it definitely isn't going to be easy,' she added. 'People like Simon Jones will stop at nothing to keep their secrets hidden.'

Chapter 24

It was dark outside the cafe and the autumnal wind was picking up. Fallen leaves, caught up in invisible eddies, were tumbling along the pavement and the theatre-goers queuing up outside the Young Vic on the other side of the road had their hands deep in their pockets and their chins buried in the collars of their coats.

Alex stared at Rowan. 'When it comes to politicians, I think you might actually be even more cynical than I am,' he said.

'With good reason,' Rowan replied. 'They're a bunch of corrupt cowboys.'

'All of them?' Pip queried.

'Maybe not all of them,' Rowan conceded, 'but certainly a good number of those who currently occupy positions of significant authority – positions they are shamelessly abusing in order to enrich themselves and their friends.'

'What do you mean by that exactly?' Alex asked. Like most people, he'd read the depressing stories about MPs over-claiming on their expenses and fiddling their second-home allowances, but Rowan seemed to be hinting at something more than either of those things.

'I mean that they're fleecing the taxpayer in order to amass huge personal fortunes, and that they're using any and every means at their disposal – legal or otherwise – in order to do so.'

'How on earth are they doing that?' Alex asked. Rowan's passion and sincerity were obvious – infectious even – but he couldn't help feeling a degree of scepticism about what she was suggesting. In spite of all his years of experience on the policing frontline, he had somehow managed to hold on to a degree of idealism when it came to human nature – a basic belief that most people, most of the time, will try to do the right thing. While he undoubtedly had his reservations about Simon Jones and he remained inclined to believe the things Becca Palmer had told him, the notion that there might be some sort of organised criminal enterprise operating at the heart of government went far beyond anything he'd previously considered.

'In two ways, mainly,' Rowan responded, undeterred and seemingly untroubled by Alex's rather obvious reservations. 'First, by privatising huge swathes of the public sector. That part's been going on for years, of course: selling off a whole range of national assets to the highest bidder, meaning that they are run for profit, rather than the greater good. And, second, by ensuring that a succession of enormously lucrative government contracts go to their preferred bidders.'

'Really?' Alex replied. 'I mean, I know all about the first bit – the privatisation of public assets – but are you genuinely suggesting that the processes for awarding government contracts are being criminally manipulated for private gain?'

'That's exactly what I'm suggesting,' Rowan replied. 'And it's happening right under our noses.' She paused and leaned back in her chair. 'It's happening all across the public sector – in prisons, in probation, in the National Health Service,' she said with a sweep if her right arm. 'And there's no doubt in my mind that it's happening in policing too.'

'Are you able to be a bit more specific?' Alex asked.

'Surely you must be aware of all the roles that used to be performed by police officers that are now being carried out by the employees of private companies,' she said.

'Like transporting prisoners to court and the forensic analysis of crime scene samples, you mean?' asked Alex.

'Exactly,' said Rowan, 'and a whole lot more besides. But that's just the tip of the iceberg. There are a number of new contracts up for grabs, and I'm certain there will be more to come. We'll have a better idea of what those might be when we hear what the Minister has to say in his keynote speech at the party conference.'

'So, give us an example of the sort of thing you think might be coming,' said Pip.

'Neighbourhood policing,' Rowan replied without elaboration.

'You mean private contractors patrolling local communities?' Alex asked.

'Why not? It's already happening in some of the more affluent parts of London.'

On that point at least, Alex had to concede that she was right. He'd seen the headlines in the *Evening Standard* a few months earlier – and the accompanying stories about uniformed civilians patrolling gated developments in the north of the capital. They'd been appearing in greater numbers ever since the Government's austerity measures had forced the Met Police to cut most of the officers and staff from their own local policing teams. For a number of observers, it had raised the troubling prospect of safer streets for those who could afford them and higher crime for those who couldn't. But the attention of most in the media had quickly moved on, and Alex had been preoccupied with too many operational concerns to have given it much more thought.

'So you think that Simon Jones wants to extend the privatisation of policing as far as he possibly can?' he asked her. 'And that he intends to get rich by doing so?' Saying it out loud somehow made it seem all the more improbable to him.

'I do,' Rowan replied. 'And I suspect he's not the only one. Partly, it's about ideology – the basic belief that private is good and public is bad; that the private sector is inherently capable and efficient, while the public sector is grossly wasteful – but, mostly, it's about money. Because that's what it always seems to come down to in the end. This is their opportunity to make an absolute fortune.'

'But aren't most of them multimillionaires already?' Alex queried.

'You're missing the point,' Rowan responded. 'These people don't think like we do. For them, greed isn't just good. It's god.'

'Remind me what I've got in the diary for tomorrow,' said Simon Jones as he turned over the last page on the document he was reading.

'Departmental meetings all morning,' Camilla replied, checking her notes. 'Then an afternoon visit to the Independent Justice Foundation at their Old Queen Street offices, followed by the fundraiser for your charity in the evening.'

'Of course, of course,' the Minister responded, his face brightening as he remembered. 'It's only Tuesday and I'm already losing track of the week. What time will Frances be here?'

'Her train gets into St Pancras just after four tomorrow afternoon,' Camilla confirmed. 'She's planning to go straight to the flat and said that she'd either meet you there or, if you're held up here, at the venue itself.'

'Excellent,' he replied. 'It's going to be a big evening for the two of us. We've been talking for a while about wanting to extend the scope of the charity's work – as things stand, we simply can't keep up with the basic level of need that exists in the poorer parts of Sheffield – and we've decided that, whatever we manage to raise on the night, we're going to double with a donation of our own.'

'Goodness me!' Camilla exclaimed. 'The press are going to love that.'

'So where do we come into all of this?' Alex asked Rowan, looking across at Pip as he posed the question. 'Why the need to speak to the two of us this evening?' Though he was doing a passable job of concealing it, his reservations were in danger of getting the better of him. If Rowan had been describing the behaviour of the rich and powerful in some far-off, tinpot dictatorship, he wouldn't have been surprised. But this was Britain she was talking about, and she was starting to sound like the kind of conspiracy theorist he'd always been swift to dismiss.

'Because I need your help if I'm going to make the connection between Simon Jones and Soteria Solutions,' Rowan replied, leaning forward in her seat again. 'I still haven't managed to find it, but I'm getting closer all the time.'

'Go on,' prompted Alex, in spite of his reservations.

'Have you been following the story of the Jersey Papers?' she asked them.

'We read about it in your blog,' Alex said, 'and we saw the *Panorama* programme about it on the BBC a couple of weeks ago.'

'The vast wealth of drug dealers and dictators,' Pip added, 'hidden away in offshore tax havens, via a maze of shell companies and enormously complex banking arrangements.'

'But it's not just the drug dealers and dictators,' Rowan replied, placing her hands on the checked tablecloth in front of her. 'It's anyone with the desire and the means to conceal their true worth.'

'So what have you found out about Soteria?' Pip asked.

'Well, this is where you're going to need to concentrate,' Rowan advised. 'Because this is where it starts to get complicated.'

Alex drank the remainder of his can of Diet Coke. 'Let's hear it then,' he said.

Rowan reached into the shoulder bag that was lying beside her feet and pulled out a hardback notebook. She opened it at a blank page and uncapped her pen. 'Let's start with the known facts,' she said. But, before she could go any further, the waiter reappeared beside their table.

'Can I get you anything else to drink?' he asked.

'How about something a bit stronger?' Rowan suggested. 'We might be here for a little while.'

'Sounds like an eminently sensible suggestion to me!' said Pip. 'Do you want to share a bottle of red?'

'Perfect,' agreed Rowan. 'A bottle of house red, please,' she said, turning to the waiter. 'And three glasses.' As the waiter departed, she returned to her audience of two. She wrote the name 'Soteria Solutions' in block capitals on the page in her notebook and drew a box around it. 'Two years ago,' she began, 'Soteria was bought by a company called Enforcement Holdings.' She paused to write the name in her notebook and, having done so, drew a line connecting it to Soteria Solutions. 'They're registered at an address in Jersey, but, prior to the recent data leak, I wouldn't have been able to tell you anything about them. The trail would immediately have run cold.'

'What do you mean?' Alex asked.

'Companies registered in Jersey – and in plenty of other off-shore locations – don't have to abide by the same rules as companies registered here in mainland Britain,' Rowan explained. 'The offshore business model is one based on secrecy. Without the material contained in the leak, I wouldn't have been able to tell you who owns Enforcement Holdings, how much it's worth, where its bank accounts are held, whether it pays any tax – any of those things.'

'So who does own it?' asked Alex.

'Chaloner Capital,' Rowan replied. 'A completely different company, this time registered in the Cayman Islands.' She added this new name to her book, with a connecting line to the first two.

'And?' Alex prompted.

'And Chaloner Capital's two main shareholders are called Sebastian Neill and Jane Hammond,' Rowan continued. 'I haven't been able to identify who Jane Hammond is yet, but Sebastian Neill wasn't hard to find.' His name went into the book next to Chaloner Capital. 'Have you ever heard of him?'

'No,' said Alex. He looked at Pip, who was shaking her head.

'Seb Neill is an exceedingly rich man,' Rowan explained. 'There are two particular things you need to know about him at this stage: one, that he's a major donor to the Conservative Party and, two, that he's funded several of the recent reports published by the Independent Justice Foundation . . .'

'Who are they?' interrupted Pip.

'The IJF?' replied Rowan, writing the initials down, with a line connecting them to Seb Neill. The diagram in her book was starting to resemble a spider's web. 'They're one of a growing number of supposedly independent think tanks – many of them based in close proximity to one another in Old Queen Street in Westminster – who really aren't independent at all. They are among the leading advocates for far greater levels of private-sector involvement in public-service delivery.'

'What does that advocacy involve?' asked Pip.

'They produce apparently well-researched reports containing headline-grabbing findings that, for the most part, serve only to advance the interests of the people who are paying for them.'

'So let me check that I've got this right,' said Alex, who was struggling to maintain his credulity. Rowan nodded at him to carry on, clearly willing to entertain his doubts without taking offence. 'Sebastian Neill owns a large number of shares in a private company that is already making millions of pounds from government contracts. And now he's funding a think tank to write reports advocating policies that would allow him to make millions more?'

'Sounds hard to believe, doesn't it,' said Rowan. 'But that's exactly what I think is happening.'

'But how can he possibly hope to get away with it?' Alex asked.

'By remaining hidden offshore,' Rowan replied. 'The fact is that, were it not for the Jersey Papers, we'd have had no idea about what was going on. Even with the leak, it's taken days and days of painstaking work to find what I was looking for and, even now, I don't have enough. There's nothing in any official record held in this country that connects Seb Neill to Chaloner Capital, much less to Soteria Solutions.'

'So what about Simon Jones?' Pip asked. 'Where does he come into all of this?'

'That's where I need your help,' Rowan explained.

'What sort of help?' Alex asked, with the sudden realisation that he and Pip were about to be ambushed.

'I need your help as intermediaries,' Rowan replied. 'If I'm going to be able to establish any sort of direct connection between Simon Jones and Soteria Solutions, I need to talk to your girl from the bridge.'

Chapter 25

'I need another drink,' said Alex.

He and Pip were walking back towards Waterloo station, having left Rowan Blake sitting at the table in the cafe with the last of the bottle of red wine for company. They had both been caught unawares by her request to talk directly to Becca and had explained that they would need to take some time to think about the implications of it, not least given the state of Becca's mental health. They couldn't – and wouldn't – do anything that might compromise or undermine her recovery. Rowan had been very understanding of this latter point, though she had emphasised that time was of the essence. 'We can't let them get away with what they're doing,' she had explained to them. She had even quoted Martin Luther King: 'Our lives begin to end the day we become silent about things that matter.'

'I think there's some beer in the fridge at home,' Pip replied.

'We should have seen that coming, Pip,' Alex said. He was feeling annoyed with himself.

'I was fully expecting her to ask us plenty of questions about Becca,' Pip replied. 'Why else would she have wanted to see us? But I hadn't quite anticipated the suggestion that the two of them might actually meet and speak directly.'

'Me neither,' said Alex.

They spent the rest of their journey home deep in conversation, with Alex wondering out loud how they'd managed to find themselves in the situation they were in. Becca's health and wellbeing were their overriding concern. They agreed that they wouldn't even raise the question of her talking to a journalist if there was the slightest possibility that it might set her back. Then there was the warning from the Commissioner's office to stay away from the Home Office. Neither of them envisaged Alex returning to Marsham Street, but they questioned whether the contact with Rowan – should it subsequently come to light – might put them in a compromising position. After all, what was it that the Area Commander had said about concentrating on the day job? Nonetheless, neither of them felt ready to walk away, either from Becca Palmer or Rowan Blake: two women with remarkable, scarcely believable, tales to tell about the man who might well be the country's next Prime Minister. Two women who were asking to be heard. Asking to be believed.

'So what do you think we should do?' Alex asked as Pip unlocked the front door to their house.

'Perhaps you could call Helen Palmer in the morning?' Pip suggested. 'She'll be able to tell you how her sister is doing, and she'll also be able to give you a considered opinion on whether or not it might be a good idea for Becca to talk to Rowan.'

'Hmm,' Alex replied thoughtfully. 'I'd need to explain to her how the connection with Rowan Blake came about – and be really clear that we haven't betrayed any confidences or passed on any of Becca's personal details,' he said. 'I definitely wouldn't want either of them to think that we'd gone behind their backs.'

'Of course,' Pip said. 'Though I don't think either of them would think that. I'm fairly certain they trust us.'

*

'Do you want the bad news or the bad news?' asked Ronnie Egan as Alex arrived at Kentish Town the following morning. She was standing in the corridor outside Alex's office and she had a grim look on her face.

'I suppose we'd better start with the bad news,' replied Alex, mirroring Ronnie's facial expression. He walked into his office and put his rucksack on the floor by his desk. 'What is it this time?' he asked as he took his coat off and hung it over the back of his chair.

'We've had another fatal stabbing overnight,' Ronnie said simply.

Alex stood and stared at his colleague, his thoughts instantly crowded and his heart immediately heavy. 'Why didn't anyone tell me sooner?'

'Because the victim only died just over half an hour ago,' Ronnie replied. 'The first officers on scene managed to keep him alive until the paramedics got there and the team at the hospital gave it absolutely everything, but – in the end – it wasn't enough. His visible injuries were bad, but the internal damage was even greater. I called you on your mobile, but it went straight to voicemail. You must have been on the tube.'

Alex tried to gather himself. He took a breath and exhaled slowly. 'What do we know?' he asked.

'Fifteen-year-old boy,' Ronnie said, keeping it brief and to the point. 'Local lad. Never been in trouble with the police. No known gang affiliations. Suspect is in custody downstairs. Sixteen years old, also local. Currently on bail from youth court for possession of a knife. Seems to have been some sort of argument about a girl.'

'What's his name?' Alex asked. 'The victim, I mean.'

Ronnie opened the hardback A4 notebook she was holding

and checked her notes. 'Cameron Hill,' she confirmed. 'Night-duty officers are with his mum, dad and two younger brothers at their home address.'

'I'll go and see them later on,' said Alex, feeling the burden of a family's grief bearing down on him. Earlier in his career, he had found it comparatively easy to maintain a healthy personal distance from the stories of strangers, but, the older he got, the harder he found it. Their sorrow was somehow his as well.

'The Commander's office have already been on the phone, wanting to know what our response is,' Ronnie added apologetically.

'Of course they bloody have,' Alex said resentfully. 'Is that the other bad news?'

'No, I haven't got to that yet.'

'Go on then,' said Alex, slumping wearily into his chair. 'I might as well hear it all.'

'One of the area cars got behind a stolen moped late last night.'

'And?' Alex prompted, already dreading the answer. Moped-enabled crime was second only to knife crime on the current list of borough concerns.

'It was two up – rider and pillion passenger – and suspected of being involved in a couple of earlier phone snatches.'

'Keep going.'

'The pursuit was authorised, but the area car crew lost them somewhere in the back doubles around King's Cross.'

'So what's the problem?' Alex asked.

'It crashed.'

'The moped?' he checked.

'Yes. We got the call about five minutes after the chase ended,' Ronnie explained.

'Any fatalities?'

'No – but both seriously injured. The rider is in intensive care.'

'And we definitely weren't behind it at the time?'

'No – but several of the usual anti-police rabble-rousers are blaming us all the same.'

'And, no doubt, the Area Commander wants a briefing about that too?' said Alex with a deep sigh. The very last thing that he and his officers needed at this point in time was a fresh round of hostile public criticism – particularly given the fact that none of them appeared to have done anything wrong.

'Of course he does,' Ronnie replied.

Alex groaned and rubbed his face with his hands. 'Could the day possibly get any worse?' he muttered.

Having called in a favour from an old contact, Rowan Blake was sitting in her flat, studying what appeared to be a recently updated membership roll for The Bridge Club. She hadn't asked too many questions about the means by which it had come into the contact's possession, on the grounds that they were almost certainly illegal.

She had two other tabs open on her laptop: one taking her to the club's homepage and another to a website offering an unofficial – and somewhat unflattering – history of the establishment. When it had first opened in the 1850s, The Bridge had been a place where those with too much time and too much money gathered to drink and gossip and, most importantly of all, to play cards. Hence the name. According to the anonymous sources quoted in the unofficial history, the club's current members had appetites for alcohol and intrigue that were comfortably a match for their forebears, albeit with far less interest in the doubles and dummies of old-fashioned parlour games. Apparently, the modern cohort were far too preoccupied with the business of amassing vast personal fortunes to have time for that sort of thing.

None of the names in the membership document came as any great surprise to her, but Rowan was nonetheless fascinated to see them all laid out in black and white. The line-up of notables included the current Prime Minister and two of his recent predecessors, together with an assortment of MPs, lords, bankers and business leaders, all defined by their positions of wealth and power. Without exception, the names belonged to men, and they were arranged in alphabetical order by surname. Geoffrey Bell, editor of the *City Journal*, was a comparatively early entry on the list, followed half a page later by Lord Peter Gier, his proprietor. The current Metropolitan Police Commissioner was also a member, Rowan noted in passing.

When she got to the 'J's, the discovery of the name of Rafe Jackson – a dozen or so places before that of Simon Jones MP – elicited a smile. Jackson was the CEO of the Independent Justice Foundation and, while the list offered no specific evidence that Jackson and Jones knew one another personally, the possibility that they hadn't at least met was diminishing significantly.

Rowan skipped quickly ahead to the 'N's and confirmed that, yes, Seb Neill was a member too. 'If the devil could cast a net,' she murmured to herself as she continued to scan the rest of the document.

By the time she got to the name of Robert Sangster – the man in charge of Soteria Solutions – on the final page of the document, the spider's web diagram in her book was beginning to look very crowded indeed.

She realised that she already had more than enough information to write an incendiary article – probably a whole series of them – about several of the names she'd gathered, but she didn't want to do anything until she had something definitive on Simon Jones.

And, for that, she needed to speak to Becca.

It was almost six o'clock when Alex remembered that he had intended to call Helen Palmer. He sighed and ran his fingers through his hair as he mouthed a silent expletive.

The previous ten hours had been overwhelming. He had spent a significant part of the morning with the family of Cameron Hill, the boy who had been stabbed, and he'd felt the depth of their pain as he'd struggled to find the words to say. On his way back to the office, he had called the leader of the council and the local MP to brief them about the killing. Evidently sensing a political opportunity, the MP – a member of the opposition front bench – had wanted to know whether the police were 'losing control of the streets' and, if they were, whether it was as a direct consequence of government cuts. Depressingly, it was the politics that seemed to matter more to him than the fact that another London teenager was dead. Struggling to hide his feelings of contempt for the MP, Alex had baulked at the suggestion that he and his colleagues were losing control of anything, but he hadn't held back on the consequences of political decision-making. Every so-called reform of policing initiated by the Government in the previous few years had made his job significantly more difficult than it already was.

Returning to the station, he had chaired an initial Gold Group meeting – a gathering of local colleagues, partners from the local authority, the Senior Investigating Officer from the murder team and a pair of trusted local community leaders who were acting as independent advisors to the investigation – after which he had taken questions from the press under the blue lamp out at the front of the building. Once the immediate clamour from the media had died down, he'd fielded a succession of emails and phone calls from Scotland Yard – including one from the Area Commander, who had proved to be as unhelpful as ever. *One of the biggest problems with people who had been promoted too quickly,* Alex thought to himself, *was that they'd spent far too little time working in frontline policing* – a significant omission that left them with little or no real understanding of operational realities. It was a situation made worse by the fact that so many of them had also been promoted beyond the level of their basic personal and professional competence.

In the midst of all this, there were two more teenagers in hospital – one of them critical – following the previous night's moped chase.

It had been a hell of a day and it wasn't over yet. As he sat alone in his office, Alex felt completely exhausted. He was also aware of the nagging anxiety humming at the edges of his thoughts. There was too much to do and too little time. There was too much going wrong and nowhere near enough resources to be able to put any of it right. There were too many people in too much pain and almost nothing he could do to mend any of it.

As he thought this last thought, the face of Becca Palmer resumed its place at the front of his mind. Perhaps there was something he could do to help her at least. One life at a time. As far as he was concerned, it was the only possible way to change the world. Like the boy on the beach with the starfish.

He reached wearily across his desk and picked up his mobile phone. He scrolled through his contacts, pressed the call button and waited for the connection. 'Helen,' he said in greeting, knowing that his number would have come up on her phone as withheld. 'It's Alex Lewis from the Met Police.'

Chapter 26

Simon Jones rang his wife to say that he wasn't going to make it back to the flat in time. He'd spent longer at the Independent Justice Foundation that afternoon than originally intended, but it had been time well spent. He had spoken at length with Rafe Jackson, who had provided him with a detailed update on all of the Foundation's latest research. Their conversation had proven to be a rich source of material for his conference speech, and he was feeling increasingly confident about the case for change that he was planning to make.

He told his wife that he'd get changed into his black tie at the office and meet her at the hotel where the charity dinner was being held. Frances responded with the news that one of the wealthiest people on the guest list had called her earlier in the day, pledging a substantial five-figure sum to the cause.

The Minister was delighted. 'That's incredible! It will make an enormous difference to the Foundation's work,' he said. 'Don't forget to point him out to me this evening. I want to make sure that I thank him in person.'

Pip was in the kitchen when Alex got back to the house just after eight o'clock. He'd texted her a handful of times during the day, so she already had some awareness of both the murder and the moped crash.

'How are you doing?' she asked, kissing him gently on the lips.

'Oh, you know,' he replied, pulling her in closer.

They stood together for a while in the middle of the kitchen floor, neither of them speaking. Pip knew that Alex needed a minute or two to begin to decompress – to slow his thoughts and acknowledge his emotions. It was something his counsellor had been teaching him to do: to recognise and accept how he was feeling, rather than trying to bury it all away as he had always done in the past. Alex knew that Pip understood, and he felt grateful. The thick band of tension running across his forehead started to ease and he could feel his body beginning to relax.

Pip could feel it too. She took half a step back and kissed him again, this time on the cheek, before reaching over to pull a chair out from under the table for him to sit on. It was only when she offered to make him an omelette that he realised he hadn't actually eaten anything since breakfast.

While Pip cooked, Alex attempted to describe his day: the ashen-faced grief of a father unable to comprehend the loss of his eldest son; the soul-deep sobs of his wife and the terrified faces of their two younger boys; the natural and perfectly understandable concerns expressed by local community members; the inevitable questions from journalists, none of them hopeful or encouraging; the ignorance and incompetence of his boss; the infuriating self-interest of the local MP. He paused to take a sip from the bottle of beer that Pip had handed to him.

'What about you?' he asked her eventually. 'How's your day been?'

Pip shrugged as she turned the omelette over. It made a

pleasant sizzling sound in the hot oil. 'Nothing much to report compared with yours,' she replied. 'Not today at any rate.'

Alex nodded. 'I called Helen Palmer,' he said after taking another sip of beer.

Pip turned around. 'Really?' she said. 'I know we talked about it last night – but didn't you already have enough on your plate?'

'It just felt like something positive to do at the end of a difficult day,' he replied.

'And what did she say?'

'She said that she'd talk to Becca, but that she wasn't convinced it was a good idea.'

'How is Becca?'

'Apparently doing much better,' Alex responded, 'which was why Helen was so reluctant to do anything to upset things.'

'Entirely understandable,' Pip acknowledged. 'That said, I can't help sensing a potential problem.'

'What kind of problem?' Alex asked.

'If Simon Jones really is guilty of the things Rowan suspects him of, and if Becca really does hold any of the missing pieces of the jigsaw,' Pip replied, 'then, one way or another, upsetting things is likely to become something of an inevitability.'

In the large ballroom at the Hilton Hotel on Park Lane, the wine and champagne were flowing and the atmosphere among the three hundred diners was celebratory. A man dressed in a red tailcoat and possessed with a booming voice took to the stage to announce that the purchase of tables for the event and the sale of raffle tickets during the meal had already raised more than seventy-five thousand pounds for the Policing Minister's hometown charity. Once the cheers and applause had died down, he informed his audience that the auction would be starting in five minutes' time. The first lot on offer would be a luxury two-week stay on an exclusive Caribbean island. It had been donated by a wealthy and influential banker with extensive offshore interests.

Simon and Frances Jones made their way back to their table. They had spent the previous thirty minutes circulating the room, posing for photographs, smiling and shaking hands, greeting old friends, making new acquaintances and encouraging their guests to dig even deeper in support of the cause.

The political correspondent from the *City Journal* was sitting next to Camilla Lane on table seven. Camilla had tipped her off earlier in the day about the Minister's plan to make a significant donation of his own, and the article celebrating the fact had been written before the event had even begun. The only detail the journalist still needed was confirmation of the exact amount of money involved. Provided the auction didn't run late, the story was headed for the following morning's front page.

Alex was not long out of the shower when his phone rang.

'You don't have to answer it, you know,' Pip said from across the room.

'It's Helen,' Alex replied as he connected the call.

'Sorry to call so late,' said the voice of Helen Palmer at the other end of the line.

Alex glanced at his watch on his bedside table to check the time. It was just after 9.30 p.m. 'No problem,' he said. 'Is everything all right?'

'Everything's fine,' Helen reassured him. 'Have you got a couple of minutes?'

'Of course,' Alex replied. 'Hang on a second though. Let me just put you on loudspeaker so that Pip can hear what you're saying.'

'Sure.'

Alex tapped the screen on his phone and Pip came to sit next to him on the edge of their bed. 'Have you spoken to Becca about our earlier conversation?' Alex asked Helen.

'I have,' came the reply. 'That's why I'm calling. If it's OK, Becca would like to talk to you about it?'

'Now?' asked Alex. He looked at Pip, who shrugged at him. *Why not?* she seemed to be saying.

'If that's all right.'

'Of course,' Alex said. 'Put her on.'

'Thank you,' Helen replied.

Alex could hear the muffled sounds of the phone being passed from one sister to the other.

'Hello?' It was Becca speaking. Her voice was quiet but stronger than it had been the last time Alex had listened to her.

'Hello, Becca,' Alex responded. 'It's good to hear you. How are you doing?'

'Definitely better than I was,' she replied.

'That's really good to hear,' said Alex. 'Have you managed to stay away from the drink?' It was a rather blunt question to ask so early in the exchange, but Alex wanted to know what sort of progress she was making.

Becca took no offence. 'I have,' she replied.

'And are you taking your meds?' he added.

'You're starting to sound like my sister,' she said. Alex could actually hear her smiling. There was a lightness in her voice that he hadn't encountered before. 'I promise you that I'm doing all the things I'm supposed to do,' she added.

'Good for you, Becca,' Alex said sincerely.

'Helen said that there might be a journalist who wants to speak to me,' she said, evidently keen to get to the point.

'Only if you want to speak to her,' Alex replied firmly. He

was determined to make clear from the outset that Becca was
under no pressure or obligation.

'Tell me about her,' Becca asked.

Alex didn't answer the question straight away. First, he
wanted to reassure Becca that he and Pip had taken great care
to guard her anonymity. 'We haven't told the journalist your
full name,' he said, 'and we haven't given her any specifics
about the job you were doing at the Home Office. All she knows
is that you were working in the office of the Policing Minister.'
More than once, he emphasised the fact that they would never
disclose her identity, unless Becca actually asked them to. He
made it clear that their overriding concern was for her health
and that he and Pip were unwilling to do anything that might
put that at risk.

Having satisfied himself that Becca understood – and was
content with – all of this, Alex turned to her actual request.
He talked about the online research that he and Pip had done
following their second encounter with her on Westminster
Bridge. He mentioned the discovery of the article written by a
freelance journalist called Rowan Blake and his subsequent exchange of messages with her. He explained that he and Rowan
had been reluctant to trust one another at first, but that they'd
found common ground in their shared distrust of politicians.
He moved on to the details of the first of their meetings in the
Waterloo cafe and was partway through summarising Rowan's
suspicions about the Policing Minister when Becca interrupted
him.

'Are you saying that Rowan believes me?' Becca asked uncertainly.

'About what?' Alex checked, not wanting to commit himself
to an answer without being certain that he had understood her.

'About the possibility that Simon might be involved in something he shouldn't be,' came the reply.

'Yes, she does,' Alex responded. 'She thinks the same thing.'

'Can she prove it?'

'That's what she's working on at the moment,' Alex replied. 'And that's why she's asked to talk to you.'

'I told you I was telling the truth!' Becca said. Alex could hear the swell of emotion in her voice. There was no sense of vindication; it was the sound of overwhelming relief.

'Yes, you did,' Alex replied. 'She believes you – and we do too.' The latter part of the statement – the suggestion that he and Pip believed Becca – was still based far more on instinct than evidence, but Alex was being sincere.

'That means an awful lot to me,' Becca said quietly. 'Thank you.' There was another brief period of silence at the other end of the line before she spoke again. 'What do you need me to do?' she asked.

The man in the red tailcoat was back on stage, looking for all the world like a circus ringmaster, minus the top hat. The auction had finished ten minutes before and, behind the scenes, someone with a calculator had been doing the sums.

'My lords, ladies and gentlemen,' he announced with a theatrical sweep of his right arm, 'I have the news that you've all been waiting for.'

He paused and allowed the atmosphere in the ballroom to build. Everyone present knew what the final bid had been for each of the auction items, but none of them knew how much the event as a whole had raised. They were about to find out.

'My lords, ladies and gentlemen,' the ringmaster repeated, 'it gives me enormous pleasure to announce that – as a direct consequence of your incredible generosity – we have been able to raise a truly remarkable sum of money for tonight's charity.' He paused once again and studied the piece of paper he was holding as the expectant buzz in the room descended to a hush. 'This evening, you have managed to raise a total of £140,000.'

The room erupted in wild cheering and applause. Everyone was on their feet – everyone, that is, apart from the *City Journal*'s political correspondent, who had retrieved a small laptop computer from beneath her chair and now had it open on the table in front of her.

The man in the red coat waited for the noise to die down and for the audience to retake their seats before he spoke again. 'But, ladies and gentlemen, that is not all,' he intoned. 'If you think that figure is extraordinary, wait until you hear what our host and hostess for this evening are about to tell you.'

The room rose again as Simon and Frances Jones made their way up the steps and onto the stage. The noise in the room was deafening as they stepped into the spotlight to acknowledge the acclaim. The Prime Minister-in-waiting was riding the crest of a wave.

Chapter 27

It was early on Saturday afternoon and Becca Palmer was sitting quietly in Helen's kitchen, alone with her thoughts. Her sister and brother-in-law had taken their son out for a lunchtime walk in the park and Becca had been left with the place to herself for an hour or two. There was a bowl of steaming soup on the table in front of her and the radio was playing Elgar's 'Cello Concerto in E Minor' softly in the background. She felt peaceful.

Earlier in the day, she and Helen had spoken at length about the fact that Becca seemed to be feeling – and doing – much better than at any other point in recent times. They definitely didn't want to get ahead of themselves – a mistake both of them had made in the past – but things certainly appeared to be a great deal more positive than they had been. Becca was in therapy, she had remained sober and, though she had been told that it might take another week or so until the full effects of her medication kicked in, she was already starting to feel the benefits of taking it.

She dipped her spoon into the bowl and tasted the soup, a winter vegetable broth that she and Helen had made from scratch while they talked. At some point during their conversation, Helen had made passing mention of the car that had been parked outside the front of the house. In response, Becca had said that she'd seen no further sign of it – or of the two men – since the day she'd run away. The passing of time appeared to have tempered her fears. Neither of them had made any mention of the lingering possibility that Becca might actually have imagined it all.

Helen had also wanted to make sure that Becca was still willing to talk to the journalist, emphasising more than once that her younger sister really was under no pressure or obligation to do so. But Becca had reassured her that she was ready and willing to go ahead.

She was just about to take another sip of her soup when she heard a knock at the front door.

It was turning out to be a beautiful afternoon. The air was crisp, the sky was piercing blue and the grass crunched underfoot as Alex and Pip walked across Clapham Common, their breath swirling like smoke in front of their faces. The leaves on the trees were the colour of fire, kindled by the late-autumn sun. They had agreed to meet Rowan Blake outside Clapham Common tube station at 2 p.m. and, from there, to walk with her to a cafe on Nightingale Lane – chosen for its proximity to Helen's home address – where Becca would be waiting to meet them.

They had taken the first half of the day as slowly as possible, with neither of them making any attempt to fight the weariness of the week gone by. Pip had been overseeing the slow progress of a complex and traumatising investigation into a series of historical child sex offences, while, at the same time, preparing for an Old Bailey trial that was due to start in a fortnight's time. Alex had spent much of the rest of the week dealing with the aftermath of the fatal stabbing. The teenage suspect had been charged with murder and, alongside the Gold

Group meetings and community briefings and the succession of unhelpful phone calls from Scotland Yard, Alex had made a point of going back round to see the victim's family. He'd sat with the boy's parents in their kitchen – as he had done with far too many other families in the past – knowing that he would never get used to the emotions associated with doing so. The sheer depth of their pain had reverberated with each of his senses in turn: the sight of their pale, sleep-starved faces; the sounds that accompanied their tears – falling some way short of words and all the more powerful as a consequence; the bitter taste of the coffee they poured him, drunk out of obligation rather than choice; the smell of the food that lay untouched on the table; the constant shiver of grief in the hands of the boy's mother as he took hold of them and tried to tell her again how desperately sorry he was. Alex had felt it all. Almost as if the grief were his own. In truth, he was still feeling the echoes of it as he and Pip reached the far side of the Common.

Rowan was waiting for them outside the flower shop next door to the entrance to Clapham South tube station. There was no sign of her oversized woollen scarf this time, but she appeared to be wearing several layers of clothing beneath a bulging navy-blue coat that was buttoned all the way up. The tip of her nose was growing red in the bright sunlight. She greeted Pip and Alex with a kind of hesitant familiarity – the inevitable reservations of recent acquaintance, mingled with the knowledge of secrets already shared.

'Is she still happy to meet me?' she asked anxiously.

'She certainly was when I spoke briefly to her sister yesterday afternoon,' Alex replied.

'Good, good,' responded Rowan as they began walking in the direction of the cafe. On the way, she updated them on her discoveries concerning the membership of The Bridge Club and reiterated her firm belief that there was a direct connection between Simon Jones and Soteria Solutions. She just needed to find it.

'Did you hear about the large sum of money that he and his wife donated to charity earlier this week?' asked Pip, in another gentle challenge to any assumptions they might be making about the Minister.

'*Their* charity,' spluttered Rowan with disdain, placing particular emphasis on the word 'their'. 'It was a PR stunt.'

'From what I read on the front page of the *City Journal* earlier in the week,' Pip responded, 'they donated more than £100,000. That's a hell of a lot of money to be giving away. And every penny of it is going to be spent in support of some of the most disadvantaged kids in the country.' Pip held no affection for Simon Jones, but, as ever, she wanted to make sure that they maintained an element of balance in any conversation they were going to have about him. Over the years, her experience as an investigator had taught her repeatedly about the enormous dangers associated with so-called 'confirmation bias' – the tendency to believe information that supports a pre-existing notion of a person or situation, while dismissing anything that doesn't. It was a failing that lay at the heart of any number of serious miscarriages of justice. As a detective, Pip had learned the fundamental importance of following the evidence, wherever it might lead.

Rowan didn't seem bothered by Pip's challenge, but she wasn't about to be swayed in her views. 'One hundred thousand pounds is certainly a hell of a lot of money to people like you and me,' she replied, 'but it's loose change to people like Simon Jones. He made millions when he sold his business up north, and, if my suspicions about him turn out to be right, he's currently in the process of making millions more.'

They had been walking for less than quarter of a mile when Alex spotted the cafe nestled in the middle of a row of shops on the other side of the road, its windows misted with condensation. They were a few minutes early, so he wasn't unduly concerned when they walked through the door and found that Becca had yet to arrive.

'Can I get you something hot to drink?' he asked Rowan. 'It's our round, I think.'

'Coffee please,' Rowan replied.

'Tea for me,' said Pip as Alex walked over to the counter. There were two other customers in the cafe: an older couple sitting at the furthest table away from the door, enjoying a late lunch and a loud conversation about their grandchildren.

Fifteen minutes later, Becca still hadn't arrived. Pip saw Alex checking his watch. 'Give her a bit longer,' she said.

They made small talk with Rowan while they waited, picking up little details from one another's lives.

Another fifteen minutes passed.

'Do you think she's actually coming?' Rowan asked eventually. She sounded disheartened.

Alex looked over at Pip. 'Why don't I give her sister a quick call?' he suggested. He stood up and, as he walked towards the cafe door, he could hear Pip re-emphasising the delicate state of Becca's health and the consequent need to be patient with her.

Helen picked up almost straight away. Alex was standing on the pavement just outside the cafe, wishing that he'd thought to put his jacket back on. The day was no less beautiful, but it was getting even colder.

'Has she found you?' Helen asked.

'She's not actually here yet,' Alex replied. 'I was calling to see whether she was still with you at home.'

'I'm not actually there at the moment,' Helen replied. 'But I suspect that she is. The medication she's been put on can make her a bit woozy sometimes and she might have got confused about when she was supposed to meet you.'

'No problem,' Alex responded. 'We're not in any particular hurry.'

'Why don't I give her a quick call on the landline and then ring you back?' Helen suggested.

'That would be great, thank you,' Alex replied.

He walked back into the cafe, blowing warm air into his cupped hands. Pip and Rowan looked expectantly at him.

'Helen's not at home at the moment,' Alex explained. 'But she's going to call the house and ring me back with an update.'

'Did she sound worried?' Pip asked.

'Not at all,' Alex replied. He explained what Helen had said about the effects of the medication Becca was taking.

'Are you all right for time?' Pip asked Rowan.

'I'm fine,' replied Rowan without bothering to check her watch.

Alex's phone rang.

'Helen?' he said by way of greeting.

'She's not there,' came the response. Helen sounded calm.

'What?' Alex replied, shooting an alarmed glance at Rowan and Pip.

'Either that or she's not answering the phone,' Helen explained. 'But I genuinely wouldn't worry too much,' she continued. 'I'm getting pretty good at reading her mood. She's been on good form today and is looking forward to seeing you. In all likelihood, she's on her way to you now.'

'Why don't I pop round to the house?' Pip suggested. She hadn't heard exactly what Helen had said, but she'd worked out what was going on.

Alex nodded. 'Pip will pop round to the house now to check

that everything's OK,' he explained to Helen. 'And I'll wait in the cafe with Rowan, the journalist, in case Becca's taken the long route to getting here.'

'Thank you,' Helen replied gratefully.

'I'll call or text you with an update as soon as I have one,' Alex said.

Pip pulled a navy blue woolly hat out of her coat pocket and put it on as she walked briskly in the direction of Helen's house. It almost felt cold enough for snow. Her eyes swept the pavements on both sides of the road as she searched for the now familiar figure of Becca Palmer.

Pip had been walking for less than five minutes when she saw her. Becca appeared from around a corner a hundred or so metres up ahead, walking at pace. There was something fiercely determined in both her appearance and her manner – as though she was trying to catch up with an afternoon that had somehow wronged her and was now threatening to get away.

She was about fifty metres away when Pip saw her face clearly for the first time. She looked furious.

Chapter 28

Becca was only a handful of paces away when Pip called out to her. Had she not done so, she strongly suspected that Becca would have walked straight past her – such was her apparent state of mind.

'Pip!' Becca exclaimed in loud surprise. She stopped in her tracks. She still looked furious.

'Are you all right?' Pip asked her.

'They broke the window,' Becca almost shouted. Her fists were clenched tight by her sides.

'Who broke the window?' Pip replied, taken aback.

'The people who knocked on the door,' Becca responded, her eyes flashing.

'Who knocked on the door?'

'I don't know . . . Probably the same people who were following me before.'

'Did you see anyone?' Pip asked as she tried to assemble her thoughts and work out what might have happened.

'No,' Becca replied, her voice falling in volume. 'But I heard footsteps – people running away.'

' "People", plural?' Pip queried. 'You mean there was more than one of them?'

'I think so,' Becca replied, though she didn't sound entirely certain.

'Are you hurt?' Pip asked, stepping forward and placing a concerned hand on Becca's arm.

'Not hurt,' she replied through gritted teeth. 'Just angry.'

'I can see you're angry,' Pip replied, consciously affirming the reality and validity of Becca's emotions.

'They broke the front window,' Becca reiterated.

'At your sister's house?'

Becca nodded.

'In which case, I'm not in the least bit surprised that you're angry,' Pip said. She reached out with her other hand and Becca stepped into Pip's firm, reassuring embrace. 'I want you to tell me everything,' Pip encouraged her, 'but why don't we head indoors before we start on the details. I don't know about you, but I'm absolutely freezing.' She reached down and took hold of one of Becca's hands, still curled into a fist. It was as cold as her own.

'OK,' Becca replied, her voice a little calmer, a little less agitated.

'Would you like to go back to your sister's or would you prefer to go to the cafe?' Pip asked her.

'Is Alex at the cafe?'

'He is,' Pip replied. 'He's there with Rowan, the journalist.'

'Then I'd like to go there,' Becca said.

Alex stood up as the cafe door opened. Relieved to see Becca walking in with Pip, he studied the younger woman's body language closely, trying to assess her state of mind. Though she seemed a little flustered, she was obviously pleased to see him. She smiled as he greeted her, and again as he introduced her to Rowan.

'It's a pleasure to meet you, Becca,' Rowan said.

'It's good to meet you too,' Becca replied quietly.

As the two women exchanged greetings, Alex tapped out a swift text to Helen, letting her know that her sister was safe.

'Becca's got rather a lot to tell us,' Pip explained as she pulled out a chair for the younger woman to sit on.

'Oh?' Alex responded, looking up from his phone.

'But first she needs a hot drink,' Pip said. She turned and walked over to the counter to place an order.

'Is everything all right?' Alex asked Becca as he sat back down next to her.

'Sort of,' Becca replied. 'Well, actually, no, not entirely.'

'What do you mean?' Alex asked, trying to interpret the expression on her face. It was obvious that she had something very particular on her mind.

Rowan glanced sideways at Alex. 'Would you like me to step outside for a bit?' she asked. 'To give the three of you some privacy?'

'No, you don't need to do that,' Becca responded quickly. 'I want you to hear this as well. If Alex and Pip trust you, then I do too.'

Pip reappeared at the table, holding two large mugs of tea. 'Why don't you tell us what happened at the house earlier on,' she suggested to Becca as she sat down next to her.

Becca looked at the three of them in turn and straightened herself in her chair. She explained that she had been sitting at Helen's kitchen table with her bowl of soup when she'd heard a knock at the front door. As she'd walked down the hall, there had been no shadows on the other side of the mottled glass and, when she had opened the door, there had been no one there. She had thought she'd heard the sound of footsteps – maybe two pairs – running away, but she hadn't thought to investigate any further. It was probably just local kids messing around, she'd said to herself. But five minutes later, having returned to the kitchen to finish her lunch, she'd heard an unfamiliar loud popping sound, followed instantly by a loud crack: the sound of glass breaking in the sitting room at the front of the house. And her first reaction had been to feel frightened. After all, an anonymous knock at the door was one thing, but a window being broken so soon afterwards? Something was going on and she didn't like it. She'd picked up the phone to call Helen but changed her mind. She hadn't wanted to spoil her sister's day. But neither had she wanted to hide in the kitchen and wait for Helen to come home. Eventually, she'd decided that she had to investigate.

'Didn't you think to call the police?' Alex asked her.

'I was coming to see you,' Becca explained. Evidently, it hadn't occurred to her to dial 999.

'Keep going, Becca,' Pip encouraged her.

Becca resumed her tale. She had tiptoed nervously back down the hall. As before, there had been no shadows at the front door, but, when she had looked into the sitting room, she had seen a series of cracks in the main window, spreading out like crooked spokes from a small hole in the centre of the glass. And that's when she'd remembered the popping sound. Surely someone hadn't fired a gun at the house? She had no idea what a real gunshot sounded like. And she didn't know what a real bullet hole looked like. But the thought had terrified her.

Chapter 29

'I'm not in the least bit surprised you were frightened,' Pip said. 'Given those circumstances, I'd have been frightened too.'

'I think we ought to send someone round to the house to check,' Alex suggested. He was still trying to process what Becca had just told them, but, in the meantime, his professional instincts had taken over. He wanted to know what had happened.

'I agree,' Pip replied.

Alex stepped back outside the cafe and selected the number for the Duty Chief Inspector in charge of the Met's main control room. When the call connected, he introduced himself to the person at the other end of the line and gave them a brief summary of the situation. The Chief Inspector agreed to task an armed response vehicle to go round to the address and take a look. 'Give them my mobile number,' Alex instructed, 'and tell them to give me a call when they get there.' He ended the conversation and returned to his three companions.

It occurred to him, looking at Becca, that, increasingly, she seemed to be considerably more annoyed than alarmed. Which didn't immediately make sense to him, given the circumstances she'd described.

'While we're waiting for an update from the ARV,' Pip said to Becca, 'why don't you finish off what you were telling us?'

Becca nodded. 'Sure,' she said. She told them that, while her immediate reaction to seeing the broken window had been to feel frightened, her emotions had changed rapidly in the moments that followed. 'Standing there in the hallway of my sister's house, it was like I had some sort of epiphany,' she explained. Whatever fear she might have been feeling had been overtaken by something much deeper and stronger. She had realised that she was angry. 'Really bloody angry,' she told them. About the situation she was in; about the possibility that there might have been someone out there trying to intimidate her; about the loss of her job and her livelihood; about the infuriating fragility of her health; about the desperately heavy price she seemed to have paid for the crime of falling in love. *Really bloody angry.* 'Sorry about my language,' she said.

'You've got nothing to apologise for,' Alex told her. There was no doubting the strength of her emotions. It was there in her voice, in her eyes and in the animated movements of her hands. Alex could feel it too. Whatever had happened to her at her sister's house – epiphany or otherwise – it seemed that she was done with feeling afraid.

His phone rang.

'That was one of the ARV sergeants,' Alex confirmed as he ended the call.

'How did they manage to get there so quickly?' Pip asked.

'They were in the area already,' Alex explained. 'Apparently, they were dealing with an earlier call just a couple of streets away – to a suspect firing what was believed to be an air weapon.'

'Oh?' Pip replied.

'They've had a look at Helen's window and confirmed that the size of the hole in the glass seems to be consistent with an airgun pellet.'

'Might that explain the popping sound that Becca heard?' Pip asked.

'It might,' Alex replied.

They both looked at Becca in an attempt to gauge her reaction to this latest news. She seemed both satisfied by the possible explanation and determined to move on – to put whatever it was that might have happened firmly behind her. 'What do you need from me?' she asked, looking directly at Rowan.

The sudden change in the direction of the conversation caught Rowan unawares, but she gathered herself quickly. 'I need your help,' she said.

Alex was feeling less ready to move on. He was still concerned by what had happened at the house – by the possibility, however remote, that there might have been something sinister going on. But he realised that there was no immediate sense in dwelling on the fact. It was time to see where the conversation with Rowan might take them.

'What kind of help?' Becca asked.

'Nothing that you're not completely comfortable with,' Rowan replied. 'I've got some questions I'd like to ask, but you don't have to answer them and we can stop at any time. I don't want you to feel under any kind of pressure.'

'I want to help if I can,' Becca said. She had a resolute look on her face.

'I'm very grateful,' Rowan replied.

'What are you going to do with what I tell you?' Becca asked.

'That's a difficult question to answer until I've heard what you have to say,' Rowan responded. 'At the moment, I'm just trying to find out some facts.'

'And then what?' asked Becca.

'I won't do anything unless it's with your agreement,' Rowan said. 'Your health is far more important than your involvement in any investigation I might be carrying out.'

'All right then,' Becca said.

The older couple who had been sitting at the table furthest from the door got up and made their way outside, leaving the four of them as the only remaining customers in the cafe. Perhaps sensing their need for some privacy, the cafe owner disappeared into the kitchen.

'Why don't you start by telling me a bit about you,' Rowan suggested.

'Where do I begin?' Becca asked.

'Wherever feels right to you,' Rowan replied.

Becca leaned her elbows on the table. She wrapped both hands around her mug and blew gently on the steaming tea as she gathered her thoughts. And, when she was ready, she started to talk. She began with the job at the Home Office and worked her way backwards and forwards in time, describing circumstances and events that were already familiar to Alex and Pip. Rowan didn't interrupt, preferring to nod her encouragement whenever Becca looked at her.

Alex studied the two of them as Becca talked and Rowan listened. One of them was young and fragile, yet possessed with a subtle inner strength that was becoming more apparent as she spoke. The other was older and far more certain of her place in things, undeniably wearied by the world, yet beguiled by the girl sitting diagonally across the table from her. Alex observed with fascination the clear similarities with the early stages of a negotiation: the fundamental importance of empathy; the significance of establishing a rapport and building trust; the basic need to encourage and allow a person to tell their story. Alex could see that Rowan was doing an excellent job of making Becca feel safe.

Becca talked about falling in love with Simon Jones and the secrecy that had surrounded their affair. She emphasised that the hidden nature of things had been very much at his insistence. She admitted to feeling guilty about his wife and children, but to being helpless in the face of her feelings for him. She had fallen hard for him – which had made it all the more shattering when he ended it.

'I'm so sorry,' Rowan said, interjecting for the first time. 'It must have been incredibly painful for you.'

'It was,' Becca replied quietly.

'Would it be all right if I asked you a little bit more about your relationship with Simon Jones?' Rowan enquired. There was nothing remotely pushy about her manner. It was obvious that she understood the need to tread gently.

Becca nodded.

'Let me try to explain where I'm coming from,' Rowan said. She was interrupted by a blast of cold air as the door of the cafe opened and a man walked in with a black labrador on a lead. The owner of the cafe reappeared from the kitchen and Rowan lowered her voice. 'I don't believe that Simon Jones is the man of the people he claims to be,' she began. 'In fact, I think he's probably a criminal.' She paused to allow this statement to register fully with the other three. 'That's why I was so keen to talk to you, Becca,' she explained. 'I'm hoping that you might be able to fill in some gaps for me.'

'What gaps?' Becca asked.

'What can you tell me about Soteria Solutions?' Rowan replied.

Becca looked momentarily blank. She turned to Alex for assistance.

'Do you remember?' he said. 'It's the name of the company you heard Simon Jones talking about on the telephone?'

'Oh that,' she replied as the memory stirred in her mind. 'I don't know very much about it, I'm afraid.'

'Anything you can tell me would be helpful,' Rowan said brightly. She produced a notebook from her bag and opened it on the table in front of her.

Becca repeated in brief the details that she'd previously given to Alex and Pip: that she'd heard Simon Jones talking about Soteria Solutions on the phone while he was in his flat and that the content of the conversations had made her suspicious.

'What was it specifically that made you suspicious?' Rowan asked.

The man with the black dog walked back out of the cafe, clutching a hot drink in a disposable cup and some sort of pastry wrapped in a paper napkin. The cafe owner disappeared back into the kitchen.

'Well, first of all, there was the fact that he only ever made or took the calls when he thought I couldn't hear him,' Becca explained. 'But I was listening. To begin with, I was simply interested in what I assumed were ordinary business conversations – because *everything* about Simon Jones interested me – but the first time I heard him emphasising the need for absolute secrecy to whoever was on the other end of the line, I began to wonder whether something else might be going on.'

'Tell me more about that,' Rowan asked with growing interest.

'Well, I couldn't hear everything he said, but it became a recurring theme in the bits of conversation that I did pick up on. Simon seemed very keen to ensure that the details of the discussions he was having remained confidential.'

'Keep going,' Rowan encouraged her.

'Sometimes, I could hear him talking about bank transfers to accounts in other countries. And the sums of money involved were huge: hundreds of thousands of pounds, sometimes millions.'

'Could it have had anything to do with his old business interests?' Rowan asked.

'What do you mean?'

'Might the conversations have been about the technology business he owned before he became an MP?'

Becca thought for a moment. 'I don't think so,' she said. 'I don't think that would explain all the secrecy – and I definitely heard him mention the Home Office on several occasions during the same conversations.'

'That's really interesting,' Rowan remarked, with emphasis on 'really'. 'Do you know who he was talking to?'

'Most of the time, I had no idea,' Becca replied. 'But there were a couple of occasions when I think he might have been talking to his wife.'

'What made you think that?'

'Every now and then, he would drop something more personal into the conversation,' she explained. 'I can't be sure, but that's the feeling I had at the time.'

'This is incredibly helpful, Becca,' Rowan said. 'I'm incredibly grateful.'

'Really?' Becca replied. 'It doesn't feel as though I'm telling you much at all.'

'Quite the opposite, I promise you,' said Rowan. 'Did you ever hear Soteria Solutions being talked about in the office?' she asked.

'Not by Simon,' Becca responded. 'But certainly by other members of the team.'

'In what context?'

'Just in a general context,' Becca replied. 'They were one of several companies bidding for government contracts.'

'Anything suspicious about what you heard in the office?' Rowan asked.

'No, nothing at all,' Becca said, leaning back in her chair.

Alex noticed that she was starting to look and sound tired. 'How are you feeling?' he asked her. 'You look like you could do with a break.'

'I'm all right,' she said.

'How about another drink?' he asked, noticing that her mug was empty.

'I'm all right,' she reiterated.

'Perhaps I could ask just a couple more questions for the time being?' Rowan suggested.

'A couple more,' Alex agreed.

Rowan looked back at Becca. 'Have you ever heard of someone called Jane Hammond?'

Becca paused for a moment. 'I don't think so,' she said. 'Should I have done?'

'Not necessarily,' Rowan replied.

'Who is she?' Becca asked.

'She's one of the main shareholders in the company that owns Soteria Solutions,' Rowan responded. 'But I haven't been able to put a face to the name.'

'And you think she might have an important part to play in all of this?'

'Absolutely I do,' Rowan replied. 'In fact, I can't help feeling that she might end up being the missing piece of the puzzle. Finding out who she is has the potential to answer all sorts of questions.'

'In which case, I'm so sorry that I can't be more helpful,' Becca said with feeling.

'You've got absolutely nothing to be sorry about,' Rowan reassured her. 'But would it be all right if I asked you about one other thing?'

'Of course.'

'Alex mentioned to me that you might have seen some documents in Jones's flat that referred to Soteria Solutions.'

'I did, yes,' Becca confirmed.

'Did you have an opportunity to see what was written on them?'

'Not really,' Becca replied apologetically. 'Simon never left anything like that lying around for long. He used the second bedroom in the flat as his office and I think he kept them in there.'

'Did you ever go in there?' Rowan asked.

'No,' Becca replied.

It was Rowan's turn to lean back in her chair. 'I would dearly love to take a look in that flat,' she said after a pause. The comment wasn't directed at any of the other three; it was simply wishful thinking, spoken out loud.

Becca looked from Rowan to Alex and back to Rowan again. 'But you can,' she said.

'What?' responded Rowan, confused.

'You can look in the flat if you want to,' Becca said earnestly.

'How on earth would I be able to do that?'

'Because I've got a key,' Becca replied.

Chapter 30

'No way,' said Alex firmly.

'No way what?' Rowan asked.

It was obvious to Alex that her mind was already racing ahead. 'No way are any of us going into the Policing Minister's flat,' Alex said, the palms of his hands raised in a whoah! motion.

'Why not?' Rowan asked.

'Because he's the bloody Policing Minister,' Alex replied. 'And because, irrespective of who they are, you don't just walk into someone else's house without their permission.'

'But Becca's got a key,' Rowan responded. Her journalist's instincts clearly weren't going to allow her to back down.

Pip interrupted the exchange. 'I think Becca's had enough,' she said, placing a protective arm around the younger woman's shoulders.

Alex turned away from Rowan and looked back at Becca. She was certainly looking tired. And, though she also looked as though she wanted to continue being helpful, Alex knew that they needed to put her health first. 'You're right, Pip,' he said. 'Of course you're right.'

'So here's what's going to happen,' Pip announced, taking

charge of the situation. 'I'm going to walk Becca home and leave the two of you here to finish your conversation. I'll come back and find you in half an hour or so.'

'OK,' agreed Alex.

'One last thing before you go,' Rowan said to Becca. 'Do you still have any of your belongings in the flat?'

'I do if he hasn't thrown them away,' Becca replied. 'Hidden away at the back of his wardrobe. Some clothes. Toiletries. One or two other bits and pieces.'

Rowan nodded as Pip stood up and turned to face Becca.

'Let's get you back to your sister's shall we?' Pip said.

Becca stood up slowly and put her coat on.

'Thank you so much for your time today,' Rowan said to her. 'I'm very grateful.

'It was good to meet you,' Becca replied.

'You did really well,' Pip said to Becca as they walked at an unhurried pace down Nightingale Lane.

'Did I?' she responded uncertainly.

'Absolutely,' Pip replied. 'How are you feeling now?'

'A bit tired, I suppose.'

'Hardly surprising,' Pip said sympathetically. 'And how are you feeling about what happened at the house earlier on?'

'Determined,' Becca replied.

Pip glanced sideways at her. 'Determined?' she echoed, encouraging Becca to keep talking.

'It probably *was* just kids being stupid,' Becca acknowledged with a shrug. 'In which case, there's really no point in getting worked up about it.' She stopped walking. Pip stopped too and turned to face her. She saw the flash of defiance in the younger woman's eyes. 'But if there was something more to it

218

than that,' Becca said fiercely, 'then I flat refuse to allow it – to allow them – to intimidate me. I've done nothing wrong, and I'm sick and tired of being afraid.'

Good for you, Pip thought to herself. She was starting to see things in Becca that she hadn't seen before. The twenty-four-year-old certainly possessed far greater depths of courage than Pip had previously given her credit for.

'Like you say, it probably was just kids,' said Pip reassuringly, managing to sound more certain than she felt.

Becca nodded and, seemingly satisfied, set off again in the direction of her sister's house.

The two women walked in silence for a while, accompanied every now and then by the lyrical tic-tic-tic call of a robin who seemed to be following them along the road.

'I'm not trying to make trouble for Simon,' Becca said as they turned off Nightingale Lane. 'But, if he's involved in committing any sort of crime, there's no way he should be allowed to get away with it. No one should.'

'Do you still think you love him?' Pip asked, remembering that Becca had said as much following the second negotiation on the bridge.

Becca puffed out her cheeks, less certain now. 'The truth is that I don't think I know very much about falling in and out of love,' she admitted. 'I can't deny that I still have feelings for him, but I do know that he hasn't been good for me.'

'You're being very brave,' Pip said.

'That's the second time you've said that to me.'

'Because it's true.'

'Thank you for being so kind to me,' Becca said. 'Thank you for believing me.'

*

Alex had given himself a few minutes of thinking time by going to use the loo at the back of the cafe. His mind was full of questions. Had they expected too much of Becca? Was she going to be all right in light of all the questions she'd been asked? Had they in any way set her recovery back? He couldn't help feeling responsible. And he couldn't help feeling annoyed with Rowan, who he thought had pushed a bit too hard at the end of the conversation.

As he washed his hands, he looked at his tired reflection in the small mirror set above the even smaller sink. He didn't want to feel exhausted when he and Pip took his sons out for lunch the following day. For years, his boys had been forced to feed off the scraps – to make the best of whatever was left of him once work had taken everything else. For the past year, he'd been trying to make sure that he gave them his best and, for the most part, he had succeeded. He desperately didn't want that to change.

When he walked back to the table, he saw that Rowan had ordered a fresh round of drinks, apparently as a peace offering. 'I'm sorry if I asked one too many questions,' she said to him. And Alex had to give her credit. She was certainly perceptive.

'I just feel very protective of Becca,' he explained to her as he sat back down. 'You remembered,' he said, pointing at the can of Diet Coke sitting on the table in front of him.

'I did,' she replied. 'You looked like you could do with the caffeine.'

'That bad, huh?' he responded. 'It's been a busy week,' he said by way of explanation for his appearance.

She added a lump of sugar to her cup of coffee and watched the dark liquid swirl as she stirred it with a teaspoon. 'I would still like to see inside that flat, though,' she remarked.

Alex couldn't blame her for pursuing the point. He would

have done the same in her position. But he wanted no part of it. 'Impossible,' he said.

'But is it?' she responded. 'Hear me out.' Rowan held out the fingers of her left hand and began to count them off. 'Number one, the flat has effectively been her home for a large part of the past year. Two, she still has some of her belongings in there. Three, she will obviously need to collect them at some point and, four, she has a key.'

Alex responded with his own set of fingers. 'Number one,' he countered, 'the relationship with Simon Jones – if there ever was one – is over—'

Rowan interrupted him straight away. 'What do you mean, "if there ever was one"? Don't you believe her?'

'As a matter of fact, I do,' he replied. 'But we only have her word for it. We don't have any actual proof. When I spoke to Jones's senior advisor at the Home Office, she was adamant that it had never happened.'

'Well, she would be, wouldn't she?' Rowan's manner was assertive without being confrontational. Alex knew that she wasn't trying to pick an argument with him. Her quarrel was with the politicians and their acolytes who were strangers to the truth.

'Fair point,' Alex conceded, before returning to count on his fingers. 'Two, she may have all sorts of reasons for not wanting to go anywhere near that flat and there's no way she should be doing anything that might upset her mental health. Three, Jones could just send her belongings to her—'

'Not if he's denying the affair ever happened,' said Rowan quickly, interrupting Alex for the second time. 'And, if I was in her position, I'd want to collect my own belongings.'

'And, four,' he continued, ignoring the interruption and

picking up where he had left off, 'it's certainly not something I'm prepared to ask her to do.'

'I accept that it would be a lot to ask of her,' Rowan acknowledged. 'But imagine if it meant finding a critical piece of evidence,' she said, her eyes gleaming.

'Speaking of evidence,' Alex said, grateful for the opportunity to move the conversation on, 'where have you managed to get to with the rest of your enquiries?'

Rowan responded by leafing back through her notebook. She found the page she was looking for and turned the book around for Alex to look at it. She had redrawn a much neater version of the spider's web diagram Alex had seen before, and had added plenty of new information to it. It reminded him of the old Anacapa charts used by police analysts to plot criminal intelligence and associations. Rowan had been able to establish the connections between any number of major players in what she called 'a profoundly corrupt system': party donors and supposedly independent think tanks and newspaper owners and various other individuals with significant access to the corridors of power – all of them with links, in one way or another, to private companies standing to make fortunes from the public purse. Many of them were members of The Bridge Club. Most damning of all was the Jersey Papers-sourced evidence that Seb Neill – multimillionaire Tory Party donor and IJF report-funder – was one of two major shareholders in Chaloner Capital, the offshore firm that ultimately owned Soteria Solutions. There was only one person left on the chart for Rowan to identify: Jane Hammond.

'So still nothing definitive on the Minister himself?' Alex enquired.

'Nothing definitive,' Rowan replied. 'But the value of the

contracts that Soteria Solutions holds with the Home Office has almost doubled since Jones became Policing Minister.'

'You're kidding?'

'I'm not. With the potential – the likelihood – of a whole lot more to come.'

Rowan explained to Alex that she had more than enough to go to press with regarding Seb Neill and Soteria Solutions, but the identity of Jane Hammond and the proof of the Simon Jones connection were the missing pieces she was holding out for.

Alex was still studying the diagram in Rowan's notebook when Pip reappeared in the cafe, flushed with colour from the outdoor temperature. She had been away longer than Alex had anticipated, but she approached the table with the look of someone bearing news.

'What is it?' Alex asked her.

'Becca wants to go back to the flat,' Pip replied.

Chapter 31

'I've got a bad feeling about this,' Alex said.

It was late on Saturday evening and he and Pip were sitting out in the small yard at the back of their house, wearing several layers of clothing and smoking cigarettes. Pip was the more regular smoker of the two – averaging four or five a day during the working week – but it was Alex who had been feeling in greater need of the nicotine hit. He used the smouldering tip of his first cigarette to light a second one.

'I honestly don't think there's any need to be concerned,' Pip replied. 'The plan seems to me to be a perfectly straightforward one. And there's nothing remotely unlawful about it.'

Earlier that afternoon, Pip had been standing on the pavement outside Helen's house, about to say goodbye, when Becca had announced that she wanted to return to Simon Jones's apartment to collect her belongings. When a surprised Pip had asked her why, Becca had said that she was looking for closure. She had already mentioned something to Pip about making a fresh start, and she'd realised that going back to the flat was something she wanted to do – *needed* to do, in fact – in order to be able to move on. She had actually been surprisingly clear-headed about it. Simply put, she didn't want to feel as though she'd left any part of herself behind. Pip had tried to question

224

whether or not it was a good idea, but, the more Becca spoke
about it, the more insistent she'd become. It hadn't taken Pip
long to realise that Becca had made up her mind and wasn't
going to change it.

The only thing was, she didn't want to go back there on her
own.

Pip had relayed all these details to Alex and Rowan after
rejoining them in the cafe and, seizing straight away on the
opportunity that appeared to be presenting itself, Rowan had
offered to go with Becca to the Minister's flat. Alex had immediately objected to the idea – for all the reasons he'd already given
– but Rowan had countered by arguing that, since the idea
was now coming from Becca rather than from one of them, it
put a completely different complexion on things. They weren't
making the decision; Becca was. Alex had remained far from
convinced and they had spent the best part of the next hour
debating the rights and wrongs of a variety of options – none
of which Alex felt comfortable with. In the end – and in spite
of his objections and concerns – Rowan and Pip had settled on
what Alex had described as 'the least worst' option.

It all came down to this: Becca had made it very clear that
she wanted to collect her belongings – something she was perfectly within her rights to do – and that she wasn't going to be
dissuaded from doing so. She didn't want to go to the apartment
on her own, but, having placed a series of significant burdens
on her sister already, she wasn't prepared to ask Helen to go
with her. There had been a shared acknowledgement of the fact
that it would be wholly inappropriate for either Alex or Pip
to go into the home of the Policing Minister, even in relation
to a supposedly private matter. Which, of those present, had
only left Rowan. Becca had other friends, but none that she

was particularly closely in touch with, and none who knew anything about the situation she had found herself in.

Rowan had pulled her laptop out of her bag and, after tapping away for some time, had confirmed that Simon Jones was in Sheffield for the weekend and that he had a meeting in his local constituency first thing on Monday morning. It all pointed to the fact that the flat would be empty throughout Sunday. For all of Alex's attempts to slow things down, the momentum of the situation had started to take over. Pip had gone back round to see Becca and, with the agreement of Helen, the decision had been made.

Sitting in the cold out at the back of their house, Pip knew that Alex was struggling with the situation.

'What is it that's worrying you the most?' she asked, pulling the sleeves of her coat down over her hands.

'I don't know,' he replied, taking another drag of his cigarette. 'All of it?'

'Think of it this way,' Pip responded. 'Becca is a private citizen. All she's doing is going to collect some personal belongings from her ex-boyfriend's flat. People do that all the time. It makes no difference that the ex-boyfriend happens to be a prominent politician. And she's taking a friend with her for support.'

'But Rowan is hardly a friend,' Alex pointed out. 'She's an investigative journalist who has an interest here that goes far beyond what might be best for Becca.'

'So it's Becca you're most worried about?' Pip asked.

'I suppose so,' said Alex. For a second or two, he was back on Westminster Bridge, trying to talk to a girl who looked as though she might fall at any moment.

'But you're not responsible for the choices she makes,' Pip

said firmly. 'She made it very clear to me that this is something she wants to do.'

Alex didn't reply. He was staring at the glowing tip of his cigarette as he remembered the silver car and the sound of screaming brakes.

'It's all going to work out fine,' Pip said. 'They can call us once they're done to let us know that everything is OK.'

'But what if Rowan is unable to resist the temptation to start rummaging through Jones's possessions,' Alex replied. 'You've seen the look in her eye. She might not be able to help herself.'

'She knows perfectly well what you and I think about that,' Pip responded. 'But she's also an adult who is perfectly capable of facing the consequences of her own actions. You're no more responsible for her than you are for Becca.'

'It doesn't feel that way,' Alex said.

Sunday morning passed slowly. Alex went for an early run in an effort to clear his head, while Pip caught up on some of the paperwork for her forthcoming court case. The boys were in good spirits when he and Pip met up with them for lunch – pizza at a place in Brixton Market that had been recommended to them – but, as the conversation went back and forth across the table, Alex was conscious of how distracted he felt by events of the previous twenty-four hours, and by Becca and Rowan's planned visit to the Minister's flat later in the day. He hoped it didn't show.

After the meal was over, the boys disappeared to play football with friends and Alex and Pip headed back to the house. Alex found himself watching the clock on the sitting-room mantelpiece as the daylight began to fade outside the window.

'Have you still got that bad feeling?' Pip asked him.

'Do you know what Ronnie said to me the other day?' Alex

replied. It sounded as though he was changing the subject, but that wasn't his intention.

'Ronnie Egan?'

'The very same,' Alex confirmed, sitting down on the sofa. 'It was earlier this week. We'd just come out of one of the Gold Group meetings for the murder and we were on our way to get an update about the two lads who were injured in the moped crash.'

'How are they by the way?' Pip interrupted him.

'Still in hospital,' Alex replied. 'But it looks as though they're both going to survive.'

'That's something, I suppose.'

'We were walking down the corridor towards my office,' said Alex, returning to the subject of Ronnie Egan, 'when she grabbed me by the arm and fixed me with one of those looks she gives me sometimes.'

'What looks?'

'Somewhere between a head teacher and a concerned relative.'

'And?'

'She looked me in the eyes and she said, "Alex, your problem is that you care too much." '

'Is that really what she said?'

'She meant it kindly,' Alex replied. 'I think she was trying to be supportive.'

'Well, you do have a certain tendency to carry the weight and the worries of the world on your back,' Pip said as she sat down next to him and rested her head on his shoulder.

'I don't know how to care any less than I do,' Alex said. 'And, to be honest, I'm not sure that I want to.'

'Even if it puts your own health at risk?' Pip asked him.

It was a question that Alex had no ready answer to.

*

Rowan met Becca outside the flower shop next to Clapham South tube – the same place that she'd previously met Alex and Pip.

'Are you sure you want to do this?' Rowan asked her.

'Absolutely,' Becca replied firmly. 'It's time to move on.' She seemed well rested and ready for whatever the evening might hold.

The two women took the Northern Line to Stockwell, where they changed to the Victoria Line and travelled a single stop to Vauxhall.

'Where now?' Rowan asked as they emerged at street level, just across the road from the not-so-secret headquarters of MI6.

'Simon's flat is about halfway along Albert Embankment,' Becca replied, pointing east along the main road that runs parallel to the Thames. 'It's not far from the old Fire Headquarters building,' she added.

They set off side-by-side, exchanging small talk as they crossed the road at the first set of pedestrian lights.

'Just up there on the right,' Becca announced after they'd been walking for about five minutes. She indicated a modern apartment block overlooking the river – one of a number that had gone up in the previous decade.

'Not exactly an ordinary flat then,' said Becca as she surveyed the impressive-looking building.

'He's a wealthy man,' Becca replied by way of explanation. 'A wealthy man with expensive tastes.'

'Which floor is his place on?'

'The one just below the top,' Becca said. 'I think it's the fourteenth. The views are amazing.'

'I bet they are,' Rowan replied with a wry smile. 'Who knows what we might see up there.'

Chapter 32

'And you're sure that you're all right with me being here?'
Rowan checked as she and Becca approached the front of the
building. 'I'm very conscious of the fact that you hardly know
me.'

'To be honest, I'm glad of the company,' Becca replied,
sounding a little less confident than she had done when they'd
met up earlier on.

'Have you got the keys?' Rowan asked.

Becca reached into her burgundy tote bag and pulled out
a bunch of three keys attached to a small wooden fob in the
shape of an acorn. She held them up for Rowan to see.

A smartly dressed man in his mid-thirties walked out of the
main entrance to the apartment block and Becca caught the
swinging glass door and held it open for Rowan to walk into
the marble foyer. There was no one sitting at the reception desk
as they walked over to the line of three lifts. Becca pressed the
button and a set of doors slid open to their left. Again, she let
Rowan go first, before stepping in and pressing the button for
the fourteenth floor. Rowan noticed a slight tremor in her hand.

'Are you OK?' she asked.

Becca nodded, but didn't say anything. Rowan chose not to

push the point, but kept a concerned eye on her companion via her reflection in the mirrors that lined the sides of the lift.

When the doors opened on the fourteenth floor, Becca stepped out and turned right. Rowan followed her.

Becca walked a handful of paces before stopping suddenly and turning around. 'Sorry,' she said. 'Wrong way!' She looked embarrassed. 'I wasn't concentrating,' she added by way of explanation.

Rowan tried to make eye contact with her, but Becca was busy searching for the keys that were back in her tote bag. The two of them walked back in the opposite direction along the broad corridor, past several pieces of original artwork hanging on the walls, before Becca came to a stop outside a solid oak door with a spyhole set into it. As she pulled the keys out of her bag, she fumbled and dropped them on the floor. Her hands were shaking much more visibly now.

'We don't have to do this,' Rowan said kindly. 'We can turn around right now and go back to your sister's house if you'd prefer.' In all her years as an investigative journalist, she had never compromised the safety or wellbeing of a source in the pursuit of a story. She wasn't about to start now.

'N-no,' Becca stuttered. 'It's just that it feels a bit strange being back here.'

'Of course it does,' Rowan replied. 'Take your time; there's no rush. And we can leave at any time.'

Becca bent down to pick up the keys, resting momentarily on her haunches while she tried to settle her thoughts and nerves. When she stood up again a few seconds later, she had a look of renewed resolve on her face. She was going to need all of that determination, and more, because the situation was about to unravel in ways that neither of them had anticipated.

*

Fourteen floors down, back out on Albert Embankment, a black Jaguar XF pulled up in front of the apartment block. The driver jumped out and retrieved a small suitcase from the boot, before setting it down on the pavement. His lone passenger – a well-groomed man with flecks of grey in his hair – got out of the rear seat and put his mobile in his trouser pocket. He reached back into the car to retrieve a brown leather briefcase.

'Thanks, Jerry,' the man said as he took the handle of the suitcase and started to wheel it towards the entrance of the building.

'Goodnight, Mr Jones,' the driver called after him. 'I'll be here to collect you at seven in the morning.'

In the corridor, Becca had selected what she thought was the right key for the uppermost of the three locks in the oak door. It slipped into the keyhole easily enough, but, when she tried to turn it, it wouldn't move. Looking confused, she glanced in Rowan's direction before turning her attention back to the door. She twisted and jiggled the key first one way, then the other, but, whatever she tried, it wouldn't shift.

'It's never done that before,' she said in an uncertain voice.

'Would you like me to have a go?' Rowan suggested patiently.

Becca stepped to one side to give her some space. Rowan removed the key from the lock and reinserted it before trying several times to coax it round.

'Are you sure it's the right one?' she asked.

But Becca no longer looked sure of anything. Instead, she looked unsettled and anxious.

Rowan removed the key and studied the whole bunch. 'Would you like me to try the middle lock?' she asked, recognising that she needed to take the initiative.

Becca nodded hesitantly. But, this time, the key she selected wouldn't even fit into the keyhole. Rowan examined both more closely and realised that the lock and key were made by two different companies: Chubb and Union.

'I don't understand,' said Becca in bewilderment when Rowan pointed this out to her. 'These are the same keys I've always used.' She looked as though she was on the verge of bursting into tears. 'He must have changed the locks,' she said.

Rowan looked back at the door. She would have been the first to admit her lack of expertise on the subject, but she could see no indication that the locks had been changed at any recent point in time. She ran the tips of her fingers over the varnished surface of the wood. There were no scratches or tool marks that she could feel or see. The finish was pristine. And, for the first time, she experienced an unsettling moment of doubt about Becca Palmer and the account of her affair with the Policing Minister. For the first time, she began to wonder whether everything she'd been told was actually true. At the same time, she remembered the note of caution sounded by Alex just the day before. 'We only have her word for it,' he had said during their conversation in the cafe. 'We don't have any actual proof.'

Somehow, Becca sensed Rowan's doubts. 'I promise you I'm not making any of this up,' she pleaded.

Pip yawned and stretched. Alex had opened a bottle of wine and they were both on their second glass. 'Slip Away' by Mumford and Sons was playing on the small wireless speaker that was sitting in the middle of the coffee table. 'I could do with an early night,' she said.

'Do you think they're all right?' Alex asked. He was still feeling distracted and hadn't really heard what Pip had said.

'Becca and Rowan you mean?'

'Who else would I be talking about?'

Pip looked at him, surprised by his tetchy tone. 'Are you all right?' she asked.

'Sorry, Pip,' he replied. 'I didn't mean it to come out like that.' He offered to top up her wine glass as a way of reiterating his apology.

'Not too much,' she said. 'I've got to be up early in the morning.'

'Do you think we should ring them to check?' Alex asked, unable to let go of the sense of responsibility he was feeling for Becca in particular. Ronnie Egan might have been a bit blunt in her assessment, but she might also have been right. He probably did care *too* much.

Pip could hear the concern in his voice. 'I'm sure they'll call us if they need to,' she said with a reassuring smile. 'They'll be fine. Simon Jones is two hundred miles away in Yorkshire. What could possibly go wrong?'

'Are you sure it's actually the right door?' Rowan asked, remembering the apparent wrong turn Becca had taken when they had first exited the lift. Perhaps it hadn't been a wrong turn after all. She still wanted to believe that Becca was telling the truth.

Becca looked up and down the corridor. 'I think so,' she said uncertainly. It was as though she was beginning to doubt herself. 'I don't understand,' she repeated in a troubled whisper.

'Could we be on the wrong floor?' Rowan asked gently. But, before Becca could reply, Rowan heard the lift doors opening behind her. Instinctively, she turned around to see who was there. As Simon Jones stepped out into the corridor, Rowan froze. Becca, who was looking in the same direction, gasped and put her hand to her mouth.

When Jones saw the two of them, he stopped in his tracks.

For what felt like several seconds, he stood in silence, staring at them with a look of incomprehension on his face.

Rowan shuffled her feet on the corridor carpet, unsettled more by the sudden and unexpected change in circumstances than she was by the presence of the man himself. She could feel Becca retreating behind her, like a child caught in the wrong.

'Becca!' the Minister said eventually, tilting his head to one side and trying to catch her eye. 'What on earth are you doing here?' There was no trace of anger in his voice, more a combination of confusion and surprise. He was very obviously struggling to make sense of the situation.

When Becca didn't reply, he put his briefcase down on the floor beside his suitcase and took a few steps towards them. His manner wasn't in any way confrontational. His movements were measured and unhurried. It appeared that he simply wanted to talk to them at closer quarters.

'Becca, what are you doing here?' he said again. And Rowan realised that, with her companion rendered temporarily mute, it fell to her to explain their presence outside his front door.

'I must apologise for the unexpected intrusion,' she said. 'We were only planning to be here for a few minutes. We've come to collect Becca's belongings.'

Simon Jones stopped in the middle of the corridor. 'What belongings?' he asked, looking steadily more bewildered. 'Actually,' he interrupted himself before Rowan could reply, 'before we even get to that, I don't think I know who you are.' His tone was curious rather than suspicious. It certainly wasn't accusing. He seemed to be going out of his way to be reasonable.

'No, you don't,' she replied as evenly as she could manage. 'My name's Rowan. I'm a friend of Becca's.'

'I see,' he responded. 'And you said that you're here to collect

Becca's belongings?' His eyebrows were arched and he was looking keenly at both of them.

'That's right, yes.'

'You'll have to forgive me,' he said, 'but, as you can probably tell, I'm a little bit confused.' He looked and sounded genuinely puzzled. 'What belongings are you talking about?' he asked. 'And where is it that you're supposed to be collecting them from?'

Rowan looked at Becca and back at Simon Jones, suddenly feeling every bit as baffled as he appeared to be. 'Her clothes,' she replied as confidently as she could manage. 'And anything else she might have left behind in your flat.'

'Left behind?' he asked, sounding even more perplexed. His brow furrowed and it occurred to Rowan that he was thinking hard about what to say next. 'Again, you'll have to forgive me,' he said at last, 'but I'm finding all of this incredibly strange.' He paused and looked sympathetically in Becca's direction. 'The thing is,' he continued, 'Becca doesn't have any belongings in my flat. How could she? She's never been here before.'

Chapter 33

'I'm sorry, what?' Rowan asked. She was struggling to make sense of what Simon Jones was telling them.

'I said that Becca has never been here before,' the Minister replied evenly. His manner was calm and sincere. His facial expression was one of concern and lingering confusion.

'That's not true!' Becca responded loudly, finding her voice at last. She stepped out from behind Rowan to face the man who she claimed had, until very recently, been her lover. 'And you know it's not,' she added defiantly. Rowan didn't need to look at her to know that she was angry. Becca took a step towards Jones, prompting Rowan to catch her by the arm and pull her back.

'Easy now,' Rowan whispered as she put an arm around her shoulders and pulled her closer.

Simon Jones raised his hands in an apparent attempt at conciliation. 'I'm so sorry, Becca,' he said, 'I promise you that I'm not trying to upset you – particularly as I know how unwell you've been.' He appeared genuinely concerned. 'The office have been keeping me up to date,' he explained, 'and I know that you've been having a very difficult time.' He directed the next question to Rowan. 'Were you aware that she's been in hospital?' he asked.

'I was,' Rowan replied.

Jones paused, seemingly trying to work out what he should say next. 'Look,' he said eventually, 'I really do have enormous sympathy for Becca's situation – it's very hard to imagine the full extent of all that she's been going through – but I hope you'll understand what I mean when I say that this really isn't the time or the place.' He paused again to weigh his words. 'I've spoken to her in the past and told her that I'd be glad to help her in any way I can,' he explained, raising his open hands again, 'but that doesn't mean that she can turn up here unannounced, late on a Sunday night, asking for things that don't exist.'

'He's lying,' Becca said to Rowan through clenched teeth.

'I'm not lying,' Jones responded, sounding unusually calm given the circumstances. He renewed eye contact with Rowan. 'I'm aware that she's told people in the office she's in love with me,' he said. 'And I also know that she's told them we've been having an affair.' He glanced across at Becca before continuing. 'But I'm afraid that none of it is true.'

'I'm going to call them,' said Alex, picking his phone up from the arm of the sofa. Mumford and Sons had been replaced by Bruce Cockburn on the wireless speaker.

'Why the need?' Pip asked patiently. 'They would have called us if they'd encountered any difficulties.'

'I just want to make sure,' Alex replied.

Pip recognised that there was nothing to be gained by arguing the point. 'They're probably on their way back to Helen's house already,' she said.

Alex scrolled through his recently dialled numbers and pressed his thumb on Rowan's name. The call went straight through to voicemail. He looked at Pip, wondering what to do next.

'They'll call us when they're ready,' Pip reassured him.

*

'How could you?' Becca demanded.

Rowan still had her arm wrapped around the young woman's shoulders and she could feel Becca's whole body quivering with a combination of anger and distress. She held her a little tighter.

'How could I what?' Jones replied. He was beginning to sound frustrated, but there was nothing in his demeanour to suggest that he was a man with anything to hide.

'Deny it all?' Becca responded. 'Deny everything that happened between us?'

'Nothing happened between us, Becca,' Jones insisted. He looked back at Rowan with an expression on his face that she interpreted as a plea for help. 'I don't understand where any of this is coming from,' he said, 'but it needs to stop.'

Rowan had no idea how to respond to him. She had accepted, almost without question, everything that Becca had told her the previous day. She had accompanied her to the apartment block that evening expecting to find evidence of an affair and hoping that, somewhere along the way – without needing to open too many doors and drawers – she might even come across evidence of the involvement of a government minister in a multimillion-pound corruption scandal. But even the thought seemed foolish to her now. What on earth had she been thinking? All she actually had was a set of keys that didn't work and a rapidly expanding list of questions for which she had no immediate answers. Who should she believe? A wealthy, powerful, well-connected man with all the facts on his side, or a virtually anonymous twenty-four-year-old woman with a history of mental illness and no proof to back up the claims she'd been making. The story of the girl on the bridge was falling apart and Rowan knew full well who most people would believe. She wouldn't have blamed them.

'I think we should go now,' she said quietly to Becca.

Becca resisted Rowan's gentle nudge forward. 'You changed the locks,' she said accusingly to Jones.

Simon Jones pulled his keys out of his trouser pocket. 'This is getting silly now,' he said as patiently as he could manage. 'No one has changed any locks. This is the same set of keys I've had since the day I bought this place.' He held them out in the palm of his hand for the two women to look at.

'Come on,' Rowan said to Becca, pushing her a little more firmly this time.

Becca very obviously didn't want to leave.

'He's lying,' she said again, her voice cracking as she spoke.

Rowan kept pushing and Simon Jones stepped to one side as they moved past him down the corridor.

'I really am sorry, Becca,' he called after them as Rowan pressed the button to call the lift. 'I'll speak to Camilla at work tomorrow and see if there's anything else we might be able to do to support you.'

But his words had the opposite of what Rowan imagined must have been their intended effect. Becca shook herself free of Rowan's grasp and turned to face him, her fists clenched by her sides. 'You're a liar,' she spat. 'And you know you are.'

'You need to go,' Jones replied firmly, 'before you say or do something to make things even worse for yourself than they already are.'

The lift doors opened as Becca fired her parting shot. 'The truth will come out in the end,' she shouted back down the corridor. 'It always does. Rowan is a journalist and she's going to find you out . . .'

'Becca!' Rowan muttered under her breath as she practically shoved her companion into the lift. It was an unnecessary disclosure that certainly wasn't going to do anything to improve the situation. She snatched a final, nervous look in the Minister's direction, and that's when she saw that the expression on his face had completely changed.

'I told you they'd call when they were ready,' Pip said as Alex reached for his ringing phone. She put her wine glass down and turned the music off as he put his mobile on the coffee table and switched it to loudspeaker.

'How did you get on?' he asked expectantly.

'Where are you?' Rowan replied. There was an urgency in her voice that neither Alex nor Pip had anticipated. They shared a concerned look.

'We're at home,' he answered. 'Why?'

'We need to talk.' Rowan's voice was clipped and purposeful.

'Why?' Alex repeated uncertainly. 'What's happened?'

'Jones turned up.'

Alex and Pip stared at one another in disbelief.

'Where?' Pip called out. 'At the flat?'

'Yes, at the flat.'

'But I thought he was in Sheffield,' Alex said, his thoughts firing in a dozen different directions at once.

'Well, he isn't.'

'Where are you now?' asked Pip, taking control of the conversation.

'Walking towards Vauxhall tube station.'

'We'll meet you outside Clapham South in half an hour,' Pip said.

'OK.'

'How's Becca?' Alex asked anxiously. 'Do you think she's OK?' He was picturing her walking alongside Rowan on the pavement, her head bowed and her mind fracturing.

'I have no idea what to think,' Rowan replied.

Chapter 34

Alex grabbed the car keys from the kitchen table. 'I told you I had a bad feeling,' he said.

'Let's get going,' Pip replied. 'We can talk about it on the way.'

Pip locked the front door and they crossed the road to where Alex's car was parked. They spent the first part of the twenty-minute drive to Clapham South wondering aloud about what might have happened at the Minister's flat, before settling on the realisation that it would be much better to wait and hear about it from the people who were actually there.

'The important thing to remember,' Pip said, 'is that no one has done anything wrong.'

'You mean that no one has done anything illegal,' Alex responded.

'Same difference,' Pip replied.

'But it's not, is it?' Alex said as they passed the large Sainsbury's on Clapham High Street. 'We were wrong to let them go to the flat.'

'It had nothing to do with us,' Pip insisted. 'It was Becca's decision to go, and Rowan's choice to go with her.'

'You know what I mean.'

'I know what you mean,' Pip replied. 'But I don't actually

agree with you. You're taking on a burden of responsibility that doesn't belong to you.'

'I just hope Becca is OK,' Alex said quietly. He was fearing the worst.

The two women were already waiting on the pavement when Alex pulled up outside the tube. He swivelled around in the driver's seat as Becca opened the rear nearside passenger door. 'Are you OK?' he asked her as she climbed in.

'We're fine,' Becca replied bluntly. She sounded tired, but the expression on her face – a mixture of unsettled discontent and jaw-set determination – surprised Alex. He had been preparing himself for something else entirely.

'What happened?' he asked as she slid along the back seat to make room for Rowan.

'What happened is that he changed the bloody locks,' Becca said impatiently. 'And that he told us a bunch of bloody lies.'

Alex opened his mouth to speak but closed it again when he realised that he wasn't entirely sure what to say. Locks and lies. He was trying to picture the scene at the apartment block. Trying to imagine what had taken place there.

'Why don't we head to Helen's house?' Pip suggested, breaking the silence. 'We can talk about everything once we're there.'

Alex checked over his shoulder and pulled away from the kerb.

Helen led the four of them through to the kitchen, where Alex introduced her properly to Rowan. Helen filled the kettle and flicked it on as they spoke. She didn't offer her guests anything stronger than tea to drink and none of them asked. To have done so in front of Becca would have been insensitive. Instead, she fetched mugs from a cupboard, milk from the fridge and a tin of biscuits from a drawer and, once she'd filled the teapot with boiling water, she joined them at the table.

'Well?' Helen said, sitting down and looking at each of them in turn. Alex and Pip were feeling every bit as impatient as she was to hear what had happened.

Becca very much wanted to be part of the conversation, but the significant demands of the day were starting to catch up with her and she was quick to agree when Rowan offered to take on the role of narrator.

Pausing every now and then to check with Becca that she was getting the details in the right order, Rowan began to describe the events of the previous couple of hours. She briefly mentioned their arrival in the building, the empty foyer and the wrong turning they had taken out of the lift. Then she talked at greater length about the difficulties they'd had with the door keys, before turning her attention to the sudden and unexpected arrival of Simon Jones. Alex, Pip and Helen were hanging on her every word.

'He denied everything,' Rowan said as she described the final moments of their encounter. 'And, I've got to be really honest with you, he was completely believable.' She was about to continue when she stopped herself and looked over at Becca. 'I'm so sorry, Becca,' she said, 'I hope you don't mind me saying that.'

'I really don't,' Becca replied. 'He's a bloody politician. He can be pretty persuasive when he wants to be.'

Alex had been listening intently, weighing once more what the evidence was suggesting against what his instincts were trying to tell him. It had been that way ever since his first encounter with Becca Palmer. The facts and his feelings remained at odds with one another. And it was clear to him that Rowan felt the same way.

'But you still believe what Becca has told us?' he asked, needing to process his thoughts out loud.

'One hundred per cent,' Rowan replied firmly.

'In spite of the fact that pretty much all of the evidence points in the opposite direction?' he asked. Here, it was his turn to apologise to Becca for seeming to doubt her. 'I'm really sorry,' he said to her. 'It's not that I'm meaning to question what you've told us, it's just that I want to make sure we're not leaving anything unsaid.'

Becca waved away his concerns. She understood.

'In spite of the fact that Becca has a set of keys that don't fit the door?' he continued, looking back at Rowan.

Rowan nodded.

'In spite of Simon Jones's clear denials?'

'He almost had me convinced,' Rowan admitted.

'So what changed your mind?' Alex asked.

'The expression on his face when Becca told him I was a journalist,' she replied.

'It's unlike you to call this late on a Sunday evening,' said Camilla Lane as she answered the phone. 'Is everything all right?'

'Becca was here,' Simon Jones announced. He sounded flustered.

'Becca was where?'

'At the flat,' he responded. 'Or, rather, in the corridor outside it.'

'What?' His aide was astonished. 'How the hell did she know where you lived?'

'I've no idea,' he said. 'She must have got the address from someone in the office.'

'And what on earth was she doing there?'

'She was with a journalist.'

'What the *fuck*?'

'It's obviously not just people in the office she's been telling tales to,' he said in an agitated voice. 'She was holding a bunch of keys that she claimed were for my front door. She said she was there to collect her belongings.'

'She must have lost her mind.'

'I think we knew that already,' replied Jones, not unkindly. 'To be honest,' he added, 'I actually feel rather sorry for her. It's the journalist who worries me.'

'Who was it?' Camilla asked.

'I've no idea,' he said. 'I've never seen her before. She said her name was Rowan, but we didn't get any further than that.'

'And did she say why she was there?'

'She just said that she was a friend of Becca's. It was Becca who told me she was a journalist.'

'And her name was Rowan?'

'That's what she said.'

'I'll make some enquiries.'

'Thank you,' Jones replied. 'What do you think she wanted?'

'I haven't got the faintest idea,' Camilla replied. 'The same thing they all want, I suppose. To dig up some dirt on someone in the public eye.'

'But there's no dirt to find,' he said. 'This whole thing is a product of Becca's imagination.'

'You actually told Simon Jones that Rowan's a journalist?' Alex said to Becca.

'I lost my temper,' Becca replied by way of explanation. She was sitting up a little straighter in her chair. She seemed to have rediscovered some of her energy.

'And what was his reaction?' Alex asked, addressing the question to Rowan.

'A mixture of anger and alarm,' Rowan replied. 'He tried to hide it, but he couldn't.'

'What did he say?'

'He didn't say anything,' Rowan explained. 'I followed Becca into the lift, the doors closed and that was that.'

'So you've no way of knowing what he was actually thinking?' interjected Pip. She was following Alex's lead in making sure that any important questions weren't left unasked.

'I know what I saw,' said Rowan. She understood what Pip was doing. She was a journalist rather than a detective, but they were both investigators. She would have offered exactly the same sort of challenge if she had been in Pip's position.

'He might just have been angry about the fact that there was a journalist loitering outside his front door on a Sunday night,' Pip suggested.

'He might have been,' Rowan conceded. 'But it looked like more than that to me.'

'What happens now?' interrupted Helen. It was clear that her only real concern was for her sister.

'We keep going after him,' Rowan said defiantly. 'He's a liar and a crook.'

'But how do we prove it?' Alex asked.

Even as he posed the question, Alex was conscious of being pulled ever deeper into a situation that had the potential to cause all sorts of professional difficulties for him. Even to land him in serious trouble. He had been warned specifically to stay away from the Home Office. He had been told very clearly to concentrate on the day job – and there was certainly a great deal that needed concentrating on. And yet, here he was, sitting in the home of someone he barely knew, talking to a journalist he'd met only a matter of days before, listening to unsubstantiated theories about the behaviour of a man tipped to be the next occupant of 10 Downing Street. In spite of all this, though, it didn't occur to him to back away. Psychologically and emotionally, he already had far too much invested in what was happening. Most of all, he felt that, having come this far, he owed it to Becca to see her story through to its very end.

'I'll keep working on the Jersey Papers,' Rowan replied. 'The proof of his criminality has to be in there somewhere; I just need to find it. I've already got enough information to make life incredibly difficult for a number of his associates, but I don't want to go to press until I've established his place in it all.'

'What are the Jersey Papers?' Helen asked.

Rowan spent the next ten minutes describing to Helen and Becca the extensive work she'd been doing on the data leak. Alex and Pip didn't in the least mind the repetition – it helped to clarify and confirm things in their own minds. Rowan explained the connections between Soteria Solutions and the Independent Justice Foundation, and between men like Robert Sangster and Seb Neill. She told them about the new round of bids for Home Office contracts. The missing elements, she reiterated, were the identity of the elusive Jane Hammond, and the particular role – if any – played by Simon Jones.

'I understand that you've still got work to do,' Helen said. 'But, in the meantime, Simon Jones has been telling lie after lie about my sister, who has lost her job – and ended up in hospital – as a direct consequence of his behaviour. How long are we going to have to wait before something is done about that?'

'Not too long, I hope,' Rowan replied calmly. 'It's all about timing.' Here she turned to Becca. 'I should have asked you this sooner, but I got rather carried away with the possibility that the visit to his apartment was going to solve everything for us. Would it be possible to have a look at your phone?'

'My phone's broken,' Becca replied.

'Why do you want to look at it?' Helen asked.

'I'd be very interested to see any personal messages that Simon Jones has sent to your sister,' Rowan explained. 'They will likely help us prove his lies.'

Becca's expression fell. 'You won't find anything like that on my phone,' she said.

Chapter 35

Becca was staring at the floor. Everyone else was staring at Becca. Alex could feel the recurring doubts about her story – those that he had repeatedly tried to dismiss – bubbling away again. Surely everyone had messages from their lover on their phone.

'What do you mean?' asked Pip, voicing the question they all wanted to ask.

'I don't have any texts or other messages from him on my phone,' Becca replied.

'Why not?' Pip asked, for want of a better question.

'Because they're all on my work phone,' Becca said quietly.

Alex was still wrestling with his doubts, but the mention of a second phone offered him a possible escape from them. 'And where is your work phone, Becca?' he asked.

Becca looked up. 'He made me give it back to him,' she said.

'When was that?'

'The night he told me it was all over,' Becca replied. 'The night before you found me on the bridge.'

'And that was the one you had all your messages on?' Alex clarified. He very much wanted to believe what she was telling them.

'He was always very particular about it,' Becca explained.

'He said it was all to do with security. We were keeping our relationship a secret and he told me that the work phone was less likely to get hacked than mine. In fact, he insisted that I never used my own phone to call him or send him messages.'

'And he made you give the work phone back to him?'

'He wouldn't let me leave his apartment until I did,' she said. 'He stood between me and the door and told me that it was the property of the Home Office and that I had to return it.'

'I bet he did!' remarked Rowan, rejoining the conversation. 'And you're sure that there's nothing on your own phone?'

Becca thought for a moment. 'I'm certain there aren't any messages,' she said, 'but there might be a photograph.'

'Really?' said Rowan eagerly. 'A photo of what?'

'Of me and him,' she replied. 'A selfie I took with him on the balcony of the apartment. I think I might have sent it to myself.'

'Now, that is interesting,' Rowan said, the expression on her face matching her words. 'How badly broken is your phone?'

'Completely,' Becca responded. 'I've thrown it away and, with everything that's been going on, I haven't quite got round to getting a new one.'

Camilla Lane was back on the phone to Simon Jones. 'I've just sent you a photo on WhatsApp,' she said to him. 'Have you seen it?'

'Not yet,' he responded. 'Who's the picture of?'

'I'm hoping it might be your journalist,' Camilla replied.

'Hold on,' he said, 'let me have a look.' He fumbled with his phone and managed to open WhatsApp without cutting her off. 'That's her,' he confirmed, putting the phone back to his ear. 'Who is she?'

'Freelance journalist,' Camilla explained. 'Used to work for the *Guardian*, but she's on her own now.'

'So we know what side she's on,' the Minister said.

'We certainly do,' came the reply.

'What's she been writing about recently?'

'All the things you'd expect,' said Camilla dismissively. 'The supposed failures of a government she clearly despises, the recent demonstrations, the Jersey Papers – that sort of thing. Most of it seems to be either on her blog or in the sorts of online publications that never get read by anyone sensible. The newspapers seem to be steering clear of her at the moment.'

'Hardly surprising,' Jones replied. 'She sounds like just another in a long procession of dull, whinging socialists.'

'I don't disagree,' Camilla responded, 'but her most recent piece does make several mentions of Soteria Solutions.' The line went quiet for a moment as she checked her notes. 'She hasn't got anything substantive, as far as I can tell,' Camilla continued. 'But she is asking one or two awkward questions.'

'Let her ask them,' Jones responded angrily. 'She's not going to find anything because there isn't anything to find.'

'You've thrown your phone away?' Rowan asked, looking and sounding surprised. 'When?'

'A couple of days ago,' Becca replied.

'Where?'

'In the bin over there,' said Becca, pointing over to the other side of the kitchen.

Everyone looked across the room.

'Has it been emptied recently?' Rowan asked Helen.

'I emptied it yesterday,' Helen replied. She suddenly looked worried.

'When's bin day in this part of London?' Rowan enquired.

'Wednesday,' Helen informed her.

'Good,' Rowan responded. 'So it should still be out there,' she said, nodding towards the front of the house.

'I suppose so,' Helen replied.

'Would you mind if I had a look?'

'If you really want to,' Helen said. 'Though I don't imagine that it will be particularly pleasant.'

Rowan stood up and headed straight for the front door. The other four got up and followed her out of the house. It was cold outside and Helen ducked straight back inside to grab a coat.

'Anyone else want one?' she asked. Apparently, no one did.

Rowan flipped open the lid on a large black wheelie bin and peered inside. She wrinkled her nose as she pulled out a large white bin liner. As she set it down on the ground, Alex could smell the rotting food inside. Rowan crouched down and undid the yellow ties at the top of the bag. After two or three unsuccessful attempts, she managed to get it open. She gave the bag a gentle shake and allowed the contents to settle. When she couldn't immediately see the phone, she shook the bag again.

'There it is,' she said triumphantly. She reached into the bag and, using the thumb and forefinger of her right hand, she pulled out an old iPhone with a shattered screen and held it up for everyone to see. It was covered with what looked like a combination of jam and toast crumbs. As she stood up, Alex retied the bag and placed it back in the wheelie bin.

The five of them walked back through to the kitchen and Helen handed Rowan several pieces of kitchen roll, which she used to wipe the phone down.

'Do you often go through people's bins?' Pip asked with a half-smile.

Rowan grinned back at her. 'Sometimes,' she replied. 'Though I try not to make a habit of it.' She turned her attention to the phone and pressed the power button. Nothing happened.

'I told you it was broken,' Becca said.

'What about the SIM card?' Alex asked. 'That's all we really need.'

'I don't know where it is,' Becca replied self-consciously.

Alex felt a renewed flush of discomfiting doubt. First, no phone messages and, now, not even a SIM card. These were obvious holes in Becca's account and they were making Alex feel uneasy. 'Isn't it in the phone?' he asked, trying hard to mask his concerns.

'No,' Becca said sheepishly, perhaps sensing his reservations. 'I took it out when I realised the handset was broken, and now I can't find it.'

'What about the cloud?' Rowan interjected. 'Surely your pictures are backed up?'

'The old ones are,' Becca said. 'But I never got round to arranging the monthly payment for the additional storage.'

Alex could feel the sands of her story slipping through his fingers.

'We might still be able to see what's stored on the handset,' Rowan continued.

'Really?' Becca asked. 'How?'

'I've got a friend who's good with phones,' Rowan said. 'Would you mind if I showed it to him.'

Becca raised her eyebrows. 'If you think it might help,' she said hopefully.

'In which case,' Rowan replied, 'I'll take it to my friend first thing in the morning.'

Chapter 36

There had been another stabbing overnight. Another teenager. Alex got the text early on Monday morning, just after getting home from a 5K run.

'Shit!' he muttered as he read it. He was standing in the bedroom doorway, covered in sweat.

'What?' asked Pip, who was busy getting dressed on the other side of the bed.

'Another one,' Alex replied with a worried frown.

'Another what?' Pip asked. She had stopped buttoning her shirt and was looking enquiringly at him.

'Stabbing,' he replied soberly. 'I need to make a quick call,' he added. He scrolled through his phone and found the number of the DI who had been dealing with the case overnight. He got through straight away and was given an update that turned out to be slightly more positive than he was expecting. The sixteen-year-old victim was still alive and it looked as though he might make it. No arrests yet, but the DI had a possible name for the suspect and a number of good leads.

Pip listened to Alex's end of the conversation and watched the emotions play out on his face. From anxiety, to relief, to concern, to acceptance of the fact that another long day's work had been defined for him before he'd even left the house.

'He's still alive then?' she queried when Alex ended the call.

'At the moment, yes,' he replied. 'Though I doubt that's going to keep the Area Commander off my back.' He gave her a weary smile. 'I suppose I'd better get into the office,' he said.

He stripped and showered in a hurry. When he reappeared in the bedroom a couple of minutes later, Pip offered to make him some breakfast.

'I'll pick up something on the way in,' he told her as he opened a drawer and grabbed some underwear.

Sitting on the tube less than twenty minutes later, his thoughts rattled and swayed in time with the carriage. He'd dealt with plenty of stabbings before, but never at a time when so many were happening all across London in such rapid succession. The Area Commander might have been an idiot, but he had every right to be concerned. Alex certainly was.

'We can't allow ourselves to get sidetracked,' Simon Jones said. 'Not with the party conference so close.' He was standing behind his desk at the Home Office and it looked as though he hadn't had a great deal of sleep. He was certainly looking a little less well turned out than usual.

'I quite agree,' said Camilla Lane, taking a seat opposite him.

'Which means that we could well do without any nonsense from Rowan-whatever-her-name-is,' he added, staring out of the window and taking a cautious sip of the double espresso that Camilla had just handed him.

'Blake,' Camilla responded.

'What?'

'Her name's Rowan Blake,' Camilla said. 'And I quite agree.'

'So what are we going to do about her?'

'Nothing.'

'What do you mean nothing?'

'Exactly that,' Camilla replied. 'I've made some calls this morning and she hasn't been in contact with any of the papers. And I've double-checked her blog. It's not had many readers in recent months.'

'I told you she didn't have anything,' Jones said, his expression relaxing a little.

'I know you did,' Camilla replied. 'And I believed you.'

'*How are you doing?*' Pip wrote in a text to Alex.

'*Fine,*' he replied. And 'fine' was an adequate enough description of how he was feeling. His mood had been lifted a little by confirmation that the injuries sustained by the victim weren't life-threatening. And it had been given a further lift with news that the Area Commander had taken a couple of days off at short notice to deal with some sort of family emergency. It meant that Alex would be spending significantly less time during the next forty-eight hours fielding phone calls and responding to emails that did precisely nothing to address the problem of knife crime in North London. It meant that he might actually be able to get on and do his job.

'*It's just that you left in a hurry this morning,*' Pip followed up. '*And I wanted to check that you're OK. You've got a lot on your plate at the moment.*'

'*We both have,*' he typed in reply. '*I promise I'm OK. The Commander's off for a few days which helps.*'

'*Not all bad news then,*' she responded. Alex imagined her smiling as she typed it. He sent a single '*x*' by way of reply and received one in return.

He settled back in his chair, closed his eyes and took a few minutes to practise the breathing exercises he'd been learning. He found that they helped him to remain steady when he had a lot on his mind. He took a deep breath in and thought about the teenage boy lying in a hospital bed, tubes and wires trailing everywhere. He breathed out slowly and felt grateful that he was still alive. He took a deep breath in and thought about Becca Palmer, sitting at her sister's kitchen table, a mug of coffee in her hand. He breathed out slowly and felt grateful that she'd been in a surprisingly positive frame of mind when he'd said goodbye to her the previous evening. He took a breath in and thought about Pip, preparing for her Old Bailey trial. He breathed out slowly and felt as grateful as ever for her love and support. Deep breath in. Slow breath out. Pulse slowing. Head clearing.

Alex was interrupted by another ping of his phone. It was a WhatsApp notification from Rowan Blake. He tapped on the screen and realised that it wasn't a message. It was a photograph. Of Becca Palmer and Simon Jones standing arm in arm, smiling at the camera. It had been taken at night and the scene behind them was out of focus, but there was no mistaking the illuminated outline of the Houses of Parliament. Alex felt an undeniable sense of relief as he studied the image. Here was proof that, when it came to the photograph at least, Becca had been telling them the truth.

'Right, well, what's the plan for today?' the Minister asked, in an apparent effort to move the conversation on.

'You've got half an hour to catch up on your reading,' Camilla replied, 'and then we've got a couple of hours set aside with the team to go through the first draft of your conference speech.'

'Good,' Jones replied. 'And this afternoon?'

'You've got your regular catch-up with the Chair of the Police Federation straight after lunch.'

'What's on the agenda for that?'

'Nothing that will come as any great surprise to you,' she

responded. 'He wants to talk to you about what he considers to be the likely long-term impact of austerity. They're running a new publicity campaign using the slogan "*Cuts have Consequences*".'

'Oh for God's sake!' the Minister replied in exasperation. 'Crime is down. Police reform is working. That really ought to be the end of the conversation.'

'I quite agree,' Camilla said. 'But I'm not sure that's how he sees it – particularly with the recent increase in knife crime in London and elsewhere.'

'He's wasting his time,' Jones muttered, pulling his chair out behind his desk and sitting down. 'Anything else in the diary?'

'Geoffrey Bell wants to meet you at the club tonight.'

'Oh?'

'He said you'd know what it was about.'

The Minister gave her a look that suggested both uncertainty and concern.

'I imagine he wants to talk to you about your next piece in the *City Journal*,' Camilla suggested.

'Ah yes!' Jones replied, looking relieved. 'That'll be it.'

'Excellent work!' Alex said to Rowan over the phone.

'I told you my man knew what he was doing,' Rowan replied.

'Where do you think the picture was taken?' Alex asked, though he knew what the answer was likely to be.

'On the balcony of his apartment, of course.'

'You sound remarkably certain,' Alex said.

'That's because I am,' she responded. 'My friend can do all sorts of clever things with geolocation and IMINT.'

'IMINT?' asked Alex, annoyed with himself for needing to ask. Normally, he was the one explaining the meaning of acronyms to other people.

'Intelligence gained from imagery,' Rowan clarified. 'My friend has studied the relative positions of landmarks in the background of the photo and compared them with other images that he's been able to find online – including one taken from the apartment block when it was still a construction site.'

'And?'

'He's as sure as he can be that it's Jones's apartment. I am too.'

'So Jones *was* lying,' Alex said.

'Well,' Rowan responded carefully, 'he certainly appears to have been lying when he said that she'd never been in his apartment.'

'But it doesn't necessarily prove that they were having an affair,' said Alex, reading the direction of her thoughts.

'It doesn't prove it, no,' she agreed, 'but I think it gives us enough of a basis to ask some reasonable questions.'

'What do you have in mind?' Alex asked.

'I'm going to draft a piece – suggesting an affair and questioning his integrity – and send it to his office for comment.'

'That's bold,' Alex replied.

'I think it's perfectly reasonable in the circumstances.'

'What will that mean for the work you're doing on the Jersey Papers?'

'There's no reason why I can't do both,' Rowan responded. 'I still haven't been able to make the connection between Jones and Soteria Solutions – but I'm hoping that questions about his integrity will at least disrupt his attempts to get away with his crimes.'

'So you're still convinced of his guilt?'

'Absolutely.'

'You'll need Becca's permission before you do any of it,' Alex cautioned.

'Of course,' Rowan replied. 'I wouldn't dream of saying or writing anything without her say-so. I'm going round to see her and her sister at lunchtime.'

It was approaching 7 p.m. when Camilla Lane knocked on Simon Jones's office door. When she walked in, his desk was clear and he was in the process of putting his coat on.

'I think you need to look at this before you head off to the club,' she said, holding out a single sheet of A4 paper.

'What is it?' he asked.

'Just look at it,' she said impatiently.

Jones took the document from her and started to read. Camilla watched as the expression in his face darkened steadily to one of undisguised rage.

Chapter 37

Alex was sitting in his office on Tuesday morning when his mobile rang. He didn't recognise the number.

'Hello?' he said.

'Is that Superintendent Lewis?' said the female voice at the other end of the line.

'Yes it is,' he replied.

'You may not remember me,' the voice said, 'but my name is Camilla Lane. We met recently at the Home Office. I work for the Policing Minister.'

Alex tensed as a swift succession of thoughts raced through his mind. Why was she calling him? Was he in trouble? Was it about Becca? Was Becca in trouble? *Why the hell* was she calling him? He was relieved that she couldn't see the expression on his face. 'Of course I remember you,' he said in his most professional voice. 'How can I help?'

'I'm hoping that you might be able to do me a favour,' she replied warmly. 'Or, rather, I'm hoping that you might be able to do the Minister a favour.'

'Of course I'll help if I can,' he said. Because that's what mid-ranking police officers were expected to say when the office of the Policing Minister called. But he hadn't the slightest idea about where the conversation might be headed.

'You'll no doubt know that the Conservative Party conference is being held in Birmingham next week,' Camilla began, 'but what you may not know is that the Minister has been invited to give one of the keynote addresses.'

'I didn't know that,' replied Alex, feeling even more confused. Apparently, she wasn't calling him about Becca. And it didn't sound as though he was about to get any kind of dressing-down.

'The Minister met with the head of the Police Federation yesterday and he wants to make sure that the voices of frontline police officers are heard in what he has to say.'

'Right,' said Alex uncertainly. He was still none the wiser.

'That's where you come in,' noted Camilla cheerfully. 'The Minister is wondering whether you might be able to spare some time to share your experiences with him.'

'Me?'

'He would be very grateful.'

'But why me?' Alex asked before he could stop himself.

'Why not?' Camilla responded. 'You impressed me when we met. I've done my research and I know that you're working in a busy part of London. You're experienced. You're respected by your colleagues. And, quite apart from anything else, you gave me your card, so I had your number to hand.'

'I see,' Alex said, struggling to know how best to respond. The request was straightforward enough – he'd briefed plenty of politicians in the past – but it all seemed like too much of a coincidence. He felt wary. 'I'll need to speak to my boss,' he added in an attempt to give himself some thinking time.

'No need,' Camilla replied. 'I spoke to the Commissioner before I called you and he was more than happy for you to help out.'

Apparently, she'd thought of everything. 'When would the

Minister like to speak to me?' Alex asked, feeling completely cornered.

'Today, if at all possible,' Camilla responded. 'The only problem is that he's got a rather packed diary between now and about six o'clock. He was wondering whether you might be willing to meet him at his flat later this evening.'

'You won't believe who just called me,' Alex said. He'd rung Pip as soon as he'd ended the call with Camilla Lane.

'You'll need to be quick,' Pip replied. 'I'm about to go into a meeting.' She sounded preoccupied.

Alex gave her a brief account of the conversation he'd just had. 'He wants to meet me at his apartment at eight this evening,' he said.

'It might be nothing,' she commented, evidently sensing his concern.

'What do you mean?'

'It might be exactly as it appears to be,' she said reassuringly. 'He might actually want your advice.'

'Don't you think that the timing seems a bit unusual?' he asked, hardly feeling reassured.

'Well, the Conservative conference is happening next week and he is giving a speech,' she responded. 'So, in that sense, the timing seems perfectly normal.'

'But that's not what I'm talking about.'

'I know it's not,' Pip replied. 'Listen, I really have got a meeting that I need to be in. I should be home by six. Why don't we talk about it then?'

'That doesn't give us much time.'

'You don't have to do it,' Pip said.

'Unfortunately, I do,' he replied. 'Camilla Lane has already spoken to the Commissioner.'

*

Unable to shift his sense of disquiet about the meeting request, Alex called Rowan. She didn't pick up, so he left a message, asking her to call him back. Then, for the next couple of hours, he tried to concentrate on the overflowing contents of his inbox. At midday, he met with Ronnie Egan and a number of other colleagues to discuss the ongoing urgency of the knife crime response in the borough. All the while, he was thinking about Simon Jones.

Rowan called him back just after 2 p.m. 'I'm so sorry for the delay,' she said. 'I've been rather preoccupied.'

'Are you OK?' he asked, picking up on the hint of unease in her voice.

'I think so,' she replied.

'You think so?' he responded. 'What do you mean?'

'When I woke up this morning, there was a terrible smell in the flat,' she told him. 'And, when I opened my front door, I discovered that the outside of it had been covered with dog shit.'

'You're joking!' he said, feeling every bit as shocked as he sounded.

'I wish I was.'

'But why?'

'I think we both know the answer to that.'

'Wait. What? You're telling me that you think the Policing Minister sent someone round to your flat to smear dog shit all over your front door?'

'Well, I think we can both be fairly confident that he wasn't involved in any sort of direct sense,' Rowan replied. 'Deniability and all that. I very much doubt that he even knows it's happened. But I don't have any doubts about where it's come from.'

'But was there anything else? Like a note or something?'

'No, nothing.'

'So it might not have been targeted specifically at you?' Alex realised that he was clutching at straws, but he was trying to establish whether there was any substantive evidence to support what Rowan was alleging.

'It hadn't been done to anyone else's front door,' she replied matter-of-factly.

'And you haven't written anything to upset anyone else recently?'

'No more than normal,' came the droll response.

'Good grief, I'm so sorry,' Alex said, his mind whirling with the possible implications of what she was telling him. He was also thinking about Becca. About the broken window; the knock at her front door; the car outside the house; the two men outside the shop. What if Becca hadn't imagined any of those things? And what if there was a connection between them and what had now happened to Rowan? Bloody hell. Surely not. 'Have you reported it to the local police?' he asked.

'Actually, I have,' Rowan replied, 'but they told me they didn't have anyone immediately available to send round. They said it was probably going to be several hours.'

'Welcome to the Metropolitan Police in the twenty-first century,' Alex said bitterly. 'Where the hopelessly limited supply of officers can't even begin to keep up with the overwhelming levels of demand.'

'Welcome to austerity Britain,' Rowan replied.

'So what did you do?' Alex asked her. 'About the dog shit, I mean?'

'I cleaned the door,' she said simply. 'The smell was unbearable.'

'I really am sorry,' Alex said.

'It is what it is,' Rowan replied. 'It's what they do.'

'What do you mean?' Alex asked. 'Who are "*they*"?'

'The people behind the people in power,' she answered, as if it were a self-evident fact. 'The people who hide in the shadows – the backers, the brokers, the moneymen – people who will go to any lengths to silence the voices of those they consider a threat.'

'You're joking!' said Alex for the second time in as many minutes. In spite of his own concerns, what she was suggesting seemed to him to be stretching the bounds of both plausibility and possibility.

'I've never been more serious,' came the reply.

'I honestly don't know what to say,' Alex remarked as he tried once more to think through the implications of what she was telling him.

'There's nothing *to* say,' Rowan replied. 'And, in any case, it's not the reason why you called me.'

'Er, no, it wasn't,' Alex responded. 'I actually rang with some news of my own,' he said. 'News that I thought might interest you.'

'Go on,' she prompted.

So Alex told her about his earlier telephone conversation with Camilla Lane and the request from the Policing Minister for a meeting at his apartment later that evening.

Rowan was immediately excited by the prospect. 'You have to go,' she said.

Chapter 38

It was just after six when Pip got back from work. Alex had got home half an hour earlier and he'd spent the intervening time sitting alone in their living room, working through his reservations about the planned meeting with Simon Jones. Neither the timing (so late in the day, and so soon after the Minister's unexpected encounter with Becca) nor the setting (in his apartment, rather than somewhere more formal or public) felt right to him. But the fact remained that the invitation had been extended and he'd had an email from the Yard that afternoon confirming that the Commissioner wanted him to go.

The only small consolation in all of it was that his younger son had called, asking if they could postpone their planned get-together that evening. He'd been in bed with flu for the past couple of days and wasn't feeling well enough. His older brother was away for the week and wouldn't have been joining them in any case. At least it meant that going to see Jones wouldn't be at the expense of his duties as a parent.

Rowan had certainly seemed to think that the meeting was a good idea. Before their phone call that afternoon had ended, she had updated him on the conversation she'd had with Becca and Helen the previous afternoon. She'd told him that Becca had been unexpectedly bullish about the proposed article. Rather than it setting her mental health back as Alex had feared that it might, the encounter with Simon Jones outside his apartment seemed to have fired her up with a sense of righteous indignation. The man was a bare-faced liar and there was absolutely no way she was going to let him get away with it.

'Is that really what she said?' Alex had asked.

'Word for word,' Rowan had replied. She'd ended the call by telling Alex to check his inbox. She'd just sent him a copy of what she'd written.

Nothing in the draft article had taken him particularly by surprise. Rowan hadn't named Becca – referring to her only as a 'junior Home Office employee' – but she'd told her story faithfully. And Simon Jones didn't come out of it well. He was an older man who had taken advantage of a vulnerable younger woman and subsequently lied about the fact. And the impact on the younger woman had been devastating. The piece made clear that the younger woman's account of events had been corroborated, though it stopped short of specifying how. It made no mention of Soteria Solutions or the Jersey Papers, but it did make a point of asking whether there might be something more to the story. There was an acknowledgement that Jones might have been lying to protect his family or to limit any damage to his public reputation, but the article had ended with a very specific question: 'Does Simon Jones MP have something else to hide?'

'Evening,' Pip said cheerfully as she planted a kiss on Alex's cheek. She knew that he wanted to talk, but, first, she needed a shower. She'd had a long day too.

When she came back downstairs, Alex was outside in the back garden, smoking a cigarette. He had a large cup of tea in his hand.

'Have you got one of those for me?' she asked, nodding at

his half-finished cigarette. He took a packet out of his pocket and gave one to her.

'How was work?' he asked as he offered her a light and tried, without success, to push thoughts of his own day to one side.

'We're as ready for the trial as we're ever going to be,' she replied, but she could see that he wasn't really listening to her answer. It was obvious that he had other, more immediate things on his mind. 'So?' she asked him.

'So what?' he replied.

'So how are you feeling about this evening?'

They spent the next few minutes talking through Alex's concerns – not least the timing of the meeting request, the content of Rowan's article and the possible connections between those two things. When Alex told her briefly about what had happened to Rowan's front door, Pip was every bit as shocked as he had been – though she was quick to point out that, unpleasant though the incident undoubtedly was, it didn't appear to have any immediate bearing on what might happen in the next few hours.

She tried to set it out logically for both of them. 'He's the Policing Minister. You're a respected senior police officer. He's got a speech to make next week and he wants to ask you some questions about it. Am I right so far?'

Alex nodded.

'Most of the rest is no more that speculation. I'm sure he knows that you're the person who dealt with Becca on the bridge, but he doesn't know that you've kept in touch with her since, or that you know about the episode outside his flat on Sunday evening.' She smiled at him. 'So, given all of that, I can't think that there's anything you actually need to worry about.'

'But I don't trust him.'

'And probably with good reason,' Pip replied. 'But it's only a conversation – one that the Commissioner has given his blessing to. You'll be absolutely fine.'

Just over an hour later, they were in the car, heading towards Albert Embankment. Pip had offered to keep him company on the journey to and from the Minister's apartment and she was doing the driving. Alex still had an uneasy feeling about it all, but, in the end, he hadn't had any choice. The Policing Minister was expecting him.

'Do you think I ought to record our conversation?' he asked.

'What? Covertly you mean?' Pip replied.

'I suppose so,' he said.

'I think you might find that you need a surveillance authority for that,' she said.

'I know, but I don't really trust him.'

'So you've said,' she replied. 'Why don't you call me before you go in,' she suggested. 'You can leave the line open and, that way, I'll be able to hear what's being said.'

'I think you might find that you need a surveillance authority for that,' he said, mimicking her comment of a few moments before.

'Maybe,' she responded. 'But there won't be any recording and I'm not going to tell anyone we've done it.' She glanced to her left to check his reaction. 'At least it would mean that you're not on your own.'

Before he could reply, his phone rang. It was Rowan Blake.

'You're on loudspeaker,' Alex said as the call connected. 'I'm in the car with Pip.'

'I've bloody got it!' came the excited response at the other end of the line. 'I know who Jane Hammond is.'

Chapter 39

'It was staring me in the face all along,' Rowan announced, her voice crackling through the speakers in the car doors. 'I just hadn't seen it.'

'Well, go on then,' said Pip impatiently. 'Who is she?'

'Jane Hammond is Simon Jones's senior advisor at the Home Office.'

Pip hit the brakes in her surprise. Slowing, she pulled over at the side of the road. There was a stunned silence in the car as she and Alex stared open-mouthed at one another.

'Are you still there?' said the voice of Rowan Blake.

'Still here,' replied Alex, finding it very difficult to absorb what he'd just been told.

'Did you hear what I said?'

'We did,' confirmed Pip. 'It's just that we're struggling to get our heads around it.'

'But it's so obvious.'

'Is it?' asked Pip.

'I thought his senior advisor was Camilla Lane,' Alex said as his mind began to click back into gear.

'She is,' came the reply.

'So he has more than one senior advisor?' Alex asked.

'No,' Rowan responded triumphantly. 'Camilla Lane and Jane Hammond are the same person.'

'Wait? What?' said Pip. 'I don't understand.'

'Camilla Lane and Jane Hammond are the same person,' Rowan repeated, obviously enjoying their confusion.

'You're going to have to explain,' Pip said.

'It's so simple,' replied Rowan. 'Camilla is her middle name. She's used it since she was at school. But the name she was born with is Jane. As is Hammond. Hammond is her maiden name.'

'You've got to be kidding me,' Pip said disbelievingly. 'I didn't even know she was married.'

'She's not,' Rowan clarified. 'She got divorced several years ago, but she kept her ex-husband's surname.'

'Are you quite sure about all of this?' Alex asked.

'I've got it all on the screen in front of me,' Rowan replied. 'There's no doubt about it.'

'He should be here in the next twenty minutes,' Simon Jones said, his mobile phone held to his ear.

'And you're happy seeing him on your own?' Camilla asked him.

'It's a conversation about current policing challenges,' he replied. 'I think I should be able to manage.'

'And about Becca Palmer,' Camilla clarified.

'Well, yes, her as well,' the Minister responded. 'But only when the moment feels right.'

'Of course.'

'I'm confident that the truth will win out in the end,' he said.

'I'm sure it will.'

As the call ended, Simon Jones stood up and poured himself a large tumbler of whisky – an eighteen-year-old Macallan – no ice, no water. It was his third since he'd got in from the office.

*

'Hold on a moment,' Pip said. 'You're genuinely telling us that the Policing Minister's senior advisor is one of the main share-holders in Chaloner Capital?'

'I am.'

'And that Chaloner Capital is the firm that, ultimately, owns Soteria Solutions – a company that earns millions of pounds from the Home Office and stands to make millions more?'

'That's exactly what I'm telling you.'

'And you can prove it?'

'Every last bit of it.'

'Bloody hell,' said Pip. 'It's almost too much to take in.'

'What a complete and utter bastard!' growled Alex, thinking more about the criminal than the crime.

'I told you he was bent,' Rowan said. There was more than a trace of deep satisfaction in her voice.

'What are you going to do with it?' Pip asked.

'I've already spoken to a contact who is still at the *Guardian*,' she replied. 'I'm taking everything in to them now. With any luck, it will be tomorrow morning's front page. And, if it is, Simon Jones is finished.'

Simon Jones had undoubtedly been rattled by the draft article about the alleged affair. He'd deny it all, of course – though he very much hoped it wouldn't come to that. If he had things his way, the smears and fabrications of an embittered former employee would never see the light of day.

He lifted his glass to his lips and drained the contents.

'You do know that I'm on my way to see him right now?' Alex said.

'I do,' Rowan replied. 'I hope it goes well.'

'You don't think I should cancel seeing him in light of what you've just told me?'

'No, I don't,' she replied. 'I don't think there's any need. I see no reason for it to be anything other than a perfectly straightforward meeting between professionals, albeit one held at a rather late hour. And, from a slightly selfish point of view, I'd very much like to know what he's got to say to you.'

'How the hell did he think he was going to get away with it?' Alex asked, changing tack.

'Because people like Simon Jones think they're untouchable,' Rowan said. 'They think they can do whatever they want – that rules are for little people and don't apply to the likes of them.'

'And to think that he was going to be our next Prime Minister,' said Pip with a heavy trace of irony.

'Not any more he isn't,' Rowan replied. 'The thing is, I don't suppose it occurred to him that he'd ever get caught.'

Ten minutes later, Alex and Pip were parked in a quiet side street next to the block where Simon Jones had his apartment.

'Are you ready for this?' Pip asked him.

Alex shrugged his shoulders. 'Ready as I'll ever be,' he replied. He dialled Pip's number on his mobile phone and, having confirmed that the line between them was open, slipped the handset into his inside jacket pocket.

Chapter 40

As Alex approached the main doors at the front of the building, he was attempting to juggle three distinct sets of thoughts. The astonishing revelations from Rowan were, perhaps understandably, at the forefront of his mind. But thoughts of Becca weren't far behind. At the same time, he was also trying to keep a clear head about the stated purpose of the meeting he was about to walk into. If the Policing Minister really did want to talk to him about current policing challenges, Alex's sense of professionalism demanded that he ought to be ready with some answers. Even if the consequences of Rowan's discoveries meant that it was more than likely a complete waste of his time. If the *Guardian* ran the story the following morning – or at any point in the coming days – the chances that the Minister would ever make his speech were slim to none.

But it wasn't only his thoughts that Alex was juggling as he walked into the foyer of the building. It was his emotions too. And he wasn't entirely sure what it was that he was feeling. He wondered whether it might be nerves, though he insisted to himself that he really had nothing to be nervous about. He was there for a perfectly legitimate purpose and with the full knowledge of the Commissioner. And he certainly didn't feel in the least bit intimidated by the prospect of talking to Simon Jones. Politicians had never impressed him.

So, if it wasn't nerves, perhaps it was anxiety. Brought on by the knowledge that he was now privy to some fairly incendiary secrets. Or by the nagging suspicion that the Minister's request to meet with him had been motivated by something other than the desire to prepare for a speech. Or maybe, like Becca, it was anger he was feeling. Anger at Simon Jones. At his treatment of his young researcher. At the lies he had told. At his apparent crimes. At his astonishing greed. Anger at all that he represented as a member of the self-entitled, lawless elite.

Yes, he was angry. That had to be what it was.

Alex gave his name to the concierge at the reception desk and told him that he was there to see Simon Jones in apartment 143. Out of habit, he produced his warrant card for inspection. The concierge picked up the phone.

'There's a Mr Lewis here to see you, sir,' the man said in an Eastern European accent, before pausing to listen to the voice at the other end. 'Very good, sir,' he replied after a moment or two. 'I'll send him straight up.' He put the phone down and looked up at Alex. 'The lifts are straight ahead of you on the right hand side,' he instructed, pointing the way. 'Mr Jones's apartment is on the fourteenth floor.'

Sitting in the car outside, Pip could just about hear the sound of the concierge's voice, though she wasn't able to make out the detail of what he was actually saying. Still, it was better than nothing.

Alex stepped out of the lift on the fourteenth floor. A discreet metal plate on the wall opposite pointed the way to apartment 143. As he turned to walk down the corridor, he suddenly became conscious of a new feeling – one that hadn't been there before. It wasn't nerves. He'd already established that. And it wasn't anxiety. At least, not the kind he was familiar with. And it wasn't anger either, though that was still very much present. It was something distinct from any of those things. It was a sense of hesitation, he realised. Almost of foreboding. He tried to dismiss it. After all, he would be back in the car with Pip in less than an hour.

When he got to apartment 143, the door was ajar. There was a crack of warm light coming from inside that fell onto the toes of his shoes. Rather than push the door open – an act that would have seemed a little too presumptuous to him – he knocked gently. When he heard no reply, he knocked more loudly.

'It's open,' a voice boomed from inside. 'Come on in.' Simon Jones sounded friendly and welcoming enough.

Alex pushed the door. It opened into a well-appointed hallway, with a large mirror in an ornate frame on one wall and an impressive oil painting of what looked like the Yorkshire Moors on the other. The floor was polished stone and spotless. Alex wondered whether he should take his shoes off, but decided that perhaps it wasn't necessary. He patted his jacket pocket to reassure himself that his phone was there and he felt an unexpected gust of cold breeze coming from somewhere ahead of him.

There were doors off to the left and right, but they were closed. Having made sure that the front door was properly closed behind him, Alex followed the hallway round to the right, where it opened out into a large, open-plan living room. Everything about the place hinted at wealth and good taste: the craftsmanship evident in the furniture, the obvious quality of the enormous Persian rug that occupied the middle of the floor, the extensive artwork on display – not just paintings, but sculptures and various smaller ornaments too – the low-lying coffee table piled high with hardback books and highbrow magazines. The far wall was made entirely of glass, with spectacular views out over the River Thames.

Alex absorbed it all in a beat, even as he realised where the breeze was coming from. At the left-hand end of the glass wall, there was a sliding door that led out onto a broad balcony. It was open and Alex could see the Minister standing just outside.

'Good evening, sir,' Alex said loudly, managing to display a level of respect that he certainly didn't feel. It was strange to feel disdain for a man he'd never actually met before. Particularly one with such a celebrated reputation. But that was the way with those who were in the public eye – politicians in particular. People formed opinions about them without ever really knowing them. Except that, in this case, Alex felt as though he really did know Simon Jones. He thought that he knew exactly what kind of man he was.

The Minister turned around when Alex addressed him and stepped back inside the apartment. He had an end-of-day look about him. His tie was loose and the top button of his shirt was undone. It had come untucked at the back of his trousers and he either hadn't noticed or wasn't bothered. He wasn't wearing any shoes. His hair was ruffled and his cheeks were red: from standing out in the cold, Alex supposed. He was holding an empty glass tumbler. He smiled – a politician's smile, Alex thought – as he hastened across the room with his right hand outstretched, addressing Alex as 'Superintendent Lewis'.

'Please call me Alex,' Alex said as he accepted the Minister's handshake. Jones was half a head taller than him, thickset and in good physical shape. Alex guessed that he had been spending time in the gym that occupied part of the building's basement. Alex had seen the signs in the foyer.

'Alex it is then,' Jones said. 'Thank you so much for coming over this evening. What can I get you to drink?'

'I'm fine without, thank you,' Alex replied.

'Really?' Jones responded, looking surprised. He raised the glass he was holding. 'I'm going to have another. Are you sure I can't persuade you to join me?' He picked up the bottle of Macallan that was sitting on the coffee table and poured himself a generous measure.

'I'm fine,' Alex reiterated. He could smell the whisky as it flowed into the tumbler. He had smelt it on Jones's breath too.

'As you wish,' Jones replied. 'How's your day been?' he asked, in a seeming attempt at small talk.

'Busy,' Alex replied, doubting the sincerity of the question.

'You had a fatal stabbing recently, I hear.'

Alex realised that Jones had done his homework. Of course he had. He was the bloody Policing Minister. 'Sadly, yes,' Alex responded. 'And another, non-fatal, one earlier this week.'

Jones gestured to Alex to take a seat in one of the expansive sofas. He sat in the one opposite. 'Both teenagers, I suppose?' he asked.

Alex nodded.

'So what do you think is driving the violence?' he enquired.

And it occurred to Alex that some of his suspicions and reservations about the meeting might have been unfounded. Simon Jones really did appear to want to talk about operational policing challenges.

Out in the car, Pip was listening intently, trying to picture the scene in the flat. As with the concierge, she struggled to hear much of what Simon Jones was saying, but Alex's voice was clear enough. She switched her phone off loudspeaker and lifted it to her ear as he answered the question about knife crime.

He began by explaining that the challenge was significantly more complex than anyone wanted it to be – and that it wasn't going to be solved by passing more legislation or by demanding tougher prison sentences and ever greater levels of enforcement. 'It isn't a problem we're ever going to be able to arrest our way out of,' she heard him say. Which meant that it wasn't something that policing was ever going to be able to deal with in isolation. He talked about poverty and inequality and trauma as the root causes of a broad range of societal ills. He described the devastating long-term consequences of austerity, not just for law enforcement, but for the whole of the public sector.

Every now and then, his flow was interrupted by the Minister. Pip was unable to pick up on the detail of the questions, but from the answers Alex was giving, she could tell that Simon Jones wasn't necessarily convinced by everything he was hearing.

She checked the battery on her phone. The display told her that it was at fifty-three per cent. She imagined that the screen on Alex's mobile would be showing something similar.

'Are you really sure I can't get you something to drink?' Jones asked when they had reached a natural break in the conversation. He was swilling the peaty liquid around in the bottom of his own glass.

'Perhaps something soft?' Alex suggested, more out of politeness than anything else. The redness was still there in the Minister's cheeks. Perhaps it actually had more to do with the whisky than the cold, Alex thought.

'Let me see what I've got in the fridge,' Jones replied, pushing himself up from his seat.

'Only if it's not too much trouble,' Alex said, maintaining his courteous manner.

'No trouble,' came the reply as Jones walked towards an open door on the far side of the room, stumbling slightly on the way. 'I can offer you a can of Coke?' he called through a few moments later, from what Alex assumed must be the kitchen.

'That would be perfect,' Alex replied. 'Thank you.'

'There was something else I wanted to ask you about,' Jones said as he reappeared in the doorway.

'By all means,' Alex responded, immediately suspicious about what might be coming.

'Ice?' the Minister asked as he walked over to a side table that held a full tray of drinks bottles, together with a small ice bucket and a collection of glasses.

'No, thank you,' Alex replied.

Jones selected a clean glass and walked back across the room. He handed it to Alex, together with the red can of Coke.

'That's very kind of you,' said Alex, easing himself forward and placing both glass and can on the coffee table. 'Now, what else was it that you wanted to ask?'

'I wanted to talk to you about Becca Palmer,' the Policing Minister said.

Chapter 41

That was it: the first crack in the facade; the confirmation of the real purpose of the meeting; the realisation that Alex had been right all along. The past twenty minutes appeared to have been nothing more than a charade: a meaningless deceit. Alex had to work hard to maintain a steady tone.

'Becca Palmer?' he echoed as though he were in the midst of a negotiation. He wasn't prepared to offer anything more by way of a response until Simon Jones had revealed a good deal more regarding his intentions. He was finding the Minister's non-verbal signals difficult to read. He was standing a few feet away, avoiding direct eye contact, seemingly staring at something beyond Alex's right shoulder. And he was swaying a little as he stared. But, while it was becoming steadily more obvious that he'd had too much to drink, he wasn't giving anything else away.

'Am I right in thinking that you were the officer who helped Becca on Westminster Bridge?' Jones asked. His manner was polite. He shifted his weight from one foot to the other, working to maintain his balance.

'I was one of them, yes,' Alex replied.

'Thank you for what you did,' Jones said, suddenly renewing eye contact. 'Thank you for saving her life.'

'I was just doing my job,' Alex responded, caught a little off guard by the Minister's apparent sincerity. 'Any of my colleagues would have done exactly the same,' he said.

'Well, it was no small thing,' Jones replied. 'I dread to think what might have happened if you hadn't been there.'

It took a moment or two for Alex to respond. The expression of appreciation was unexpected – as was the fact that it sounded so genuine. He wondered what the Minister was up to. 'I'm glad I was able to help,' he said eventually.

Jones swallowed another mouthful of the single malt. 'Did you know that Becca was working for me until very recently?' he asked casually.

'She mentioned the fact, yes,' said Alex.

'Have you had any contact with her since?'

'I was called back to the bridge a second time,' Alex replied, choosing very deliberately to say no more than that. He had learned that it didn't necessarily require a lie to hide the full truth of a situation.

'Oh, so that was you as well, was it?'

'Yes it was.'

'Then I owe you my thanks twice over,' Jones said, his voice rising a little in volume as the whisky continued to work its effect on him. Alex watched as he finished his glass. The bottle on the coffee table was half-empty and Alex wondered how much of it had been drunk in the past couple of hours.

'As I said before,' Alex replied, 'I was just doing my job.'

'Becca is a remarkable young woman,' Jones said, changing the direction of the conversation. 'Intelligent, resourceful, capable. She was a rising star in my department. What's happened to her is incredibly sad.' In the absence of a question, Alex offered no answer. 'Having dealt with her on the bridge,' Jones continued, 'you're no doubt aware of the challenges she's been facing with her mental health.'

'I know that she's been having an incredibly tough time,' Alex replied, continuing to measure and limit his answers.

'It's her mental health that I wanted to talk to you about,' Jones said.

'Oh really?' Alex responded, his suspicions returning to the fore. 'Why's that?'

'I'm told that she's been saying things about me.'

'Oh really?' Alex replied. 'What things?' He was all but certain that he knew the truth, but he wanted to hear the Minister's version of events.

'Damaging things.'

'I'm sorry, sir, you're going to have to explain what you mean to me,' said Alex patiently, determined to make him do the work.

'She's told people that we've been having an affair,' Jones said.

Alex maintained his silence. He was waiting for Jones to incriminate himself. He hoped that Pip could hear what was being said. He found himself wishing that she was in the room with him.

'Obviously, it's not true,' the Minister added.

I don't believe you, Alex wanted to respond, though he was able to check himself once again. He was determined to find out exactly where Simon Jones was heading with his lies.

'I was wondering whether you might be willing to speak to her?' the Minister asked.

Another crack in the facade. A significantly larger one this time. Alex knew exactly what he needed to do. He began to feed the Minister rope – in the form of simple, open questions – and the Minister obliged each time by taking hold of it. Lowering his voice and adopting a pained expression, Jones told Alex that the allegations of an affair – the *false* allegations, he reiterated more than once – had come as an immense shock to him. He had been deeply upset by them and now they were casting long shadows over both his work and his personal life. He had been completely open with his wife about the situation and, though he knew he had her trust and support, it was inevitably distressing for her as well. He was a devoted husband and father and he hated to think that the situation might become a source of enduring pain for the people he loved. It all seemed so unfair.

As he paced around the room, steadying himself every now and then against the back of a chair or sofa, his story began to flow as smoothly as the whisky. Becca Palmer was a junior member of staff, who, right from her earliest days at the Home Office, had displayed significant potential. Everyone had noticed it. He'd tried to do the right thing by investing in her personal and professional development, but she'd somehow started to become fixated with him. And he had been at a loss to understand why – he certainly hadn't given her any reason to regard him as anything other than her boss. Her boss's boss, in fact. But, in the weeks that followed, it had become increasingly apparent that she was unwell. Even then, all that the Minister and his team had wanted to do was help and support her. But her attendance at work had become increasingly patchy and elements of her behaviour had become steadily more chaotic. In the end – and with enormous reluctance – he and his senior advisor had agreed on the need for her to take some time away from her role. It had therefore been suggested to her that she should take a break from the pressures and demands of work.

Alex had been listening intently for several minutes – not just to the words spoken by the Minister, but also to what was being left unsaid. He had been trying hard to maintain an element of objectivity, but the lies and half-truths appeared to be piling up. And when Jones suggested that Becca had been told to take a break from work, he felt that he had no option but to step back into the conversation. 'Becca suggested to me that she'd actually been fired,' Alex said. It was his first challenge to the narrative Jones was offering, though he was careful to ensure that it was no more than a gentle nudge. There was nothing noticeably confrontational in his tone.

'Goodness me, no,' the Minister replied with arched eyebrows. He stopped pacing the room. 'I'm positive she was told that we wanted her to come back when she was feeling better. That's certainly how I understood it.'

Had Alex not known better, he might almost have been persuaded to take Jones at his word. He was definitely continuing to sound plausible enough. But Alex did know better. He decided it was time to move the conversation on. 'So what did you want me to talk to her about?' he asked, cutting to the chase.

'Ah ... yes ... well ... that's the sensitive bit,' Jones blustered, pouring himself a fresh glass of malt. 'The thing is,' he continued, 'I was hoping you might be willing to have a quiet word with her – and ask her to stop saying things about me that aren't true. I'm sure you can appreciate how damaging these sorts of unfounded allegations can be. Particularly for a man in my position.'

'Why me?' Alex asked, finding it increasingly difficult to maintain a neutral tone. The apparent deception was becoming increasingly hard to bear.

'Because I'm hoping that she might be willing to listen to you,' Jones responded. 'You're the man who saved her life after all.'

You bastard, Alex thought. *You complete and utter bastard*. He could scarcely believe what he was hearing. Having apparently pushed a fragile young woman to the very edge of life, Jones was now asking a man he had only just met to help him cover his tracks. It was sickening.

'The situation has become rather more pressing,' continued Jones, clearly oblivious to what Alex was thinking and feeling, 'because I'm told that she's been talking to a journalist.'

'Oh?' replied Alex, saying no more for fear of saying something he might regret.

'Some sort of freelancer,' Jones explained. 'No one important. But you can see my dilemma.'

Alex was perfectly well aware of the Minister's dilemma, and he knew full well that it wasn't the one being portrayed. 'What do you mean?' he managed to ask.

'Well, as you know, I've got this speech coming up at the party conference,' Jones explained. 'And it might well just be the most important one I've ever been asked to make. We're at a critical stage in our public-sector reform programme and we really can't afford to be distracted by the made-up stories of someone who isn't well.' He stopped himself. 'I must apologise,' he said with raised hands. 'That probably came across as rather harsh.'

'Yes it did,' Alex said bluntly. He could feel the anger rising up again from somewhere very deep inside him. He had reached the point where he no longer felt able to measure his words and he spoke again before he could stop himself. 'Particularly as I believe that Becca Palmer is telling the truth.'

In the street below, Pip gasped. She and Alex had tried to rehearse the conversation with Jones on the way over and they had covered what they thought were all the likely possibilities.

One thing they had definitely agreed on was that Alex wasn't going to confront the Minister – that he was going to listen to what Jones had to say and then he was going to make his excuses and leave.

'Shit!' she muttered to herself.

Chapter 42

Back in the apartment, Simon Jones was staring at Alex with a strange expression on his face. Eventually, he broke the silence. 'What did you just say?' he demanded.

'You heard what I said,' Alex replied firmly, fixing the Minister with his gaze. He was done with the deception.

'I'm not sure that I did,' Jones replied slowly. There was an edge to his voice that hadn't been there before, as though he was defying Alex to repeat what effectively amounted to a direct accusation that he was lying. And it seemed clear from his manner and tone that he was expecting Alex to back down.

But Alex was doing nothing of the sort. 'I said that I believe Becca Palmer is telling the truth,' he repeated.

Jones opened his mouth to respond, then closed it again. A swift succession of expressions and emotions passed across his face: from anger, to confusion, to frustration, to fear. Alex could see the inner battle Jones was fighting as he tried to work out what to say, and he felt no sympathy whatsoever for him.

Alex recognised that he'd gone further in the conversation than he and Pip had agreed he should, but he had no regrets. In any case, he wasn't sure that it could have turned out any other way. The lies had become too brazen and too great. And the Minister's shameless attempt to use Alex to run interference for him was a disgrace. There was no way he could have allowed that to pass without challenge.

'What on earth are you talking about?' Jones said at last, attempting a kind of bonhomie that was both forced and contrived. He seemed to have settled on redoubled denial as his chosen approach.

'I think you know exactly what I'm talking about,' Alex replied.

'Well, I'm afraid you're going to have to spell it out for me,' Jones remarked obstinately, his words beginning to slur.

'I believe Becca Palmer,' Alex said simply. His voice was calm, but his words were damning of the man he was speaking to.

'What do you mean, you believe her?' Jones spluttered, his face starting to become blotchy.

'I believe her when she says that you had an affair with her.'

'But it's not true,' Jones insisted, almost stamping his foot as he did so. His mood was starting to become more unpredictable and he was retreating desperately towards the familiarity of his lies. 'And, in any case, it's just one person's word against another's. How can you possibly believe her and not me?'

Alex stood up and looked at his watch. The constant denials were exhausting and he could see no point in prolonging the conversation any further. 'I think perhaps I should go now,' he said.

In the car outside, Pip relaxed just a fraction. She wanted Alex out of there. There was certainly no point in him staying. She'd only been able to hear one end of the conversation in the apartment, but it was obvious that Jones was sticking fast to his story.

At the same time, she was also thinking about Becca: a young woman without wealth or power or connections, who had paid such a heavy price for the actions of an older man who had taken advantage of every single one of those things in order to take advantage of her.

Fate being what it is, it was at precisely that moment that Becca Palmer suddenly appeared, crossing the road in front of Pip, seemingly headed straight for the apartment block.

'But you haven't answered my question,' Simon Jones complained as Alex made to leave. 'Why would you believe her and not me?'

So many reasons, thought Alex to himself, but he spoke only one. 'Because I've seen the photograph,' he said.

'What photograph?' responded Jones with a look of alarm on his face.

'Does it really matter what photograph?' said Alex wearily.

'Of course it does,' Jones replied. 'If I don't know what you've seen, how can I possibly hope to explain it to you.' He took yet another large gulp of whisky. Alex had completely lost track of how much he'd drunk.

'It's a picture of the two of you, standing out there on your balcony, with the Houses of Parliament in the background,' Alex clarified, gesturing towards the still open door.

'What?'

Alex could tell that Jones was stalling. 'You and Becca, arms around one another, out on your balcony,' he said.

'So what if we were?' Jones complained evasively. 'It's hardly proof of an affair.'

'Perhaps not,' Alex replied. 'Were it not for the fact that you have said quite clearly that Becca Palmer has never been in your apartment.'

And, as he said it, the crack in Jones's facade opened up into something more closely resembling a chasm. His face fell as the implications of what Alex had just told him found their mark.

'How can you possibly know that?' he said, in a voice that was trying to be assertive but that sounded very much like defeat.

'Becca told me,' Alex replied, watching the Minister's shoulders slump as his lies found their way back to their source. 'You said it to her on Sunday night, in the corridor outside your front door.'

'So you knew she was here?'

'I did.'

'And you knew there was a journalist with her?'

Alex nodded.

And, for a brief moment, it looked as though Jones might respond in anger, perhaps with some sort of self-righteous allegation about there being a conspiracy against him, worked out between the police and the press. But the inclination to fight back seemed to desert him just as swiftly as it had appeared. 'Is she going to run the story?' he asked meekly. The rope that Alex had been feeding him was beginning to form a noose around his neck.

'That's none of my business,' Alex replied. 'My job is trying to stop people jumping off London bridges.'

'But she's lying,' Jones insisted, clinging to the fragments of his story like a drowning man to the debris of a shipwreck. 'And her lies are going to ruin me.'

'Becca!' Pip shouted urgently as she shoved the car door closed with her foot. She was pressing her mobile to her ear with one hand while using the other to cover the phone's microphone in an effort to muffle her voice. It made running awkward. The younger woman had already disappeared out of view. By the time Pip rounded the corner, Becca was practically at the door to the block. 'Becca!' she shouted again.

Becca stopped and turned around. The look on her face was one of pure determination. She didn't seem at all surprised to see Pip.

Pip stopped running and caught her breath. 'What on earth are you doing here?' she asked.

'I've come to collect my things,' Becca replied evenly as if the answer was obvious.

'Your things?'

'I've come to collect my belongings from Simon's place.'

'But why?' Pip asked. 'Why now, I mean?'

'Because I know Alex is up there,' Becca replied, glancing up towards the top of the building. 'And I thought that him being there would make things a little bit more straightforward.'

'How did you know he was there?' Pip asked.

'Rowan told me.'

'Does she know you're here?'

'No.'

'What about your sister?'

Becca shook her head.

'Where does she think you are?'

'She probably thinks I'm still in my room.'

'Oh, Becca,' Pip responded. 'You can't keep doing things like this to her.' It was an unwitting echo of almost exactly the words Alex had used in the back of the van on the night that Becca had run away.

Becca looked at her with a mixture of surprise and shame. It seemed to Pip that she'd got it into her head to come to the apartment and that she hadn't the slightest thought to the impact of her actions on anyone else. Pip knew Becca wasn't

294

trying to be unkind. She understood that it was a symptom of her illness: of her still fragile and unpredictable mental state.

'You need to come with me,' Pip said gently. She still had her mobile phone held to her ear. She was trying to listen to Alex, even as she was talking to Becca.

'Where to?' Becca asked reluctantly. In spite of Pip's challenge, it was apparent that she still wanted to continue into the building.

'To the car,' Pip replied. 'It's parked just around the corner. We need to call your sister and then we need to talk.'

A couple of miles away, in King's Cross, Rowan Blake had been holding court in a large conference room at the headquarters of the *Guardian*. The recently appointed editor of the paper was there, along with a number of her colleagues and the senior in-house lawyer. There was an array of paperwork laid out on the large table in the middle of the room and everyone present had been listening intently to Rowan's every word.

'Well, I'm satisfied,' the editor announced, once Rowan had finished answering a lengthy series of rapid-fire questions about the evidence she'd presented. 'What about you?' the editor asked, turning to the lawyer.

'It seems pretty clear to me,' the smartly dressed woman agreed. 'I'll need to read the copy before we go to press, but the facts appear to be sound.'

'Then we run with the Soteria Solutions story tomorrow morning,' the editor instructed, 'follow it up with the affair on Friday, and cover the fallout from it all on Saturday.' She turned and looked at Rowan. 'Bloody good work,' she said. 'Make sure you give Jones and the Soteria Solutions people an opportunity to comment before you file.'

*

Pip walked Becca back to the car. The open line to Alex was on her work phone, so she retrieved her personal phone from her coat pocket to ring Helen. She was about to make the call when she looked at Becca and put her finger to her lips.

Alex had run out of patience. Simon Jones had continued with a flurry of self-pitying denials and protestations and Alex could think of no good reason to take the conversation any further. 'I really think that I should be going now,' he said, glancing over his host's shoulder, towards the hallway and the front door.

'Wait!' Jones pleaded. 'Please sit back down.' He was looking and sounding increasingly desperate.

Alex chose to remain standing, but made no immediate move to leave. He watched as the Minister's face betrayed another stumbling succession of emotions and wondered what possible fiction the politician might try to conjure up next. Jones remained silent for several long seconds, perhaps wondering the same thing.

'Can I ask you a question?' he said hesitantly.

Alex shrugged.

'Even if there were some truth in this ridiculous notion of an affair,' he ventured uncertainly, 'would you really stand aside and allow it to ruin a man?'

'So there is some truth to it?' Alex responded, feeling a burst of contempt for the man standing in front of him. But Jones was far too preoccupied with his own train of thought to hear the challenge.

'Would you really stand aside and allow an allegation of a meaningless affair to ruin a man?' the Minister repeated. 'To ruin his marriage and his family? His career and his reputation?' The agitated questions spilled out of him. The depth of his self-absorption was extraordinary to behold.

'But what about Becca?' Alex demanded.

'What about her?' Jones replied, looking genuinely surprised by the question.

'What about the effect that all of this has had on her?'

'Why should that matter?' the Minister asked, sounding confused.

'Seriously?' Alex replied. He was struggling to believe what he was hearing.

'What the hell has she got to lose?' Jones spluttered. 'I am a minister in Her Majesty's Government. I have a home and a wife and young children. I'm the one with everything to lose.'

'But Becca Palmer almost lost her life,' Alex replied.

Chapter 43

'Don't be so ridiculous!' Jones responded irritably. He was pacing backwards and forwards again, staring at the floor.

'What do you mean?' Alex asked, not giving an inch of ground.

'Suggesting that she almost lost her life,' the Minister complained. 'That's ridiculous. You're making her out to sound like some sort of victim.'

'But isn't that exactly what she is?' Alex replied, his voice firm and clear. 'The victim of a powerful man and his lies?'

The expression on the Minister's face changed in an instant. It became suddenly hostile and aggressive. It was obvious that he wasn't used to being challenged in this way – to having his failings and deceptions held up in front of him like a mirror. 'Oh, for fuck's sake!' he shouted, losing for a second both his composure and his control. 'She's the one who seduced me.'

There it was. In a single, unguarded, angry, drunken moment, the final disintegration of Simon Jones's facade. And, with it, a grotesque shift from denial to blame. Because it wasn't his fault. It was hers.

Alex stared at him, struggling to find the words to say. Simon Jones was proving himself to be exactly the sort of shallow, hollow man who represented practically everything that Alex despised: manipulative, abusive, misogynistic, truth-twisting, arrogant, self-serving, corrupt. Alex had to resist the urge to take a swing at him. 'She seduced you?' he asked in disbelief. 'You cannot possibly be serious,' he continued, making no attempt to disguise the anger he was feeling. 'Becca Palmer is a junior member of your staff. She's twenty-four years old. She's incredibly vulnerable. And you're a middle-aged, married, senior politician.'

Jones closed his eyes, his sense of self-righteous rage seeming to vanish as swiftly as it had surfaced. He had the look of a man undone; of a man caught in a snare of his own making. 'Would you mind if we got some air?' he said very quietly.

'You can do whatever you want,' Alex responded bluntly. 'I'm leaving.'

'Just for a moment or two,' Jones pleaded. 'I've made a terrible mistake.' All of the bluster was gone. All of the hubris and conceit of a man who had thought himself untouchable. He looked like a two-bit salesman with nothing left to sell. Had Alex not known the truth of the situation, he might almost have been tempted to feel sorry for the man.

Jones reached out with a shaking hand and poured himself yet another glass of malt. And, against his better judgement, Alex followed him as he shuffled, shoeless, out onto the balcony.

It was bitingly cold outside. Alex was wearing a shirt and V-necked woollen jumper beneath his jacket, but, even in combination, they offered precious little protection against the elements. The Minister, dressed only in a shirt, suit trousers and socks, seemed oblivious to the significant drop in temperature.

The only distraction from the cold was the view, which was even more spectacular now that they were out in the open air. To his left, Alex could see the Thames winding its silvery way towards Hammersmith and beyond, flanked on either side by towering riverside developments, interrupted every now and then by the run-down remains of an older London. Huge barges pulled at their moorings in the centre of the strong current, as the four smokeless chimneys of Battersea Power Station stood like sentries to the east of Chelsea Bridge. To his right, for all the compelling sights of Parliament and the city beyond, Alex was unable to look past Westminster Bridge: the place where he had first met Becca Palmer. He could see the exact spot where she had been standing, on the wrong side of the balustrade.

'It was just an affair,' Jones mumbled, as much to himself as to Alex. 'People have affairs all the time.'

Alex was barely listening. In his mind, he was back on the bridge, watching the slow, shuffling movements of Becca's feet on the terrifyingly narrow ledge.

'Has she suggested that I've committed any crime against her?' Jones asked. His voice was a little louder this time. He stood up a little straighter. He appeared to be searching desperately for a way out.

'Not against her, no,' Alex replied, his mind jerking back into the present. He wanted to get back inside, into the warm. Then he wanted to leave. He was sick of the sight and the sound of the man.

'Then why write about it in a newspaper?' Jones responded, missing the nuance in Alex's answer. He'd drunk too much for subtlety. 'Why ruin a man over something so insignificant?'

'Insignificant?' Alex snapped, the anger rising in him all over again. Jones appeared utterly incapable of seeing the world from any perspective but his own; unconcerned about the impact of his behaviour on anyone else. It was perfectly obvious that it had only ever been about him. Insignificant? Alex looked back at Westminster Bridge. Back at the place where he had been. Where Becca had been. *It wasn't insignificant to her*, he thought to himself. 'Insignificant?' he repeated. 'Is that what it was to you?'

Jones shrank back in avoidance of the question. 'What am I going to do?' he asked, in a slurred attempt to change the subject. The effects of the whisky were becoming steadily more pronounced. He swallowed another mouthful. 'My reputation is going to be ruined,' he whimpered.

From denial, to blame, to self-pity.

You probably should have thought about that before you decided to take advantage of Becca Palmer, thought Alex.

Jones turned and looked at him with an expression of desperation on his face. 'What am I going to tell my wife?'

'I'm afraid that's not a question I can answer for you,' Alex said.

And, at that, Simon Jones started to cry. Large tears pooled in the corners of his eyes and rolled down his cheeks.

'I think we should go back inside,' Alex said as his basic sense of humanity momentarily overtook his immense, intense dislike of the man.

But the Minister didn't seem to hear him. He turned away to face the river and, as his faltering feet tried to follow the inebriated movement of his upper body, he stumbled. Reaching out to steady himself against the balcony rail, he succeeded only in knocking the glass tumbler out of his own hand. It fell, end over end, and disintegrated on the polished white stone at his feet. The metaphor wasn't lost on Alex: the falling glass and the falling man. It would have been almost perfect, were it not for the fact that Jones had yet to hit the ground.

'I'm ruined,' he whispered as he sank to his haunches, one hand still hanging on to the metal railing next to him.

In spite of all that had gone before, Alex actually felt a

301

measure of concern for him. 'Careful where you put your feet!' Alex called out as he noticed the Minister adjusting his weight and position. But his warning came too late. Alex heard the unmistakable crunch of glass beneath stockinged skin. 'Careful!' Alex repeated more loudly, taking a step closer.

'Leave me alone,' Jones insisted. He seemed to be no more aware of the glass than he was of the cold. He struggled to his feet and began to move along the balcony, further away from Alex. As he did so, he left a smeared trail of blood on the paved floor.

Down in the car, Pip's concerns were growing. Jones's last remarks hadn't quite been loud enough for her to pick up on, but she'd heard Alex's raised voice – the warning to be careful about where Jones put his feet – immediately beforehand. She had absolute confidence in Alex's ability to handle whatever might be happening, but, all the same, she was beginning to wonder whether she ought to start making her way to the fourteenth floor.

Just in case.

Becca was sitting quietly in the seat next to her, unable to hear what Pip could hear, but seeming to understand that her own questions and concerns needed to wait.

'Call your sister,' Pip said quietly, handing her other phone over to Becca to use.

'We need to get you back inside,' Alex said to Jones, stepping forward and closing the gap between the two of them. The Minister's face was turning a shade of purple-tinted blue. The loss of blood combined with the effects of the cold was obviously getting to him, whether he was aware of it or not. For the moment, Alex's instincts as a police officer and as a negotiator were overriding every other consideration.

'I thought you were leaving,' Jones replied.

'I'm not leaving you like this.'

'Like what?' responded a confused Jones.

'Look at your feet,' Alex instructed him.

Jones stared blankly at the ground.

'You've cut them,' Alex explained.

'Have I?'

'Yes, on the broken glass.' Alex reached out and took hold of the Minister's arm. 'Let's sit you down inside and I'll take a look at the damage.'

Pip opened the car door and stepped out onto the pavement. 'Stay there,' she said to Becca, who was in the process of tapping her sister's number into Becca's phone.

Leaving Becca in the vehicle, Pip walked around to the front of the building. The reception desk was unoccupied and the entrance was locked. She gave the doors a rattle, but there was no response from inside. She turned her attention to the keypad mounted on the wall and considered disturbing the occupants of one of the other apartments in order to gain access to the foyer. But, from what she was able to hear, things appeared to have settled down upstairs. Alex seemed to have the situation under control – for now at least.

Reluctantly, she decided to wait.

Feeling immensely relieved to be in from the cold, Alex slid the glass door closed and walked the Minister slowly to the nearest chair. Though he was limping heavily, Jones displayed no signs of feeling any pain. The scarlet scuffs of blood on the floor marked his progress across the room.

'Let's have a look at you, shall we?' Alex suggested.

'I need a drink,' Jones replied.

'No you don't,' Alex countered, placing a firm hand on the Minister's shoulder as he attempted to stand up. He pushed Jones back into a seated position, crouched down next to him and started to carefully peel his socks off. It was an incongruous sight: a drunk, bloodied and confused Member of Parliament being attended to with great care by a plain-clothed police officer acting out of duty rather than affection. 'Have you got any kind of first-aid kit in the flat?' Alex asked. Having successfully removed the socks, he was examining a series of cuts on the soles of Jones's feet. He could see several fragments of glass half-buried in the callused skin. The bleeding wasn't particularly heavy, but it was persistent.

'There might be something in the kitchen,' Jones replied drunkenly.

'Let me see what I can find,' Alex said as he stood up. 'Are you going to be all right if I leave you there for a minute or two?'

'Of course I will be,' mumbled Jones, his body listing over to one side.

Alex reached out a hand to steady him, before turning and walking towards the door in the corner of the room. He checked over his shoulder to make sure that Jones was still seated and upright before disappearing into the kitchen.

Pip had retreated back to the warmth of the car when Alex's voice came through clearly on the line. Becca had finished speaking to her sister and was sitting quietly in the front passenger seat. Alex was speaking in a whisper, but appeared to have taken the phone out of his jacket pocket.

'Are you getting all this, Pip?' he asked.

'Some of it,' she replied keenly. 'Are you OK? What's happening up there?'

'Long story,' he whispered, 'but I'm fine. Jones has cut himself on some broken glass and I'm in his kitchen, looking for a first-aid kit.'

Pip could hear the sounds of drawers and cupboards being opened. 'Do you want me to come up and help?' she asked. She'd made the swift decision not to mention the fact that Becca was sitting alongside her in the car. She didn't want to give him anything else to worry about.

'No need,' he replied. 'I'm going to patch him up and then get the hell out of here.'

'You're sure?'

'I'm sure,' Alex responded. 'He's drunk, but he's not going to give me any bother.'

'What's he said to you?'

'I'll tell you everything when I come down in a few minutes,' Alex replied, 'but he's admitted to the affair.'

'Bastard!' Pip snapped before she could stop herself. *Bastard*. She flicked her eyes left, concerned that the expletive and her brief show of emotion might have unsettled Becca. But Becca seemed unperturbed. She was listening intently, obviously trying to work out what might be happening up in the apartment.

'You're being far too polite about him,' Alex replied. 'I actually came very close to punching him.'

'That doesn't sound like you,' Pip responded.

'It's not, which is why I didn't do it,' Alex said. 'But he is a truly vile human being.'

'So why are you bothering to look after him now?'

'I've been asking myself the same question,' Alex replied.

*

Alex put his mobile back into his jacket pocket. The line to Pip remained open, but the battery was down to ten per cent. As he resumed his search of the cupboards, he could hear the ringtone of another phone breaking the silence in the next-door room. The call went unanswered. A moment or two later, the same phone rang again and Alex heard the sounds of movement.

'Stay where you are,' he called through the half-open door. 'I'll be with you in a moment or two.'

There was no reply from the Minister.

Alex opened the last of the kitchen drawers and, having found nothing resembling first-aid equipment, instead ran some warm water into a medium-sized mixing bowl. He tipped a generous helping of salt into the water and grabbed a couple of fresh tea towels from a neat pile at one end of the heavy marble worktop.

When he returned to the main room, Jones was no longer sitting in his chair. Alex looked behind the door and saw that the Minister was standing next to the tray of glasses, with a new bottle of whisky in his hand.

The phone was ringing for a third time.

'Don't you think you should get that,' Alex asked, looking at Jones with a mixture of frustration and exasperation. He was starting to feel as though he was completely wasting his time on a man seemingly ungrateful for even the smallest amount of compassion or care.

'It will only be my wife,' Jones mumbled. As if she didn't matter.

'But it might be important.'

'It rarely is,' the Minister replied, attempting to fill a clean glass from the bottle and spilling much of the drink on the floor.

'You really don't need that,' Alex said, nodding at the glass.

'I'll be the judge of what I do and don't need,' came the prickly reply.

Alex put the bowl of water and the tea towels down on the coffee table. 'I still need to look at your feet,' he said, deciding reluctantly that he should make one last attempt to help the Minister before making his final excuses and leaving.

'I'll be fine,' Jones responded, with a dismissive wave of his hand.

The phone rang a fourth time and, through some combination of irritation and innate inquisitiveness, Alex picked it up from where it was lying on the sofa. 'It's Camilla Lane,' he announced, holding the screen up for inspection.

'What the hell does she want?' Jones complained as he stumbled towards Alex, spilling more of his drink in the process. He snatched the phone from Alex and connected the call. 'What?' he demanded impatiently.

Alex could just about make out a female voice at the other end of the line, but he couldn't hear what Camilla was saying. Instead, he watched the change in Jones's body language and facial expressions. As the seconds ticked by, the looseness that comes with drunkenness was gradually replaced by the onset of an unsettled – and, for Alex, unsettling – rigidity. The Minister's brow deepened. His eyes darkened. His cheeks flushed an even brighter red and then drained of all colour.

'What the fuck did you just say?' he yelled into the phone.

Chapter 44

As soon as Pip heard the Minister shout, she was straight back out of the car. 'Stay where you are,' she ordered Becca, before sprinting back round to the front of the building.

'Fucking hell!' she heard Jones bellow.

'Did you fucking know about this?' Jones was still holding his phone, but he was addressing his enraged question at Alex, flecks of spittle scattering as he spoke. His demeanour and mood had shifted beyond all recognition, and in a matter of moments. He was incandescent.

'Know about what?' Alex replied as calmly as he could manage. The atmosphere in the apartment had changed as markedly and rapidly as Jones's mood. It was crackling with intensity and aggression and menace. Instinctively, Alex found himself rechecking the layout of the room – noting the positions of each item of furniture and looking for potential obstacles and hazards. Jones was once again standing between him and the hallway. Between him and the way out of the flat.

Alex was partway through his rapid visual sweep when Jones drew his arm swiftly backwards and hurled the glass he was holding. It missed Alex by a fairly comfortable distance – smashing noisily against a wall somewhere behind him – but, as a statement of hostility, it hit the mark. Instinct kicking in, Alex took a couple of defensive steps backwards.

'About the fucking *Guardian* newspaper,' Jones shouted. 'Some kind of article tomorrow morning about Soteria-fucking-Solutions.' His eyes were wild and there was now a pronounced vein running in an erratic line up the centre of his forehead. The hand that had been holding the glass was now a fist.

From denial, to blame, to self-pity, to rage.

Alex was the one who had confronted him about the affair. Alex had known about Becca's visit to the flat. He had known that Rowan was there too. And that Rowan was a journalist. Somewhere in the back of the Minister's storming, surging, whisky-addled mind, the idea seemed to be forming that the police officer now standing across the room from him was somehow responsible for the story that the *Guardian* were planning to run in the morning. Jones must have realised that he was done for. Completely and utterly done for. And Alex was about to become the focus of all his fury.

'I don't understand,' Alex said, taking another uneasy step back in an attempt to give himself both space and time to react.

Jones started to advance towards him.

'Easy now, Simon,' said Alex, addressing the Minister by his Christian name for the first time. He had his hands raised defensively in front of him and was trying to keep his voice steady. He knew that he needed to calm the situation down. He took several swift steps to his right, ensuring that one of the large sofas was positioned between him and the man who was presenting an increasingly significant threat to him.

Jones was halted momentarily by a loud and insistent voice at the other end of the phone line – Camilla Lane trying to reason with him, Alex suspected – but the Minister's response to whatever she might have been saying was to pitch the mobile handset at Alex. It missed his head by inches and broke into several pieces as it skidded across the stone floor.

Alex pulled his own phone out of his pocket. 'I need a hand up here, Pip,' he said quickly.

'What the fuck do you think you're doing?' Jones snarled.

Outside on the pavement, Pip had heard the sound of first the glass and then the phone smashing. She had heard the Minister's raised voice and his menacing tone. Most clearly of all, she had heard Alex asking for help. From the tone of his voice, she understood straight away that he was in real trouble and when her concerned reply to him yielded no further response, she began pressing a rapid succession of doorbells, willing someone – anyone – to answer. With all her focus on the intercom and the door and whatever was happening upstairs, she didn't see Becca approaching until she was standing right next to her.

'What's happening?' Becca asked, her face taut and her voice a mixture of fear and concern.

Before Pip could respond – before she could yell at Becca to go back to the car – a male voice crackled on the intercom. 'Hello?'

'Police,' Pip shouted, her heart pounding. 'I need you to let me in right now!'

After a moment's hesitation, she heard the buzz and felt the mechanism in the door ease. She shoved it open and sprinted into the foyer. Giving up on the idea of sending Becca back to the car – realising that she might, in fact, be able to do something useful – she reached over the reception counter and grabbed the desk phone. 'Call 999,' she instructed bluntly as she pushed the handset into Becca's anxious grasp. There was no time for pleasantries. 'Ask for the police, give them the address, and tell them there's an officer needing urgent assistance.' She placed particular emphasis on the words 'urgent assistance'. As soon as the operator heard them spoken, Pip knew that they would prompt an immediate reaction. It was a distress call. *The* distress call. The one radio message guaranteed to get police officers from all around to drop whatever they were doing and to get to a location as fast as they could. 'Have you got that?' she shouted back over her shoulder as she started running in the direction of the lifts.

Becca was already dialling. 'Urgent assistance, yes,' she replied, half to Pip, half to herself. 'Police,' she said as soon as the person at the other end of the line asked her which emergency service she required.

'Wedge the front door open,' Pip yelled back down the corridor as she repeatedly pressed the call button on the lift, 'and wait there for them to arrive.'

'Who are you talking to?' the Minister spat, his face a picture of suspicion and hostility.

'Just a friend,' Alex replied, leaving the line open and putting his phone back into his pocket, his eyes not leaving the man on the other side of the sofa.

When Jones moved one way, Alex moved the other. They were like two boxers circling a ring. Albeit one without rules or referees. All the while, Jones remained between Alex and the front door – barring the only possible route of escape from the apartment.

'And is your friend fucking in on it too?' Jones demanded aggressively, picking up the original whisky bottle that was still sitting on the coffee table and taking a large swig from it.

'In on what?' Alex responded, his palms still raised in an attempt at conciliation.

'This fucking plot to ruin my fucking life,' Jones growled as he stumbled over a chair leg.

'I'm not involved in any kind of plot, Simon,' Alex insisted. 'I'm only here because you asked me to be here, remember? I'm here because I was told that you wanted to talk to me about current policing challenges. That's it. Whatever else it is that you're talking about now is none of my business.'

'I don't fucking believe you,' Jones snarled as he started to boil over. He put the bottle down and picked up an expensive-looking bronze bust of a galloping racehorse and pitched it two-handed at Alex, who managed to duck just in time. It thudded hard against the wall and fell harmlessly to the floor behind him. But Jones was just getting started. He followed it up with a table lamp that snagged on its own power cable as he threw it and fell short of its intended target. Then he reached out and grabbed hold of a large book of *National Geographic* photographs and raised it above his head.

'You don't believe me about what?' Alex shouted, all of his senses on edge. He realised that he was dealing with a man who was fast vanishing beyond reason and that the threat he was facing was only likely to intensify. If he could just manage to keep Jones talking, he might be able to find some sort of way to defuse the situation.

'I don't believe you about anything,' Jones bellowed, allowing the book to drop to the floor. 'You're a fucking liar and now you're going to fucking pay!' And with that, he launched himself forward with such unexpected speed and ferocity that Alex was unable to react in time.

Jones leapt onto the sofa that had been offering Alex his only real protection and hurled himself over the back of it. The two men collided and crashed to the floor, knocking the wind out of Alex. As he gasped for breath and wrestled furiously to defend himself, he realised immediately that the man now on top of him was significantly stronger than he was.

The lifts seemed to take forever to return to the ground floor. Phone still held to her ear, Pip could hear Alex trying to reason with Jones and she could tell that the situation was worsening. She contemplated taking the stairs but knew that it would have been self-defeating. She needed to save every last bit of her energy for whatever was to come.

When the doors finally opened, she stepped inside and jabbed the button for the fourteenth floor. Then, as the lift started moving, her phone went dead. She stared at the hand-set. No reception.

'Shit!' she yelled.

Alex was on his back on the floor, struggling frantically, his body surging with anxiety and adrenaline. Jones was on top of him, trying to gain control of Alex's flailing limbs. The toxic blend of whisky and wickedness and rage meant that he had lost all control of himself.

Somehow – he wasn't sure how – Alex managed to pull his right arm free. But he knew not to punch. The only thing a punch was likely to achieve was a collection of broken fingers. So he drove the heel of his hand into the bridge of Jones's nose with as much force and ferocity as he could muster. He heard the crunch of cartilage and bone as he found his target. And he heard the howl of pain as he felt Jones's weight shift to one side.

Summoning up every last ounce of his strength, Alex heaved upwards and managed to push his assailant to one side. Jones collapsed against the back of the sofa, his hands clutched to his face.

Alex struggled to his feet and started hobbling towards the hallway, his movement hindered significantly by a heavy blow to the hip that he must have taken when he fell to the floor.

He had made it as far as the entrance to the hallway when a flailing Jones rugby-tackled him from behind. As Alex hit the ground for the second time, his head smacked hard against the stone, leaving him momentarily at the edge of consciousness.

It was all the advantage Jones needed.

The lift doors opened on the fourteenth floor. Pip checked the sign and raced in the direction of apartment 143. Thank goodness she'd double-checked the number with Alex earlier in the evening.

She reached the solid oak door and pushed hard against it. It didn't move.

'Alex!' she shouted as she hammered on the wood. At the very least, she wanted him to know that she was there. That she was doing absolutely everything she could to get to him.

Alex's head was pounding. His thoughts were foggy. He was face down on the floor and Jones was on top of him, pummelling his upper body with a succession of heavy blows, while he spewed out a series of hate-filled obscenities.

'You fucking bastard . . .'

'You've fucking ruined me . . .'

And finally, 'I'm going to fucking kill you.'

Chapter 45

Simon Jones had taken complete leave of his senses. Something had snapped inside of him and he had become untethered from both sanity and reality.

And it seemed that there was nothing that an increasingly desperate Alex could do about it. He didn't have sufficient breath to respond verbally. And he didn't have sufficient strength to respond physically. He was struggling with everything he had but finding it almost impossible to land any blows of his own. Jones was too heavy. Too powerful. Too deranged.

He could hear Pip shouting in the corridor. He could hear her banging on the door. But it was of no use to him.

He realised that he was fighting a losing battle.

On her side of the door, Pip could hear them fighting. She could hear the threats from Jones. She could hear the punches landing. She could hear the groans as the breath escaped from Alex. And she was feeling frantic.

Somehow, she managed to keep a clear head.

She leant her full weight against the door to feel whether or not there was any give in it. She wanted to know how many of the three locks were in use. To her relief, she realised that it was only the middle one. Just the Union one. The other two locks hadn't been turned. Which meant that it might just be possible for her to force her way in.

Somewhere off in the distance, she thought she could hear the sound of sirens. But the help was still too far away. It was all down to her.

She took a couple of steps back and threw herself at the door, shoulder first. But it held firm. She stepped back again and, this time, aimed the sole of her right foot as close to the middle lock as she could. No change.

She could still hear the struggle.

'Hang on, Alex,' she yelled. 'I'm right here.'

Alex could hear her. But 'right here' in the corridor, on the other side of a locked door, was no good to him. He'd been involved in a fair few fights over the course of his policing career, some of them serious, some of them resulting in injury. But rarely off duty. Rarely without his kit and equipment, limited though it had always been. Rarely without the immediate backup of his colleagues.

This time, he was on his own. And there was nothing to be done about it.

His head hurt. His body ached. And what little was left of his strength was fading fast. Perhaps sensing this, Jones lifted his weight a fraction, grabbed the fabric of Alex's jacket and spun him violently over, so that Alex now had his back on the ground. Jones pinned Alex's arms to his sides and settled his full bulk back down on his chest, leaving Alex fighting for breath.

As Alex stared up at his attacker's bloodied and broken nose, Jones pulled back his right fist and smashed it into Alex's face.

*

Pip had sprinted back down the corridor, past the lifts and into the stairwell. There, she'd found what she was looking for: a large fire extinguisher. She unhooked it from its wall mounting and ran with it back to the door of the apartment.

For the first time, she could hear no sound coming from inside.

'Alex!' she howled in desperation.

Taking hold of the neck of the extinguisher in her right hand and the base in the left, she drove it with force into the door, right at the point where the middle lock met the frame. The blow left a significant dent in the wood, but the door itself didn't budge.

She repeated the move. Twice. Three times. Four times.

She paused, bent double, trying to catch her breath.

The sirens were closer now. But still not close enough.

Somehow, the blow to his face hadn't knocked Alex out, though it had almost certainly broken his eye socket. The pain was excruciating. His vision was shaky. His ears were ringing. His lungs were burning.

'You don't have to do this,' he managed to whisper. The survival instinct was still there. He hadn't given up.

'Fuck you,' Jones muttered as he placed his hands firmly around Alex's throat and began to squeeze.

And, for the first time, Alex felt truly afraid. He tried to struggle, but he knew it was no use. He thought of Pip and he thought of his boys as his eyes started to swim and he began to lapse into unconsciousness.

It was all over.

He was done.

Chapter 46

The door splintered and the lock gave way on what must have been the eighth or ninth blow with the extinguisher. Pip dropped it to the ground and gave the door one final heave with her shoulder.

At last, it swung inwards on its hinges.

Pip saw nothing of the fabric of the apartment. Nothing of the fancy decor; the expensive furniture; the original artwork. None of it. All she saw was Alex prone on the floor and Jones straddling his body with his hands wrapped around Alex's throat.

Alex wasn't struggling. He wasn't moving.

And Pip didn't hesitate.

She covered the distance in a fraction of a second, snatching up a heavy stone paperweight that was sitting on a small side table and, in a single arcing movement, crashing it against the side of the Minister's skull.

Jones's head dropped and his whole body went limp. He began to keel slowly over to one side, releasing his grip on Alex in the process. Pip added her own furious force to the movement and sent the Minister sprawling across the hallway. There was blood already oozing from an ugly gash in the side of his head. He was out cold.

But so was Alex.

Pip dropped to the floor beside him and grabbed his wrist, frantically searching for a pulse. 'It's me, Alex,' she said with urgent, whispered intensity. 'I'm right here.' She moved her shaking fingertips backwards and forwards over the surface of his skin, one moment thinking she could feel the trace of a heartbeat, the next thinking she must have imagined it. 'Come on!' she pleaded, willing him to live.

Outside in the corridor, she heard the sound of several pairs of feet, approaching at speed from the direction of the lifts. She looked up in time to see two unformed PCs appear in the doorway, swiftly followed by two more.

'We need an ambulance!' she yelled at them. 'Now!'

One of the PCs – a middle-aged officer in a well-worn uniform with 'Constable Mills' displayed on his name badge – rushed forward and knelt down on the floor next to her. 'You must be Pip,' he said. 'The girl downstairs told me your name,' he explained. He possessed the calm, authoritative demeanour of someone who had seen and survived most of what policing was ever likely to demand of someone, and his presence was a source of immediate reassurance to Pip. She wasn't on her own any more.

'That's me,' she replied without actually looking at him. 'And this is Superintendent Alex Lewis,' she added, nodding down at Alex's motionless form. In the background, she could hear one of the other officers calling up on their radio with an 'Active Message', asking for an ambulance 'on the hurry up'.

PC Mills reached out and carefully took hold of Alex's fore-arm. 'I've got a pulse,' he confirmed a couple of seconds later.

Speechless with relief, Pip put a gentle hand on Alex's chest and was able to feel the shallow rise and stuttering fall of his breathing.

'Do you have any idea what the full extent of his injuries might be?' PC Mills asked with concern. Behind him, two of the other uniforms – one male, one female – were crouching down next to Jones, who had started to moan quietly. The fourth officer had stepped past them and kept going into the apartment, presumably to check whether anyone else was present.

'I've no idea,' Pip answered helplessly. She could feel the tears pricking at the corners of her eyes. 'It took too fucking long to break down the door. I should have got to him so much sooner.' At the edge of her vision, she caught sight of Becca appearing in the doorway, but Pip was far too preoccupied with Alex to say anything to her.

'Well you're with him now,' the PC responded, placing a reassuring hand on her back. 'We all are. And the ambulance is on its way.' He was wearing an earpiece, meaning that Pip wasn't able to hear the radio updates being given to him by the control room.

'How long until they get here?' she asked, anxiously checking the time on her watch.

'They haven't given an ETA,' came the reply.

Before Pip could respond, they were interrupted by one of the officers who was kneeling beside Jones. 'Do we know who we've got over here?' he asked. The fact that Jones was lying on his front meant that his face was largely hidden from view. The flow of blood from his head injury had further obscured his features.

'The suspect,' Pip responded bluntly, not shifting one jot of her attention away from Alex. She couldn't have cared less about Simon Jones.

'He's lost quite a bit of blood,' the male PC replied as his female colleague got onto her radio and asked for a second ambulance and for someone to bring a first-aid kit up from the back of one of the patrol cars. 'How did he get his injury?' the male officer asked.

'I hit him with that paperweight over there,' Pip replied, pointing to where it was lying on the floor. 'As hard as I fucking could,' she added. She didn't notice Becca taking a couple of tentative steps towards her former lover.

'No kidding,' the PC responded as he continued to check Jones's body for other injuries.

But Pip was no longer listening to him. Her hand was still on Alex's chest and it seemed to her that his breathing might be starting to become a fraction stronger. She glanced at PC Mills, looking for reassurance. He was still holding Alex's wrist. He nodded and smiled. Apparently, Alex's pulse was getting stronger too.

'Can you hear me, Alex?' Pip said gently.

He didn't reply, but his lips moved a fraction. He groaned in pain and his head rolled slowly to one side.

'Can you get me a cushion or something?' Pip asked PC Mills. 'Anything to make him a bit more comfortable.'

'Of course,' the officer replied. He jumped to his feet and jogged into the main living area of the flat.

'Try not to move, Alex,' Pip whispered gently. 'The ambulance is on its way.'

Meanwhile, the two officers tending to Jones had been joined by Becca, who crouched down next to them and placed a trembling hand on his shoulder. Rather than ordering her back out into the corridor as he should have done, the male PC asked her a question. 'Do you know his name?' he enquired.

'His name's Simon Jones,' Becca replied in a voice that was shaking as much as her hand.

'Are you a relative of his?'

'No, I'm not.'

And you shouldn't bloody be here, Pip thought as she glanced over at them. But she didn't say so.

'A friend perhaps?' the PC asked.

'Something like that,' Becca replied uncertainly.

'Do we know what's actually happened here this evening?' the female officer asked.

'It's a long story,' Pip interrupted before Becca could reply. She was trying to concentrate on Alex, but she also knew that she needed to assert at least some semblance of control over what was happening. There was no way of knowing how Becca might answer the question and Pip desperately wanted to avoid adding possible confusion to an already complicated and difficult situation. 'But you might want to get your Duty Inspector up here,' she said. Once everyone had worked out what was going on, and who was involved, Pip knew that all hell was likely to break loose. After all, they were in an apartment belonging to the Policing Minister. And it was the Policing Minister who was lying semi-conscious on the floor, in a pool of his own blood. All sorts of people – very senior people – were going to be demanding to know what had happened.

Alex groaned again and Pip went straight back to ignoring everyone and everything else. 'You're going to be all right,' she insisted to him. 'The medics will be here soon.'

PC Mills reappeared next to her, holding a large pillow and an expensive-looking blanket, evidently retrieved from a bedroom.

'Thank you,' Pip said, taking the pillow and easing it gingerly under Alex's head. She leant closer in to him. 'You had me worried there for a moment,' she whispered in his ear. She took the blanket, unfolded it and laid it over him.

From the general hubbub in the communal corridor, Pip could tell that several more officers had turned up at the scene. In her experience, that was always the way with Urgent Assistance calls. Everyone responded.

'Cancel any more units,' said one of the officers into their radio. 'We've got more than sufficient on scene. We just need the two ambulances asap, and the Duty Officer.'

A young officer Pip hadn't seen before hurried in through the front door, carrying a large green canvas bag. PC Mills – who appeared to have assumed some sort of unspoken responsibility for the whole scene – waved him over to where Jones was lying. The Minister appeared to be regaining some form of consciousness. Pip could see the intermittent movements of his arms and legs.

The young officer unzipped the first-aid kit and his colleagues immediately grabbed a handful of dressings and bandages and started applying pressure to the wound on the side of Jones's head.

'Did I hear someone say that his name was Simon Jones?' PC Mills asked Pip. She saw the knowing look on his face and realised that he had worked it out.

She nodded.

'Would that be Simon Jones the—' Mills began, but Pip cut him off.

'The very same,' Pip said briskly. 'And, when he regains full consciousness, one of you can have the pleasure of arresting him.'

But Pip had spoken too soon.

Chapter 47

'W-what's happening?' It was Simon Jones speaking. He was still lying face down in the hallway. He was groggy and thoroughly disorientated.

'You've had a bang to the head,' the female PC said calmly. She was still applying gentle pressure to his wound. 'I need you to lie still for me. There's an ambulance on its way.'

Jones pushed her hand away and rolled slowly onto his side. The bloodied dressing that the PC had been holding fell onto the floor. 'Who are you?' he asked in laboured tones, his eyes slowly coming into focus.

'My name's Laura,' the PC replied. 'I'm a police officer.'

Jones appeared confused. 'What are you doing here?' he asked as he attempted to sit up.

'Lie back down for me,' the PC responded evenly. Her male colleague assisted her in easing Jones onto his back and lowering his head gently onto the floor. The blood from his head wound was starting to congeal, forming a matted mess in his hair.

'I asked what you were doing here,' Jones reiterated, more impatiently this time.

'We were called here,' the PC replied without elaborating any further.

'By who?' came the irritable response.

'By a member of the public.'

With no further explanation forthcoming from the officer, Jones retreated into a brooding silence.

Pip looked across at him. He seemed to be trying to get his head together – to work out what the hell was going on. She wasn't sure whether the PCs had picked up on it, but there was a sense of prickling tension building in the hallway. She had no idea how much Jones had had to drink, but suspected that alcohol – in addition to his injuries – was a significant factor in his condition.

Turning her attention away from him for a moment, Pip looked back down at Alex. His eyes were still closed and his face was a mess, but his pulse and breathing were steady and growing stronger. She told herself that he was going to be all right. That everything was going to be all right. Then she glanced across at Becca, who was leaning against the wall a few feet away from her. Her whole body was trembling.

Pip nudged PC Mills and gestured across at her. 'Might it be an idea for someone to take her into the flat and sit her down?'

Mills nodded in agreement. 'Good idea,' he said. 'What's her name?'

'Becca,' Pip replied. 'Becca Palmer.'

What happened next blindsided them all.

The simple mention of Becca's name had an impact on Simon Jones that was not unlike the effects of a defibrillator. His body jerked violently and he sat suddenly bolt upright. 'Becca!' he said loudly, shrugging off the two PCs next to him as they tried to take hold of his arms and settle him back down. His eyes cast wildly around the hallway until they settled on her. 'Becca!' he shouted – his voice a mixture of drunken shock and rapidly materialising aggression.

Before anyone could react, he sprang to his feet in a manner utterly inconsistent with his injured, intoxicated state and grabbed hold of her. Becca screamed. He swung her body around in front of him and clamped his right forearm around her neck. 'Get away from me!' he snarled at the two PCs closest to him.

Pip stared at him in horrified disbelief. His eyes were wild, his movements fierce and threatening. He looked like a cornered animal. Pip's negotiator's instincts took over. 'I need you to look after Alex for me,' she whispered urgently to PC Mills, before rising slowly to her feet. 'Simon, look at me,' she said.

'Stay where you are,' he growled as she took a couple of very tentative steps towards him.

Unable to escape his grasp – barely able to move at all – Becca had been rendered mute with fear. She stared at Pip in panicked desperation.

You shouldn't bloody be here, Pip was thinking, even as she was trying to work out how on earth to help her.

'Simon, look at me,' she repeated, more firmly this time. As she spoke, he was edging to one side – to Pip's right – with his back pressed against the wall. 'Give them some space,' she instructed the two PCs who had both adopted a defensive stance – one foot planted in front of the other and their hands raised in a silent attempt to calm the rapidly escalating situation. Jones kept moving slowly sideways, getting closer all the time to the side table that Pip had earlier grabbed the paperweight from. Pip didn't see the wooden-handled letter opener until it was already in his hand. 'Simon, no!' she shouted desperately as he pushed the sharp metal point of it into the side of Becca's neck. Becca let out a strangled cry of distress.

*

Lying on the ground, Alex was improving gradually, but he remained only distantly aware of what was happening around him. He could hear Pip's raised voice, but his shaken brain was struggling to make sense of what she was saying. Who was Simon? The name was familiar, but he was struggling to put a face to it. He tried to stir himself, but there was someone kneeling alongside him – someone he didn't know – who was telling him to remain still. What was happening? Where was he? He needed to get to Pip.

'Simon, please!' Pip pleaded. 'You don't need to do this.' The letter opener hadn't yet broken the surface of the skin on Becca's neck, but it was obvious that it would require only the smallest amount of additional pressure from Jones for it to do so.

'Back off,' Jones snapped as he started to edge backwards with Becca, away from the front door and further into the apartment.

Pip realised that she needed urgently to find a way to release some of the pressure and tension from the situation. 'I'm backing off,' she said firmly, gesturing at the two PCs to do the same. She was aware of other officers gathering in the hallway and in the corridor outside. 'Nobody else move,' she shouted as an instruction to all of them. She might have imagined it, but she thought she noticed the faintest relaxation in Jones's hold on Becca as the officers complied.

Pip tried to slow her breathing. She snatched a glance back at Alex. PC Mills was still with him. One less thing to be concerned about. She was aware of everyone watching her, waiting to see what she was going to do next. Pip realised that she wasn't certain herself. There was no time to come up with any kind of coherent plan. It was all about instincts now.

327

'Simon,' she said as calmly as she could manage, 'I need you to look at Becca.' She supposed that, if he had ever had feelings for her, it might make sense to appeal to those.

But Jones didn't respond. He continued to walk backwards into the apartment. He was now at the entrance to the main living area and he was still holding the letter opener to Becca's throat. Becca's face was a picture of dread-filled despair.

Hoping that she had allowed for a reasonable distance to open up between them, Pip took a couple of steps forward. She wanted to be close enough to maintain eye contact with him, and to be able to talk to him without raising her voice.

'Stay right where you are,' Jones hissed.

'Simon, you're hurting her,' Pip insisted.

'So fucking what?'

'You don't want to hurt her!'

'How the fuck do you know what I do and don't want?'

It was clear to Pip that he had no more of a plan than she did. He was drunk, he was badly injured, he was aggressive and he was afraid. The fact that he didn't appear to have a single rational thought in his head made him all the more dangerous. 'I don't think that you want to hurt anyone,' she replied, in an attempt to reason with him.

But he was beyond reason. 'She's the one who's fucking hurting me!' he yelled.

'What do you mean?'

'She's the one talking to the press and spreading lies about me.'

'What lies?'

'About being in a relationship with me.'

'But she was in a relationship with you,' Pip responded. She wasn't trying to provoke him. She was trying to give him a reason not to harm her. 'She cared about you,' Pip insisted. 'She fell in love with you.'

'Oh, for fuck's sake,' he shouted. 'What are you talking about? It didn't mean anything. She's just a fucking girl. She's nobody. And now she's trying to destroy me.'

And that was all it took. For Becca to abandon all her fears and give herself over completely to the righteous fury that was surging unstoppably inside of her. *Just a fucking girl? Nobody?* She drew her right foot up and slammed it back down onto Jones's bare foot – the one that still had shards of tumbler glass embedded in it.

The sudden, searing pain caused him to drop the letter opener and to loosen his grip around her neck. Her instantaneous response was to lean forward and, with every ounce of strength and rage that she could muster, to drive her elbow back into his already broken face. He bellowed in agony and dropped to his knees on the floor.

Within seconds, the nearest PC had him in handcuffs and Becca was safely in Pip's arms.

Alex blinked uncertainly. His head and his face were pulsing with pain. His whole body was aching. But Pip was kneeling next to him, and that meant that everything was all right.

'What happened?' he mumbled quietly. 'Did I miss something?'

Pip smiled weakly at him. 'Nothing that Becca and I couldn't handle,' she replied.

Chapter 48

Ten Days Later

The press were having a field day. Ten field days, to be more precise. And the coverage was showing no signs of letting up.

What had started out as the story of a denied affair, and developed into a tale of corruption and greed at the highest levels of government, had turned very quickly into something even more sensational than either of those things.

Simon Jones, Member of Parliament for Fulwood in Sheffield, Minister of State for Crime and Policing, had been charged with the attempted murder of a police officer.

Sitting quietly at home, sipping tentatively from a cup of freshly made tea, Alex had been doing his best to block out all the noise. Pip was curled up on the sofa next to him. She'd been given time off work to look after him and the two of them had been taking the days slowly.

Alex had been discharged from hospital the week before, following a lengthy but ultimately successful operation to repair the damage caused by Jones to his eye socket. His vision was likely to remain blurry for a while longer, but he had been told that he should make a full recovery. In the meantime, the side of his face remained swollen and bruised and there were a number of purple-coloured weals, the shape of finger and thumb prints, clustered around his throat and neck. Much of the rest of his body thrummed intermittently with a succession of dull aches and pains. There was a box of strong painkillers lying open on the floor next to his feet.

He and Pip had been ignoring the newspapers for the past few days and they had confined their TV viewing to the comfort and distraction of old box sets. Fictional drama in place of the real thing. Though things were starting to settle down, Pip had spent a significant amount of her time fielding phone calls and responding to messages from concerned friends and colleagues. Even the Area Commander had texted, albeit with a follow-up message asking when Alex was likely to be back on duty. There had been a handful of visitors too. A pair of DCs had spent several hours sitting at the kitchen table, taking lengthy statements from both Alex and Pip, followed the next day by a forensic photographer who'd recorded each of Alex's injuries in close up, high-definition detail. And Richard Wells from the Hostage Unit had called by with a large case of beer, together with a get well card that had a picture of a duck on the front of it. 'So you remember what to do the next time someone throws a punch at you,' Rich had explained. Alex might have laughed harder if it hadn't been so painful for him to do so.

The most welcome of all their visitors had been Alex's two sons, who had spent an entire evening with them. Once they had both reassured themselves that their dad really was OK, they had bombarded Alex and Pip with a succession of questions about what had happened. They wanted to know absolutely everything and Alex had humoured them with as much detail as he thought appropriate, glad of their company and delighted to have an excuse to spend more time with them than usual.

It was his boys he was thinking about when Alex suddenly

remembered something he'd been meaning to mention to Pip for the past couple of hours. 'Was that Becca I heard you speaking to on the phone earlier on?' he asked, turning gingerly to face her.

'It was,' Pip replied.

'How's she doing?'

'Remarkably well, actually,' said Pip. 'She was pretty shaken up by what happened, but she's feeling a whole lot better now that she knows you're on the mend. She's sticking to her meds, she's staying off the booze and she says that the counselling is going well.'

'It would be good to see her at some point in the next few days,' Alex said.

'I'm sure she'd love that,' Pip replied. 'Though there will come a time when you're going to have to stop feeling quite so responsible for her.'

'Am I that transparent?' Alex responded.

'Only to me,' said Pip with a grin.

'I just seem to find it a whole lot harder to let go these days,' he admitted.

'That's hardly surprising in this particular case,' Pip reassured him. 'You could live a dozen lifetimes and never come across anything remotely like it again.'

'Do you think she's going to be OK?' Alex asked. Buried somewhere deep inside him was a recurrence of the idea that he needed her to be all right in order to be all right himself.

'Actually, I do,' Pip replied. 'She knows that it's going to take time, but she told me on the phone that she's starting to feel more hopeful about the future.'

'That's a good thing,' Alex said.

'It's a very good thing,' Pip agreed.

Their conversation was interrupted by the buzz of Pip's

phone in her pocket. She pulled it out and checked her messages.

'It's from Rowan,' she said, looking up from the screen.

'Oh?' replied Alex enquiringly.

'She wants to know whether you're up to receiving visitors this afternoon.'

Alex hesitated. Rowan was still more of an acquaintance than a friend and, though he was starting to both like and admire her, he wasn't entirely sure that he was ready for all the inevitable talk about Simon Jones. 'What do you think?' he asked Pip.

'It's entirely up to you,' Pip replied. 'But it might be a good thing. I know we've been taking a much-needed break from reality, but we're going to have to get back to it at some point.'

'I suppose,' Alex said, scratching at the ten days' worth of stubbled growth on his chin. He wouldn't be shaving for a while yet. Not while so much of his face remained so tender.

'She needn't stay for long,' Pip responded. 'I'll tell her that we're good for half an hour. I'm sure she'll understand.'

'OK then,' Alex replied, leaning back and resting his head on the sofa cushions.

Rowan Blake ended up staying with them for a whole lot longer than half an hour.

Having got to their house not long after three in the afternoon, she was still talking animatedly with them as the hands of the clock on the kitchen wall moved towards nine in the evening. By then, she and Pip were partway through their second bottle of wine. Conscious of not wanting to mix his pain medication with alcohol, Alex was sticking to fruit juice.

Rowan had been deeply shocked by Alex's appearance and, within moments of arriving, had tried to take at least some of the blame for his injuries. After all, she said, she had encouraged Alex to attend the meeting with Jones. In reply, Alex had assured her that he took full responsibility for the decision and that, quite apart from anything else, the Commissioner of the Metropolitan Police had asked him to go. Neither he nor Pip blamed her in the slightest for what had happened to him.

Settling down at the kitchen table, they had talked at length about what had happened in the apartment, and Alex had described, in unsparing detail, the Minister's descent into madness. *From denial, to blame, to self-pity, to rage.* It fell to Pip to tell the story of how it had all come to a sudden, unexpected end.

Over the course of the late afternoon and early evening – having reassured them that she was paying a social visit and that whatever they said was off the record – Rowan managed to ask them even more questions than Alex's sons had. 'I would dearly love to have been there for the moment when he was arrested,' she had said with a glint in her eye.

After that, it had been Rowan's turn to describe what had happened to the original articles she'd taken to the *Guardian*. She explained that they had been run more or less as planned, not least because they'd given the paper an exclusive angle on the Minister's arrest. In fact, the editor of the paper had been so delighted with both the content of the pieces and the reaction from readers that she'd actually asked Rowan whether she might be interested in returning to her old job. And though Rowan had declined to go back on the payroll as a full-time employee – explaining that she preferred the freedom and flexibility afforded by freelance work – she had agreed to keep writing for them. Not least about the continuing fallout from the arrest of Simon Jones.

Because Jones wasn't the only one in serious trouble.

Sebastian Neill had been arrested and was on police bail for a lengthy series of fraud offences. Camilla Lane had been questioned by police too, though she was publicly claiming to have no knowledge of either Chaloner Capital or its parent company, Enforcement Holdings. She had employed the services of a PR agency and there were stories already being sown in the press, suggesting that Jones had registered the shareholding in her maiden name without her knowledge. Rowan was far from convinced by any of this and, sitting in their kitchen, she made it clear to Alex and Pip that there was no way she was going to let the subject lie.

The Directors of Soteria Solutions had convened an urgent board meeting and Robert Sangster, the company's CEO, had wasted no time in issuing a series of emphatic public denials that he and his senior colleagues had been involved in any form of criminality or wrongdoing. Whether or not that was true, the Home Secretary had already confirmed in a statement to the House of Commons that all existing Soteria contracts with the Home Office were under urgent review and that they would not be considered for any new business until those investigations were complete. In the meantime, the firm's share price was in freefall.

While all of this was happening, The Bridge Club had reportedly lost more than half its members and the Old Queen Street offices of the Independent Justice Foundation appeared to have been closed down. Its CEO, Rafe Jackson, wasn't taking any calls.

Rowan suggested that the stories were likely to run and run. Except in the *GB Today* and *City Journal* newspapers, whose coverage of it all remained suspiciously muted.

'So what happens now?' Pip asked as she refilled Rowan's wine glass with a generous measure.

'Oh, this is just the beginning,' Rowan replied casually.

'The beginning of what?' Alex cut in, trying and failing to stifle a yawn.

'Well, there are endless uncomfortable questions for the Government – and for politicians in general – to answer: about the less-than-transparent connections between MPs and a broad range of wealthy commercial interests; about politicians and the second jobs that so many of them appear to hold; about the decidedly murky funding arrangements for a number of think tanks that are far from independent; about political donations and the purchase of influence; about the nefarious role played by certain sections of the media; about labyrinthine back channels and secretive old boys' clubs. Need I go on?'

'Do you really think it runs that deep?' Pip asked.

'Absolutely I do,' Rowan replied. 'The system is completely broken. The whole thing has been rigged – by the few, for the few. And they will continue to get away with it for as long as we allow them to.'

'Blimey, that's depressing,' said Pip.

'It's the truth,' Rowan countered.

Alex yawned again. 'I'm so sorry,' he said. 'I'm completely done. Do you mind if I leave the two of you to carry on putting the world to rights. I need to go to bed.'

'Of course,' Rowan replied, standing up to say goodbye to him.

'Do you need anything?' Pip asked him.

'I'm fine,' he replied, giving Rowan a hug and Pip a kiss.

As he reached the bottom of the stairs, he could hear the resumption of their conversation.

'There's something about Simon Jones that I'm still struggling to understand,' Pip said.

'Go on,' Rowan prompted.

'I don't understand what it is that would compel a man who already has everything to risk the destruction of it all in the pursuit of more,' Alex heard Pip say.

'It's really not complicated,' Rowan replied. 'We talked about it before. It's greed, pure and simple. A motivation as old as time.'

Alex closed his eyes and allowed his head to sink into the pillow. The voices of the two women downstairs were no more than a murmur now.

As the exhaustion washed over him in waves, his mind began to wander and weave. He thought about Simon Jones, the self-made, self-destroyed Conservative MP who would be going to jail for a very long time. He thought about Rowan Blake, the fearless investigative journalist who had never trusted police officers, but who had learned to trust him. He thought about Pip Williams, his lover and best friend.

But, one by one, he left them all behind as he was drawn inexorably back towards the centre of the city: back towards St Thomas' Hospital and the angled shadow of Big Ben; back towards the girl on the bridge. He could see her up ahead of him, silent and still, on the wrong side of the green balustrade, staring down at the water below.

He stopped a metre or so away from her and called out her name. 'My name is Alex,' he said as she turned to face him. 'I'm with the police and I'm here to help you.'

Acknowledgements

As ever with a book, there are plenty of 'thank yous' to be said.

To the incredible Laura Williams, who remains the best agent in the business.

To Fran Pathak, who commissioned *The Fallen* and is an entirely brilliant editor to work with.

To Sarah Benton, who inherited me from Fran, and has rapidly become an incredibly important source of guidance, inspiration and encouragement to me.

To the rest of the team at Orion, all of whom I love to bits: not least Leanne Oliver, Tom Noble, Lucy Brem, Alainna Hadjigeorgiou, Paul Stark, Ellie Clegg and Katie Espiner.

To Jade Craddock, copyeditor extraordinaire.

To Ronnie Egan, who lent her name to one of the characters in the story. Ronnie won a competition held to raise funds for *Police Care UK*, an amazing charity that supports serving and former police officers, staff, volunteers and their families.

To Phil Williams, dear friend and former Head of the Hostage & Crisis Negotiation Unit at Scotland Yard, who remains the inspiration for the character Pip.

To Christian Guy and Robert Palmer, for their time and expertise.

Oliver Bullough's outstanding book, *Moneyland: Why Thieves*

338

& *Crooks Now Rule the World & How to Take it Back* (Profile Books, 2019) was a valuable source of research, as was the documentary film, *The Spider's Web*, directed by Michael Oswald.

As always, the final – and most important – 'thank you' goes to my family. To Bear: you are the best friend I ever had. To Jessie, Charlie & Emily: what wonderful human beings you are growing up to be. I love all four of you with all my heart.

The Fallen is dedicated to the memory of four young men I never met, who became four young men I will never forget:

Kodjo Yenga
Ben Kinsella
Milad Golmakani
Dogan Ismail

Four victims of knife crime, murdered in parts of London where I was based at the time of their deaths, they remain with me even now.

Credits

John Sutherland and Orion Fiction would like to thank everyone at Orion who worked on the publication of *The Fallen* in the UK.

Editorial
Sarah Benton
Lucy Brem

Copyeditor
Jade Craddock

Proofreader
Linda Joyce

Audio
Paul Stark
Jake Alderson

Contracts
Dan Herron
Ellie Bowker

Design
Charlotte Abrams-Simpson
Joanna Ridley
Zane Dabinett

Editorial Management
Charlie Panayiotou
Jane Hughes
Bartley Shaw
Tamara Morriss

Finance
Jasdip Nandra
Nick Gibson
Sue Baker

Marketing
Tom Noble

Publicity
Leanne Oliver
Alex Layt

Production
Ameenah Khan

Operations
Jo Jacobs
Sharon Willis

Sales
Jen Wilson
Esther Waters
Victoria Laws
Toluwalope Ayo-Ajala
Rachael Hum
Anna Egelstaff
Sinead White
Georgina Cutler

If you loved *THE FALLEN*, don't miss John Sutherland's electrifying debut novel . . .

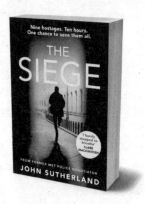

Nine hostages. Ten hours. One chance to save them all.

Lee James Connor has found his purpose in life: to follow the teachings of far-right extremist leader, Nicholas Farmer. So when his idol is jailed, he comes up with the perfect plan: take a local immigrant support group hostage until Farmer is released.

Grace Wheatley is no stranger to loneliness having weathered the passing of her husband, whilst being left to raise her son alone. The local support group is her only source of comfort. Until the day Lee James Connor walks in and threatens the existence of everything she's ever known.

Superintendent Alex Lewis may be one of the most experienced hostage negotiators on the force, but there's no such thing as a perfect record. Still haunted by his last case, can he connect with Connor – and save his nine hostages – before it's too late?

AVAILABLE TO BUY NOW

If you enjoyed *THE FALLEN* don't miss the
highly anticipated new novel from
John Sutherland . . .

THE STALKING SEASON

Following the successful conclusion of another immensely
demanding negotiation in south London, Superintendent Alex
Lewis and his partner Pip head for a much-needed break in
the Scottish Highlands. But, the morning after their arrival
on the Castle Craigie estate, they find themselves caught up
in an attempt by an armed gang to kidnap a well-known
Scottish Earl. In the desperate hours that follow, Alex and
Pip must call on all their years of negotiating experience to
save not only the life of the Earl, but their own lives too.

OUT MAY 2024

Prologue

Superintendent Alex Lewis pushed open the heavy fire door and stepped out of the damp, drab stairwell into the fourth floor corridor of a decaying southeast London block of flats. It was just before 3am on the first Saturday in July.

The concrete floor beneath him was cracked and worn, and the strip light above him was making a constant, dull buzzing noise as it flickered on and off. Immediately in front of him, the facing wall was lined in single file with more than a dozen officers from the Met's Territorial Support Group, dressed in full riot gear – helmets on, visors down. Half of them were holding full-length Perspex shields, resting on the scuffed steel toecaps of their black boots, while the other half were carrying smaller, round versions of the same thing on their forearms. All of them were silent. On edge. Waiting for a word of command.

Alex looked along the corridor to his right, his eyes following the line of officers all the way to the entrance to what he had been told was flat number 42. He could see the splintered remains of the faded red front door hanging loosely from its hinges, with much of the rest of it lying on the floor further along the corridor. Standing immediately in front of the space where the door should have been were two more TSG PCs with their long shields interlinked, barring the doorway. They were in a tense, half-crouched position, their eyes firmly fixed on whatever was ahead of them. Behind them, another officer with the white epaulettes of a Sergeant on the shoulders of his flameproof overalls, was talking quietly but insistently to someone who was out of view, inside the flat.

'I need you to try to stay calm for me,' the officer was saying, the palm of his left hand raised in a *"easy now"* motion, his right resting uneasily on the handle of the yellow Taser that was strapped to his hip. 'Most of all, I need you to stay calm for your baby.'

Taking a deep breath, Alex started walking towards them.

Less than two hours earlier, he had been soundly asleep when the shrill ringtone of his mobile had snatched him unceremoniously back towards consciousness. He'd been on the Met's Hostage Negotiator call-out rota for the preceding five nights, but this was the first time that the phone had actually rung.

He reached over to his bedside table and fumbled to connect the call. 'Alex Lewis speaking,' he mumbled groggily.

'Sorry to wake you at such an ungodly hour,' said the familiar voice at the other end of the line. It belonged to DCI Richard Wells, a long-time colleague and friend, and the officer in charge of the Met's Hostage and Crisis Negotiation Unit.

'Morning Rich,' Alex whispered as he eased himself slowly out of bed. 'Give me a moment or two to clear my head and get downstairs. I'll call you straight back.'

'No problem,' Rich replied before ringing off.

Alex glanced back over his shoulder at his partner Pip – like him, a serving police officer and an experienced negotiator. She had barely stirred. Over the years, they had both grown accustomed to the sound of phones ringing in the middle of the night – and to somehow managing to sleep through the disruption if they were not the ones on call. Taking care not to wake her, Alex stood up, crossed the bedroom, grabbed his rucksack and hurried down to the ground floor of their small terraced home.

Switching on the kitchen lights and blinking in their sudden brightness, he walked over to the sink, ran the tap, and splashed some cold water on his face, before sitting down at the table and making the call. Rich picked up straight away.

'What have you got for me?' Alex asked, reaching into his rucksack for a blue Bic biro and a thick pad of yellow Post It notes.

'It's a Domestic Violence job,' Rich replied.

And Alex felt the immediate check in his chest: the sudden surge and stop of adrenaline. Of anxiety. He had been responding to DV calls since his earliest days as young PC and, in his experience, they were rarely – if ever – straightforward to deal with. On occasions, they became the stuff of unimaginable nightmares.

Among those he had dealt with as a negotiator, there was one in particular that had seared itself into his memory and remained there – one that had ended with the fatal police shooting of the suspect: a man of sickening violence and rage who had beaten his wife unconscious before taking her and their three young children hostage. And, despite the fact that Alex had done everything right, despite the fact that he'd succeeded in saving the lives of the victim and her children – he'd carried the burden of that day with him ever since. It was one of a number of cases that had left him with a legacy of post-traumatic stress disorder: a deeply debilitating condition that he was finding ways to live with, but that retained the capacity to blindside him from time to time. For the briefest of moments, listening to Rich speaking at the other end of the line, he could hear the sound of gunfire. He could see the man fall.

'Are you still there Alex?' Rich asked, filling the lingering silence.

'Sorry, yes,' Alex replied, doing his best to shake his mind free of the troubling recollection. 'Go ahead with the details.'

'Male suspect with previous for violence and sexual offences has forced his way into his ex-girlfriend's flat, assaulted her and thrown her out. He's now holed up inside with their six-month old daughter.'

'Six months old?' Alex queried in alarm. In his mind, the past vanished from view as the present came jarring into sudden focus.

'That's what I've been told.'

'Bloody hell,' Alex responded, his mind already racing. 'Is she alright?'

'As far as we know, yes.'

'Then there isn't any time to lose,' Alex said. 'What's the address?'

The moment Rich had rung off, Alex had called the Met's main control room and requested a fast car run to the scene. A decade of middle-of-the-night call-outs had taught him that a high-powered Traffic Patrol BMW – unconstrained by red traffic lights and statutory speed limits – would likely get him to the scene a whole lot quicker than attempting to make the journey in his own car. Letting someone else take responsibility for the actual driving also helped him to keep his head clear and concentrated on his responsibilities as a negotiator.

Fifteen minutes later, he was waiting impatiently at the end of his road when he heard the approaching sound of sirens. He flagged down the marked car as it came into view and pulled his warrant card out of his jeans' pocket to identify himself to the crew. Then he threw his rucksack into the back seat, jumped in after it and, following the briefest exchange of introductions, the PC in the driver's seat spun the car round and put her foot down.

As they raced through the largely deserted streets of south-west London, Alex took the time to prepare himself as best he could for whatever might lie ahead. Rich had not been able to give him many details – the important thing, he'd emphasised, was to get Alex there as quickly as possible. As a consequence, there were all sorts of gaps in Alex's knowledge and his mind filled with a quick-fire succession of questions. What was the DV victim's name? What was the extent of her injuries? What about the suspect? What sort of psychological state was he likely to be in? What kind of threat might he still present? And, most pressingly of all for Alex, what about the baby?

He felt the full weight of her little life resting in his hands.

The traffic car drew up outside the flats just as an ambulance was pulling away on blues and twos. Alex thanked his driver and operator, jumped out of the back seat and ran the last fifty metres towards front of the block. He passed a number of unoc-cupied police vehicles – including three TSG Mercedes Sprinter vans – before spotting a small group of officers assembled by the main entrance into the building.

As Alex got closer, he could see the TSG inspector among them – identifiable by his well-worn flat cap and flame-proof overalls – along with a second, female inspector. Alex guessed that she must be the local duty officer – the individual in over-all charge of the unfolding incident. Seeing Alex approach, the two supervising officers turned to face him.

'Alex Lewis,' Alex said, extending a hand in greeting. 'I'm your negotiator.'

'Laura Swain,' the duty officer replied, shaking his hand. 'Thanks for turning out.'

'No problem,' Alex replied, immediately reassured by her calm, professional demeanour. Here was someone he could work with. 'There should be one or two other negotiators on the way, but I'm it for now. What have we got?'

'That was the victim on her way to hospital,' Inspector Swain replied, her expression darkening as she gestured in the direction the ambulance had just taken. 'Her name's Chloe Thompson,' she continued. 'Just turned twenty. And she's in a bad way. Blunt trauma head injury.'

Alex felt his heart fall. 'Life threatening?' he asked, his mind immediately snatched back to another point in the past: to a DV murder scene he'd attended early on in his policing career. Despite the passage of time, he could recall every last detail of what he'd seen and done there that night. Another block of flats in another part of town. A young victim who had been stabbed multiple times by her partner. Alex had helped one of the paramedics carry her down the narrow stairwell to the waiting ambulance. And he'd travelled to hospital with her, watching on helplessly as the medics tried in vain to save her life. It took no more than a fraction of a second for the forensic detail of the recollection to crash through his head.

'It's certainly not looking good,' Inspector Swain admitted grimly. 'Chloe was unconscious in the corridor outside the flat when we found her and she's not shown much sign of improvement since.'

'What about the baby?' Alex asked, attempting for the second time that night to set aside an unnerving memory, and demanding of himself that he spend every last part of his energy and attention on the here and now. There was very little he could do for the stricken Chloe, but there was still a chance that he might be able to help her daughter.

'Unharmed as far as we can tell,' the inspector replied evenly. 'In the physical sense at least. Six-month old girl called Riley.'

'Have we got eyes on her?' Alex asked, trying to picture the scene four floors up.

'Last I heard – a couple of minutes ago – yes we have. Apparently the suspect is holding her while the TSG are trying to talk to him.'

'And what do we know about the suspect?' Alex asked, continuing to focus his thoughts on the people and circumstances he might actually be able to exert some sort of influence over.

The inspector glanced down at the decision log that she was holding and scanned through her handwritten notes. 'Harvey Jackson,' she said a moment or two later. 'Thoroughly nasty piece of work. Thirty-five years old. Chloe's ex. Believed to be Riley's dad. Big drinker. Previous for drugs, violence and sexual assault. He's been arrested at this address on several recent occasions and he's currently on bail for rape. Three weeks ago, Chloe finally threw him out for good. Our Domestic Violence Unit helped her to get a restraining order against him only yesterday.'

As he listened, Alex was forming a mental picture of Harvey Jackson – and it was a decidedly ugly one. A man of violence. A domestic abuser. Fully fifteen years older than the target of his misogynistic rage. A drinker and a drug user. A suspect for rape. As he narrowed his concentration to the likely demands of the next few minutes, Alex realised that he was about to begin a negotiation with a man he already despised.

The rapid turnover of his thoughts was interrupted by the buzz of his phone. It was a text from Rich to say that he was en route, but still at least half an hour away. It meant that, for the next little while at least, Alex was going to be doing the negotiating on his own.

'Those previous arrests you mentioned?' he asked the duty officer as he tucked his phone back into his pocket. 'Has Jackson ever come quietly?'

'Never,' the inspector replied.

As he walked along the fourth floor corridor, Alex could see the unsettling evidence of Chloe's blood congealing on the floor immediately outside the flat. Breathing in sharply, he made a conscious effort to slow both his pace and his pulse. At the same time, he tried to bury his hostile preconceptions about the suspect. Because he knew that any trace of anger at the man and his crimes – no matter how justifiable – would be entirely counterproductive. The overwhelming urgency of the situation demanded absolute clarity and calmness.

He glanced down at the palm of his left hand, at the three names he had written there in marker pen: a simple safeguard against stumbling over – or momentarily forgetting them – under the inevitable pressure and intensity of whatever might be about to happen:

Harvey
Riley
Chloe

As he reached the three officers stationed at the door, the sergeant glanced to his left and offered Alex a grim nod of acknowledgement. His face had a lived-in look about it: a little frayed around the edges, but somehow familiar and reassuring – the steady appearance of a man who had been there and seen it all before. Alex nodded in return, as he moved cautiously forwards to stand alongside him. And, from this new position, he was able to look inside the flat for the first time.

Beyond the two PCs and their long shields, a cheap-looking dining table had been tipped on its end and wedged into the doorframe in the form of a makeshift barrier. Two of its legs had apparently broken off in the process and were lying on the floor next to it. After the table came a dimly lit, Lino-floored corridor with two doors leading off to the right, one to the left and one at the opposite end, heading into what looked to be the kitchen. And, standing square and hostile in the middle of the corridor, was the suspect: tall – certainly taller than Alex, who was 6'1' – paunchy, unshaven, with pale, pockmarked skin and untidy black hair, dressed in a white vest, dark grey jogging bottoms and a pair of expensive-looking trainers. He had a single, garishly-coloured tattoo of a naked woman on one arm, with the initials "C.F.C." and the outline of a lion on the other. He was holding a baseball bat in his right hand. And the baby with his left.

'Who the fuck are you?' the suspect hissed aggressively, his eyes narrow and his jawline tense.

'I'm Alex,' Alex responded, trying to ignore his immediate sense of prickling unease at the obvious fragility of the situation – a feeling complicated by a surge of deep loathing for the man now standing in front of him. He could smell the alcohol on the suspect's breath from several metres away. As his eyes adjusted to the dim lighting inside the flat, Alex looked more closely and was astonished to see that the baby somehow appeared to be fast asleep – seemingly oblivious to all that was happening around her. He could see the gentle rise and fall of her chest and the occasional fluttering of her eyelids: a gentle kind of stillness that formed a stark counterpoint to the angry, agitated restlessness of the man holding on to her.

'And what the fuck are you doing here, *Alex*?' The suspect spoke Alex's name with deep hostility.

'I'm with the police,' Alex replied steadily, his eyes flicking rapidly between the suspect, the baseball bat and the sleeping infant. 'I'm here to help you.'

'Fuck off!' the man spat in a strained whisper. 'We don't want your help.'

'We?' Alex queried, in an invitation to the man to keep talking.

'Me and my little girl,' the suspect replied, glancing down at his sleeping daughter. And Alex thought that he could detect the very faintest softening of the man's features as his attention was directed towards the child.

'I'd like to be able to help both you and your daughter,' Alex said.

'I told you,' the man growled, 'we don't want your *fucking* help.' And with that he turned around and disappeared through the door on the lefthand side of the corridor.

Alex glanced uncertainly to his right.

'It's been like this for the last hour and a bit,' the TSG sergeant whispered to him, pushing the visor of his riot helmet halfway up to make communication a little easier. 'He talks to us for a while, then he disappears into one of the rooms and we don't see him for the next few minutes. Truth is, we haven't been able to make a whole lot of progress.'

'You and the team are doing a great job,' Alex reassured him. 'You've bought us some time, and the most important thing is that the baby doesn't appear to be hurt.'

'Poor little thing,' the sergeant responded, almost to himself.

'Hmm,' Alex agreed, the face of the sleeping baby already

354

fixed firmly at the front of his thoughts. 'I don't know whether you noticed,' he continued after a pause, 'but the suspect's mood seemed to change a bit when his attention was away from us and on the little one.'

The sergeant nodded. 'I did,' he said.

'It might give us something to work with.'

'You think?'

'I certainly hope so,' Alex replied. His colleague's seeming reservations were unsettling. Alex hoped so, but he didn't *know* so. Uninvited doubts began to surface. How was this one going to play out? How was it going to end? His mind started to slip back to another part of London, to the domestic siege that had ended in a hail of gunfire. In his imagination, he could see the line of armed officers crouching in front of him, fingers resting on trigger guards.

'So what happens now?' the TSG sergeant asked.

The sound of the sergeant's voice hauled Alex back into the present. He made eye contact with his colleague in an effort to ground himself. 'We wait,' he said quietly.

'What the fuck are you two whispering about?' the suspect demanded menacingly. He had chosen that moment to reappear in the corridor. He was still holding both baseball bat and baby and, somehow, the child was still asleep.

'We were talking about your daughter,' Alex replied instinctively, his mind instantly re-engaged with the reality before him.

'What about her?' the man responded, marginally less aggressively.

Alex heard the slight change in the suspect's voice. And it renewed in him the sense that he should try to keep the focus of the exchange on the child, rather than on the man holding her. 'I'm worried about her,' Alex said simply.

'She's not yours to worry about.'

'All the same,' Alex persisted, 'I'm not sure that this is the best situation for her to be in.' He chose his words with great care – anxious to avoid any suggestion of accusation in his phrasing. He was inviting the suspect to reach his own conclusion.

'Of course it bloody isn't,' the man bristled, his tone starting to shift once again.

'And I was hoping that you and I might be able to do something to change that,' Alex ventured, deliberately allowing for the idea that the suspect might form part of the solution, rather than the entirety of the problem.

'Such as?' the man snorted derisively.

'Such as letting one of us look after her for you?' Alex suggested, putting it deliberately as a question, rather than as a statement.

'Fuck off!' the suspect spat, struggling now to keep his voice in check.

As he tried to keep pace with the volatile switches in the suspect's behaviour, Alex recognised the need to temper his own approach. 'You obviously love her very much,' he said gently.

'Of course I bloody love her!' the man responded, his voice growing louder. 'She's my daughter!' The baby's eyes flickered and she sighed, a small sound that momentarily distracted her father. 'It's alright,' he whispered, rocking her gently. 'Daddy's gonna look after you.' Alex could see his grip tightening on the baseball bat as he spoke.

'What's her name?' Alex asked, already knowing the answer to his question, but using it in an effort to establish a connection – any kind of connection – with the suspect.

'Riley,' the man replied, his eyes not leaving his daughter. 'Not that it's any of your business.'

'Riley,' Alex echoed. 'That's a pretty name.'

The suspect offered nothing more than a grunt by way of a response.

'And, am I right in thinking that your name's Harvey . . . ? Harvey Jackson?' Alex asked.

Jackson ignored the question. 'Why don't you lot just leave us alone?' he rumbled.

'You know we can't do that,' Alex replied quietly but firmly.

'Why the hell not?' Jackson demanded, his face growing fierce again.

'I think you know the answer to that question,' Alex replied.

Before Jackson could offer any further response, Riley took an audible breath, blinked her eyes open and started to cry, the tiny fingers of her left hand curled into a tight ball. 'Now look what you've fucking done!' Jackson hissed. 'The two of us were doing just fine until you wankers got here!' He turned on his heel and disappeared once again into the room on the left.

Alex looked back to his right.

'Told you,' said the sergeant.

'You did.' Alex replied, experiencing both a fresh swell of concern at Riley's plight and a renewed sense of outrage at the suspect's behaviour: anger and anxiety knotting themselves together somewhere deep inside him. The weight of the situation was starting to rest not only in his hands, but on his shoulders and in his chest. *Steady now*, he cautioned himself, slowing his breathing once more, and reminding himself of a phrase that Pip often used. *"Negotiators are optimists"* she would say, any time he started to doubt himself or a situation. And she would remind him that it was an outlook born not of idealism, but of hard-won experience. In the past decade – over the course of more than fifty deployments – Alex had only ever lost one person: the man at the domestic siege.

He insisted to himself that wasn't about to lose another one, least of all a six-month-old baby.

By the time Rich arrived in the corridor some twenty-five minutes later, the sense of stubborn optimism that Alex had been trying to nurture was starting to wane. The suspect had re-emerged twice more into the hallway of the flat – still holding the baseball bat and the once-again-silent Riley – and, on both occasions, Alex had persisted in his attempts to establish a rapport with him. But, each time he had thought that he might be getting somewhere, Jackson had found another reason to lose his temper and disappear again.

Rich placed a reassuring hand on Alex's shoulder. 'How are you doing?' he whispered.

'I'm knackered,' Alex responded wearily, all the while trying to work out what he was going to say the next time Jackson appeared.

'I'm not surprised,' Rich responded. 'Here, have a mouthful of this,' he said, handing Alex a disposable cup of hot, sugary tea.

'Thanks,' Alex replied, taking a grateful sip, his eyes not leaving the doorway. 'Any news from the hospital?' he asked.

When Rich didn't immediately reply, Alex turned his head to look at him. And the expression on his old friend's face – the pursing of his lips, the slow blink of his eyes, the barely perceptible shake of his head – told him all that he needed to know.

'Dear God,' Alex muttered as the realisation started to settle in. But, this time, he managed to catch his heart before it fell. And, in place of despair, he dug deeply into a sudden sense of fierce determination. There was nothing he could do for Chloe now. But Riley was still alive. Which meant that there were any number of things he could try to do for her. And, for the moment at least, that had to be the only thing that mattered.

'What about the little one?' Rich asked, as though reading Alex's thoughts. 'How's she doing?'

Before Alex could respond, Jackson reappeared with Riley in the corridor. 'And who the fuck do we have here?' he demanded, glaring at Rich. Straight away, Alex could see the change in Jackson's appearance and demeanour. His pupils were dilated, his nose seemed to be running and there was a certain swaggering, simian looseness to his movements – all of which Alex recognised as symptomatic of likely cocaine use.

'This is Richard,' Alex replied steadily, knowing how vital it was to respond to each new display of hostility with a show of measured calm. 'He's a friend of mine who's travelled halfway across London because he wants to help us.'

'I thought I'd made it very fucking clear that I didn't want any help from any of you!'

'You did,' Alex acknowledged. 'But, as you already know, it's not only you we're worried about.' He looked at Riley, who was now wide-eyed and unblinking. Though she still had no visible injuries, Alex knew full well that the harm being done to her would have a lifetime of consequences.

Jackson stood and swayed and stared. He reached out with his right fist – the one still grasping the baseball bat – and steadied himself against the wall. 'Riley's fine,' he mumbled. 'She just needs her dad.'

You're the very last bloody thing she needs, Alex thought but didn't say. Instead, he decided to try something different.

'I'm a dad,' Alex said indicating a possible point of connection between the two of them.

Still swaying, Jackson stared blankly at him.

'I'm a dad, same as you,' Alex reiterated, compelling himself once more to suspend all hatred of the man and his unimaginable crimes.

'And?' Jackson responded, seemingly confused by the change in the direction of the conversation.

'And I know exactly what it's like to want to protect your children . . . To want to do only what's best for them.'

A look of recognition spread slowly across Jackson's face. 'Too fucking right,' he said firmly. Then he leaned forwards and kissed his daughter gently on her forehead. 'That's my girl,' he slurred. Riley blinked and stared back at him.

Alex sensed an opportunity. 'There's nothing quite like it, is there?' he said, trying to draw Jackson deeper into the exchange.

Jackson looked back up at him. 'Like what?' he asked uncertainly.

'Like the connection between a father and his child.'

Jackson glanced from Alex to Riley and back again, and nodded in unexpectedly thoughtful agreement.

'I've got two boys,' Alex said, willing himself to make the most of any brittle affinity he might be starting to find with the man in front of him.

'Boys?' Jackson queried, his interest apparently piqued.

'They're Chelsea fans, just like you,' Alex said, nodding at the initials and lion tattoos on Jackson's left forearm. Over the years, Alex had learned to identify and make the most of every possible negotiating option – however unlikely or insignificant it might first have appeared – and the tattoos were something he had noticed right at the start of his encounter with Jackson. Now, they were suggesting to Alex the possibility of further common ground. He was leaning on a hunch that Jackson's love for his football team might be the only other thing that came remotely close to his love for his daughter. And the reaction he got was exactly the one he was hoping for.

Jackson's face visibly brightened. Without disturbing Riley, he slowly rotated his arm to offer a better view of the inked signs of his sporting allegiance.

'Who's your favourite player?' Alex asked, looking for a way to reinforce the connection that seemed to be developing between them.

'Of all time?' Jackson responded, his attention distracted for the moment from the overwhelming seriousness of the situation he found himself in.

'If you like,' Alex replied, swiftly rehearsing in his mind his sons' likely answers to the same question.

'Super Frankie Lampard, of course,' Jackson said without hesitation. 'What about your boys?' he asked, evidently warming to his subject.

'Lampard, definitely,' Alex agreed. 'And they've always loved Didier Drogba.'

Jackson nodded approvingly. 'Good shout,' he said. 'Best striker Chelsea have ever had.'

'What about Riley?' Alex asked, carefully drawing the focus back to the situation in hand.

'What about her?' Jackson asked, his eyebrows raised.

'Is she going to be a Chelsea fan too?'

'Of course she bloody is!' Jackson said proudly.

Alex knew that they had reached a critical juncture in the negotiation: an inflection point. Jackson appeared significantly more biddable than at any time since their initial exchange, but Alex knew better than to rely on that remaining the case – particularly given the unpredictable effects of the cocaine that

Jackson had apparently taken. Alex needed to make the very most of the moment.

'Look at her,' Alex said gently, his eyes fixed on Riley.

'What about her?' Jackson responded, his attention returning to his daughter.

'She's beautiful,' Alex said.

'Too bloody right she is,' Jackson replied.

'What's the first thing you think when you look at her?'

'That I fucking love her,' Jackson replied with surprising tenderness.

'That you love her,' Alex affirmed quietly. 'I'm not surprised,' he added. 'That's exactly what I think when I look at my boys.'

Alex allowed the silence to linger for a moment, mentally rehearsing the wording of his next question before speaking it out loud. 'Is this what you want for her?' he asked when the moment seemed right.

Jackson looked up. 'What are you talking about?' he asked, his tone quizzical rather than hostile.

'All of this,' Alex repeated, gesturing with both hands at the grim reality of their immediate surroundings. 'It's perfectly obvious to me how much you love your daughter. And I reckon that you want more for her than this. Much, much more.'

It was Jackson's turn to pause. He looked first at Alex, then at the upturned table and the two TSG officers crouched silently behind it. With a shrug and a heavy sigh he leaned his weight back against the wall.

'So what are you suggesting?' Jackson asked eventually, his head tilted back, his eyes closed.

Alex felt a rush of something approaching euphoria and had to check himself against rushing into an ill-considered reply. Riley's safety was suddenly within near-touching distance and it would have been all-too-easy to say the wrong thing – to undo all the progress that he had been able to make in the negotiation. Alex needed Jackson to feel as though he still had some control over what was happening – that he was part of the decision-making process, rather than the subject of it.

'Well,' Alex said eventually, 'we could start by giving you a breather and allowing me to hold her for a bit?' Once again, he phrased it as a question rather than a statement.

'And then what?' Jackson asked uncertainly.

'And then we can talk a while longer,' Alex suggested. 'Talk about what you think is best for Riley.'

Jackson lapsed back into silence, his forehead creased in an agitated frown. Silently, Alex willed him to make the right choice, even as he fought off the urge to interrupt the slow-moving quiet.

It took a seeming eternity for Jackson to speak again.

'So you're telling me that, if I let you hold Riley, you'll stay here with her and we can talk together about what happens next?' he said eventually. The uncertainty on his face matched the hesitation in his voice.

'That's exactly what I'm telling you,' Alex replied, his hope surging again. He had given no thought to what might happen beyond the possibility of Riley being handed over to him but, for the time being, it hardly mattered.

'You promise?' Jackson asked, taking a tentative step towards the pair of TSG officers.

'You have my word,' Alex replied, his heart hammering.

The next few moments and movements happened in seeming slow motion.

Alex hardly dared breathe as Jackson approached the doorway. Releasing his grip on the baseball bat and allowing it to fall to the floor, he carefully took hold of Riley with both hands, lifted her above the table and the riot shields and allowed Alex to take hold of her.

As Alex drew her precious, fragile little life into his arms, he felt a surge of relief beyond almost anything he had known in his life before. It was matched only by the plunging depths of exhaustion he experienced as the last reserves of his adrenalin emptied out of him. His legs buckled and he needed Rich to reach out and steady him.

One last effort, Alex demanded of himself, even as he wondered whether he had anything left to give. He looked down at Riley, needing to reassure himself that he hadn't somehow imagined it. That he really was holding her. That she really was safe.

Meanwhile, Jackson was standing and staring at him, wide-eyed and restless, waiting to see what happened next. True to his word – and in spite of a compelling urge to do otherwise – Alex made no attempt to move away from the door, or to hand Riley over to anyone else. Because he understood how important it was to keep his promises. Because he knew that the negotiation wasn't over. Because Jackson was still inside the flat, unaware of the fact that his ex-partner was dead, and that he was going to be arrested for her murder. Alex now needed to find a way to persuade him to surrender peacefully, without placing his TSG colleagues at risk of any harm.

At least, that would have been the plan if Riley hadn't started to cry.

Alex felt it before he heard it: the sudden tensing in her tiny frame; the sharp, silent intake of small breath.

And then the noise.

The reaction from Jackson was instantaneous. 'Riley,' he called out in frantic alarm, pushing forwards against the table and the riot shields. The two PCs at the door crouched lower and steadied themselves.

Alex drew Riley into an even closer embrace and pleaded wordlessly with her to settle.

But she didn't.

'Give her back to me!' Jackson demanded furiously.

Alex looked Jackson in the eye and tried to hold his unfocused gaze. 'I can't do that,' he said, as calmly as he was able.

'What the fuck are you talking about?' Jackson responded, his voice rising and his fists clenching.

Out of the corner of his eye, Alex could see the TSG sergeant gesturing down the corridor for the line of waiting PCs to move up closer to the flat. And he could feel Rich's hand in the small of his back, grabbing hold of his belt, getting ready to pull him clear.

Riley's cries grew louder still.

'I can't give her back to you,' Alex tried to explain. 'It's not safe for her in there.'

Jackson responded with a guttural roar of fury. Stumbling back from the upturned table, he snatched the baseball bat up from the floor and slammed it double-handed into the wall next to him, sending splinters of paint and plaster flying in every direction.

'Harvey!' Alex shouted out in alarm, trying desperately to re-engage with him.

But Jackson had fallen far beyond reach. Far beyond any semblance of reason.

It was all over in a matter of seconds.

Raising the baseball bat high above his head, the screaming, spittle-flecked Jackson hurled himself at the table – which snapped in half like matchwood – and into the two long shields.

Having anticipated what was coming, the two PCs at the door managed to survive the initial impact and hold their ground.

As this was happening, Alex felt the urgent nudge from Rich. Wrapping both arms round Riley and covering her head with his hands, Alex spun round and hurried back down the corridor. At the same moment, the TSG sergeant was yelling a rapid series of instructions, summoning the rest of his officers in the opposite direction, towards the door.

Having failed in his first attempt to break out of the flat, Jackson picked himself up from the lino, and started raining blows with the baseball bat down onto the shields. The response from the uniformed officers was instantaneous. Reinforced by their colleagues behind them, the two PCs holding the long shields charged forwards and unceremoniously flattened Jackson – pinning him to the floor while the rest of the team swarmed into the flat to help detain him.

A minute or two later, a bloodied Jackson was being carried away face down, handcuffs and leg restraints in place. He was spitting and struggling and bellowing obscenities, but utterly powerless to resist his detention.

It was almost eight o'clock in the morning when Rich dropped Alex back at home in Stockwell. They hadn't spoken much on the way. Alex was feeling shattered – both physically and emotionally – and Rich had been happy to give him some space.

'Good job tonight,' he said as Alex climbed out of the van.

'Thanks,' Alex replied with a smile that was more of a grimace. The burden of responsibility he'd felt over the previous few hours had weighed more heavily on him than in any other negotiation of recent times. He had left Riley in the care of one of his colleagues, but that fact that she was safe – and that he had played his part in saving her – was the only positive he was able to draw from the whole dreadful situation. Her mother was dead. Her father was going to be behind a cell door for a very, very long time. And that just left Riley. With a life sentence of her own. What the hell was going to happen to her now? Where was she going to live? Who was going to care for her? What kind of ruined future was she facing? Alex's brief involvement in her life might have come to an end, but the seemingly endless list of challenges she was facing had only just begun. The ghosts that haunted Alex were of the living as well as the dead.

He unlocked the front door and closed it quietly behind him. Allowing his rucksack to drop to the floor, he walked slowly into the sitting room, slumped onto the sofa, leaned back and closed his eyes.

The next thing he knew, Pip was crouching on the carpet next to him, easing his shoes off his feet, and asking him if he was okay.

'What time is it?' he asked uncertainly.

'Just after eleven,' Pip replied quietly. 'How did it go?'

And so Alex told her.

'You need to take some time off,' Pip said sympathetically as he finished his account of the night's events.

'We both do,' Alex replied. He knew full well that Pip was as much in need of a break as he was. Her job as a DI on one of the Met's sexual offences units – alongside her own additional duties as a negotiator – had taken every bit as much out of her as his professional life had taken out of him. She was a good deal more measured about it than he was – much better able to maintain a distance between their work and home lives – but, in the end, the impact on them both was much the same. Policing London just felt relentless: seemingly every kind of carnage and chaos every single day. The demand was endless and, at times, it felt as though the sadness was too. The calls just kept on coming and so he and Pip – like the vast majority of their colleagues – just kept on going. He knew that they both needed to stop, if only for a while.

Pip nodded slowly and thoughtfully in agreement. 'We're both due some leave,' she acknowledged. 'What say we take two or three weeks – just the two of us – and get away from it all?'

'No phones?' Alex asked.

'No phones,' Pip readily agreed.

'No emails?'

'Definitely no bloody emails.'

Alex paused for a moment, before offering her a weary half-smile. 'Then I think I might know just the place,' he said.

Reader's Guide

Police negotiators need to possess a whole range of skills – but the most important one of all is the ability to **listen**.

(1) Why do you think that is?
(2) What sort of qualities does a person need to be a good listener?
(3) What is the difference between 'active' and 'passive' listening?

Sometimes, it feels as though we are getting worse at listening to one another – particularly to people who see the world in a different way to us.

(4) Why do you think that might be?
(5) What might each of us be able to do to improve the situation?

One of the main themes of *The Fallen* is **trust**: in our politicians, in the police, in one another.

The fact is that trust in both politicians and the police has declined in recent times.

(6) Why do you think that is?

(7) What can politicians do to rebuild our trust in them?

(8) What can police officers do to rebuild our trust in them?

And two final questions:

(9) Which character in the book did you most relate to – and why?

(10) Which part of the story stayed with you longest after you'd read it – and why?